Everything She Didn't Say

Center Point
Large Print

Also by Jane Kirkpatrick and available from Center Point Large Print:

All She Left Behind
This Road We Traveled

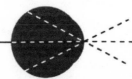

Everything She Didn't Say

Jane Kirkpatrick

CENTER POINT LARGE PRINT
THORNDIKE, MAINE

This Center Point Large Print edition
is published in the year 2018 by arrangement with
Revell, a division of Baker Publishing Group.

Scripture used in this book, whether quoted or
paraphrased by the characters, is taken from
the King James Version of the Bible.

This book is a work of historical fiction based closely on
real people and events. Details that cannot be historically
verified are purely products of the author's imagination.

The text of this Large Print edition is unabridged.
In other aspects, this book may vary
from the original edition.
Printed in the United States of America
on permanent paper.
Set in 16-point Times New Roman type.

ISBN: 978-1-68324-950-4

Library of Congress Cataloging-in-Publication Data

Names: Kirkpatrick, Jane, 1946- author.
Title: Everything she didn't say / Jane Kirkpatrick.
Other titles: Everything she did not say
Description: Center Point Large Print edition. | Thorndike, Maine :
    Center Point Large Print, 2018.
Identifiers: LCCN 2018033717 | ISBN 9781683249504
    (hardcover : alk. paper)
Subjects: LCSH: Large type books. | GSAFD: Christian fiction.
Classification: LCC PS3561.I712 E95 2018b | DDC 813/.54—dc23
LC record available at https://lccn.loc.gov/2018033717

Dedicated to Jerry
Thanks for walking the trail beside me

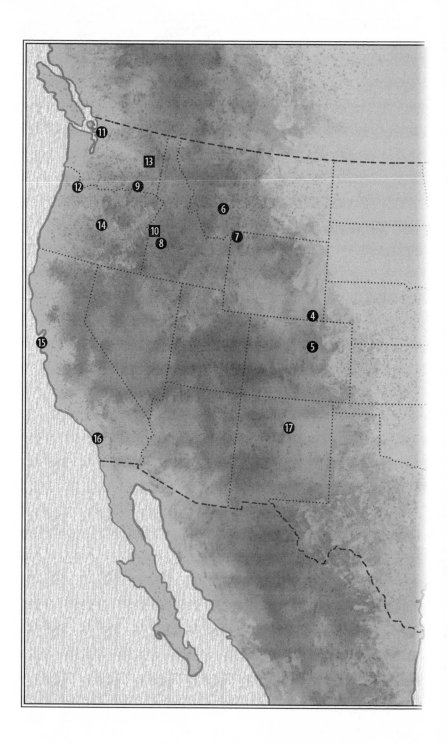

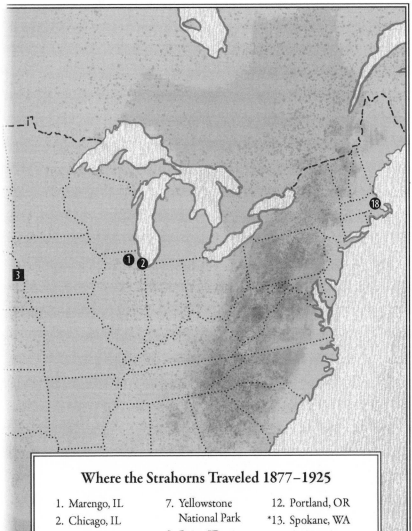

Where the Strahorns Traveled 1877–1925

1. Marengo, IL
2. Chicago, IL
*3. Omaha, NE
4. Cheyenne, WY
5. Denver, CO
6. Helena, MT

7. Yellowstone National Park
8. Boise, ID
9. Walla Walla, WA
*10. Caldwell, ID
11. Fairhaven, WA (Bellingham)

12. Portland, OR
*13. Spokane, WA
14. Bend, OR
15. San Francisco, CA
16. Los Angeles, CA
17. Santa Fe, NM
18. Boston, MA

* Robert & Carrie's permanent homes

I want to be famous in the way a pulley is famous,
Or a buttonhole, not because it did anything
   spectacular,
But because it never forgot what it could do.
                  Naomi Shihab Ney from *Famous*

Tell all the truth but tell it slant. . . .
   The truth must dazzle gradually. Or every man
   be blind.
                       Emily Dickinson

Character List

Carrie Adell Green Strahorn, writer, wife of Robert

Robert E. Strahorn, writer, railroad investor, husband of Carrie

Mary Green Waters, Carrie's older sister and journalist

Christina Waters, Carrie's niece, daughter of Mary

Hattie Green Lacy, Carrie's younger sister, physician

Jay Gould, Union Pacific Railroad president

H.R. Harriman, Union Pacific Railroad president

James J. Hill, Great Northern Railroad president/owner

Pace Caldwell, friend of Carrie; wife of Senator Caldwell, business partner with Robert

William Judson Boone, first pastor of Caldwell Presbyterian; president of the College of Idaho in Caldwell

Presbyterian women of Caldwell and Carrie's friends

Elizabeth Meacham, widow, treasurer of the Presbyterian Society

Delia Gwinn, croissant maker

Marvel Gibson, widow, secretary of the Presbyterian Society

*****Hester Adeline Brown**, member of the Presbyterian Society

Carrie Gwinn Blatchley, treasurer of the Presbyterian Society

Annie Bloom, wife of pastor William Judson Boone

Beatrice Little, member of the Presbyterian Society

*****Kate & Kambree**, **Bunting,** twins

Elizabeth Larrabee, Fairhaven friend, wife of founder

*fully imagined character

1

What's in a Name?

Life if anything must be an adventure, one we make ourselves from whatever comes our way. Tomorrow I begin my greatest adventure. My Robert is whisking me away to the wilds of the West as his bride. I will pick up my fiancé at the train station; we'll marry and then we leave for Cheyenne on the Union Pacific. My thoughts are on the newness, not what I'll leave behind in Marengo, Illinois. There'll be new twists and turns like the Mississippi River that meanders. Surely there'll be waysides and green oxbows where I can adjust my bustle and catch my breath following this worldly man whose book has been published to rave reviews. I shall make light of trouble should there be any. That shall be my motto, to remain in the happy lane of life which is where I am today, September 18, 1877.

Carrie Adell Green

I have a stack of foolscap papers tied in lavender ribbons written and preserved from my elementary school years when I discovered the power of words. I began a new notebook for my life as Mrs. Robert Strahorn. I hold it now. I'll write a memoir if my life is adventurous enough and if I'm strong enough to tell the truth to myself, and others, without whining over the hard times nor becoming overbearing at those ace-high moments. These journal entries will be the ore I mine for memoir.

Scared, that's what I was, though I don't think I'll mention that in my memoir.

I'll make light of the concerns my parents had about sending me off to the unknown wilds of Cheyenne as a new bride. I know they hoped I'd marry someone from the university, but I didn't. And after the years went by, my sister Mary married and I was still "at home," as the census recorder noted, so perhaps they welcomed this unknown entity—a westerner—and trusted my judgment. I know he endeared himself to them when he left out the word "obey" in the wedding vows. I thought that quaint. I didn't realize then how obedience can have a certain comfort to it, a certainty in an otherwise uncertain world. That is, if both confess obedience.

I was twenty-three years old and Robert was twenty-five. We had a minor crisis with the printer misspelling Robert's last name on the invitations, but I was more concerned with my father's melancholy as he pondered our nuptials.

"I hope he can support my little girl. Writers don't make much money, do they?"

I had no idea.

Before I knew it, I stood in the First Presbyterian Church (Marengo, Illinois) with my sisters fluffing my hair and me trying to make light of the worries in their eyes. Mary, my older sister, tall and slender, wore the most concern. She'd been married three years, was now a mother herself. "I love my Willie," she said, "but marriage takes more than love."

"You're the wise sister," I told her. And to Hattie I said, "And you're the most beautiful sister and that leaves me with being . . . the most adventurous sister. I'm off to the wilderness. Everything's going to be fine."

"But he calls you 'Dell,' as though the name our parents chose for you isn't good enough." Mary stood before me. We shared strong chins, high foreheads, blue eyes, and hair the color of chestnuts, though mine frizzed like spewed baby bubbles, tiny and soft at my temples in the September heat. "You're Carrie and will always be Carrie to us." She reached for the ivory combs, pushed them into my hair. She straightened the sleeves of my satin dress, the scent of lavender left over from the dressmaker's hands bringing comfort. "Did the two of you discuss him calling you Dell?"

"I don't really mind." His first fiancée, my

15

friend Carrie, and I had shared given names. She had died. I missed her.

Hattie held Christina, our one-year-old niece, in her arms. I loved that child. Nieces and nephews, they can be such a comfort. "It's diminishing, calling you Dell."

"No. I . . . it's just that Carrie Lucy has passed and I don't think he likes being reminded of her death by using any part of her name for me."

"Do you love him?" The wiser older sister asked.

"I do. I really do." I sank onto the wide arm of the horsehair-stuffed couch. I didn't want to wrinkle the satin dress that fit around my curves nor bust the bustle, either. I didn't remind them that I was twenty-three years old, college-educated, and there weren't a lot of men willing to take on an oldster like me. Robert was. He was charming, and yes, I did indeed love him and his western garb of cowboy boots, his closely tailored sack-suit with wing-tip collar and tie. He didn't don the Stetson hats we'd seen on Texans coming up the Mississippi but instead wore the stylish Homburg made of black wool.

"I saw him care for her, grieve when she died. I watched his tenderness as he held her hands in his, and the attentiveness he extended to Carrie's family and to me while he dealt with his own grief."

Hattie smoothed my dress. I could tell she held back a thought. She was nineteen and not yet with a steady beau. She was the beautiful sister with eyebrows as though painted perfectly on, and quick-witted.

"My accommodation to his simple request to not have to call me Carrie is a little thing I can do to make him happy." I reached for the rouge and dabbed my lips. "Marriage is made up of little sacrifices like that, isn't that so, Mary?" She didn't reply.

His request to call me Dell had come after he arrived on the Union Pacific and told me his grand news about his book—and new job offer. We were in the carriage heading to my parents' home.

"Omaha? I thought we'd be heading to Cheyenne." I'd been looking forward to the more exotic life of Cheyenne, putting down roots as deep as the sage. "Carrie would have loved Omaha."

That was dull of me, bringing up her memory.

Robert removed his hat, ran his hands through his thick dark hair. He closed his eyes as he leaned his head against the backrest. I sat across from him. He was tall and slender and quite handsome, with thick eyebrows and sideburns framing a jaw cut from sharp scissors. "Yes, Carrie would have loved Omaha." He paused. "About that."

"We'll be fine there. I'll adjust my imagination."

"No, about what Carrie would have liked. Or more, Carrie's name." He cleared his throat.

"She was my best friend, Robert."

He leaned in, patted my hand, held my fingers, forearms on his knees. "What I wonder is, would you mind if I called you Dell instead of Carrie, from your middle name?"

I must have flinched, as he quickly added, "It makes you unique to me, having a name that doesn't bring up loss."

"But—"

"I know it's a great deal to ask of you. And I wouldn't want you to give up your name legally, just what I might call you. I know I'm marrying Carrie Adell Green and looking forward to it, absolutely." His smile could melt cheese. "But when I say your name in the sweetness of an hour—or when I tell stories of our adventures, and there will be those—well, I'd love to have no startling memories rise up with the sound of 'Carrie' in my ears. Does that make sense to you?"

I wanted to tell him to separate the two of us some other way. I wanted to say, "Change how you feel," because people can do that, change how we feel. We do it all the time, from one anxious moment anticipating the arrival of one's fiancé to worrying that something has gone wrong on the tracks to flashing to a beloved memory of sadness, all within seconds. He could have changed how he heard my name, given himself some time to associate me with it and not his first fiancée.

"Men are named Del, aren't they?"

"Yes, but it's spelled differently."

I didn't tell him that didn't matter to the ear. "It'll take a bit of getting used to."

"One of the things I love about you, Dell, is that you are open to trying new things. We're partners in that, or 'pardners' as the cowboys say. We're on a track that will take us to amazing places with remarkable people, the most important being you and me, working together."

"In Omaha."

"In Omaha, where everyone will come to know you as Dell Strahorn."

Carrie Adell Green had stepped off the caboose.

He at least could have called me Adell, but I suppose the old printer in him knew that the *A* took extra space in a line and good writers are all about saving space.

"I'll call you Pard," I offered.

"Good, that's good. We are partners in all things. I like that."

So Dell and Pard got married, and arrived in Omaha. I adapted. It isn't written in the marriage vows that one must adapt, but it ought to be. Somehow I'll find a way to explore that in my memoir—if I write one—remembering the happy lane from my journal, but sprinkled with a little Mark Twain making fun of things too serious to explore. It's not a lie to not tell all the truth.

"I say, mother, I made our new son promise to put in a hundred bushels of potatoes every fall, but if he stays in Wyoming I think he will have to rustle some when its credits now are only wind and Indians." "Well, pa, don't worry," mother replied, "It does seem a long ways to be from home if things don't go right, but so long as daughter can sing as she does now she will never go hungry for they do say there are churches in Cheyenne just the same as here. . . . You know she is a pretty good judge of human nature and maybe he'll surprise us all someday by living up to her ideal. He don't seem to know much about women, but he does seem dreadfully fond of our girl. It was really funny last night to hear him tell Rev. Hutchinson, the minister, that the bride-to-be wanted the word 'obey' left out of the ceremony because there is Woman's Suffrage in Wyoming, and suggest, 'If you don't want to leave it out entirely, just put it in my part, for I've been running wild so long I just want to be obliged to obey somebody.'"

2

The Alchemy of Marriage

Brides are the alchemists of emotion, enduring new challenges and telling ourselves it's part of the arsenal of elixirs we'll mix throughout a lifetime. A pinch of hopefulness, a dash of delight, baked inside a dish of dependence on one's more western and successful husband. I've been dependent on my father for years and now I make sunshine out of shadows cast by my new husband's choices. It hasn't been easy, taking in Omaha. Especially when, as I settled in, Robert changed the formula I'd been mixing as a new bride. I'd married a writer, but he was soon to be a railroad man as well. And that means change. Lots of it. I'm not sure how I feel about that.

October 5, 1877

Robert's book garnered rave reviews. I'd have thought a title like *The Handbook of Wyoming and Guide to the Black Hills and Big Horn Regions for Citizen, Emigrant and Tourist* would have set some reviewers off, but it didn't. The book unveiled Robert's capacity for seeing what wasn't always there, the "passionate sense of the potential," as Kierkegaard wrote. As we rode the train toward Omaha, Robert pointed out valleys he thought could be good sites for dams or rivers, with wide swaths beside them that could be an easy route for a railroad track. The geology of a place spoke to him the way musical notes speak to me, with unique and fresh visions that others might not always see. *Wyoming Handbook* was published at the perfect time, adding fuel to the fires burning in the East about the possibilities of the West.

Robert's rendering of landscapes, of mountains and deep valleys still marked on maps as "unexplored regions," created paths for those seeking to leave behind the eastern crush and move to open spaces and yet find a way to survive. Or better, thrive, which Robert did in those wilderness places. He was more at home beneath tall timber, riding through buckbrush and fording streams on horseback, than he ever was in the parlors of the powerful, and yet, those parlors would become our future—now and then—and Robert would master them.

I remember an evening a few months into our marriage. We were in Omaha with General Crook and his wife, and the men discussed former battles in Indian country. The general's eyes shined with the memories of leading good men toward a common mission and how Robert, though not commissioned (he was a journalist covering the conflict), had served his country above and beyond, not only as a reporter, but as one of the "soldiers" who fought as needed. They didn't go into details—those who experience conflict rarely do, I've found, leaving the talk of glory to the others. But the comradery, Robert included, was highly praised by the general.

I wondered if the general sometimes woke with a start in the night, breathing hard and fast and shouting with sweat pouring off his chest, as though he'd run a hard race to save his life. Robert did. His nightmares scared me to death, I can tell you. I didn't know whether to wake him.

Listening to General Crook, I discovered my husband through the eyes of others and by reading what he wrote and what brought light to his eyes, hoping that my presence did so, as much as geological formations or chatting with an old friend did.

※※

It turned out, Omaha was a wind-filled place where a three-story courthouse towered over the town like a medieval city without the wall. I missed my hometown. But then, I often longed for where I'd been and where I wasn't. It was a lesson of living I hadn't yet learned about, finding the blessings of each moment.

Small houses dotted the prairie that at first looked flat but proved to be rolling, its formation camouflaged by tall grasses turning brown as we arrived that September. One of those houses was to be ours. And then it wasn't.

I had unpacked the boxes of wedding gifts and linens and such, seeking an armoire of some size for our clothing. We hadn't brought furniture with us, and there was nothing to be found in Omaha. I ordered in oak and located a craftsman who could deliver what I needed, while putting through a request for items from Illinois that would arrive by train, now that I knew what would fit. I was certain that not a single house in Omaha had a closet. Merely hooks on the wall. None we'd looked at had linen, changing nor bathing rooms either. Those would come in time, Robert assured me, when we could build our own estate, if the book sold well and if he could write another.

That first fall, Robert took the train to Cheyenne to finish up an article he'd been commissioned by the UP (Union Pacific) to write, then returned to me with a light in his eyes that came from a story rather than the home-making advances I had to show him.

"They want me to head up a new publicity office for the Union Pacific. I'll write books and pamphlets that will bring people west. What an offer, Dell."

"That's wonderful." I kissed his cheek, then turned my gaze to the table I'd had built. Too large for the space, I could see that now.

"It'll mean travel though, and a lot of it. They want people to move into unknown places, new sites where the railroad will one day come." He was following me around the table, stopping when I did to check a potential ding in the edge. He bumped into me. I stopped. He turned my shoulder so I looked at him, saw the passion in his eyes for this new role he'd been asked to play. "I'm to be the lead man, identifying, describing, whipping up that pioneering desire. A blend of wide vistas and words. Dell, it's a dream job."

"Yes, it is." I was happy for him, I was. "Tell me again about the traveling part."

"The thing is, it means going into unknown wilds identifying terrain suitable for towns, for railroad termini, spur lines. The new law gives railroads free access to entire sections of government land on either side of the tracks they lay. That land can be resold to settlers who arrive by the very same train. Railroads have to lay tracks or repay the treasury. It's a license to make money for them, expand our country's hold on vast vistas between the Pacific and the States, and give people meaningful work. It taps everything I've ever loved—adventure, engineering, the great outdoors, the writing of it."

"You'll operate out of Omaha or where?"

"Sometimes here, Cheyenne perhaps, then wherever UP chooses to bump up interest. But mostly, I'll be on the road. Helping to make the railroad in advance." He took my hand and walked me into the living room. "I know this is a change of plans for you, making your way with me gone most of the time. You can visit your family as often as you might like, bring them out here even."

As he spoke, I could feel my shoulders tighten up like a rope pulled around them and my chest. We'd come all this way to where I knew few people and I'd do what without a husband beside me?

"I know you wanted a home of our own, and this way I'll be able to afford a place worthy of you, where we can entertain when I'm home and you can learn to fix blood soup or something." There were many Polish immigrants in Omaha known for their fine foods like blood soup, though baking and cooking weren't strengths of mine. I wasn't sure what my strengths were. I'd certainly ordered too large of a table for the dining area.

"You'd like that, wouldn't you?"

"What I'd like is to have a life with my husband. Maybe—" I hesitated here to speak of such intimate things, but it had to be said— "maybe start our family. That'll be a bit hard to do with half of the equation riding into the sunset alone." I'd smiled, a little embarrassed to be championing procreation so boldly.

He looked as though he saw me for the first time. There'd certainly been no lack of interest in our marriage bed, so why he looked astounded by my mention of a family, I didn't know.

He held me then, his suit-coated arms a comfort. "I'm such an idiot. Of course, that's what you want: a home, family." He stroked my hair, the back of my neck.

"You close by, maybe even helping you with your writing now and then. Editing. I do have skills in that area, Robert. I earned A's in composition at Michigan."

"Yes, yes, of course." He released me, kept hold of my hand. "Let's think about this. Let's think about this." He often repeated himself when he was nervous. "A cup of tea? I'll fix it."

He headed to the kitchen and blew on the cookstove coals to heighten the flame beneath the teapot. I joined him and pulled out pastries I'd purchased that morning from an Italian baker.

As though he was out on the prairie over a campfire, Robert whistled as the water heated, and he put the loose-leaf tea into the porcelain pot my sister Hattie had given us as a wedding present. He did it as he did all things, it seemed, with such ease. I watched, wary of where this conversation of family planning might be going and wary too of the tightness in my chest.

"Sit." I did, at our new dining room set. He handed me the tea.

"I could go with you." My enthusiasm overflowed.

"That makes no sense." *Our having a family?* "Too many hardships." He ran his hand through his hair. "There's almost nothing out there, no people."

"You'll need someone to look after you."

"The UP would never go along with that."

My world was swinging like an unhinged gate. I wanted a home, settled, a family like my sister Mary had, like women of my station did. And yet, I had already chosen a different route, following my husband west where women were few but hardy.

Thunder rolled in the distance and I noticed the wind had begun to pick up too, rattling dust against the windowpanes. "It could work, Robert. Once we had a family coming, well, of course I could come back here. Or Cheyenne, if that's where your home base would be. Or Denver. It wouldn't matter. But until then, what keeps me from coming along?"

"It . . . the danger. Indian country much of it. Wild outlaws and miners, those we're likely to encounter. Stage stops peopled by strangers and a wide range of proprietors whose cleanliness will vary as the wind. Lack of, uh, bathing arrangements. And then there are the elements themselves. Storms. Blizzards. Temperatures hot enough to blister your skin in the shade. No safe place really in scrappy clapboard boarding houses, if we're lucky. Or unlucky."

"I can manage bedbugs."

He laughed. "The least of our worries, I suspect. Privacy might be unheard of."

"Not all the time, surely. With such wide-open spaces—" I let the image linger.

He sipped his tea. Stared at me. "Gould will never agree." Jay Gould was the head of the UP.

"You'll have to persuade him, then. That's what you do, isn't it?" A thought occurred to me. "My presence could add to the aura, Robert. You're out there looking at townsites, at land acquisition where engineers can ply their trade to lay tracks, while I bring along the sense of civilization. If a society woman can endure those hardships with spirit and spunk, then surely the hardy pioneers with their half-dozen children behind them will find the same possibility you want for your farmers and entrepreneurs to pull them west. I'll represent home and family and churches and schools, what it takes to make a town the railroad wants to dot the West. It'll be the women and children who settle this land, Pard." I emphasized my name for him, reminding him that we were partners in all things. "Every happy woman has a true Pard and will follow him anywhere if she thinks they're on the same team. Women do have choices, you know. Not many, I admit, but women in Wyoming can vote, so they figured something out. And didn't you say you'd 'obey'?"

Robert laughed out loud. "Are you ordering me to obey you, Mrs. Strahorn?"

"If that's what it takes, yes."

"Oh, Carrie."

He sighed but didn't look at me and I didn't know if he was bringing forth the image of his first love or if he forgot for a moment and saw me as I was.

But who was I? I'd proposed a future of hardships on horseback or stages and occasionally trains taking us to the end of their tracks. I'd agreed to look after him, as that was how he'd described my strength, being his "Pard," but I'd thought it would be welcoming him home as my mother had my father, at the end of a weary day, children flocked around. Proximity was necessary for reproduction, that was certain, but he'd been evasive about family, hadn't he? And yet that was one thing for certain I did know: I wanted a family, and should I conceive, it might very well be a challenge to carry the infant to term if I was jostled about on a stagecoach. I'd bridge those notes when I knew the music better.

Corporations tended to make their decisions on what was best for their shareholders and not their employees. I hoped I'd given Robert a good argument for allowing me to be his "partner" in this endeavor. "I'll go with you to see Gould."

"Not a chance. But you'll be there in spirit. And I think you've just given me the best argument I could make about the influence of women in advancing the cause of the West. I couldn't have said it better."

From *Fifteen Thousand Miles by Stage,* vol. 1, by Carrie Adell Strahorn (page 11)

But if there is ever a time in a woman's life when she will endure hardships and make sunshine out of shadows it is when she first leaves the home nest to follow the man of her choice.

3

Pioneering without Protest

Today, Robert meets with Jay Gould, and I find out if I'm to be the first woman to go hither and yon into wild places with my Pard. I have been first before: I was the first to solo in Italy and France when our choir toured. I admire women who take the initiative, like Francis Case and Mary Robinson, the first women to summit Mt. Hood in Oregon. But the idea of a pioneer, that "dust-laden dress of the weary," bothers me. They seem beaten down and I don't want to ever be that. And I don't like people in their aging years looking back as though what had gone before was the highlight of their lives. I want to be talking about amazing things happening now and ahead, even as I grow older. I want to anticipate the possible, always. If I write a memoir, I'll look back, of course—that's what a memoir is, a reflection of a life or a time period or an adventure sprinkled with epiphanies of wisdom to give others insights without making mistakes. But one can be a pioneer without letting the past hold one hostage. Pioneer means "foot soldier," the one who goes before. So that's what I need to consider: if all goes well with our proposal to the UP, I will indeed be a pioneer but one who goes before and looks forward, not back.

October 30, 1877

"I used your words about a society lady demonstrating the partnerships of pioneers. Gould was wary about a woman going out west and he didn't like the additional costs involved for two instead of one traveler. But he went for it."

"Oh, Robert, I'm so pleased."

He kissed me soundly. I might have lingered on that kiss, but he was all into his success and paced the room.

"I told him I wouldn't do it unless you came with me."

"You didn't."

"I did. They'd already convinced themselves that they wanted a book like *Wyoming Handbook* written for every territory or state, anywhere the tracks might lead, so they weren't going to let me go, now were they?"

"Awfully risky to test it, though."

"Wait, don't you want this?" He stopped his pacing and touched my shoulder, his white shirt-sleeve peeking from his tweed jacket.

"Of course I do. When do we start?" I gulped with getting what I wished for.

"We move to Cheyenne first, to a boarding-house. It'll be our base. We'll be on the road so much there's no need to buy a house and try to keep it up."

"Oh." Visions of entertaining in between our stints hither and yon faded like an often-washed dress. "What should I do with—" I spread my hand around our rented house stuffed now with furniture from back east or craftsman-made in Omaha.

"Sell everything. Or we can box it up and ship it back to your parents' home. Put big items into storage with the railroad perhaps. Yes, a warehouse would hold all this if you wanted, though by the time we settle down, these might be outmoded fashion." He picked up one of the brass candlesticks. "I suppose brass never goes out of style. I'll ask for a drayage to come help you pack and load."

"Won't you be here?"

He shook his head. "You'll join me in a week in Cheyenne. I'll try to meet you at the station, but if you don't see me, hire a livery and head to the Tin Restaurant. I'll have secured a boardinghouse or maybe a Single Room Occupancy hotel and gotten my marching orders by then. I'll meet you there for dinner. We'll eat steak on their tin plates. Oh, and I got passes for both of us on all conveyances, including stage lines and ferries and trains, of course, even if they aren't UP's. We can go anywhere we want!"

Now, that was a delight to this travel adventurer.

❧❧

I spent the next few days sending my beloved furniture to a warehouse, putting linens in trunks and shipping them back home to Illinois. I wrote to my mother about "storing things," deciding I wanted a little more time to describe exactly what I'd be doing for the next few months. I thought it would be months. I didn't imagine pioneering my entire life.

I did decide to keep one small trunk for bed-sheets I could pull out at a less-than-clean stage stop and to store my unmentionables. I added a few silk gowns for those receptions I hoped to hostess. Then it seemed that certain wedding gifts should travel with us—wool blankets, pillowcases with lace edging, Hattie's teapot. One can always get a good night's sleep with a cup of tea and a special pillowcase. I threw in the down-filled pillows Mary had insisted I take wherever I went.

Perhaps I'd conceive before long and wouldn't need the worry of managing my monthlies, though that would mean a significant change. Robert surely wouldn't allow me to continue once I was with child. But western women rode horses, tended sheep, did all sorts of things while carrying a child. I so wanted a family . . . but I also wanted to be with my husband not only until but throughout.

⌘

Cheyenne was a madhouse in the shadow of snow-capped mountains. Wagons, horses, mule teams; men with wild gold-pursuing eyes bought up every shovel, pan, dish, and Nobel's dynamite, followed by black powder, cheese, and canned milk that was available in that mountain town. Dogs barked while stagecoaches were loaded with mounds of supplies—sluice boxes, wire, gun powder boxes, sides of pork—and men hanging on to stages wherever they could, all heading to the Black Hills for this new gold rush amidst cooling October mornings. They headed east while we'd be mining the possibilities of the west.

I stepped down from the train, looking for Robert's black hat to bob above the rest of the mostly men gathered. A wind gust pushed against my straw hat and I jammed it against my head. At least there was no humidity here to frizz up my hair. Not finding my Pard, I headed to the livery. Then I spied him and fast-walked toward him. He swooped me into a bear hug, and for the one hundredth time I wished I was fine boned like Hattie instead of laden with curves and hips that filled out a dress like a thick blanket of snow over hills and valleys. Perhaps all this travel I'd be engaging in would change my terrain.

"My little pioneer woman," Robert said as he kissed me discreetly on the cheek.

I struck him on the arm but laughed. "You know I never ever wanted to be a pioneer." Wind whipped my skirts around my legs. "Pioneer means *foot soldier* and gives me images of aproned women with their hair in tendrils sweating over open fires while children chase chickens and tend a log house in the background. A man with a mule plows his field without an ounce of energy left to sing a merry song or attend a cake walk to raise money for the new church piano."

Robert laughed, took my elbow. "Foot soldiers are the heart of an army." He directed the livery-man to pick up my three trunks. He frowned as the third one was hoisted onto the wagon, but he didn't say anything, continued instead to praise foot soldiers. "They go before the rest of us and that's exactly what we're doing, Dell. We are leading the way for those stalwart souls to come marching forth to tame the land. And make the railroad rich. And maybe us too."

"Is that thunder?" I scanned the sky.

"Indeed. Let's hurry to Angie's."

We arrived at the boardinghouse, unloaded, and had just come downstairs into the parlor when the storm struck. Hail the size of prize onions crashed through the window, tore open a cane chair, struck the oak floor beneath, and bounced back up to make yet another hole in the chair seat. I thought of what we'd have looked like if such a storm had hit us while we were beneath a mere canvas tent out on the prairie. I shivered.

An engineer at heart, Robert took out his measuring device. "Seven inches in diameter. Now that's hail."

"Quick, quick." Our landlady handed us baskets and urged her boarders to follow her out once the storm had ceased. The air was crisp and cool. I soon had a basket full of hailstones, wondering what on earth she intended. "I'll make us a batch of iced cream and we'll have a hailstone party," she announced. And she set to it.

"That's the spirit." Robert cheered her. These Wyoming souls were enterprising and, yes, pioneering.

❊

While we waited for our first assignment, I sought out a church choir. I always did better while waiting for the unknown if I could sing hymns or arias. I loved to solo, but I also had no difficulty stepping back into the choral line, being simply one of the voices raised to the rafters. It was where I found my greatest peace, being both out in front and blending in. I was discovering that those qualities were exactly what my marriage required.

After a few days of careful listening to Angie, our landlady, the wives of some of Robert's UP colleagues living in Cheyenne, and the Territorial Secretary's wife, I found a Congregational church. I asked the choirmaster if he was interested in another voice, auditioned, and then began singing. It was what I needed while Robert met with dignitaries and railroad folk to arrange our itinerary. And so I whiled away my days singing in Cheyenne.

❧❧❧

"They've issued our passes," Robert told me before Christmas. He didn't make eye contact with me. "Uh, we aren't always—we aren't always on the same rail lines and we might have to meet up along the way now and then."

"We won't travel together? Aren't we going back to Illinois for Christmas?"

"Yes, yes, we are. But we'll head home from there at different times. I need to make a quick trip to Salt Lake City after the new year."

"I could come with you."

"Your pass is for Cheyenne to Chicago, then a return to Denver."

"Denver?"

"It'll be fine. Pack up everything when we leave from here. We won't be coming back to

39

Cheyenne." He lifted my chin with his warm hands, looked me in the eye. "I need a few more details for *To the Rockies and Beyond*. The rail agents will take good care of you." I could have helped him with the final edits of his latest, but I didn't suggest it now. He'd made up his mind. I would simply obey.

※※

I kept the knowledge of this separate travel from my family while we enjoyed the holidays with taffy pulls and hot cider, soothing scents drifting over the greens on the mantel and lifting the already sinking pine boughs to rise yet one more day until freed of their ornaments and candles.

On New Year's Day we all celebrated my twenty-fourth birthday. Robert gave me a gold necklace with a tiny cross. He clicked the clasp around my neck, kissed me in front of my family. "This woman is the light of my life, the gold of my heart, her presence the balm of love and wisdom that soothes my soul. Thank you all for allowing this woman to be my beloved wife."

My family burst into applause. I felt myself blush and blinked back tears.

Hattie said, "Such beautiful sentiments. You have a way with words, Robert. No wonder your book is doing so well."

"I have a good editor in Dell," Robert said. He tapped my nose, something he did in affection.

I never told Hattie that I'd written those words in a card to Robert on *his* birthday last May. I took it as a compliment that he chose to edit them and give them back, but a little part of me felt cheated too. They were my words, but my family would always know them as his. *Sunshine out of shadows.*

During those holidays, I thoroughly engaged myself with Christina, my niece, fifteen months old and bright as an evening star. There is something about the lack of all guile in a loved and happy child that brings tears to my eyes. I treasured the smell of her after her bath, the giggle that grew from her belly, the words she put together as she pointed her dainty finger at the dog.

"No baby news?" Mary watched me make faces just to hear my niece laugh.

"Not yet, though not for lack of trying." I felt myself blush with my frankness.

Mary laughed. "He is a handsome man, no doubt about that. And attentive. A new job, too, in addition to another book contract so soon. That speaks well of him."

I nodded. "They'll publish fifty thousand copies and the Union Pacific is giving them away for free, to promote the West and reduce the fear and anxiety for those considering heading in that direction."

"This one's about the Rockies?"

"And the flora and fauna and valleys and ridges and the nature of the soil, of course. Farmers always want to know about that. And the rainfall. Timber projections. All a little . . . technical, but I've urged him to put a bit of flower into his words, make the dream of new beginnings more vivid."

"He appears to have flowers in his words to those he loves. You have a way with words too. Mama reads your letters out loud to us." She lifted Christina from my lap, as the child had reached out to her mother. "These books he writes, they're establishing a new kind of genre?"

"In part. They're a bit of history, geology, science, business, agronomy, and inspiration too. Pioneering of a sort. Emigration is an important issue these days, and Robert's words speak to those looking for something better, hoping they'll find it in the West."

She held Christina close, patted her back, then looked at that angel face. "Time for a lunch and then a nap?" Christina nodded. "That's one of the advantages of motherhood." She turned to me. "The pleasure of nursing, then putting your baby down for a nap and taking one with her."

"I look forward to such blessings." And I did.

❧※❦

White flakes began blanketing the ground as Robert prepared to leave ahead of me.

Prognosticators predicted more snow to fall, but Robert was packed and out the door. I waved.

"He's going without you?" Hattie grabbed my elbow.

"We'll meet up in Denver. I'll leave in four days. It's fine. I know how to do this, Hattie. And I get extra days with you this way."

In truth, I didn't know for sure how to "do this." I'd never traveled so far without a companion of some sort, my sisters or parents. Carrie, my friend when we were in college, and now deceased, shared transport back and forth to Michigan. An entire choir with chaperones joined together when we toured Italy. On this journey, I'd be alone.

"So much for marriage bliss," Hattie teased.

"We're perfectly happy doing what we need to do: he needs to be in Salt Lake and I don't need to be there. We'll meet in Denver where we both need to be." I made it sound like my idea.

"I'm sort of envious that you get to travel by yourself. You can be anything you want if someone asks who you are." She paused. "Aren't you worried about your safety?"

"I'm Mrs. Robert Strahorn and I'm sure no one will harass a Union Pacific employee's wife."

"Is that status written on your forehead?"

I rolled my eyes and changed the subject to what she'd mentioned on Christmas Eve, that she was going to go to medical school. I'm good at distraction.

That evening I turned out the gaslight in my old room, marveling at my little sister becoming a doctor. Taking after our father's profession was a good thing. She'd be doing worthy work, as was Mary as a mother and wife. And what was I about? Being a pioneer.

From *Fifteen Thousand Miles by Stage*, vol. 1, by Carrie Adell Strahorn (page 14)

In all my girlhood, the one thing I wanted to avoid in my life was to be a pioneer. So often had I listened to tales of my elders of " '49 and the spring of '50," etc., that it had made me say many times that I would never be a pioneer and be called the oldest settler in a town or country, or one of the early ones in any State history. Yet, there I was at the very threshold of a new land where I was to be the first woman in many then unexploited regions, and the title of "old settler" was to be indelibly and forever attached to me and mine.

4

Obstinate or Resilient

This will be a short entry. I'm on the train but wishing I wasn't. That must be the definition of suffering, wishing for something one doesn't have or hoping to be somewhere that they aren't. I am suffering the elements made worse by my foolishness in insisting that I continue on despite the blizzard. I hope I'll be alive to write more later. For now, I need to blow on my gloved hands to keep them from freezing brittle as a stick.

January 5, 1878

I could have enjoyed lingering over waffles and beefsteak with my sisters, watching cardinals visit the feeders, bright red against white snow. Perhaps I could have spent some hours posing in my wedding dress if the photographer was available. Such exposures made even a year after the wedding were common practice among my social set, a way of celebrating the bride more than the wedding itself. Besides, I'd never wear the dress again, and it deserved to be taken from its tissue a last time. Maybe my daughter would wear it. But Robert had set up my transit and I was nothing if not obedient to his wishes. So four days after he set out, so did I.

Truth is, I was ready to leave, though I love my family, I do. But I didn't want to have to explain anymore about what it was we'd be doing and how that was going to work, because frankly, I didn't know myself and I didn't like not having answers and I didn't like looking at their eyes that I thought held pity.

I kissed Christina, hugged my parents and sisters, wiped a tear from my father's cheek, and waved my goodbyes wearing a smile born of determination, then boarded a short line whose name I shall not mention but it wasn't the UP. Once at the station, one of the old conductors insisted I wait a week, what with the snows also having fallen over most of the western territories as well. "Trains are delayed, Missus. It's dangerous for a woman."

I might have let his experience and my family's worry override my persistence, but when he added "for a woman," I was determined then to show him wrong. If men were getting on the train to Denver, then so would I. How could I let a little weather hold me back? What kind of a pioneering soul was that? It wasn't the last time my insistence overruled my good judgment.

The conductor relented and let me on, but the Chicago cars were a blight, well used up with holes in the floors showcasing the tracks beneath. It was nothing like those I was accustomed to traveling in. I wondered if the good cars were caught in snow or if that railroad line was protecting its better ones. I stepped up and we headed out, engine steam rolling back like fog in the cold air. I was the sole woman on a very long train.

It took us twenty-four hours to go sixty-five miles and the cowcatcher pushed snowdrifts all the way. The lunch of ham sandwiches I ate turned out to be all I would have until the following day. I had thought there'd be a depot with food available. But storms have a way of unsettling everything, the whistles sounding forlorn as we chugged past trees whose limbs broke from the weight of the heavy snowfall. Often I couldn't tell if it was still snowing or if the engine and cars swirled up the mounds of fluff. We were in a world of white framed by the wooden windows we stared through. The small stove inside the car hoarded its heat. At least there were entire seats empty and I sat with my back to the window, my booted feet up, my cape and hood keeping me as warm as they could. I didn't disturb anyone else while I made the effort to sleep. The weather was so ominous that the other passengers kept to themselves, perhaps praying as I was that we wouldn't be stalled, run out of coal for the engine nor our little stove, the whole affair requiring search parties sent to find our frozen bodies.

At some point, I wrote a quick note to my sisters making light of my plight, thinking I'd send it from Denver. I entered a sentence or two in my journal. Even as my fingers numbed, I wondered why I had insisted I take this train. Why didn't I wait? Was I fearful Robert would think me weak or not part of the game? Did I want to somehow "stand out" in my family, prove to them how brave and adventurous I really was? Why couldn't I change my mind, incorporating the wisdom of others?

The third morning out, the cold lessened and the snow turned to rain. We were delayed yet another six hours because of a freight wreck ahead and then all passengers were transferred to another train brought in. We had to walk past the wreckage, and I was doubly relieved that I'd purchased rubber boots in Marengo before we left, as the slush and sludge beside the tracks proved more than ankle deep and my wool socks felt barely dry from laying them on the train's little stove after trudging through snow. This happened two more times—being moved to another train— with each car being worse than the first, until I was bunched like a handful of carrots with other stalwarts onto the only passenger car on the line, all the rest bearing freight. We were a motley mix, cranky and worn. I didn't even try to cheer the men up, nor did I lament their total lack of interest in my well-being by not even asking how I was doing. They probably thought me daft for being there and may have resented my presence preventing them from swearing as they might have to express their frustration with this travel.

At Omaha where I switched lines, I was at last on a UP car. I leaned back, grateful that we were aligned with a more reputable company than those I'd experienced so far. Still, they had gotten us all where we hoped to be, if not when. And even the UP couldn't halt the weather-related damages . . . being held up two more days waiting while more than 1,000 feet of track torn out by floodwaters was replaced. The station at Ogallala, Nebraska, wasn't meant to hold delayed passengers, but UP did its best to bring us food and keep the station warm.

At least during this wait there were children to watch and distract to help their tired mothers and fathers. Children's presence, even those tearful or sad, always brought me from my self-pity.

⁂

Cowboys shot up the town outside our station and I held no small amount of trepidation hoping the outlaw gangs said to be in those hills wouldn't burst through the door. Rumors spread that such thieves often tried to rob trains down the tracks.

The UP's security forces roamed the station, offering their confidence, and a few rode on the trains themselves. Mary's words about being safe dribbled into my consciousness. I swept them aside. No sense worrying about the future.

Robert's need to be in Salt Lake City without me began to wear on me like a bit of sand in my shoes, though. Then as if nothing more could go wrong, my monthlies began in that station. I hadn't expected to be out and about when this occurred, so I had only a towel and no belt, but for once I was grateful for thicker thighs to hold the towel in place, and I didn't hope to be walking much at all. But it saddened me. I had not yet conceived.

My disposition made no good gains and I longed for my sheep's wool. I made a note to always travel with readiness in the future and to perhaps have a few words with Pard in Denver about this whole business of traveling alone.

But my longing to have words with him had to wait, as Pard wasn't in Denver when I finally got there after a week on the tracks. Instead, I had a telegram from him urging me to Laramie, where I headed the next morning, arriving to once again wait. He wasn't there. But at least I was warm, in a nice hotel, with bubble water for a good, sound bathing, my monthly unmentionables secured, and later ate hot food in the dining space.

I people-watched, a favorite pastime of mine.

It made eating alone less troubling. After a day or two, the waiters knew who I was and kept good care of me, which lifted my melancholy. It had been a tough week of travel and that was all by train. What would it be like once we began our sojourn by stage to more primitive places? I liked the idea of slipping into clean sheets and laying my head on my hand-packed pillowcase. Would it get tiring, traveling from here to there, following Robert around?

This lack of routine would only continue until we started our family, I decided. Until then, I would focus on Robert, listening to his sound advice, being where he arranged for me to be and taking in what sights I could in between. Maybe one day I'd write about them. Yes, this whole living in the unknown uncertainty was research for a life I'd write about. I'd mine these experiences like a gold rusher, seeking the ore of insights that yielded treasured meaning. I resolved to make notes—but to tell the truth in them to better recall what was really happening in my heart and soul.

With my new resolve, I headed up the stairs to my room. To my amazement, this hotel in Laramie had electric lights, not gas. They were bright with fewer shadows cast as I washed my face in the basin, put a little lard on the dry spots of my cheeks where they were snow- and wind-whipped pink, if not frostbitten. Then the long pull on my frizzed hair thick as sheep's wool. My toilet finished, I looked around.

I didn't know how to turn the electric lights off!

There was a bell line to the clerk that I located, but the idea of calling for help for such a simple thing seemed beneath me. I, who had traveled through blizzards and waited out floods and sloshed through ankle-deep misery changing trains, I surely could figure out an electric light. After a search I found the little button on the single lamp. I held my breath and touched it, not sure if I'd be shocked or thrust into dark. I faced the dark with absolute delight, switching it off and on at will. I got up from my bed and wrote a note to Hattie, telling her that in the middle of the wilds of Wyoming I'd discovered electricity and wasn't that grand when most of Illinois and the East still settled for gas. Wyoming led in more than women's suffrage. I slept contented in that progressive place.

❧❦

Robert's train arrived the next morning, and thankfully, he was on it. He rocked me in his arms, as we exchanged horror stories, and he expressed genuine concern that my trip had been rife with trials.

"It was good practice," I told him, "for what lies ahead, I suspect. But I really would prefer we travel together."

"As often as we can." He held my elbow as we walked. "We'll go back to Chicago together in March for the book finishing and release. You can stay at your parents' if you'd like. Or the UP will put us up in Chicago proper. It's where I'll need to be, closest to the printer."

"I'll think about it. But for now, here we are in Laramie and we've been more than a week apart. What do you say we celebrate with a lovely lunch right now in this fine hotel that has electricity?" I clapped my hands like a child.

He grinned. "My adventurer." He motioned for my glasses, I gave them to him. He cleaned them with his handkerchief. "I've got to meet with some people, Dell. The day's committed, I'm afraid. But I'm yours for the night."

"Could I help? Are you working on the book?"

He shook his head no, hooked my glasses frames over my ears. "Talking with potential principals in where a line might go out. It would be a dull day, I'm afraid. They have a library here." And he was off.

I wondered why he wanted me to meet him in Laramie. Why not wait until he could come to Denver or, for that matter, simply return to Cheyenne, our home base, and meet me there? I could have sung in the choir on Sunday. And if I'd listened to that train conductor or heeded the wary eyes of my sisters, I could have simply enjoyed more time with them. My headstrongness

53

could be a liability in this adventuring . . . but wasn't willfulness on the other side of resilience? Making new discoveries—whether finding electricity in the wilderness or the insights about ourselves—required that we step into uncertainty, take risks. I suppose it was possible that one could face a challenge and not learn anything from it. I didn't want to be of that ilk. But I'd need to make certain that I didn't blithely go along with Robert's itinerary of our lives. I could question him now and then, even though he surely knew more about the western terrain than I did. But what did he know about the terrain of the human heart? That was what would make the western expansion—passion.

From *Fifteen Thousand Miles by Stage*, vol. 1, by Carrie Adell Strahorn (page 21)

When it was too late, I began to feel repentant for my willfulness and to think that the wishes of others should have been given precedence.

5

On the Road at Last

These past months of travel and rootless-
ness wear on me. Or perhaps it's the
immediate demands of attention that have
my stomach in a swirl. We await word
on whether we can go forward or not.
Oneida, a small Mormon town, is sweet
and it houses a number of us. Robert and
I are hoping to reach Helena in Montana
Territory within the week. But the
Bannock and the US military are at war,
and the conflict has reached us on the
Utah-Idaho Territory border. We passed
burned-out ranches and have huddled at
this stage stop for safety, not intending
to leave while the conflict continues. The
army is unable to position enough soldiers
to protect so wide an expanse while still
engaging in conflicts. I won't write to my
mother of this day, nor my sisters. I am
praying that this will not be my last entry
into this journal or any journal.

July 15, 1878

There'd been Indian wars before and this one
was no different, having raged on since early

June, stockades packed with frightened settlers. They were fighting over land, which is almost always the case. Your land; my land; settler's land; the railroad's land—all of it initially Indian land. I had mixed feelings. Who could blame the Bannock for warring? I'd heard that a former Oregon missionary, Josiah Parrish, had met with the tribe, hoping to dissuade them from their latest fierceness, and at least one group had returned to their reservation convinced of the futility of their conflict. But others pillaged on in the very country that we must travel through to reach Montana Territory.

We had boarded the stage in Utah and were in good hands with the well-known and respected *jehu*, or stage driver, but even Jake Farson acted nervous now. I wondered if I should insert my lesson from that terrible trip last Christmas and suggest we not start out. We stood in front of the stage station, the Concord loaded to the hilt on the top, with long-delayed mail stuffed between luggage, shipments of ordered goods. Red streaks in the sun-setting sky belied dangerous war clouds that couldn't be seen but existed nonetheless. I watched as Robert's eyes drifted away and wondered if he was back in Crook's Army, in one of his four Sioux campaigns. A little moisture beaded on his forehead. His breathing sounded funny.

I handed him my handkerchief. "You're

sweating, Robert." I touched his face with my gloved fingers. It was hot, but a lady still wears gloves.

"Am I?" The action toward something of the senses like that seemed to bring him back. He removed his hat and used my handkerchief to dab at his head, his neck. He was short of breath and his eyes looked glazed, wild even. Maybe he was tired from helping load, but I suspected it was more than that.

"I've got my little revolver here," a New York passenger boasted. "We'll make light of those heathens, won't we, Jake."

"That's Mr. Farson to you." Our driver wasn't one to be called "Jake" by a stranger.

"Making light of warriors isn't advised." Robert chewed his lip. "Why don't you wait inside, Dell."

I hesitated but then did as Robert asked, lifting my skirts up as I took the steps slowly to listen to him talk to Jake and the New Yorker. A bird someone called a meadowlark chirped a cheery tune in the air perfumed with sagebrush. The evening heat was oppressive, and I felt perspiration beneath my corset. I left the door open to the sunset, leaned against the doorframe, fanning myself with my fingers. I could tell that Robert was considering something—namely suggesting we take a separate trip, again, that he head to Helena without me.

I certainly didn't want to wait for peace in

Oneida—which might take months or years—though the little Mormon town was pleasant enough. It would be less so without Robert. I wanted to be with my husband no matter what happened, rather than wait as the wives of soldiers did, for word of his life or his death. I think it was the first moment that I considered my mortality—and Robert's. What would I do if something happened to him? I didn't linger long with those thoughts. Instead I urged the cook at the station to finish up the fried chicken to take with us.

Through the window I watched as Robert gestured with his hands, the two other men nodding their heads, looking my way. Then Robert took the steps in a long stride, his mind made up to leave me behind, I knew it.

I grabbed our dinner box and met him at the door. "Pardy," I said, reminding him that we were all for one and one for all. I touched his evening-stubbled cheek. "We've plenty of fried chicken to get us to the next stop if the Indians don't take it from us. Let's be on our way." I handed him the hamper before he could protest, asked the New Yorker to help me up, which he did, casting wary eyes at Robert. Then the bulky man plopped across from me, squeezing himself between stacks of mailbags.

Robert stood at the stage door by then. "Dell—"

"Hand me the food. I'll hold it on my lap.

Doesn't appear to be any other room except next to me, and that's where I expect to see your handsome frame." I gave him my warmest smile and refused to let him see any of my own trepidation. "Doesn't it look grand? Red at night, sailor's delight." I scanned the blazing horizon, then back at him.

He looked at the sunset. His eyes glazed again.

"Smell that chicken. Yum." I took a deep inhale.

Robert inhaled too, his eyes thawed. Then he handed me the hamper, which I placed on my lap.

"Let's go, Jake." Robert lifted himself into the stage, pulled the door shut, while Jake from on top gave the shout to his team, ribbons in his able hands, and we were off.

Mailbags stashed like sausages were stuffed everywhere, including where other paying passengers might have sat: on leather seats, beneath them, lashed onto the outside where our luggage rode. Inside, we were locked into a single position, unable to stretch our legs and barely able to move our bottoms. Like pickles in a jar, Robert and I held each other upright while the New Yorker—James Randolph—sat like a sausage between gray bags marked *U.S. Mail.*

"We're so packed in here I can barely pull my rifles." Robert looked toward where the weapons rested, barrels down, on the other side of a mailbag next to the door. I saw for the first time what he was seeing: a situation where bravado wouldn't be enough. We were in a war zone and the poor man was stuck with one other good soldier—the driver—and two misfits when it came to self-defense. I vowed to have him teach me how to shoot once we arrived in Helena, if we arrived. Meanwhile, I needed to reassure him that whatever happened, I was here because I wanted to be and because he'd had the confidence in me to push the railroad to let us be a partnership in the first place. I wasn't going to fail Robert nor the railroad, and I didn't want him to assume blame for whatever might happen next.

"It'll be alright." I patted Robert's knee. "It's been quiet for more than a week now. You're a good shot. Jake's skilled. I can follow orders. Maybe tomorrow you can show me how to reload so I can at least hand the rifle to you." He nodded, swallowed. "I admit I'm scared. But my father always said fear wasn't a sin at all, not when you did what had to be done. I heard General Crook say he'd rather be with you on the battlefield than any other man." I pushed my palm through his elbow, pulled him to me. "We're in good hands."

He looked me in the eye then and seemed to forget our New Yorker was eavesdropping on our lives when he said, "I love you, Carrie Strahorn." That's when I knew how scared he was.

"You'd better. My love for you would be pretty lonely if it didn't have a pardner."

Being jostled in a stage while scanning the

horizon is not my idea of a good time. But as we traveled at night—the moon didn't rise early—it was soon dark, with stars dotting the sky like sequins on a black gown. I vowed to never utter a moment of complaint, even when my legs ached to be lifted and rested on the seat across from me, when my knees tired of the hamper pressing against them, when I sneezed from the dust and couldn't reach my reticule now stuffed under a mailbag somewhere beneath my seat. I won't mention the urge my body had. Robert handed me his handkerchief that turned out to be the one I'd given him when moisture dotted his head. We didn't talk much, listened to Jake urging his team on. The New Yorker soon snored. We were so loaded that we couldn't move as fast as I knew both Jake and Robert would like, and if spotted by warriors, we'd be easily overtaken by the Bannock's faster ponies. It seemed a good time to keep praying.

Dawn greeted us and I would have liked to relieve myself, but daylight was not only the most dangerous time but privacy was absent. We rambled on, gnawing on the fried chicken, wiping our hands on now dry towels. They'd been moist when I'd put them in the hamper. We changed out the horses at a small station. I found a sagebrush to relieve myself. And returned to learn that Jake and our trusty team would remain. The new driver spoke little and Robert knew nothing of his skills as a defender, which added to his wariness and mine.

We were more alert now, watching for signs of Indians. We stopped once beside a stream while the men carried buckets of water to the horses and I found a spot to squat. Then we were off again, movement being our best defense, but not so hard our dear horses would collapse.

Robert didn't talk much, which was rare for him. His caution reached out to me and I felt small in the landscape where we rode vulnerable as newborn babes. We all have some say in the things that happen to us, even being at the wrong place at the wrong time. Somewhere along the way we made choices. I remembered a college friend say she'd survived three hurricanes and wondered why she had been singled out for such tragedy and then one day asked herself, "Could it have something to do with where I live?" She moved after that. I was here—we were here in this wilderness by our own choices, and no one else bore responsibility for what happened to us.

As night approached again, we reached the next stage stop, such as it was. Four stalls and feed awaited the weary horses. The other half of the building housed our quarters. The sign over the station door read "Hotel de Starvation, 1,000 miles from hay and grain, 70 miles from wood,

15 miles from water, and only 12 inches from h—." I guess the stationmaster had a lot of time to make up signs but in a moment of sensibility left off the last letters of this one. Or he ran out of paint.

A single room served as kitchen, parlor, and sleeping arrangements. More signs stating "God bless our home" followed by "Wanted—a nice girl for general housework. Apply within" were scattered around the room papered with pictures from what appeared to be a police gazette with garish photos of death and destruction, not the perfect antidote to the previous twenty-four hours of fear. I was certain any "nice girl" would want to change the paper at least. I could hear the horses kick and paw on the other side of the thin partition between the animals and us.

"What news do you hear?" Robert asked the proprietor, who was also our cook.

"Not so good. The last stage was burned out, horses stolen, and the driver killed. No passengers, fortunate for them."

Robert looked at our driver, whose eyes had gotten larger.

"Will you stand by us if there's trouble?" Robert put the question to the jehu.

Our New Yorker took offense. "There's no call for accusations like that. We're in this together."

"Some would say. But I've known drivers to cut the traces and ride off on one of the mounts when trouble approached. Will you cut and run?"

The jehu's face turned bright red, but he said he'd stay with us, though he looked aside. I wasn't confident, but there was little to be done about it. Then our New Yorker glared at the driver and said that Robert and I would be looking out either window seeking enemies but that he'd have his pistol pointed at our jehu, and if there was any cut and run to be done, we'd all ride out together.

We left at night again, with a full moon. This stage was smaller, called a mail jerky, with canvas top and sides, so we lacked even the safety of a wooden conveyance. My back felt like an ice pick had entered it. At midnight, we reached the next station, but there were no fresh horses.

"Most likely the tender was too scared to go out to bring them in," Robert whispered as we huddled by the stage door.

"He says the Indians drove the horses off," the jehu said. He watered the team, murmured to them.

"If they had, they'd have burned the place and killed him," Robert said.

"You'd best stay." The proprietor stood in the door now. "I heard tell there were Indians near, less than a few hours before you arrived. You'll be safer here."

I looked at the clapboard structure that to

me offered no more "safety" than our canvas jerky. I'd already climbed into the stage and listened as the little man's voice shook with fear camouflaged by his angry tone.

"If you won't stay for me, then at least stay for that woman's sake."

Robert said, "That woman is my wife and she'll decide."

From *Fifteen Thousand Miles by Stage*, vol. 1, by Carrie Adell Strahorn (page 75)

The Bannock War of 1878 was at its height and no one knew what terrors might befall an unprotected stage at any hour of that five days' trip between there [Oneida] and Helena.

6

The Abyss

I'm alive to write yet another day in my journal. How easy it is to let others make choices, then sit back and comment on whether they were good or poor. I wonder at how my parents worked their differences out. Did my father make the decisions and my mother implement them? Did they discuss it and then choose? Were they true partners or was one—my father—the ultimate judge when they reached an impasse? Maybe it depended on the weight of the issue, how strong one felt about the wall paper or what breed of dog. But what of life-and-death issues? Was it an honor or a curse to have the power to decide?

July 17, 1878

Lantern light flickered on their faces as the driver and Randolph—the New Yorker—turned to stare.

I didn't want the responsibility of deciding our fate, but for a partnership to be true means bearing the weight at times. Robert had the most experience with our circumstances. He'd fought in Indian wars, he knew what to expect. Why had he handed the decision to me? Did he favor my opinion that much? The weight of judgment felt heavy as a wet cloak, and I understood in part what a general must feel about the impact of his choices for his soldiers.

I took a deep breath. I guess it was Robert's way of truly inviting me into the partnership. Two for all, all the time. My heart still pounded though.

"The moon's bright. We can see anyone coming at us, and we've enough horses for all of us to try to outride them if we need to." I did know how to ride, though it wouldn't be easy sitting astride a wide-backed cross-breed of quarter horse and draft horse more used to pulling a stage than carrying a woman. I nodded toward the proprietor wringing his hands. If he came along we'd be a horse short. "If we stay here, we're sitting ducks. This stage is leaving. We need to leave with it." I thought of the man we were leaving behind. "You could come with us, ride with the driver. Be the coach gun."

"And have no horse?" He was little enough we could have shared a mount. I said as much, but he interrupted. "Can't leave my post. Besides, someone needs to be here to spread the word of your foolishness when they report your demise." He stomped back into his little station, and with a deep breath, we headed out.

For a time afterward, his warnings crackled like a low-gas lamp about to go out.

"That was good reasoning, Dell." Moonlight brushed Robert's strained face. We'd rolled the window shades up as far as they'd go, allowing each of us a view. He kept his rifle on his knees. Randolph had decided to sit close to the driver up top, watching the jehu as much as the landscape. "You've a good head on your shoulders and are compassionate too. I'm not sure I would have invited the old guy along, though I suspect he can shoot alright."

"Which is more than I can."

"We'll remedy that, come Helena."

I wanted to tell him about the conflict of feelings racing through me when he'd deferred to my wisdom or lack thereof in our decision. But I needed a little more time to consider what his referral really meant.

Dust billowed up through the open curtains. I could smell it, but it was hard to see now. We'd put out the lanterns to make ourselves as invisible as possible as we tensed our way through the night.

Robert righted himself when the stage jerked us forward and back. He was all of twenty-six years old but had already seen what old soldiers had. He'd been a printer, a newspaper reporter, a soldier, an author, and now the head of the Union Pacific's new Communications bureau, writing pamphlets and the *New West Illustrated* that came out three times a week. I wrote my mother three times a week to assure her I was still a "lady." I wondered how he'd write of this, as his copy was meant to inspire people to leave their pasts and burdens behind and bring their families to the mountains, plains, valleys, and vistas of this previously unexplored land.

"What if people really do come out here because of your good words?"

"That's the hope, Dell." He didn't look at me as we whispered, his eyes always on what happened outside—or might happen.

"But would you want them to experience this?" I coughed from the ever-present dust.

He patted my hand. "Shhh. Sound travels far in this landscape. Risk is a part of any new undertaking."

"But some people don't do well with this kind of uncertainty. They've been known to go mad with worry," I whispered.

"Women mostly." Robert's words stung. He'd given me the decision, then suggested that the female form is prone to go mad? I wished I could have seen his eyes. There was no humor in his voice.

"Then you took a risk giving me the choice for our being here or staying back at that station."

"I knew you'd make the right call. And that's in part why people—men included—go mad in these circumstances. They lose sight of the possibilities and let their emotions rule their reason. Your train trip at Christmas is an example. I talked to some of the railroaders on that same line. They told me they could almost see you think, the way you were concentrating. Gave them confidence too. A level head in a time of trial, that's admirable." He paused. "And a belief we have some say over our destiny with the courage to live or die with the consequences. It's what keeps a soul from going mad. It's one reason why I wanted you with me on this venture. I knew you had that kind of ability to see clearly and take the consequences without laying blame on another."

A compliment, certainly, but it also framed an expectation that would define me for years to come.

"Are those fires?" I leaned farther out the window and saw flickering at a distance I hadn't before. My mouth went dry. The horizon was dotted with flames. "Are they trying to burn us out?"

"They're communicating with each other." He leaned back. "They'll have stationed braves along the way. They're watching us move across. Not sure what's keeping them from pulling down on us, but so far I've seen nothing coming at us."

I was quiet. That many fires meant a great many warriors and we were "moving ducks" but as much a target as if we'd sat and waited at that station. The only difference was, we had some hope of making it to the next stage stop where fresh horses and maybe soldiers waited.

The moon rose and now I could see an Indian behind every sagebrush, as it was nearly as light as day. I had a night's work ahead, keeping my imagination from racing to our certain death. My old pattern of memorizing Scripture came in handy, and I repeated a psalm as a mantra: "Be still and know that I am God." I saw it as a promise that God would have our backs rather than as a chastisement to be quiet. The repeated words calmed my pounding heart. Then the stage pulled up, horses stopped, and the driver jumped down.

"Robert. Is that jehu—is he cutting the trace?"

He was out of the stage in a second, his voice raspy and breathless as he called up to Randolph. I thought he was trying to whisper loudly. "What's the word?"

Every muscle in my body was stiff as old leather. I remembered my doctor father saying fear sent scads of chemicals through our bodies to heighten sound and senses.

Silence. Then the New Yorker's words to Robert: "Loose wheel lug. Gotta tighten it." I sighed relief. They finished their work as Randolph warned the driver, "Next time, you jehu, best you tell me what you're about. I don't want to mistake your effort for safety for something else and shorten your life."

We heard the driver grunt his assent and the soft sound of Randolph re-holstering his pistol. Robert stepped back up into the stage. His breathing came short. Must have been the dust and tension. I would have liked to have stretched my legs, but we jerked forward on that rocky road, heading on to what fate we didn't know. My teeth were gritty with dirt. We drove on into an abyss lit by fires of war and flushed by those chemicals of sustained fear keeping us filled with necessary alertness, proving that the human spirit can live despite hour after hour of uncertainty.

From *Fifteen Thousand Miles by Stage*, vol. 1, by Carrie Adell Strahorn (page 82)

Thus the night wore on, while the sage-brush shadows seemed ever to conceal a dusky form, and the rumbling coach on the rocky roadbed sounded like the roaring of Niagara to our over-strained ears.

7

At the Table

Sustained uncertainty can either bring a person to their knees or it can open them to the reality of what is before them, in those moments of heartbeats that remind us that we live. I write this now so full of gratitude for the opportunity to breathe in that dusty Montana air, to hear the sounds of horses chewing at their bags, smell the sagebrush, watch the soldiers march in early morning drills. I love the feel of the rough lumber creating the makeshift fort's gate. My heart swells at the sound of the trumpet. Small things become larger and matter more. I write filled up by the tiniest of joys. I may not be able to tell my mother of what transpired to bring me to this place, but I will remember and will find some way to write of it in that someday-memoir.

July 20, 1878

We arrived at the stage stop at nine o'clock in the morning. The station bustled with life. Wagons pulled in carrying settlers from far-off ranches seeking safety; dogs and children scampered, oblivious to the dangers as they chased hoops close to a high stockade surrounding the corrals. Best of all, protecting the horses and the people were armed United States soldiers. Yes, the military had arrived during the night from the direction we were heading, and we learned those Bannock signal fires were not following us so much as monitoring the troop movements. The Indians had been pushed back, seeking their own safety.

It was comfort, relief for however short we'd have it, that there were others seeking safety just as we had. Fresh horses awaited the stage when it would pull out again. And meanwhile food filled us and we walked around. Free at last from anxiety, my legs moved me forward.

I spoke briefly to the proprietor of the station, a Mrs. Corbett, thanking her for allowing us pitcher and bowl to freshen up and for her fine viands.

"Would you like a room? That lovely jacket must weigh an extra five pounds with the dust. I hope the tooth powder helped. You'll surely stay."

I would have liked to have had a bath, slept in a bed, washed out a few unmentionables. Behind me I heard someone at the table tell Robert we were "foolhardy" and thought for a moment what that word really meant, made up of "fool" and "hardy," both words applying to pioneers in many ways and, yes, to us.

"Stage is leaving. Mail has to get on its way and we should take advantage of this Indian calm to make it to the next stop and one day closer to Helena." This was Robert.

"I guess I won't be needing a room, but thank you for the offer," I told the proprietor.

Mrs. Corbett took my hands in hers and nodded, a shared moment of women's understanding. "I wish you'd stay," she said. "We could have a nice conversation, two women finding themselves in a foreign place."

"It would be pleasant. A rare treasure." I released her hand, pointed to the stage. "We're rolling on."

"It's what we do, we women."

By impulse, she pulled me to her, held me as a sister. Her back felt bony yet strong, her arms firm and warm. We held each other for a moment, wiped tears as we let loose our embrace.

"God go with you," she said.

"And stay with you here."

She nodded, returned to her kitchen, and I savored that sweet gesture of kindness, let it nourish me as fatigue leached away into wonder.

Once outside, I rolled a hoop back to a girl about six years old, with two missing front teeth awaiting their replacements.

"Thank you, Missus." Her eyes lowered and she curtsied, well-mannered. I imagine it was the silver pin at my throat, a once-white blouse with high collar still buttoned, a blue-dyed linen skirt and jacket that stood out among the calicos that suggested to her I was from a far-off place. Or perhaps it was my hat with feather bobbing that inspired such formal manners. I was a contrast to the local women wearing aprons and bonnets, their faces strained with worry about the safety of their children and the status of their chickens and goats and milk cows that they'd left behind at their homesteads as they sought safety at this station. They carried uncertainty on their work-and-worry-stooped shoulders. How long could they remain at this partially fortified post where the horses, not the people, were protected behind the stockade? They'd have to decide when it was safe to go home again or if it would ever be safe once they returned. Or their husbands would decide, unless they were men like Robert who shared the load and made a mar-riage a true partnership. I remembered what Robert had said about the spirit going mad if it had no say in its destiny. Did these women have a voice?

I stepped up into the stage, still looking at the mothers rounding up their children to get them out of the way. Mrs. Corbett waved at me from the doorway. The scent of horseflesh filled the crisp morning air. A child I assumed to be an older sister spit on her handkerchief and wiped a smudge from her struggling sibling. These were the very souls Robert's books and articles were designed to lure to these dust-laden climes. These people, not the railroaders, would take, then tame, the West.

For the first time I really understood what the railroad had in mind with this new kind of development. They wanted towns already established, with buildings built up, crops and products stacked at the depot waiting to be shipped back east before the railroad even arrived. In fact, the UP wanted entire towns to be raised up with the promise of the railroad to come, bringing more people and goods but having a full train of paid product to take back to feed the East. The railroad tycoons wouldn't be delivering people to the end of the line waiting for them to create a town; the town would be waiting for the trains.

That meant the hard work of building would be done as Helena and Boise and other towns had begun: with hopes and dreams of a better life created by plows and lumber moved by horses and wagons and the spunk and hardiness of people like those waving as we pulled out.

I wanted to interview them, ask them all the questions about how it had been, how they'd decided to come to this remote place. What did their ranches consist of? How had they endured the hardships of tent-living for months, of the dust clogging their children's eyes, of burying a baby for lack of medicine, their ranches being too far from medical help. Had their families been here for forty years and thus built up a ranch and constructed a house with lumber from their own land? Were they asked their opinions? And what of days and nights alone while a husband and maybe an older son took a meager crop to the nearest town or drove cattle miles through Indian country to where the railroad ended to trade for rice and beans and real coffee. Viands.

I'd never mock the simple fare spread out at these distant posts or farmsteads. These settlers themselves were viands, the "meat" of life, that French word growing from the Latin *vivere*, meaning "to live," and giving rise to "victual," revive and survive. They did all that, these foolhardy women.

And when the time came for a big feast to celebrate the forming of a town and the railroad coming to it, I vowed that day I'd make certain that women like these came to my table too to lend viand as they dined and told their stories to the politicians, corporate heads, and city leaders who wouldn't be there without these weary-lined faces having gone before them.

From *Fifteen Thousand Miles by Stage*, vol. 1, by Carrie Adell Strahorn (page 84)

It was surely a place devoid of all comfort except that gleaned from a table well-laden with pork and beans, bread and black coffee, all of which better satisfied a hungry stomach than all the dainties at a rich man's table though not the viands an epicure would select.

8

Mates

The proprietors of the Cosmopolitan Hotel laughed when we asked for a key to our room, because no one in Helena ever locked their doors, which surprised me, it being a mining town. We weren't approached on the street by beggars either, never saw anyone without a purpose. I suspected that the churches found little to do for charity, though with the brewery up and running, there'd soon be temperance and poverty to address. Here freedom to come and go and be oneself wafted the streets like the cool mountain air that we drew from the wide, blue-sky vista all around. The telegraph lines had been cut by the Indians, but it made little effect on those Montanans. People carried on without news from the outside except from those like us, and they seemed the better for it. Business, mostly at the brick assay office, carried on, and we were given that tour, shown scales that could weigh a single thread, not to mention a tiny speck of gold dust. They had me write my name on a piece of paper that had been weighed

and then weighed my signature. The result:
1/264 of a grain. This I would surely write
to my mother about.

August 23, 1878

Robert got all the politics about Helena, the territorial capital. His news came not only in meetings and interviews but in those lax moments at a fishing hole when men calmed by streams awash with trout let down their guard. As their hands slowly stripped a line luring a fish toward a fly, they might reveal an insight about a political rival or even express a worry over some piece of territorial legislation. I wasn't invited on those little excursions, sadly. I'd fished in Europe and found dropping a worm into water to be a soothing activity.

What I really longed for was purposeful activity. A life without a purpose is a story without an ending.

Robert was driven to write his books. He'd also started a newspaper of sorts that the railroad circulated. When he felt he'd met with all the major influencers who would sing the praises of a railroad—and made copious notes, wrote his weekly *New West Illustrated* articles—he was ready to head for shorter trips to places like Butte and Virginia City, keeping Helena as a base for a time. The Cosmopolitan was our new home.

I suggested writing a piece for the female reader

for Robert's *New West Illustrated*. "Men need mates," I said. "And women will be interested in where they might fit in." I served him cold tea. The water here was so bracing, surging out of mountain streams, that even the oldest tea leaves sparkled to life.

"Has it occurred to you that in these mining towns there's little need of women?"

"Then these towns are doomed. Sugar?"

"Think about it, Dell. Chinese chambermen clean houses and do the laundry. Boardinghouses and hotels serve hot meals, provide baths, a change of linens now and then. Saloons offer a brew without a clicking of one's chastising tongue and not an ounce of disparagement. Why would a miner want a mate at all?" I figured Robert was teasing—at least I hoped so.

"The mines will peter out and then they'll be alone." It didn't seem like a strong argument. I embellished. "For companionship, of course, that's why they need their wives. For shared dreams and hopes and to live through the hard times. To start families as men begin to see their efforts amount to little if they have no one to hear their stories of exploits, of successes and failures as they form legacies to leave behind. Yes, families, that's why men need mates."

"Could be a good theme to explore." He set his tea aside, lathered his face for his shave. "Yes. Write a bit on that. Give male readers words to convince their women to let them come west." He added more soap to his face. "I'm off to Butte this morning."

"You'll spend our first anniversary without me?"

He looked at me in the mirror. I think he'd forgotten.

"Helena's beautiful. We'll celebrate later."

"And what am I to do here?" I pouted, I know, my back up against the high headboard, my stocking feet not yet slipped into my high-tops, though I had donned my corset, soft bustle, slips, and stockings, and my ruffled dress. My hat and gloves were on the table beside the door. I held a crocheted bird, like one we'd handed to guests as wedding mementos. It was stuffed with goose down and I pressed it between my fingers. Along with the linens, it was my way of making each room we found ourselves in, our "home."

"Read to the sick perhaps? Visit the library. It's old, been here since the town was called Last Chance Gulch. A subscription one. I'll give you coins. Write that article. Rest your pretty head on our linens and sleep in a morning or two. Aren't you exhausted? Don't you want a little rest?" He stood before the mirror in our Cosmopolitan room, more spacious than most, with furniture hauled across the prairies from some eastern town. I needed to give his hair a trim.

"Do you? Want rest?" I shifted the pillow behind my back.

He smiled at me in the mirror, wiggled his eyebrows. "If we're never separated, how can we ever have that joy of reunion?"

"I suppose I could write yet another letter to my mother, but she must be bored by my descriptions of mountains and valleys and all nature of hustle and bustle in towns. And her letters to me and my sisters' missives don't catch up in a timely fashion, so it's hard to respond to what's happening in their lives, how Christina is growing, how Hattie's studies progress."

"I bet Fisk, from the *Herald*, might like something about your observations. Maybe you could send a post back to the eastern papers, a woman's point of view from the West." He turned to me. "You've convinced me that women need to see themselves as part of the future of these towns."

"Would you have me tell them of the hard work that awaits them? The separations from their husbands?"

"Some women might like time away."

"Would you?" A man could get a shave and haircut without a mate's assistance too.

I left my place of comfort on the bed and brought the straight razor across his foamed cheeks as he sat now before the mirror. "I suppose separation does offer a natural kind of birth spacing."

"There, you see?" He reached his arm around and patted my bustle.

"But we've no need of such separations. The

opposite, in fact." I approached this delicate subject with a razor in my hand. But he didn't take
my bait.

"I'll talk to Fisk. Your words are more . . .
conversational than mine, more—" He searched
for the word.

"Colorful? Dramatic? Plot-filled?"

"Invitational. They read like a letter you're
sending home to a friend. You bring a kind of
intimacy to your writing, something that my
words of stats and numbers lack."

"And yet you have the published books. The
reviews are excellent all the way to the New York
Herald."

"Because you edit them before I ever send them
off to the New York editors—Ouch!"

"Sorry. Did I nick you?"

"Maybe a little."

"Serves you right for trying to distract me from
going with you to Butte. We'd better get this
straight, Robert. From what you've just said,
you need me in Butte with you. You need my
perspective, my invitational ways. And maybe,
occasionally, my way of saying things. How can
I do that if I'm stuck here, away from you?" I
wiped his face with a towel. The little spot where
I nicked him still bled, so I pulled alum from my
kit and dabbed it.

"I'm listening," he said.

"I know that in these established places like

84

Helena, it's the push to bring the rail lines to them. Helena will survive the gold bust if she's got other businesses, and the railroad promises that transition from gold to other commerce. I do understand that. But I also understand what you're trying to do to form unknown towns in places not on any stage route, places where the railroad will be promised *after* the town is there. I have to see what will make it possible for the Buttes and Helenas to persevere even after there's no mining and somehow write things down about that resilience for women, so they'll take the risk that their new town can endure too. And the better for it because of the railroad. For women, it's not all about fighting the elements or fleeing to posts for protection when times get tough. We need places to tend and others to befriend. Some of us are lucky to have our best friends be our pards, but others aren't. Love gets lost in work, challenge, and disappointment. Or in distance. I don't want that happening to us."

He pulled suspenders over his shoulders that had been lying on either side of his white shirt and checked the nick on his chin. "Wise, as usual. All right. We go to Butte. Together."

I squealed. "And every other place. As you convinced UP I needed to."

He nodded. "The survey team that's here is heading to Yellowstone as soon as the warring stops. They've invited us. Would you like to make that trek?"

"You couldn't keep me from it. That would give me something to write home about!"

"It would. I'll let the captain know he'll be having a lady along."

"Unless I'm with child by then."

"We can hope for good timing then between babies and wars. Best you get things packed up, Mrs. Strahorn." He swatted me on my bustle as I moved by him.

"Indeed, I will, Mr. Strahorn. What are mates for, if not packing up."

He grabbed me by the hand and pulled me to him. He looked at me directly and appeared about to say something, but he kissed me instead— which led to other things mates are known to do.

From *Fifteen Thousand Miles by Stage*, vol. 1, by Carrie Adell Strahorn (page 96)

Pard was a veritable Corliss engine at pumping up statistics of the various products and prospects of every foot of land. . . . There did not seem to be much left for me, except just little, every-day things as they come and go in frontier lands . . . yet with the coming of the dainty matron, the real homemaker, the whole western world brightened, and it was no wonder the great and glorious pioneer cried for a mate.

9

Paradise Road

Yesterday I felt the consequences of what we're doing. It was at the top of a mountain people called Paradise Road, but it wasn't a paradise. The family we met looked exhausted, the horses worn as two young boys and a man walked them to an area where scraping snow would bring them brittle blades of grass if they were lucky. The woman, the mother, a child at her side and one at her breast, blamed her misery not on the elements but on the author of a book, some "Strahorn," who had convinced her husband to take his family west. None of us in the stage said a word. I couldn't think of a comforting thing to say to her or to Robert.

November 15, 1878

My eyes shared the woman's tears along with a saddlebag of guilt. We were near the Red Rock divide in western Montana. Some called it Inspiration Pass and it could be, on a summer day with vistas that rivaled a Tuscan landscape for its breath-taking-away beauty. There was little inspiration for that family that November dusk, though, as six of us rumbled by stage on our way to Virginia City. Winter pushed its nose into the tent of that family we encountered while we were snug as bugs in a blanket inside the Concord. They were not. I felt terrible for them.

The family had made camp while wind blew from the north, whipping a steady snow down on them. A bent-over man tried to catch the wagon canvas slapping in the wind and the wet. Crabby children serenaded and the woman who spoke held a fussy infant in her arms, its little limbs pushing out from the tight blanket she'd wrapped to keep the child warm. A losing battle in that wind and wet. The woman made her pronouncement blaming "that Strahorn" for bringing them to this desolate place.

I looked at Robert. He lowered his eyes.

Our driver broke the silence. "You've stopped at the top of this pass and it can get brutal up here on a night like this. A little protection waits a mile down the hill."

We had no room to take them with us, though we could have brought the children inside, if only for a moment.

The man in the party thanked us. We didn't say a word about the author of that promise that had led them to this horrible night being said author sitting in the safety of a stage, blankets around his legs. I reached beneath my own rug and lifted the still-warm brick the hotel had given us to keep our feet toasty. I handed it to Robert.

"What?"

I pushed it at him, nodded toward the woman.

"Oh." He opened the door to a swirl of cold and snow. "It's not much warmth but it'll offer some comfort to your babe." An older child took the brick, put it to his cheek, then gave it to his mother.

She was too weary to speak. Her husband shouted to the lads with the lariats and horses, and they began the tedious process of re-harnessing. I was glad to see they were taking the driver's advice as he flicked the ribbons and put us back on our way.

No one spoke. Then Robert began talking about the rough elements of weather and land, how exhausting wind and snow were. He spoke of his own trials during the Sioux campaigns— the bitter cold, threadbare blankets, empty stomachs of the soldiers and the reporters, like himself, covering the war. He could list by name the various men and their newspapers who counted on them writing under terrible conditions, their words important for Congress to read to ensure the best possible resources for the soldiers, and for the citizenry and families to know what was happening so far from their heated homes.

"War is never a picnic." This from a general who was another passenger. He bumped his companion when the stage wheel rolled over a larger than normal rock, and Robert's reminiscences were cut short by the driver pulling up.

"I can't see the road ahead." He was a good jehu, so this was worrisome. "Too much snow and wind." His words whipped around him like the scarf that held his hat on, flapping him in the face. I felt a moment of panic. We should have stayed another day at our hotel, but I honestly never knew when to go and when to stand firm.

The general knew this country well, and he and another passenger—the "hanging sheriff," as he called himself—departed the stage with lit lanterns. They ducked their heads to the gale, braced themselves against the windy howl, each stomping a parallel track with their own feet so the jehu could ease our stage forward. Robert and the other passenger offered to relieve them, but they insisted they knew the land best and pushed on until we reached the valley floor and the snow turned more to a drizzle as we pulled into Salisbury, our stop between Helena and Virginia City.

"You shouldn't feel badly about what that woman said," I told Robert, who had become unusually quiet as we prepared our evening rituals in the mountain town. I didn't know if he felt badly; I did. A part of me hoped he had a little remorse for having made everything sound so sweet. But I took it as my duty as a wife to encourage him against memories of war and the shrill words of the woman on the pass.

He helped me float clean sheets from our trunk onto the bed that appeared in the pale light to be void of bugs. I made a mental note, hoping that Virginia City had laundry service so I could get our linens cleaned.

"What did you say?"

"The immigrants we came upon. Her words about 'Strahorn's paradise.' Don't let that discourage you. It's a verification that words—your words—have power. We knew that. We knew that what you wrote would inspire dreaming, a desire that the human spirit has, a longing that's like an ache for something better. 'Desire realized is sweet to the soul.' That's what Proverbs says." He looked at me then. "Those immigrants will make it and they'll tell the tales of how they struggled, just as you remember your war experiences. They pursued their desires and they'll beam that they did it all themselves. Found that sweetness. Imagine." I felt some of that longing myself. That infant's crying tweaked my desires. "But maybe temper your words."

"It's a bit discouraging to think someone's misery is the result of what I wrote."

"You wrote what matters to you—this country,

its beauty and grandeur. One day that woman will see the beauty when the snow melts and they're where they want to be. It's always worse when you're not where you've been, yet not where you're going to be. You can't sit down and think too long about it, you have to keep going. And it's easier to blame someone else, if you can, for your misery while you're in the middle of it. I do it all the time."

He smiled. "No, you don't."

"Maybe not out loud."

He stripped down to his long johns while I found my flannel gown and wool socks and even a bed cap to keep whatever heat my body generated within. The room lacked a stove, but the quilts floated warmth over us. Robert put his head on my shoulder that night. I pulled the quilt up around his neck, held him to me.

"They looked so cold."

"They did."

"You at least thought to give them a warm brick. I couldn't even move. Her words were . . . That flapping canvas. You know they'd hear it all night with the wind. No letup, no relief." He shivered. "And my words brought them to that place of despair."

I pushed his hair from his forehead. "Your words are already written, Robert. You can't take them back and you wouldn't. She needed someone to blame for their plight and better you than her husband that she's dependent on to get them off that mountain. You rescued him." I kissed his forehead. "Let it be a reminder that what we do and say carries meaning."

"You always have another way of looking at things, Dell." We heard a gust of wind push against our window. "I do adore you. Can't thank you enough for putting up with me. I don't deserve it, not a whit."

"Think of the woman's words like a bad review," I offered. "You read the words until you get those first ugly adjectives, then use it to line the bottom of the birdcage."

"It's what I should do with good reviews too, toss them aside."

"Yes, but read them all the way through first."

I felt him chuckle against me and knew we'd crossed a bridge between his own bad memories and the reality of the present and future power of his words.

❖

We spent but a few days in Virginia City, visiting gulches that might become railway passages, hearing of the potential for a growing town, the mining operations. Sometimes a surveyor would go with us, which Robert was always grateful for. It added depth to his work and would please the engineers he'd be sharing his observations with, not to mention the support those other men

93

offered when Robert met up with Jay Gould, the head of Union Pacific.

Robert made notes in his leather-bound book, sketching rock formations, stream width and direction. That notebook was mentioned now and then by newspaper reporters who shared a kinship with him, I suspect.

Occasionally, a news article even mentioned me. The Helena *Weekly Herald* reported that "Mr. Strahorn has a clever assistant in his wife, an educated lady and enthusiastic literary worker who is his companion in this Montana tour of sightseeing."

I beamed. Robert grunted. Did I sense a tad of jealousy? I did.

Sightseeing, that's what I wrote in my journal. Of course it was more than that. The landscape and people worked my literary muscles. I wanted to write of them too. Robert worked on yet another book, *The New West*, and we'd be heading to Chicago before long to see to its publication. But for now, I made notes about the people we met, how they looked, funny stories they told. I had an ear for accents and could detect North Carolinian from Missourian, Germans from Wisconsin, as different from those settling in Texas. I remembered names and faces—something Robert struggled with—so I could whisper who approached in a hotel dining room and even give him a hint of where we'd met before that hand reached out to shake Robert's as he stood. I wasn't sure then what I'd ever do with those observations I wrote down, but the activity fed me, gave me something to nurture.

The stage companies now turned to a winter schedule that was really no schedule at all. No night travel allowed except some evenings when the moon might be full or the weather projected by the width of the ring around the moon suggested rainless roads. Or we'd be awakened and told to be ready to leave in an hour, though it be three in the morning. Sometimes we stopped early afternoon; other times not. And we were at the mercy of the openings a stage had as we rode on passes paid by the railroad. We couldn't bump other passengers who might have found a better schedule.

"It's really inconvenient, Robert." I rushed about to put the linens into the trunk, folded the wet towels that never dried overnight in this cold country, wrapping them in newspaper to keep the damp from affecting the linens, knowing those towels would come open with words inked all over them, lifted from the newsprint. I might never get the latest column out.

"That it is, Dell. But we can't complain. If word got back to UP that we railroader freeloaders were whining about the conditions, we'd never hear the end of it. Just be as gracious as you always are. One day maybe we'll be able to pay our own way and then we can assert our preferences."

"I know. At least I can complain to you, my Pardner."

He dragged the trunk toward the door, the exertion causing him to catch his breath. He often had that sort of breathing issue. I didn't know why. "I'll alert the clerk and get some help with this. You bring your bag as soon as you can."

"I'm hurrying."

He came back in and turned me around toward him. "We're meeting people we'll have as friends for a lifetime, seeing places that sear the mind with beauty. You're free of drudgery—well, most of the domestic drudgery—and adventure awaits. That's how we must look at the inconveniences. And we're doing it together. What more could you ask?"

"You're keeping me from packing, Mr. Strahorn. Off with you."

"See you at the front desk." He saluted me, turned on his heels as his boots clicked the wooden floor toward the stairs.

I turned back to the mirror, settled the fur-lined bonnet over my head, and tied the red ribbons beneath my chin. I could see my breath in the cold air. "What more could you ask?" I spoke to that pudgy-faced image. What I was thinking was this: *To be in a warm home of my own, holding an infant in my arms.*

From *Fifteen Thousand Miles by Stage*, vol. 1, by Carrie Adell Strahorn (page 97)

Then a sharp, shrill voice piped up from the wagon tongue saying: "If this is Strahorn's paradise, as his book calls it, I just wish he had to live in it, that's all, but I wish I was back in Missouri whar we 'uns come from," and then she burst into tears. She did not know that the man "what write the book" was enclosed in that stage-coach, or she might have said more.

10

The Elasticity of Love

*I consider myself still youthful and that we
have time yet to begin a family. I must not
dwell on this but instead find other avenues
to nurture that part of me that longs to
mother. We are too far flung for me to spoil
Christina, my niece, and Robert's brothers
are equally spread across the country, so
we have little contact with them or their
fine children. I could teach, perhaps. But
we travel so much. Maybe I could write
children's stories of the West. None would
take the place of telling stories to a child
of my own. Our own. There I am again,
longing for what is not in my present life.
Such suffering sucks out vitality and I must
not let that happen. Where is that happy
lane that seemed so easy to stay inside of?
At least when I'm with my family, I feel at
home.*

December 27, 1878

In the year of our marriage, I had learned to unravel
the hurts of words spoken in haste, or sometimes
a dismissiveness Robert could give, especially

when he was pulling his notes together and found any interruption difficult to manage. I felt shuttled off, or worse, it might take long seconds before he acted as though he even heard me, so engaged was he in his work. I envied that. And the usual tricks I'd developed as a middle child to manage the "green sickness," as Shakespeare called it, of an excelling older sister or a beautiful younger one, both who nevertheless got our parents' attentions more easily than I did, eluded me. I had enjoyed walking at a good pace through our old Marengo park, sitting beneath sumac and oak, expressing frustration to a Being I believed loved me despite my complaints. Or I could sometimes ride out on manicured paths atop good horseflesh from a nearby stable. But singing with a regular choir—which always gave me new sustenance—escaped me in Montana despite good, sound people and a landscape worthy of singing about.

We spent days on the stagecoach—and nights. Even in small places like Butte or Deer Lodge, there'd be meetings, trips to interesting sites, but as a lady I had to be as though handing out calling cards, always alert, smiling, gracious, lest I upset a city father or two. Or their wives. I had no friends, really. Always wondering if those who invited me to tea in fact were courting favor with my husband. When Robert wanted me to plan a salon, I knew that was exactly what he intended: to influence, cajole, even manipulate.

Once Robert came upon a stage stop where the proprietor had a copy of his book. He bravely asked him if the tome was worth reading. The man said it was a great book by a feller who's "got 'em all skinned on drawing the long bow." Robert knew what he meant and asked for a bit of clarification, wondering if the man thought his descriptions or numbers were deceptive. He was told that there wasn't a single "gol darned lie," but that the writer had the "darndest way of telling truth of any man you ever saw."

Would the man describe a con artist the same way? Robert invited people to find their dreams in the West, at the behest of the railroad. Hyperbole? A bit, but with good intentions.

〰〰

Speaking of intentions, I have the best of such in writing to my family of my happy-lane moments, leaving out the painful ones.

Mary, my sister, suggested as much when we returned to Marengo for Christmas that year. We were in the dining room having a late breakfast, the others having gone off for final Christmas shopping.

"Are you happy?"

"Who couldn't be happy? The townspeople treat me like royalty. We get the best rooms in the hotels, and one town father even gave us a room in their own home for whenever we're there. That saves on expenses for the railroad, which makes Robert look better and keeps them happy about the extra expense of his traveling companion."

"But what do you do all day?" Christina, now a toddler, fed herself from her high chair while her mother chattered with me. A silver spoon pounded the tray now and then.

"What ladies do. I have my toilet, though it's abbreviated as we often leave at a moment's notice. I read to people if the town has a hospital. I do laundry unless the Chinese chambermen are available. Such efficient men they are."

"Men do the laundry?"

"You're deprived of the ways of the West, my sister. The Chinese lay rail lines, dig in mines, cook, do laundry, sleep in colonies separate from others, and they send all their money home to family. Those old miners have no regard for washing their own pants. And, I've watched in the laundry houses: those stiff pants are often dusted with gold that those Chinese brush into a tin. It wouldn't surprise me if some of them are millionaires."

"Surely not."

"Surely yes. I even considered taking it up."

My sister laughed at that. "Have you had to do the wash?"

I shook my head. "Now and then, but I always secure the help of local women, or the chambermen, so I'm not hauling heavy tubs of water."

"And, is there a little Strahorn in the future? You won't be hauling tubs of water then for sure."

"Not yet," I chirped. "We have had a fair number of nights when I shared a room with more than Robert."

"You didn't."

"I did." I pressed the loose tea, squeezing out the leaves. "Some of the places we stay in are built with green lumber, and as they dry, there are gaps between the boards that separate the rooms and us from the outdoors. I tack my linens up for privacy and hope no gust of wind unveils my unmentionables while still on me."

"You ought to write these things down, Carrie. Like the letters you send us that we read in the evening as a kind of respite for our days. Charming all the way, though I do wonder what you're not telling us. Do you keep a diary?"

"Robert's the writer in the family. His *New North West* is well received and he's also published a paper on Montana. It's for sale in time for Christmas."

She didn't notice my avoidance of the diary question. I didn't want others to know what I might be writing down to draw upon later for a memoir one day, perhaps.

"Nothing personal to your Pard, but I find his books dry," she continued. "Willie does too, but he finishes them. And they have gotten better with a little more life to the statistics."

"I've encouraged him to add a few illustrative vignettes."

"Yes, that's likely what makes them more readable."

Christina pounded her bowl on the tray.

"Youth needs attention at regular intervals," I said. "May I lift her out?"

"Of course. Carrie . . ." My sister hesitated then, as Christina sat on my lap playing with the strand of pearls I wore. "I've gotten something published."

"Mary, that's wonderful! Now who's been holding back. Why didn't you say?"

"I didn't want you to feel badly. It's a short piece, about a small business run by a woman here in Marengo. Human interest, they call them. The *Tribune* picked it up from our little paper, giving it a wider distribution."

"I'm proud of you, I truly am."

"You don't feel badly that I've published, do you? You did so much better in composition classes than I did."

"I'm more envious that you have Christina here." I took my pearls off and draped them over my niece's head. She slipped off my lap to look in the mirror.

"Someday you'll have a family."

"I hope so, though traveling right now with an infant would be a strain." I remembered the family at Inspiration Pass. I would stay home rather than put my child in that kind of peril, but then one never knew what the weather and landscape might conspire to do. Tornadoes plowed through Illinois with some regularity, so having a roof over one's head in the midst of a city didn't necessarily protect one's family either.

I was happy for my sister, but there was also a little twinge of green envy, not jade so much as olive. "At least I can sing better than you can," I teased.

"No contest there." She stood to take Christina's dish to the sink while the old Labrador eased in from the other room to lick up the cracker crumbs. I scratched the dog's graying head.

"Did I tell you I encountered one of Daddy's old patients, way out in the wilds of the Idaho Territory? We had to travel through some rough country with the Bannock war going on. At this remote stage stop, this man approached and said he was one of 'ol' Doc Green's patients' and he recognized me. Isn't that something? It made me terribly homesick."

"You're here now and I'm so grateful." She hugged me and I felt tears press against my eyes.

"Let's go into Chicago with Robert tomorrow." I lifted my voice to its happiest timbre. "While he's at his publisher's, we can visit some of the shops. That's the one thing I'm totally deprived of, though Helena and Omaha both have some fine stores. It takes a long time for the fashions to catch up to them."

"I don't mean to be obtuse, but where do you wear the latest fashions?"

I laughed and relished the telling. "They hold fetes for us, dances, dinners. I have to look the part. They know why we're there, promoting the railroad, and the newspapers follow our every move like Hansel and Gretel, hoping the railroad tracks will soon be in their region. There are articles like 'WH Todd and wife'—they never name the women—'of Benton, accompanied Mr. and Mrs. Strahorn to the grand hotel reception.' Things like that. Or this article: 'The trip to Yellowstone National Park has been postponed and the Strahorns travel on to Butte next week.' That lets the next town know we're coming. They can line up the dignitaries to glad-hand Robert about the railroad. I sometimes think I can hear them whispering at every turn, 'Bring it here, bring it here, bring it here.' Like the chugging of the steam engine itself."

"You were going to Yellowstone? Oh my goodness."

"If the war ever stops and we're still around when the survey party enters. We've been invited."

"That's a first for a Green sister."

"What is?" Our father entered the kitchen. His office was located through a separate entrance into the house.

"Carrie gets to go to Yellowstone."

"When it's safe." I didn't want him worrying.

"That sounds like a fine trip, Carrie." He moved to fix himself coffee.

"Of course, you won't go if you're with child, will you?" Mary asked.

"I do see a fair number of pioneering women riding like their men, astride, with rifles in the scabbards and burgeoning bellies, and no one bats an eye in the West," I told her.

My father frowned. "You're surely not counting on children, are you, Carrie?"

Mary said, "Why wouldn't she, Daddy?"

"Do you know something I don't know?" I kept my voice light as a feather, but my heart beat like a racing metronome. Sometimes our hearts know things before our heads can react.

"Well, I, uh, Robert . . . that is, uh. Oh my. I thought—" He cleared his throat. "Robert had mumps. During one of those terrible Sioux campaigns. He nearly died. I don't think . . . that is, orchitis is a condition that, well, it would be unlikely that he could . . . I thought you knew."

From *Fifteen Thousand Miles by Stage*, vol. 1, by Carrie Adell Strahorn (page 64)

Youth is often deeply hurt, but so elastic that it bounds back into happy line again with very little encouragement.

11

Baby Steps Forward

At least I was surrounded by the safety of family when I got the news of Robert's condition. Mumps! Infertility from mumps isn't certain, of course. There are miracles. It's the absence of Robert's telling me that hurts. I can hardly write of it here, the fracture in the possibility of the joys of motherhood so deep. I can make excuses for him—he didn't want to assume we couldn't conceive; didn't want to bring up an issue needlessly. Still.

December 28, 1878

"The joys of motherhood" had in that moment of my father's words slipped into sorrow. Mary put her arms around me, held me. "I'm so sorry."

"I'll . . . I'll be fine. There's nothing certain, is there, Daddy?"

"Well—"

"I'm sure Robert didn't mention it because he didn't want me to be discouraged. He adores me."

"Yes, he does."

"I . . . I think I want to be alone now."

I excused myself and went up to my old room that was now the bedroom that Robert and I occupied. I wanted to be by myself and had forgotten that he would be there, at my desk.

Upon hearing me come in, he spoke without looking up. "Wait just a moment, Dell, while I finish this section."

A moment could mean anywhere from five minutes to two hours when Robert was writing. I didn't respond. I sat myself up on my old bed, pillows behind my head, and stared forward. Oak branches scraped against the window and a rainbow formed from the sunlight, reflecting against the cut-glass vase on the dresser. After waiting ten minutes or so, I left. He never heard me leave. At the front door, I donned my rubber boots, muffler, and hood, threw my cape over my shoulders, and opened the outside door.

"I'll go with you." Mary set her crocheting aside and stood as I held the door against the cold. "Mother and Hattie are back. They can watch Christina."

"I'd rather go alone."

She stopped and the old lab, Casey, bumped right into her.

"I'll take Casey if he wants to go."

"He always wants to go. You're sure being alone is a good idea? Where's Robert?"

"Working on his book. I'm fine," I lied. "Please."

She nodded assent.

"Come on, Casey. Let's see if we can find a rabbit in the snow."

I knew I needed to speak to Robert. First, I'd gather information from my father's medical books. We could visit specialists, of course. But the greatest pain came from Robert's not sharing. When I didn't conceive and wondered out loud what was wrong with me, he'd remained silent. That's not true. He had held me and told me not to worry, that we'd have a fine, full life until that time arrived. Perhaps he didn't know that infertility could happen. Yes, I wanted to name his betrayal ignorance, not willful omission.

Casey left the path shoveled by the good citizens of Marengo, and I followed his footprints in the light snow. He searched for rabbits, I thought, or maybe he wanted to see different terrain, since this was the route my mother often walked him. We were both on new paths. All the visions I had of seeing myself with child, carrying an infant in my arms, juggling marriage and parenthood—all I had imagined drifted away like feathers on a windy day. No substance to them at all.

Jingle bells rang on the carriages going by. Laughter whispered into the dusk, and I felt such longing I thought my heart would break. I stopped, leaned my back against an oak, my cape so thick I couldn't feel the bark. The cold air stung my cheeks and made me stay in that moment rather than morosely sinking into self-pity. The dog stopped suddenly, turned, then limped back toward me. "You're better at noticing my movements than Robert is." I scratched his head again. "Maybe I'll get a dog. Except dogs would be even more difficult to travel with than a child. Come on, let's head back."

The gas lighter approached, lifted his long-handled starter to the lanterns, and light burst onto the path. He tipped his hat and went on down the street, illuminating as he went.

Casey barked then, and I looked up. In the distance, I saw a man whose gait I knew was Robert's. He walked fast and then started to wave and I could see his eyes above the scarf that wound around his chin and nose. "Dell!" I waved back and as he reached me, breathless, he said, "I'm so sorry. Your father told me. I—I have no words."

"Did you know that mumps could cause infertility? Did you keep it from me?"

"Only out of my own fear. I didn't know until after we married how incredibly important it was for you, for us, to have children. I should have. I'm dense. I'm really dense."

"You are that."

"But I remembered when . . ." He hesitated. "When Carrie was ill, I remember you telling her she'd get better and that, yes, she might not be able to have children but that that wasn't the end of the world. There were lots of orphaned children who need help. Lots of babies whose mothers or fathers couldn't keep them. You made such a convincing case that I thought that, well—"

"I was encouraging a sick woman, Robert."

"But didn't you mean what you said?"

"Then, yes. For her. And perhaps I will again, for me, but it is a blow."

He put his elbow through mine, making sure my gloved hand didn't pull out of the muff. "I'll work a lifetime to make it up to you, I will. Anything you want. Anything."

"Right now I want to go home, and when you leave for Omaha on the train, I want to be with you and not left behind like last Christmas."

"Consider it done."

He held me then as we stood beneath the lantern light. But something had changed. I saw a crossroads and how I dealt with it I knew would make a difference for our entire lives. The youthful wound was deep, but I remembered a word in my father's medical book—*incarn*. It meant to grow new flesh. That's what I'd have to do now and hope that every time I saw a child, it wouldn't reopen this wound.

≈≫≪≈

After Christmas, we stayed in an Omaha hotel a few months, then moved on to Denver, where

Robert's latest published article raised talk of immigration. It was that "army conquering a wilderness as it follows the trail of the pioneer" that made me wonder if the needs of those many people could make me forget my hopes of motherhood in the more traditional sense.

"I didn't expect my work to be controversial." Robert held the Denver *Rocky* newspaper in his hand while I packed us for the wilds of Idaho, Robert's new data-gathering site. The Union Pacific wanted another pamphlet on that area. The Montana Territorial government had allocated money for more copies of Robert's book about Montana, and there was much discussion about the good and bad of luring so many "tenderfoots" west.

"People want commerce, but they also hate to give up their way of life with new people arriving." He read a few of the letters to the editor, including the one chastising that "author Robert Strahorn."

"Change threatens people, Robert. And you're whipping up change like Mama whips up egg whites. They'll make a fine meringue, but meringue can go soft and sticky in the right conditions."

"I guess the UP is getting what it wanted. Interest in the West. They'll have to live with the demands that'll come for running the tracks 'through my town. No, my town!' " He acted out a town meeting with raised fists, depending on which town got chosen for that short line.

"Let's hope we don't get run out on those rails when they arrive to a site that rivals another. People won't take kindly to that rebuff." I had no idea how prescient I could be.

I tried to put the news of Robert's mumps and the repercussions from my mind as we rode the train west. I'd focus on the adventure. It might have even been then that I began to think about those developing towns full of hopeful pioneers and how I might mother them rather than children.

⊰≫⊱

We grabbed the thrice-weekly stage one morning later that summer and approached the many soda-laden springs after days of travel toward Idaho. More than one hundred pools of water gave the place its name Soda Springs. A pungent smell wafted upward from some circles; others looked clear as crystal, no steam above any of them, merely tiny bubbles.

Our guide was another military man originally from Boston but now the owner of a lovely home in view of the sulphur springs that had become a kind of oasis for travelers on what people called the Oregon Trail. The Codmans had traveled all over the world with Mr. Codman as a former sea captain, and these were the waters he and his wife wanted as their summer view. No steam—so no bathing in this place like the hot springs we'd visited in Montana—but good water for horses and laundry. Some pools cast off strange smells.

"Check that pool over there." The captain directed my dear Pard toward a pond maybe five feet across. "You leave your mount right there and take in a nice deep breath at that spring. Breathe in. You'll like it." The captain winked at me.

Robert always listened to men with "Captain" or "General" before their names. He leaned his lanky frame over and inhaled.

His legs buckled under him and he fell in.

"Robert!" I shouted, then lifted my skirt over the hook on my saddle, catching it as I dismounted. By the time I reached the spring, the now very chastened captain had pulled Robert out by his boots and my husband stood dripping wet and coughing up a storm. "What were you thinking, Captain?"

The captain had been fast on his feet, I gave him that. He'd pushed past the ammonia smell and had Robert back in seconds. Robert coughed and vomited.

"I wasn't thinking, ma'am. I'll never joke with that again. Didn't think the fumes would fell him like that."

"I should hope not."

"Don't be hard on him, Dell. He didn't mean it. I—I've had tuberculosis." Another assault on fertility and the lack of frankness in our marriage. The immediate demanded my attention.

"You could have drowned." I glared at Captain Codman, who kept his distance from me. I clucked my tongue in disgust. Silly men, one playing jokes, the other brushing it off. "Let's get him back. Dry clothes are in order for you both, wouldn't you agree?"

"Yes, ma'am. My Tilly will rustle up some Boston chocolate for him. You'd make a good captain, Missus."

I was in no mood for cajoling.

Sometimes Robert's charm and the way he had of deferring to others to inflate their ego led people to believe he was a tenderfoot. My Pard may have behaved as such by doing what the captain asked. I'm sure that old captain would call me hawkish for being a shadow watching over my husband, but Robert could be naïve. I'd just seen another example of it.

He dripped, wet. His horse wasn't too happy to be so close to the smell, and the animal skittered, taking a bit of time and attention from a sound we heard next: a woman's voice, frightened.

"Lacy, you come back here."

A small girl, maybe five, her thin dress flowing out behind her as though she raced the wind, had darted away from her mother's hands. We saw the child dance toward the same pool that had overcome Robert.

"Lacy!" Her mother deserted her scrub board, ran.

"Can you grab her, Captain?" I shouted.

Curiosity, the lure of the fascinating, maybe even seeing Robert plunge in, then be pulled safely out, all tumbled the child into the fetid water. The captain was right there, held his breath as he plunged in. I prayed for that child, that mother.

The captain pushed her out into her waiting mother's arms. But it was too late. She had aspirated the noxious stuff into her lungs and lay limp, her bare toes looking so cold.

"No, no, no, no." I heard that mother's words for days after that, as her husband, then perhaps a brother and a sister-in-law, swarmed around her. One man took the child from her arms. Tears marked his dusty cheeks as she thanked him.

I hear her still, echoing in my own lament, that cry of wishing for what isn't. We each mourned the shortness of life but also railed at what we could not control. I struggled with what it all meant, the death of innocents. What was this desire to go forward into a new land, to *pioneer,* and how would this mother, like mothers past, put the death of this child to rest so that she could move on? How did any of us come to terms with disaster and disappointment; keep ourselves from despair?

There was nothing we could do now. But on

the ride to the captain's quarters these thoughts filled me when it should have been gratitude that my husband was safe. His larger body (than the little girl's) and the fact that he had fainted from the fumes before falling in likely kept him from greater damage to his lungs.

"What's happened, John?" Captain Codman's wife welcomed us and Robert's wet clothes; her husband's too. Their home displayed seafaring motifs.

"One terrible disaster and one rescue from a joke gone bad," the captain told her.

She looked at me and nodded toward our room. "I'll have hot water brought in. And chocolate." She gave orders to a housemaid while her dear captain put his head to hers in what must have been a familiar gesture of affection for this childless couple. She lingered but a moment, then returned to her hospitable duties. She was all generosity and grace as she wrapped her arms around me. "I'm so sorry for whatever has made you all sad." She didn't try to cheer us up as I might have. She then walked me arm in arm to our room, gave us hot chocolate and a blanket for Robert that I soon wrapped around him after helping him strip from his soaked clothes.

We waited for the steaming water of a bath. "I'm sorry, Dell. Sorry for everything."

I put my head to his and we sat that way, breathing in each other's breath. I knew he spoke not of this latest episode but of the greater loss.

"It would be too difficult to have a child now anyway," I said. "They're hard to keep safe and—"

My voice cracked and he held me then.

"Maybe I'll mother towns into being," I offered.

"Shhhh. You don't have to try to fix this."

I remember those days in early 1879 as discomfiting. I was as vulnerable as a Boston lobster during its first year of life when it must shed its hard shell so many times in order to grow larger. Oh, the vulnerability while it grows!

From *Fifteen Thousand Miles by Stage*, vol. 1, by Carrie Adell Strahorn (page 146)

The joys of motherhood have often been envied as fond parents watched the budding and maturing intellects of their children and noted their development into men and women of honor and refinement, but it is no small compensation to help make towns and cities spring from earth in answer to the demands of an army conquering a wilderness as it follows the trail of the pioneer.

12

The Chivalrous West

Tonight I sleep with 26 men. Should I ever write my memoir, I'm not sure I will include this episode except that it speaks to the chivalrous West, where even the most crusty rancher removes his hat at the sight of a lady, holds it to his chest, and with watery eyes calls me "Ma'am," as though he approached royalty rather than a bedraggled, dust-shrouded woman. Robert had warned me about the lack of privacy at times, but this is surely the prime example.

April 15, 1879, at a stage stop somewhere in the West

They were as miserable as I was. The worst for me was that I couldn't undress and there were no bathing options, except for the pitcher and water bowl provided (and refilled by the agent).

But the occasion did affirm what I was coming to learn: chivalry was alive and well in the West. Yes, this country was wild, with whole towns overtaken by corrupt lawmen and gun-toting inebriates who intimidated, raped, and pillaged.

119

(Robert didn't write about that. He didn't want to scare off the travelers seeking their dreams. And I certainly didn't write of that kind of thing in my epistles to my family.) But they were brought under control by good men and women bravely stepping up to take their towns back. It would be those same kinds of people who built the settlements that Robert promoted.

Indeed, those miners and buckaroos sharing their blankets were examples of what I wanted to believe was the real West. And it's true: Sir Walter Raleigh had nothing on the cowboy. Those wiry men remove their hats in church; and when a lady enters a room, western men hold those weather-worn John Stetson beaver hats or simple felt chapeaus to their chests. Men give up their horses and walk in rough terrain so a woman can ride. They even take the outside windows in a coach, despite the closer attack of dust surging through the openings allowing air in but also assault by the elements.

We'd traveled through forty miles of such sagebrush desert with no water along the way except what was carried for the horses, only to find ourselves in that room with twenty-six men, all of us stuck in the only structure at the station. We'd rattled through ashy earth, clouds of dust shrouding the stage wheels as though snow poured up from the ground instead of down from the sky. We breathed through scarves over our noses. Everyone in the stage looked like racoons, eyes framed by dust. Or like bad bandits hiding behind our bandanas.

"We can't accept all these blankets," Pard told the men that night. "We have enough with our own. Let's all be as warm as we can. But we thank you for your generosity."

"Well, take the place by the stove then." This from a miner with one bad eye he kept patched.

Pard agreed and then they all moved as though choreographed as one unit, away, so we could lay our blankets down.

Those twenty-six men were all as dusty as we were. The room we were in had but one small window, though a wide gap at the bottom of the door let in skiffs of snow and dust and bracing March winds. Robert took one of those proffered blankets and used it to stuff the opening under the door. Our spot by the stove felt heavenly despite the hard floor. I held gratitude that we weren't trying to stay warm in the coach.

I didn't mean to shriek when a chivalrous traveler grabbed my ankle instead of a chunk of wood in the night as he hoped to stoke up the fire. It was a miracle he didn't faint dead away with my screech. My mother was of the belief that a woman's ankles were as untouchable as her bosom. I, on the other hand, had read a suffragette say that "until we get control of our ankles we women will never have control over our brains."

I had control of my ankles; my scream proved it as he dropped the blanket like a hot poker.

The poor buckaroo (that's what they call cowboys in that Idaho country) apologized profusely, but I assured him he was forgiven and Robert insisted he'd take no revenge on his wife's limb being mistaken for a log.

"At least you didn't imply he'd touched your property," I whispered when we'd settled back down beneath our blanket.

"And have you beat me over the head with your umbrella? You're no property of mine, dear woman." I felt more than heard his chuckle. I wished he could have seen my grin with his recognition that I belonged to myself and not to him as chattel.

And that was another thing about the West: women were seen more often as equals, despite that cowboy's horror that he'd touched another man's wife's ankle. Wyoming allowed women to vote as early as 1869. Oregon's married white women could own property in their own name from 1850. Even single women could own land there. Robert opined that suffrage for women came to Wyoming before anywhere else in the States because there were few women, and men didn't feel threatened by them getting the vote. I, on the other hand, suspected those men granted the vote to attract more strong women. Granting franchise was a golden glow to many women that could lure them west even without a husband to accompany them. Robert's West was also a place that could bring new beginnings to women who might be seeking a mate or an independent life. If they were willing to work for it, their male neighbors would grant respect to their efforts, if sometimes a bit grudgingly. Those twenty-six men I bedded down with (I didn't write it that way when I wrote to my mother) likely hadn't seen a woman for weeks or even months. They treated me with such deference so as not to scare me off.

There was no begrudging my presence that night, and there is something to be said for opportunities for generosity. Giving makes us feel better about our own circumstances and receiving can be a gift as well. Our accepting that warm place by the fire appeared to be a gift to all those men.

In the morning, their generosity continued with Robert and me allowed to sit on chairs at the table while others stood. We knew we'd all be heading out again into the same dust and chilled weather they spent their days in until they reached the mines clutched in the mountains' hands. There'd been no bed within twenty miles of that stage stop.

We departed that morning, six of us inside and another six up top the coach. They were farther from the dusty wheels but more exposed to the mercury hovering below freezing, at least until the sun came up. Our fellow passengers spoke of trials, of longing for family not seen in months or years. One started to speak of a child's death by a rattlesnake, and I coughed, interrupting.

"Maybe some references to danger in your pamphlets would be good," I suggested to Robert that evening. We had a room to ourselves for that night.

"I don't want to frighten people."

"No, but they must know it's not always soft pillows and popped corn. Perhaps telling of an occasional tragedy would be a providential warning so there'd be no claim that they were misled." He seemed to consider my suggestion, tapping his lead against his lip. I added more. "And perhaps share the message that despite the hardships, people endure. That immigrant family from Inspiration Pass is doing well in Montana, didn't you tell me that?" Robert had followed up on that Missouri family.

He nodded.

"So you see, a few authentic stories of pain and the resilience of recovery could be good additions in your books."

"It'll appeal to the adventurous side of a woman too, I imagine you'll try to tell me."

"Yes, the adventurous side. The mountain-climbing, ferry-operating, boardinghouse-owning, gold-mining woman. Just the kind to win over a western man."

"They like ladies too, I've noticed. Beautiful ones, like you."

"Charm will get you anywhere with me, Mr. Strahorn."

He returned to his writing and I filed my nails, feeling a little lost despite his appreciation of my suggestions and his compliment. I picked up my little wedding-favor bird, squeezed it. I'd have to find another purpose besides hoping one day to have a family of my own or merely playing second fiddle to a maestro. Without that, I'd become morose and bring Robert down with me. No, I was still an adventure-seeking woman. I just had to let her come out.

From *Fifteen Thousand Miles by Stage,* vol. 1, by Carrie Adell Strahorn (page 153)

I was the only woman, but there were twenty-six men, all looking for a place for a few hours' rest; yet almost with one voice every man demanded that I should have his blanket, insisting that he did not need (?) them, and instantly putting them in a pile down by the stove. . . . It was a strange night and I wondered what the good folks at home would think if they could have had a glimpse of our surroundings.

13

What Fools We Mortals Be

Doing what I haven't ever done before has become a kind of purpose for me. This month, I proposed something truly exciting. Robert had conceded that it could be exhilarating. He also has an adventure planned for me "if we survive."

May 10, 1879

The day before Mother's Day, we were going to cross over the 650-foot Dale Creek chasm coming out of Cheyenne toward Salt Lake City with the steaming power of the train pushing us forward while we rode the cowcatcher. All because we could. Robert negotiated favors with the UP, allowing us to do things most people couldn't.

The cowcatcher fanned out in front of the engine and I gripped the iron with my gloved hands that day. I anticipated that the thrust of the wind as we raced down the grade at ninety feet to the mile (those are Robert's statistics coming out of me now) would drive us back against the cowcatcher so fiercely that we couldn't have moved if we'd wanted to. Still, the engineer's admonition to "hold on tight for it is sure death if you loosen your hold even a little bit!" did make me think we might want to lash ourselves on. We didn't, trusting to Providence, though I'm not sure Providence would intervene in such willful foolishness.

"We're really going to do this!" I could barely keep from giggling.

"Yes, we are, and if we survive, I will ask to have my head examined by the nearest physician."

"Oh, Robert. It'll be such a joy. Hang on—"

The train jerked into movement, slowly at first. The thin air felt cool, then cold against my face as we picked up speed, the engine noises making any speech impossible, the metal's cold seeped through the stays of my corset. Wind in our faces pushed at the ribbons I'd wrapped over my hat and tied beneath my chin to keep it on. The smell of smoke wafted around us as we gained speed, two engines and a string of cars with passengers and freight surging behind us. Then we were racing, racing down a mountain with trees and rocks whizzing by us on either side. I screamed, the wind shoving even my joy back into my mouth. My face felt frozen. With effort, my cheeks flapping, our bodies vibrating, I looked at Robert, but he stared straight ahead, his jaw clenched. He wore no hat.

And then we were slowed upon the Dale Creek Bridge itself and all scenery backed away and there was only sky on either side. It was as though we were in the clouds. I tried to peek over the edge to see the depths, that sliver of silver that was Dale Creek, six hundred and fifty feet below us. I pressed back after a glance.

We picked up speed again, racing through high sagebrush desert and then suddenly, darkness.

It was the blackness that began my panic. "What's hap-pen-ing, Ro-bert!"

He left his grip to put his arm in front of me as if to protect me from an unknown assailant in the dark cavern of what I realized must be the snow-shed, a place for the trains to be protected from the heavy snows that would otherwise close the tracks in deep winter. But why the dark? Usually lanterns lit the way. It was like a coffin. And then we were in a long tunnel, equally black, the echo of the engine in that dark cavern rattling against my ears, the surrounding darkness pressing like a great weight against me. I had trouble breathing. I wondered if we had somehow died, the smoke a heavy presence with no escaping allowed.

Or perhaps the engineer had purposely plunged us into darkness so we'd never again use our pass.

But when we hit daylight again at the end of the tunnel, we slowed, then stopped. Trainmen jumped from the side and two on the ground came running toward us. I could see from the engineer's face that he was horror-struck. We learned why. The keeper of the lights had become ill so there'd been neither light in the tunnel nor assurance for each train that the track ahead in the tunnel was safe. By the time the engineer realized no lanterns lit the snow-shed, it was too late to stop, and once inside the tunnel, he couldn't stop or the smoke from the train would have suffocated everyone.

Robert and I were both shaky and grateful. He walked us beside the train to the Pullman car so we could recover. Me, to search for my breath.

"Maybe that was foolish," I gasped.

"We survived." He coughed. "And you talked your malleable husband into doing something he really would never have done on his own. You're quite the adventurer yourself, Mrs. Strahorn." He kissed me, touched his fingers to my wind-and-hat-smashed hair.

"Indeed."

And I was. Quite the adventurer.

"Now it's my turn to offer up an excursion," Robert told me a few weeks later. We'd arrived in the Idaho town of Bonanza and in the morning headed up the mountain by horseback, taking narrow trails no wider than a horse's steady foot in places. I kept my eyes on Robert's horse in front of me, my stomach queasy from the depth of the ravines on either side of that ridgeback. I wasn't feeling well that morning, the "mocking monthlies" having arrived while on the train.

And I hadn't really wanted to go to the mine. Close places made me clammy inside, increased the pace of my breathing. My temples would throb. Heights were not a problem, but narrow passageways were.

I remembered as a child having my sister Mary and her friend roll me up in a carpet. I thought it great fun until I couldn't move my limbs, couldn't see out, the wool fibers so close to my nose I thought I'd inhaled a sheep. My cries were muffled, so my sister thought I giggled. By the grace of God, my mother walked in at that moment, assessed the situation, and unfurled me. Snot ran from my nose and I clung to her in tears.

"I suffocate," I told her.

She didn't correct my grammar, chastised my sister and her friend who got sent home while Mary spent the rest of the afternoon in a corner. The smell of a wool carpet can take me back there in an instant. Even the thought of a closed space causes my heart to race.

Which was what my heart was doing, pounding like a steam engine. Plus, I didn't feel like being my sweet and funny public self that morning, watching my Pard glad-hand potential investors in the railroad's future.

But I did love horses and a good ride through grand vistas, and Robert promised me I'd have that. Staying behind in the hotel lent itself to self-pity, a never-pretty condition that is often remedied by putting oneself into challenges that require one's total absorption. The greatest antidote to tiredness was engagement. I'd let the steep trail up to the mine consume me. I didn't have to do more than arrive. I could say no to going down into the mine shaft.

I forced myself not to think about the closed-in shaft that awaited me and turned as I had before to the landscape to bring me calm.

The trek up to the Montana Mine was glorious. I'd never seen such timber thick with birdsong drifting through the firs. Then rocks and walls dotted with lichens, patches of snow leading to a steep ascent where I held on to my horse's mane to keep from sliding back as the gelding lunged upward to the top, areas having been axed out so the animals and people could stand level. Wide as an arena. A hardy wildflower pushed itself between a craggy crack, while stacks of ore waiting to be hauled by mules down the mountain looked like mountains themselves.

And there gaped the wide hole in the earth—the entrance to the vertical tunnel. I soon wore a raincoat and gum boots, and I peered into a gold mine shaft of the Montana Mine at the top of Mt. Estes in the shadow of the Saw Tooth and Salmon River mountain ranges of Idaho. A railroad had been built from Challis to Bonanza, a distance of thirty-five miles for the cost of $30,000, and it saved days of travel and offered spectacular vistas. I'd remember that cost later when railroad building became a part of the Strahorn agenda.

It was a narrow shaft, wet from melting snows and thus the rain gear and rubber boots we were given by Captain Hooper, the superintendent. The only way down the shaft was hand over hand on a ladder that clung precariously to the wet sides. Loose ropes hung from different levels of the ladder to be grabbed in case of emergency. *Emergency such as a woman suffocating from the confining space.*

"I'm the biggest man here," the superintendent announced. "I'll put the rope around me and the other end around you, Mrs. Strahorn. You wrap it around your middle there."

"I . . . I don't know. It might be better if I stayed on top. Keep the horses company."

"Nonsense," the superintendent said. "You don't want to miss out on such an experience. Few women ever get inside a mine."

"You're usually up for adventures," my Pard encouraged. He took the other end of the rope and slid it around my jacket, secured the knot. I removed my hat. He handed me my safety lamp. I'd have to hold it while I descended, my right hand doing double duty.

"Let's attach the lantern so you can use both hands." The superintendent latched it to my wrist, the flame secure behind an iron mesh that let in air, he told me, but didn't allow the flame to set off the gases that permeated the mine. *Gases? Flames?*

Pard patted my back. Had I ever told him of my fear of close spaces?

"I'll be above you on the ladder," the superintendent assured. "That way, if you lose a step I'll hold you back."

"If I don't pull you down with me."

"You aren't that much of a weight, madam."

"Too much for the winze basket," I said. The winze basket worked on a pulley to bring ore up to the surface. "It only holds one hundred pounds, I'm told."

"It isn't running today. The pulley needs to be restrung, I'm afraid. The ladder is our route." Then as an afterthought he added, "Besides, you can't weigh much more than one hundred pounds."

"I didn't know military men to be such diplomats." I had forty pounds over that.

He grinned, tipped his fingers to his hat. Other guests chattered. An investor and author who was another major. He and Robert had spoken of publishing issues and the military, as the major's book was a history of a certain Pennsylvania cavalry. I hadn't considered it until then, but since the Roman times, men have written both of their exploits and regrets in war. Robert gravitated toward these kinds of men, trusted when they proposed new investment ideas. Superintendent Hooper had been a captain for the Union.

I felt like a calf attached to a child preparing

to pull me onto a parade grounds with my roped waist leaning into the hole. I took deep breaths, imagined myself beneath a blue sky and not in that shaft we stood above.

Why am I doing this? Because I'd made a bargain with Pard? To force new experiences? To take advantage of the opportunities my unusual life offered? To forget that the next day was Mother's Day? I honestly didn't know.

Four men started down, their lanterns bobbing; then Robert, then me. The superintendent was the last to grab the ladder, his larger bulk blocking the daylight above me. All seven of us were on that rope at once.

One hundred fifty feet into the depths of the earth we went, the very channel sweating. I kept my eyes on the ladder, did not look up or down, ignored the jerk and pull of others. When I gained a rhythm with hands and feet, I closed my eyes to keep the closeness out. My gloves soon became damp and my fingers cold, but I hung on, the gum boots wanting to slip from the wet. The sounds of dripping water serenaded us. I could hear my heart. Prayers came to my clenched jaws. *Please don't let me suffocate.*

My legs wobbled as we hit the shaft's floor, Robert there to help me with the last rungs. I stood with a sense of satisfaction. Half the journey completed. I only had to get back out.

It was cramped but a wider space had been

clawed out where miners could swing a pick and load ore into the winze basket when it was in service. We congratulated each other, the tenderfoots did, as we were handed our own tools from two miners awaiting us. "You're the first woman in this mine," Captain Hooper told me. "You'll want to dig for a little gold."

"Perhaps one day I'll write of it." My voice sounded shaky. We sloshed around with our spades, poking and picking the walls. I could not imagine working here eight or twelve hours a day. The cramped space, pale lights, the hard work, that small shaft, the dampness—although in the summer, the shaft was apparently bone dry.

"I've picked out a rock." I held it up. "Is it gold?"

"It is," the major said, rolling the nubby ore around in his hands. "It's yours to keep as a memento of the day."

"Ephemera," I said. "That part of the historical record that is neither documents nor maps. The truly treasured things."

"Just remember," Robert said. "That ephemera you put in your pocket has to be carried back up. By you."

"A gentleman would help a lady out."

"A gentleman wouldn't have let a lady come down here," Pard teased. "Unless the lady was an adventurer."

The climb up was much more grueling than

going down, and it was at that point that I wondered at Shakespeare's *Midsummer Night's Dream* and words, "Lord, what fools these mortals be." It was a prayer for certain, the answer to which could only come from the Divine. My arms were weak from pulling that one hundred forty pounds of me up out of that hole while fighting back a sense of panic. It was only later—much later—that I permitted myself to feel a certain pride in having accomplished that climb in and out. I'd let go of the terror as we made our way down the mountain. I had not allowed fear to prevent me from taking on a challenge. I remembered a verse from Philippians with the apostle Paul saying he must leave the past behind and seek the goal God gave him. I thought having a family was my métier, but I no longer knew what that call was.

From *Fifteen Thousand Miles by Stage*, vol. 1, by Carrie Adell Strahorn (page 167)

All kinds of encouraging words were echoing down the long dark passage, but in spite of them, the one thought of "What fools we mortals be" seemed uppermost in my mind. We were praised for our courage but felt that those who remained at the top were the only ones with a grain of sense.

14

Backtrack to Bonanza

Robert is leaving me. He says only for a few weeks, but he needs to look over a timber stand and check mining conditions in an area impassable by stage right now because of flooding streams, and the only horses available for me to ride are not trail broken. I vowed to make the best of this separation, knowing I'll soon be moving on again. This vagabond life may have adventure written on it, but there is little room for friendship building.

June 25, 1879

I accepted that the swollen streams and lack of ferries was a good reason to remain behind, but I was as good a horse rider as Robert and they surely could have found a seasoned mount for me. They had wanted to go without me. Pard too. At least he made no complaint when Mr. Norton set down "the law." I think he rather relished going off with a good guide and the author major, camping out as in his "days of old" when he was twenty-two instead of now at nearly twenty-seven.

There were distractions in Bonanza, I admit, and people were warm and generous. We packed picnics and climbed heights to carve our initials in trees. Where the streams had sent their swollen flows onward, we found good fishing. One gentleman sought to improve my fly-fishing and said kind things about my skills. It was something I found peace within, that flick of the wrist, watching the line drift in the stream toward a spot I thought a trout might be resting in a shady pool. Several of us planned a weeklong fishing trip, in fact, that got cut short when two horses disappeared and after two days of searching could not be found. So instead of riding all the way out, men went ahead a mile, then left a horse tied tightly (this time!) until walkers came to pick up those mounts. We women would ride until the next marked area, usually a mile or two down the trail. We'd leave the horses tied for the walkers/riders behind us. Walk two miles to the next tied mounts, get on, ride a mile or two, and so it went for twenty miles until we made it back to Bonanza.

Where I was not happy. This separation agitated me. It was a dangerous trip Robert engaged in and my imagination knew no limits. I wondered if I waited as a widow without knowing.

Pard's traveling partner, a military man and attorney, had left his office key with me. I tried the diversion of writing at his pine table. After

I wrote to my mother describing the office in detail, including mentioning the scent of old pipes and a few colorful paintings on the walls, I sketched out through words what was happening in my heart. My worry over Robert. The feeling of aloneness despite the kind people to spend time with. The uncertainty of the future. I even penciled a scene with us sharing mounts on that interrupted fishing trip. And I expressed on paper how upset I was that Mr. Norton had made the decision about my remaining and that Pard had not dissented. Writing the words made me feel better. And I vowed to write more often of what I felt and not just of everyday observations. So as not to worry my mother, I didn't mail that one, kept it for myself.

I was in the major's office writing when I saw riders approach through the window and recognized the officer's mount. Without waiting to see Robert, who was surely behind him, I straightened up my papers and bundled them as I stepped outside to greet my darling Pard. I'd missed him!

He wasn't there. Only Major Hyndman and the guide.

"He's gone on to Boise. Everything's fine. You're to wait here until he returns."

I had a range of emotions to write about that afternoon, I can tell you, though I no longer had the use of the major's office. Once again, I had been left behind with no say in it. I broke a pencil pressing so hard on the paper expressing my thoughts about my dear "pardner" who gave me no recourse, assumed I'd do as he said. Didn't I always?

❧❦

Writing, and the hospitality of the people, helped calm my grievances, but after two weeks more, I wanted to get back to where there was a railroad so I would more likely get into contact with Robert. I felt adrift without him, though I would never have shared my loneliness with the fine people of Bonanza. They only saw my "happy lane."

"He won't want you to make that trip to Salt Lake on your own," the major insisted. He had kind eyes.

"He'll be grateful in the end that he doesn't have to backtrack to Bonanza to pick me up." The words *Backtrack to Bonanza* sounded like the title to a novel I might write about a woman left behind and how she dealt with her wayward husband. Alright, he wasn't wayward, but it was a novel. I could make him any way I wanted. My Pard, my liege lord, was willful, however. I could be too.

"A stage is my second home," I told Major Hyndman, grateful he didn't ask where my first home was because I had no answer and I realized then how very sad that made me.

I headed to Challis. At the stage stop there, I encountered a ticket agent for the UP in Omaha who had just come through and he urged me not to make the trek. "It's alkali and lava rock, hot and miserable as any place I have ever been. I will not go back that way until I can go by train. Reconsider, Mrs. Strahorn."

But I didn't.

The first stop at Big Butte would have been uncomfortable with its mix of private travelers, their teams, and stage passengers all packed into a rather small stop. But Providence reigned and a US Marshal and his wife were there. I knew them slightly and they graciously looked after me. He had booked a room and he suggested his wife and I share it, as it had recently been cleared of a rattler by a snake-killing dog.

It was at that stop that I was reminded of the stalwart women who peopled this untamed country. Cooking and cleaning for guests day after day, fighting dust and snakes and dealing with uneasy men with guns. My life was so privileged by comparison. And when I spoke of my gratitude for the fresh water in the basin in our room or mentioned how good the johnny cakes were or asked "However do you keep your dishes so clean in this alkali country? You're remarkable!" my words brought tears to their eyes. The effect of a compliment seasoning hard, dreary days was something I could give and vowed to do that more. Kindness. To notice small moments of service, even asking for a woman's name, brought joy out of proportion to the simple act. We all want to be known.

In the morning, the marshal arranged for me to ride atop with the driver when we left, a marginally better seat for finding a smidgeon of fresh air. But there was no avoiding the powdery grit. We pulled bandanas up over our noses, and the driver—his name was John Johnson—slapped the ribbons on the horses' rumps and we started out. I wondered how the animals breathed. They too needed bandanas.

The grit seeped through our scarves, clogged our throats, filled our noses, shrouded our clothing, so when we disembarked one could barely tell us from the dusty earth.

I had several days rumbling through that barren country. If I never see another lava rock, it will be too soon. Salt Lake City was a mecca of warm water, a place to put my feet up and write. There'd been no such option on that journey south.

"Can you locate Robert Strahorn for me? He's likely in the Boise country. That's my husband. He works for the railroad."

The UP agent stood as though at attention. "I'll send a message to track him down for you straightaway, ma'am. No problem at all. Thought I knew that name."

It wasn't the first time that I wondered if Pard might have backtracked to Bonanza while I headed to Salt Lake but given his intention to go all the way to Boise, I figured it would have been weeks, if not months, before he returned for me.

After two days, I received a telegram. *"Go home to Omaha. Stop. Grand Central Hotel. Stop. There soon."* He signed it *"Love, Robert Strahorn, Chief, Union Pacific Public Relations."*

Did it mean we'd be staying in one place now? Had Robert written all the books, traveled to all the places in the West that the railroad needed, and now he'd be drawing on those trunks of copious notes to write more pamphlets? Perhaps they'd identified the places where new towns would now be promoted. I danced around the room, holding the telegram.

Chief of the Union Pacific Public Relations Department. A promotion.

We'd have much to talk about in Omaha. Might this mean a home of our own? A place to consider taking in an orphan or adopting a child or two? Maybe I could get published as my sister had. As my husband was. The idea felt welcoming, and after weeks of travel mostly without my Pard, I looked forward to that place called Omaha, seeing it with now more experienced and hopeful eyes.

From *Fifteen Thousand Miles by Stage*, vol. 1, by Carrie Adell Strahorn (page 170)

After a few days in Bonanza my liege lord and two companions left for the Saw Tooth range and the Wood River country 150 miles southward on horseback. I was left among new-found friends, with a good horse and saddle, and they thought I was also left with the conviction that the trip would be too hard for me. . . . Mr. Norton, the godfather and oracle of the camp, had said it would not do to send a woman over that rugged Saw Tooth range with such swollen streams and an untried horse, and his word became the law. Several most delightful weeks were then spent among Bonanza's hospitable people.

15

Home, Sweet Home

We're to have a place of our own at last. I can take furniture out of storage, keep a scrapbook of notes and adventures already taken and anticipate the next to come. I will take cooking classes and learn to knit. Volunteer at the library. I'll be a woman "at home." At last I will have a home and not the Single Occupancy Hotel. Eventually.

July 1, 1879

Robert's new position and the UP moving its main offices to Farnham Street in Omaha took up most of Robert's time. He was on-call almost twenty-four hours a day. The offices were built on the only hill in Omaha, with a grand view of the Missouri and the flat valley below, though my dear husband had little time to gaze at the landscape. He was ensconced in an office with one window.

Our reunion in Omaha after the Bonanza episode left little time to discuss my frustration with his having abandoned me in that mining town. Reconnection was the order of the day. I did so love that man! I could hardly take issue with Robert for his choice to go to Boise without me, as he was delighted with the outcome of his travels, inspired by his new appointment and the chance to glean the next publication from his notes, the work to be fully funded by the railroad.

He showed me a building site on 18th Street, out of the commercial area, that would be our very own home. How could I be upset with a man who does that? We would stay at the Grand Central until the house was built, but then we'd have a house my sisters and parents could visit.

Pard set to work with the general manager of the UP right down the hall from his office, where he was called in often to talk about grades, passes, rock formations, and all that he'd seen. In the meantime, he hired people to help him, while I visited the building site daily, pointing out features I wanted (an indoor water closet, piped-in water to the kitchen sink, three bedrooms). I had the builders order in transoms with horse heads etched into the glass. My mother sent me money for my "enjoyment" and I purchased paper instead of the linen so many women in Omaha used on their walls. I did my best not to annoy the builders and we soon came to an agreement about how things should be done. I overheard one of them refer to me once as "bossy" and I'm not. I just knew what others should be doing.

Once our house was built and we moved in, Robert announced that we'd have boarders—two men who worked with him in the Public Relations office, Mr. Gleed and Mr. Blackburn.

"Oh" was all I said.

The river flooded that year, which did not affect us but did the city and the railroad. Robert had to put out press comments about when the five miles of track that had been flooded out would be back in service. He became friendly with the reporter from the Omaha *Bee*. And then there was the adobe mud that Omahans rarely speak of. I had not experienced it before that winter in the valley, but getting stuck in it one day and having to be rescued by a passing stranger is not an occasion easily forgotten.

Within a few weeks of our moving in, Mr. Gleed and then Robert became ill. If it had been only one of them, I would have been fine, but nursing two men without a housemaid or cook proved daunting. And worrisome.

Our other boarder was fine literary help in Robert's office. Mr. Blackburn carried a cane and likely secrets, as he was often melancholic. He would leave the Farnham office, arrive at our home, take to his room, and begin to play his old Stradivarius while lying on his back. I learned of that position when I once knocked on his door to tell him supper was ready and he invited me in. There he lay, the bow and violin resting on his chest. He was quite a good violinist and I had sung with some of the best.

"I'll come for supper when my tunes bring me to a reel," he told me in his soft, nasal voice. "My violin takes me from here to there, and when I'm there, I'll be here with you. I hope that's agreeable?"

I nodded that it was and backed out. After that, I waited until that reel or an *allegretto vivace* piece took over the bow, for then I'd know his sadness had turned to joy. He'd come to supper cheerful and chipper, the way Robert described him being at the office. Music can do that to a person and so can writing.

I didn't have much time to ponder or write though, as caring for the two men consumed me, while also making sure fresh linens awaited our violin-playing guest.

We'd hired cooks while I was growing up, and I could remember standing on a high stool beside one while she made crepes or dipped strawberries in chocolate. I never wanted to help with the everyday meals like scrambling eggs or frying bacon or making broth—the latter easiest for my two patients to consume. No, it was the party things I liked, the new recipes, the exotic dishes, decorating the tables. My admiration grew for those pioneering women who served dozens in a day at stage stops with a prairie rose in a jar. I could never do what they did, never.

The sickness in our home concerned me, and neither fine music nor good books nor my gruel or broth helped them make progress. Robert's attempt to keep writing despite the malady seemed to help him until he became more ill. I suggested fatigue as the cause. He had a slight fever. Then complained about chewing. I called in the doctor, who diagnosed ague, common among the Missouri River communities.

"Or perhaps a recurrence of his TB?" I asked. Sometimes doctors need help.

But then Robert swelled up and his throat hurt, and this time when the doctor returned he diagnosed mumps. Both men had mumps.

"But I've had mumps," Robert told him.

I was incredulous too.

"Whatever you had before, it wasn't mumps," our Omaha doctor insisted. "You can only have mumps once. This is mumps." He pointed, then finished packing up his leather bag. "It's contagious, which is probably why both of you men have it. Gotten from a sneeze or cough. You'd best be careful, Mrs. Strahorn. Wear a mask or bandana when you care for them. They'll pull through with good nursing. Especially since your husband has had it before." That last he said with mocking, but I didn't get into it with him.

"Infertility?" Robert asked.

"Nonsense. That's an old wives' tale spread by infertile women to blame men."

Now that did get me up on my high horse. "Excuse me, but my father is a physician and he indicates that orchitis is often the result of mumps in adult men."

"Orchitis? Your father must be a quack to think that."

"Dr. John Green was well schooled by the military. He is one of the first physicians in the army to use anesthesia west of the Mississippi River. And my sister is in medical school this instant. I suspect they've kept up on things."

"Green, you say. In Marengo?" I nodded. "I've heard of him. He best buffer up his medical information though," our soon-to-be-former doctor said. I had to remember that physicians, in 1880, had usually less than two years of schooling with maybe a year at an eastern university studying surgery, while ministers of the faith had seven or eight before being sent out to the tributaries. This man had had no military experience and was unschooled, but that didn't mean he wasn't right. I opened my mouth to protest, but he stopped me with a raised hand.

"All I'm saying is that it's likely he never had mumps before, has them now, and it shouldn't interfere with his progeny. Send a messenger if he gets worse. I'll alert the UP who is paying me, madam, that he's on the mend. Good day."

The infertility up until then may well have been on my end, if indeed there'd been a misdiagnosis with Robert years before. Or if my father was misinformed about infertility related to mumps. Maybe it wasn't very common and it was an old wives' tale, though I'd take issue with our former doctor's reasoning about how such stories began.

After he left, I said to Robert, "Can the UP get a different physician? I'll make a complaint."

"I'm sorry, Dell. I really am."

I sat on Robert's bed. I'd made up one for myself on our divan each night since he'd been ill. That probably added to my irritable disposition.

"I hope you don't get it."

"It was probably at the New Year's Eve birthday party," I said. "I do remember hearing sniffles and coughing, and I think Mavis has been down with something that I now suspect might well be mumps. It's my own fault for having such an affair."

"I loved that party. You throw quite a festive event, Mrs. Strahorn."

"Do I, Mr. Strahorn?" I leaned over and kissed his forehead. It was warm. "It was such fun to plan for, get the invitations printed. Create the decorations. Order in the inexpensive meats and make them rich with sauces." I let my mind go to somewhere pleasant in the past, pushed aside that unease about fertility.

"Those snowman doughnuts were exceptional, Dell." I shrugged at his praise. "And you did it in the midst of tending our home, our boarders,

151

me. I wish my salary was a little more so you'd have help." He coughed. "One day, we'll have a grand home and you won't have to plan your own birthday party."

"I love that part, but a mansion would be lovely."

"It'll have two indoor baths and a dozen bedrooms."

"For all those children we'll have?"

He took my hand. "Wash this beautiful hand after I've held it."

He wasn't going to pick up on my question, so I moved along. "I've the constitution of a horse, my father always told me. Perhaps this extra weight serves me well in fighting off disease." I fluffed his pillow. "You were skinny before this hit. Now look at you. Skin over bones, hardly any flesh." He did look gaunt. "Much as I like Omaha, let's go to the mountains and get you well. We'll ask UP to hire a nurse for Mr. Gleed."

"You change the subject, Carrie. I heard the question." He swallowed hard. I gave him water to sip. "I am sorry. Whether your father's right or this doctor is, I know you want a home and children. For now, we have each other. I want that to be enough."

It was his longest sharing of something personal with me, ever. I didn't know what to say to have it continue. Silence might have been best, but I've never been good with silence.

"It is enough as long as we're on the same team," I said. "I hated it when you left me in Bonanza, when I didn't have any way to be in touch with you unless I made an arduous trip across that lava moonscape. We have to talk about things, Robert, and decide together. I'm not one of your employees, you know." He nodded. "Maybe I need some sort of . . . focus, something I'm working on so that when you are gone I don't feel abandoned. I want to see your absence as though I've been given a gift of more time to pursue whatever project I have. Working with the builders was great fun."

He winced. *Maybe the builders complained about my involvement?*

I heard Mr. Gleed ring the bell I'd given him to call me when he needed something.

"You go. You're Nurse Dell now. A whole new adventure for you. Perhaps that's your new calling."

"Very funny." I stood, washed my hands with the lavender soap, then spritzed a few drops at him before I dabbed his face, then wiped my hands with the towel. I'd embroidered his initials onto that linen, ordered from back east. I used gold threads and gave him a shaving mug with gold leaf initials on it too.

"I'll get better," he said.

"You will. If you feel up to it, we can work on that pamphlet. You dictate, I'll write."

He nodded.

"I love you, Robert Strahorn."

"And I you, Dell Strahorn."

After I tended Mr. Gleed, Robert and I worked together for a time until he tired.

"Mama's coming for a visit, in a week or so. To help out. I hope that's alright."

"Your mother is always welcome. She'll be disappointed, I fear, that you've had to work so hard on your own. That we have boarders."

"She has to find something to complain about. She wouldn't enjoy herself if she didn't."

He laughed, then closed his eyes and was asleep. I headed out to the kitchen area, passing the china cabinet where I'd put my precious things, including that chunk of ore, my ephemera, from the Montana Mine. I'd conquered a fear there as I climbed out seeking new light. There might be hope yet for a family if the quack was right about progeny. We had a permanent home now. All we had to do was fill it up.

From *Fifteen Thousand Miles by Stage*, vol. 1, by Carrie Adell Strahorn (page 176)

For the winter of '79 we settled down to a quiet, orderly life in Omaha.

16

A Stray

Mother arrived in Omaha. But she was not pleased that our time together involved, not shopping or walking the new park, but instead getting Robert better and helping me pack. I had no time to write, to journal. Robert opened an office for the UP in Denver, but they wanted him back out in the field. Mr. Gleed improved and took a job with the Atchison, Topeka, and Santa Fe railroad, much to Robert's chagrin. Our violin-playing boarder found himself a wife (he said he was inspired by our connubial bliss) and made his own home in Omaha while we headed to Denver and I prepared for at least a year of travel living again in hotels.

May 1, 1880

My mother insisted that I come home for a rest. Robert, much improved, agreed, and Mother and I were soon on the train back to Marengo.

"Why don't you stay here instead of returning to that hotel in Denver, let him do this surveying and writing." My mother fluffed the pillow behind my head. She'd brought me breakfast in bed.

"I've thought this through, Mama. He's my husband. I'm a help to him with all his contacts. Even with his writing. Besides, what would I do here? Walk old Casey? Knit?"

She sighed. "I wish you were closer to having the life you really want."

"I've chosen this one, Mama. It's alright."

It wasn't alright, but I didn't want her to worry and I kept a cheery attitude, let her pamper me, and we reminisced about old times. I saw Mary and my niece and walked old Casey too. All I was missing was Robert. And my Omaha home that was no more. Two weeks later I waved goodbye when I caught the train to Denver. From Denver, Pard and I traveled out like spokes on a wheel. I lost track of how many mines we visited, struggled as I wrote to describe the gold and silver workings in a new way. I'm not sure how Robert did it. Well, he didn't. His reports read like statistics books where the reader had to find some way to distinguish the Ruby mine from the Gothic or a timber stand in New Mexico from one in Montana. My notes were about the people we traveled with and the nature of the stages or train cars. And a surprise family connection too when Robert learned his brother was bringing his wife and three children to the Ruby

Valley in Madison, Montana. Robert's words now had a direct impact on his own family's desire to find a new direction in the West. Sadly, we had little contact with them. Maybe because we were always on the go.

I'd read my notes and comments to Pard, giving a little room between the experience and memory of it. He'd be sitting at the table looking over his notes, and I'd be on the bed, stocking feet wiggling back and forth in nervous twists, my corset off, a wrapper on. "What do you think of this? 'In spite of the altitude of Irwin, the mountains rise around it in emerald heights over a thousand feet, and rich forests extend almost to the tops that will make the whip-whine of the saw resound for many years.' "

"That's good, Dell, I like that auditory image of the 'whip-whine of the saw.' Why, I can almost hear the sound, musical, and the reader will too." He also liked my rendition of a horse giving me a disgusted look after I'd given it poor rein instructions. I'd said it was like the look of a "hunting dog when a shot has failed to bring down the game." He laughed out loud at that. Or after my description of an uncomfortable, strenuous encounter with a wretched passenger on the stage, Robert said, "That guy pushed his way onto your seat on top that I paid for! I didn't use the pass, I used cash." My words had brought both the moment and his intense feelings back. "Good thing you got me inside that stage, Dell. No telling what I might have done to that barbarian."

"I was very ill."

He paused, pencil in hand. "Yes, that's right, you were. I'd forgotten that part, just remembered how impudent he was."

I didn't tell him that his making a scene about it had made me feel worse than what that barbarian had said of my illness, which was probably why Pard forgot that I was sick. He'd wanted me getting fresh air in a seat next to the driver, and the selfish man had said, "It serves her right; a woman has no business traveling in this country." Maybe, at that point, Robert was feeling a bit guilty about having me with him when I was sick, not able to nurse me as I had nursed him those months before in Omaha.

I'm kidding myself: illness of others sent Pard like an arrow from a quiver toward a faraway target.

Stage stops were no place to recuperate, and at Manitou Springs or Gunnison, Colorado, or even lovely Santa Fe, he had to be in the railroad's employ, looking at hay fields or those mines to report to potential investors and bring inspiration to home seekers while pushing for possible stations for growing railroad wealth.

It's also true that my observations sometimes appeared as his words in articles he wrote for the New York *Herald*, for example. "I hope you don't mind," he said once when I lifted my eyes about a turn of phrase I recognized as my own. "You have such a colorful way of putting things."

"I don't mind. I'm flattered."

At that moment, I was. But I was also—I couldn't find the right word. Beguiled, maybe a little bewitched? We were "pardners," weren't we? Why did I grimace at his cavalier explanation? I was pleased to see my very words in print. But I also understood, as I hadn't before, why my sister Mary's "by line" in the local Marengo paper must have thrilled her. "By Mrs. William Waters."

Looking back, I see where that interchange might have been the impetus for my doing something that Robert was more likely to do than I was: I invested in real estate.

It was at Crested Butte, a mining camp eight miles east of Irwin, in Colorado. Because of its lower elevation and access through four mountain passes and a nearness to Gunnison accessible by stage, Crested Butte expected to be the terminus of the railroad. Or so I thought, listening to Robert's discussions with the locals. It was in beautiful country, and I could see the mining owners, railroad people, and store owners make their homes there, a thousand feet below the mines but where trainloads of goods could serve surrounding camps and take out ore from those same.

I kept Pard in the dark, but it was soon out. Men cannot keep secrets. They call us women gossips, but they're much worse.

"Why didn't you tell me? I don't mind at all. Surprised, though. Aren't we partners?"

I shrugged my shoulders. I cut his toenails with my little scissors in our Denver hotel. Later, he'd snip mine.

"It was fun to see if I could manage the transaction. It's a good-sized lot."

"Not in the residential area, I hope, should there be one."

Snip. "I fancied a commercial site. I'll sell when the railroad comes, make a tidy profit."

"It does suggest that you need your own bank account, Dell. So you can do these things more easily."

Snip. "I used money from my allowance and the household account. I've little need of the latter, really, when we're far from having a house." I kept my voice light, lest he think I was unhappy back on the road. There was much to like about not fixing meals twice daily and having the hotel tend to our laundry. "An investment account would be good. In my own name. Maybe one day I'll have money from my earnings to put in there."

"Earnings from what?"

"From my buying and selling." I cleared my throat. "Or maybe . . . writing."

"You'll have to be careful about that. All my

160

publications are a result of the railroad and my employment with them. You wouldn't want to get in trouble with them by having a by line that someone suggests you have inside information because you're married to me. Come to think of it, they might think that about your real estate dealings."

I felt like I'd been slapped. I could respond with quick wit to every stage jehu or rude passenger I met, but with Robert, I needed time to ponder. And maybe "grow new flesh." I hadn't thought that short, passing moments in a marriage could both linger and sting, but perhaps that's what marriages are made up of—series of little interactions, some blessed, some trials. I wondered if other couples who spent so much time together, worked together (at least I had always thought we worked together), planned and hoped together, found themselves at times saying things that failed to build the other up.

The snipping of his nails was the sound to break the silence. After I scrubbed his feet, scraped off a callus, rubbed his arches with a sweet-smelling cream, I said, "I'll use a nom de plume. Maybe Dell Green."

"How about memorializing Carrie's name? Make it Carrie something?"

Did I ask for your assistance, Robert Strahorn? Fury flushed my face but I kept my calm. I know he wanted the best for me, he really did.

"Perhaps C. Green. So they'll think it's a man writing and pay more attention to it."

"That's a good thought." He stood to take the scissors, rinsed them, and got fresh water for my foot bath. "Ready?" He held the basin like a restaurant waiter.

"Let's do my toes later," I said. "I think I'd like to take a walk."

"I'll come with you. It's late."

"No. Please. Work on your tome. I'll be fine." I hooked the buttons on my shoes. "Taking a stroll around the block."

I came to a few conclusions on that short journey. Alright, I went three times around the block.

First, I would begin to submit some of my writing to newspapers. I'd use the by line *A. Stray* for Adell and half of Robert's name and hope Robert missed the pun. I felt like a stray calf left outside the corral. But it was Adell, that middle initial that gave Pard his Dell and it was Dell who was the stray. Carrie Adell Green Strahorn would find a way to make her mark not just as the wife of the famous Robert Strahorn.

That very evening, I wrote a little piece about a woman buying a lot in a mining town. I would submit it to the *New Northwest*, a weekly published in Portland, Oregon, all about women's issues in the western region. Even eastern women would like that story and it wouldn't rob from Robert or from the railroad. I also wrote to my sister and invited her to visit. We would talk writing and its challenges, and I wouldn't have to worry that I'd stepped on anyone's toes.

⚜

Mary's arrival thrilled me more than I had expected. Extended family could bring salve to a burdened soul. Mary said, "It's such beautiful country. I really had no idea, even though your letters describe everything so grandly. But these mountains!" She swirled around outside the Denver station.

"I wish you could have seen our Omaha home."

"Mama said it was quaint."

"She would. But truly the scenery here is more astonishing. I have adventures planned."

Mary clapped her hands like a happy child.

"First to Colorado Springs, and if you think you're up to it, we'll climb a mountain."

"We can?"

"Indeed."

"Well, let's get to it! It's so good to see you, Carrie." She hugged me tight. "Christina begged to come, but Willie said no daughter of his was going into that wild country."

"You can decide how wild after our little adventures."

"Can't be that much drama when you're looking robust."

163

"I don't get enough walks in, though." I patted my curvy hips. "Climbing Pikes Peak will do me good."

"Climb as with ropes and such?"

I shook my head. "We'll ride horses up as far as we can, then walk the rest of the way."

"A little bluff climbing, like back along the Mississippi. That'll be fun. We can picnic in the shelter on top, can't we?"

I smiled. "No shelter. We'll be exposed to the elements."

Robert greeted her with a warm hug, carried her bags himself up the stairs to a room in the hotel we'd booked beside ours.

"Hardly a wild country with furnishings like these." She ran her hands down the brocade drapes, oohed at the large bedstead and the marble top of the cabinet holding the water basin.

"You won't spend much time here. We'll have supper and after breakfast be on our way to Colorado Springs."

"We're glad Willie let you come," Robert said.

"He could hardly say no to a 'professional woman.'" She winked at me. I didn't know what she was talking about and I frowned. "Didn't I tell you? I'm acting as a correspondent for the Freeport *Journal*. I'll be sending missives back about our travels, so be careful what you say." She laughed. "You might end up in my story."

"Oh. Why, that's wonderful. Another by line?"

"This time, 'Mary Waters.' "

"That's . . . that's grand."

"You aren't distressed?" She reached to touch my elbow, squeezed it.

"A little envious, I confess."

"Dell can't really write under her own name, with my UP association, except a letter now and then." Mary frowned. Robert added, "Your dispatches can only help our cause to bring people west, if not as permanent settlers, as tourists wanting new sights and sounds. Wait until you see the Garden of the Gods in the Springs area. Magnificent."

"What makes you think I'll only write glowing reports, Robert? I'm not my happy-lane sister."

She'd silenced him when I couldn't.

⧽⧼

We were soon in that fabulous Garden of the Gods, with a guide to take us through spectacular rock formations as though a giant child with blocks and stones of odd geometrical formations had placed them precariously to see if they would stand the test of time. Mary was in constant awe. She made notes as soon as we finished our ride. Actually, all of us were busy scribbling while the horses tore at sparse grass reaching through reddish dirt. When I looked up at Mary and Robert with their sketchbooks and pads, I laughed. "Look at us! This beautiful scenery,

165

God's own creation, and we have our noses in our foolscap." I put my book down and inhaled the clear air, took in the deep blue sky and the color contrast of the stones. I felt a bit light-headed but let the landscape fill me up. I refused to let Mary's success steal mine. We both had a way with words. That was what I would hang on to.

The next day, Mary and I headed by horseback to Pikes Peak where the mild winter had left the last feet of climbing bare, unusual for June. The vista was stunning. Mary couldn't stop smiling. We spent the night at Manitou Springs and took the baths. "I'll write about this day," Mary said. "From the top of a mountain to the bottom of hot springs. Strenuous and slackening, all in the same day." She never complained about the weather, the stage, our itinerary. "It's nice having someone else decide everything."

"Next stop, Estes Park. Pack a smaller valise," I told her. "We'll be gone three weeks and roughing it in more primitive cabins. No fancy brocades."

"Oh, my heavens. I can hardly wait. It's a good thing I'm here for two months, if three weeks of it will be taken up by a single trip."

Robert remained with us in Estes Park, where we fished and walked and rested. Then he planned to go overland on horseback, and we arranged a rendezvous at Middle Park a few weeks forward.

I didn't mind him going off without me, not with Mary at my side. This was my world—as being a superior mother was hers—and I wanted to share it with her, even the strenuous sides. Besides, a little time without one's husband isn't a bad thing when it's by mutual choice. To go with him, we would have had to travel by cross saddle, and neither Mary nor I wanted that. I found the saddles quite uncomfortable, built for men as they were. And in that rough country Robert was headed into, sidesaddles left a woman in a precarious position, easily brushed from her pillion. That had happened to me once, resulting in a concussion, but I didn't tell Mary of it.

While Robert rode overland, Mary and I took the first stage out to Longmont. "At least they have iron handles at the windows to grab," Mary observed. "It helps keep one a little upright at the turns." Our fellow passengers were all complacent and pleasant, having vacationed for a few days in that gorgeous country.

At Longmont, we took the train to Denver, where we rested a few days more, shopping and staying up late, talking. "It does annoy me some," Mary said as she curled her hair with a hot iron, "that Willie is quite the detail person in his work, but he can't see his underdrawers in the middle of the room to pick them up. He knows I'll do it for him."

"Robert is fastidious about his mustache being

kept trim, but he never cleans the bowl afterward. It's like he's blind." We both giggled. How grand it was that I could complain about Robert's idiosyncrasies without Mary turning on him, and she told me tales of her Willie, and neither of us thought the less of the men we sisters had married. I had no close friend with whom I could be in safety except my sister. Friendships take time and presence and I was rarely available for long at any one place, and I always knew we'd be traveling on. I was a stray. Turning that into belonging was the challenge.

From *Fifteen Thousand Miles by Stage*, vol. 1, by Carrie Adell Strahorn (Page 185)

It was a joy, indeed, to flee from the hot bed of the smothering Missouri valley to the cool, sweet air of Denver, and as soon as Pard's office was well established in the new stone Union Pacific depot building, there we departed for the mountains and began the most strenuous year of our travels.

17

Voices

I must speak of a mysterious "power."
Sometimes we are placed where we are
because we have listened to another voice.
This happened while Mary visited, and I'm
grateful I had a reasoned source to explore
with me how what happened could have
occurred. We were leaving Georgetown.
We'd been ready to board, five adults and
four children. An ill man and his small son
sat atop the stage in the cooler air at their
request and having paid the extra price.
The rest of us piled inside. And then this
amazing thing happened. It's hard for me
to write about it and yet I must.

August 14, 1880

"The sardine ride," Mary quipped as we tried to
settle our bustles and bags into the stage. A nanny
had the four children under control—I hoped.
Their mother looked pale.

Then as the driver was about to lift the reins,
a man reading the paper by the Barton House
stood up, shouted for the stage to halt, said that
he *had* to be on it. "I'll get my coat and bag. Five

minutes most." He was a brawny sort and he rushed about, while groaning occurred from the pale-faced mother and the man atop telling the stage driver to head out. Mary and I were in no hurry, but I could see where a mother with four children might want to reach her destination as quickly as possible.

For some reason, even though the jehu already held the ribbons and whip ready to flick above the lead team's ears (a horse was never whipped), he pulled up, allowing the brawny man to join us. The straggler huffed and puffed as we resettled ourselves inside, squeezed even more into that sardine state.

A child coughed as we started out. The nanny picked up another to hold on her lap to give a bit more room to the grown-ups, and then the newest passenger introduced himself as George Washington Giggy. A rancher, he was headed to Georgetown to ride a horse there for a man, but here he was, going the opposite direction, seventy miles. And he told us of this strange power that had insisted he get on our very stage.

Call it intuition. Men say that about women's ways. But this man had listened to something and he was willing to see where following that inner voice would take him. He looked embarrassed as he told us of his experience, but I find myself with that same expression when trying to make sense of mystical moments—and that's how I described it.

We rattled along easy enough, feeling the jerks of a six-horse team that from the uneven stride told me they had not moved as a six-hitch team for long. Or the jehu was new to them. More surging and a sense that the horses took all his effort to hold back. I didn't say anything to Mary about my observations, but when you ride a stage as much as I did, you begin to recognize the skill of the driver, the inexperience of the team, the condition of the Concord. As we rounded a third curve with more speed than required, three of the four children threw up. A stage like that could remind one of sea travel, and apparently it did to these children. I had to fight back joining them, with the smell now permeating the interior. We helped the nanny clean up, but they kept up their discomfort, moaning.

At a mail stop, we had a brief respite, though Mary and I stayed in the stage. The nanny got out with the four children to give them a little fresh air, and the jehu wrapped his ribbons around the brake while he loaded and unloaded mail bags. No one at the mail post stood to calm the horses, who jerked forward and back, restless as a woman's legs after a long ride astride.

And then, as though as one, the horses lurched forward, the brake slipped off and in seconds they surged at full speed. Without a driver. The sick man atop couldn't gain the reins and his boy attempted to jump off, then slipped and fell between the wheels. I knew we'd run over him. Mary couldn't see what made me gasp.

Mr. Giggy sat across from me, jostled by the thrust, his hands in prayer, his face contorted. Then his countenance brightened. "If I can get up to get the lines, they're still wrapped around the brake, I can halt—" His words were shoved back and forth as the stage rocked. I knew we'd soon approach a length of corduroy road which, if we hit it crooked, would flip the stage and drag us to our deaths.

Then before I could even complete my own prayer, Mr. Giggy wrangled his large self out through the window and atop the stage to the front boot, where he grabbed the lines, shouting, "I have them!" That did not stop the rolling, rattling stage, however, as no man can hold back six runaway horses. But we could pray he could guide them enough that they would hit the corduroy directly and, in time, tire themselves out and slow themselves down.

As the stage roiled like a ship on a dark sea, I believed in that moment that we were going to die.

There was no panic in me. I didn't have my life flash before my eyes. A sense of calm flooded my spirit, and I felt badly for Mary and for Robert, as I knew he'd blame himself for sending me on, for not accompanying us. There was no white light as I had heard people speak of when they thought they were about to die. It was an . . . acceptance, that God was with us and we might live or we might die, but in the end, it would be alright. I was very reassured by that calm.

"No, no!" Mary's words took me from my peace. She grabbed at the mother, who clutched at the door handle, trying to open it.

She screamed, "I must return to my children!"

"They're fine. If you jump out, you'll die." Mary took her hands.

I looked into her terrified eyes. "He's gotten the reins. The horses will tire." I used my most steady voice. But she wasn't all there, her fear wiping all reason from her. I lunged to help my sister then, to hold the woman in as we bounced around like stones in a swirled bucket. The woman sobbed and fought us through her crying.

I felt, then heard us hit the corduroy road, breathed gratitude that we'd struck it square. We rattled on a mile or more and once off of it, our savior Mr. Giggy turned the team into a fence where the sweating horses stopped, hung their heads, breathed hard and snorted.

"I'll bring them about," he called down to us. "We'll head back. They're tired now. It'll be alright, ladies, gentleman." He spoke to the ill man who moaned about his son.

Not long after turning back, we met the driver fast-walking toward us and he took over from Mr. Giggy. I would have liked our angel to have remained atop, as he was being thanked profusely. He walked back to the mail stop where Mr. Giggy opined, "I guess I know now why I was supposed to take this stage."

Not a one of us disputed his claim.

It was a day to celebrate Providence's intervention, the boy who had fallen was not killed. He was badly hurt, though. His ill father stayed with him at the postal stop where the children were also reunited with their mother. Much hugging and kissing and crying, though the nanny had kept close tabs on them. That family stayed and would return to Denver in the morning.

Mary and I and new passengers from the postal stop all traveled on to the Middle Park Hotel at Sulphur Springs. Getting out, I wobbled to the front of the team, patted the neck of one lead animal. "Quite a day you've had." The big animal lifted its head and jangled the bridle. I saw blood at his mouth where he'd held the bit. "You'll tend these horses well tonight, won't you?" The jehu nodded, looked sheepish, it seemed to me. He knew of his part in this catastrophe. That boy's broken bones would take some time to heal.

❦

Mary and I sat at the edge of one of the hot springs where a cooler stream rushed through—there were more than twenty springs—with fifty cabins set around. "What do you think of all that happened today?" Mary asked. All I could see of her was her head that held a bathing cap, the ruffles limp in the steamy water. Lit candles with a lavender scent gave more an illusion of light than being able to see. She moved closer to the edge where it wasn't as hot and could be refreshing. "The role of Providence in our rescue," Mary continued. "There's no denying that Mr. Giggy was where he was meant to be."

"I suppose one of us might have wrangled ourselves through that window and crawled up to the boot, but we'd have little knowledge of how to operate that set of reins once we got there." I shivered. "And the horses would feel that. They'd know they had an amateur at their helm. Mr. Giggy is a horseman. He had the size and bulk and had obviously managed smaller teams. He was the right one."

"And he listened. I think that's the hardest part of this life journey." Mary's body sat out farther still, seeking the cooler edges. The water steamed off her legs. "Knowing how to listen to all the different voices that talk to us."

"Mary, are you hearing voices?" I teased.

"I'm not jesting. We all hear voices inside. Things Mama told us when we were little that remind us of some action to take in the present. Husbands tell us things we let stew inside our heads and hearts, even when they aren't present. It's not always for the best."

I thought of Robert's words about my writing under my own name or how I sometimes didn't do what I thought best because I knew Robert would have done it another way. I'd do it his way instead of my own way, so I didn't have to defend if questioned.

"It's so hard to know if the voice we're hearing is Providence. Or some tempting devil." Mary got out of the water and dabbed a towel to her face.

"If we're familiar with the voice, that would help," I posed.

She brushed beads of sweat from her face. "That means time in silence, doesn't it? A mother labors to find such time. I envy you those long walks you write about."

"Music is where I hear the voice of God," I said. "Not so much when I'm singing as when I'm preparing to sing, in those moments of silence before the first notes. I sometimes think silence is the first note. Then I get lost inside the music."

"I'll tell you a secret. When I'm writing, that's how I feel. It's like I'm there allowing another voice to speak."

"Even when it's about practical things like your piece on how to make a perfect cherry pie? It had lots of humor in it. I loved that."

"Even then. I imagine I'm making someone's day brighter, offering them a small respite. It's nothing like a book, of course, I know that. But I think everyday moments can be divine.

Mr. Giggy's story is a divine revelation that there is still mystery in the world, unexplained phenomena. Miracles."

"People don't call much miraculous anymore. We've gotten cynical. But I have no trouble calling it that. All the little things, too, like our working together to keep that mother from jumping out. And bigger ones, the boy not dying. At least I hope he won't die. And most of all, Mr. Giggy being willing to go in a totally opposite direction from what he'd planned for today. How many people are willing to look foolish?"

"You did, when you married Robert."

I thought about that. "I guess I did." I laughed.

"All those other voices telling you it was crazy to go off with him and plan to travel the West by stage and train and horseback, without a home to come back to. It's quite a different path for a lady to take. Mama says that often."

"I'm sure she does. But has it benefited the life of anyone? Or was it just a selfish wish on my part, to indulge in my own dreams and adventures?"

"You were here today to keep a woman from jumping to her death. You nursed Robert and what was his name?"

"Mr. Gleed."

"Both men were brought back to health. You've given Robert sound advice. And I suspect there have been other moments where you were present to offer a kind word when someone needed it."

All those stalwart women at the stage stops, the ones I'd paid a compliment to. Could such a little thing really be divine-inspired?

I may not manage a runaway team but working with my sister, I did listen to common sense and help a woman face terror.

I got out of the pool. "When we were racing along today, I had the most tranquil moment. I wasn't afraid. I accepted whatever would happen. I'm reassured that when my time comes, I won't be terrified because I know I'm not alone."

"Tranquility. Who knew one could find it in the wildest of moments." She sighed, wrapped the towel around her shoulders. "I could stay here for the rest of my life."

"Willie and Christina would come find you. Two months to let you go is a very long time." I never loved her more than at that moment. "I'm so grateful that you're here."

"Something told me it was time to see my sister. I listened."

From *Fifteen Thousand Miles by Stage*, vol. 1, by Carrie Adell Strahorn (page 204)

Then a feeling came over him so strong that he must take it [the stage] that it was like a power not his own that impelled him to demand the stage to wait for him.

18

Singing in the Snow

Landscapes ask us to ponder our inner being. Dutch painters coined that word— landscape—when they moved from painting seascapes to capturing the beauty of a land, her mountains and valleys and rivers. Wish I could paint what feelings the West's grand landscapes inspire in me.

October 10, 1880

"Remember the cancelled trip to Yellowstone?"

I nodded. Autumn had arrived and I was homesick for Marengo.

"Well, it's back on." Robert grinned. We were at our hotel in Virginia City, the city bustle active outside our window. "The owner of the stage route will himself drive us on the official first run. Just you and me as passengers."

"I hope it's not too late in the season." It was October.

"Marshall says we'll do fine. We've got to load up with felt for our boots, though, take mittens, scarfs, overcoats, a felt skirt, heavy woolen shawl, blankets, pillows. We need to finish shopping and get you a pair of thick-soled boots. The ground there is said to be too hot for your thin leather soles, and if we encounter snow, too thin for those too. Come along."

He dragged me out of my moroseness that had settled after Mary left. The lack of fashion of the boots I eventually bought made me grimace. "They're not very attractive, are they?" I said. Heavy soles of thick rubber held leather sides.

"They'll keep your feet dry and your ankles safe. You have such dainty feet." He lifted my foot as I sat at the mercantile. He rubbed my calf above the boot top.

"They weigh a ton."

"All the better to protect you, my dear. That's my job on this trip and those boots are my partners."

※※

Once on the road in our private stage, Robert teased me about those heavy boots, said they looked like how he imagined Mary Shelley's Frankenstein's monster boots must have looked. "I had no idea you had such big feet, Dell."

To silence him I said, "I'll wager you five dollars that I could get both my dainty feet inside one of your boots."

"I accept your bet. Now prove it."

"When we settle for the night. I'm not taking them off in this stage." The weather brought cool but clear skies, and the leaves had begun their annual turn toward amber, red, and cinnamon woven between deep greens of pines and fir. A vast stillness shrouded the place as we stopped by Henry's Lake. Teal and canvasbacks and mallards quacked their calls to fellow ducks. I'd stepped outside the new coach to stretch my legs and heard an elk's bugle. Then soft sighing through the trees, broken by the sudden clatter of antelope racing beyond snowcapped mountains shadowing tiny green plants. Pine scented the air. It was a place for tourists, that was certain.

"You're the first woman to come into the park," Marshall said. He was Robert's height, older though, and carried himself as a man who found strength in the elements.

"First white woman, I imagine," I countered. "No Indian woman would have kept her distance from so grand a landscape as this."

"I hadn't thought of that," Marshall said. "When Colonel Vandervort of the survey team was here, he wrote that 'no lovely woman's sweet voice had ever floated across Henry's Lake.' No longer true now, thanks to you, Mrs. Strahorn."

It wasn't true before, I'm certain of that. Sometimes men didn't listen and for a moment I wondered about that Arapaho or Shoshone, Crow or Blackfeet woman who might have sung a song heard in this natural cathedral.

Several hours later, we came upon our rest

stop for the night. It was a two-story house that a ranger had built but then, with Indian troubles, had abandoned, taking out the glass windows and doors for fear the house would be burned and he'd lose those costly items. Canvas flaps were hung to keep out the wind. There were no beds inside, only a crude table and chairs.

Mr. Marshall rustled up supper for us. "I hope you like cold beans."

"Beans make anything a complete meal," Robert said. He did like his beans. After we ate, Robert said, "We'll head out to the stage for the night. Best place to keep warm."

"No, no," Mr. Marshall insisted. "The upstairs has hay. It'll be softer and warmer. You take this candle lantern and head on up there. I'll bed down in the stage, keep the horses company."

I made a quick foray for personal things left in the stage and became aware of how cold and tired I was. My bones ached. In the darkness I heard the serenade of crickets, the crunch of horses chewing; then I returned and climbed the ladder to the loft. Robert waited with the candle lantern that the wind kept blowing out. I wondered why they'd hauled hay up above the living space in the first place, but there it was. I was cold, tired, hungry, and my feet hurt, and I'd take what comfort the loft provided. I'd slept in a stage. It was not a pleasure.

Robert made a bed of sorts over the hay and

rubbed my gloved hands trying to warm them. I started to cry, I'm not sure why. I didn't often, but the contrast of being in that magnificent park by day and in this primitive accommodation by night overwhelmed.

"I'd let you sleep with those boots on, but we need to dry out the felt. Besides, I wouldn't want anyone to mistake your limb for a log." I knew he teased to make me feel better, but it wasn't working.

I began the unhooking of the heavy boots, no easy task, as my fingers were slowed by cold. "My feet have got to have a rest from these."

Pard helped pull them off, massaged my stocking feet. "Now's the time to determine if your five-dollar wager brings me five more." He removed his boots, handed me his big brogan. "OK, let's see you get both of your dainty feet into my boot." Our eyes had adjusted to the darkness. The moon gave off pale light through the cracks in the roof and walls.

"Robert, please."

"Oh, come on. We might as well have fun as be miserable. There's a choice."

I sighed, stuck my stocking-clad foot in Robert's boot; took it out. Then I daintily slipped in the other foot, and took it out. "Done. I win." I reached for a blanket.

"Hey, wait a minute. You were supposed to put both feet into my boot."

"I did. Where's my five dollars?"

"No, no, no, no. At the same time."

"I never wagered that. I said I could get both of my feet into your one boot and I just did. Pay up."

His mouth hung open. "Well, I'll be." He tossed me a five-dollar gold piece but in the pale light I missed it and it landed in the hay.

I scrambled to find it, patting up dust, messing up the blankets. He knelt too, and pawing, we both started laughing. It took half an hour until, voilà, I had it in my hand.

"Woman, you are amazing." He re-spread the blanket, rolled onto it, and motioned me there too. Then he pulled another wool blanket over us. And the first white woman to visit Yellowstone Park giggled in the arms of her hero, five dollars richer than the day before.

Love drives out tiredness.

※※

After a heartier breakfast than our supper, we continued our tour by stage, stopping whenever we wanted to gaze and be amazed at the grandeur. "Thank goodness this is protected now," I said. "No railroads, correct?"

"Not likely. But the railroads will bring people to the entrances, and stages and horses will bring them into the interior."

Mr. Marshall had a half-built cabin that awaited

us for supper. He planned to bring his wife here, leaving in the winters. This time we had both a stove and a bed. In the morning, rangers brought horses around and we began our tour by horseback, really a better comfort than the stage, though more exposed to the elements. We kept our mounts far back from some of the stranger park oddities.

Geysers greeted. "Astonishing." I couldn't say the word enough. I made detailed notes each evening, writing the names of the geysers, the height of their explosions, how long they stayed in the air. Hot springs, boiling lakes, rainbow-colored pools, it was all so intriguing. Some of the geysers sent a kind of spray over my notebook that preserved my lead pencil writings as though they were etched in stone. Someone had thrown socks in one pool, and though they were white as snow, they were brittle and broke when Mr. Marshall tugged them up. We slept without tents that night, heard the horses being restless for a time, continued our journey in the morning, and had ridden several miles before Mr. Marshall told us he'd found bear tracks not far from the horses when he went to saddle them that morning.

"Should we head back?" I asked. Being the first white woman to be a bear's breakfast didn't appeal at all to my adventurous spirit.

"We have a few miles' ride to Yellowstone Falls. You wouldn't want to miss that." Mr.

Marshall spoke to my husband's happy nod.

We slept out under the stars and I put aside thoughts of bears and in the morning peered at the glorious lake with pelicans and swans as we began the twenty-mile ride around the lake. We'd picked up the superintendent of the park by then—Colonel Norris, who led us—and we carried on, knowing we had another twenty-five miles to ride to reach the falls. Storm clouds hovered and by midafternoon . . . sent a calling card of snow. And then hail.

"Dismount! Rest the horses!" came the colonel's order.

Darkness closed over us in a steady rain as we figured we were five miles from the falls. We'd make that trek easily in the morning, I was assured. Robert had gone on ahead to shoot an elk for our dinner and the superintendent had left Mr. Marshall and me, too, to find the best camp. When we found Colonel Norris's choice for where to spend the night, it was in the open instead of under trees. Rain pelted down that would turn to snow. I said nothing and I knew Robert would never question a colonel's choice, but truly, if I'd had the strength, I would have complained and offered up another solution, one that included trees for shelter.

Robert returned without our dinner and pulled canvas over the bedding, hoping to keep it dry. He said nothing about the campsite. Bread and bacon was our fare that night. Snow fell as we kept the fire going to find scant warmth.

I awoke after a miserable night, cold and shivering, to Mr. Marshall's mutterings and learned that our horses had departed without their riders. Robert was livid and said words to Mr. Marshall, who hung a sheepish head, adding, "I lost my pipe too," as though that was the real disaster. *Men.* The horses had already been gone for two hours, but in daylight the men hoped to track them. I was given an extra blanket with a canvas draped over me and a rifle for protection. *Bears.* They stoked the fire with wet limbs, then left me alone while the men made their search to take us back the thirty miles to any kind of supplies. I prayed they'd find those horses or we'd be walking back.

You can learn a lot by sitting and thinking. A person could freeze to death in circumstances like these. My feet were this side of wet inside those boots. Thank goodness for wool socks, wool skirts, wool coats and hats. I didn't see my life flash before my eyes, yet. I almost wished it would. I got up, stomped around, sat back down. Memories of my childhood did come back though: my sisters and I slumping through snow, the light from our house a beacon as we walked home from school in the early dark. I imagined a warm fire. The one in front of me lacked sufficient fuel. I remembered my mother's words in her letter after I told of our plans for Yellowstone, of how cold meals are not good for a person. What would she say about cold everything? I tried to write but couldn't hold the pencil in my wet-gloved hands. I was grateful I wasn't pregnant, the first time that bit of gratitude had pushed its way into my brain. And I'd have a story to tell. I considered singing but didn't . . . it might attract a bear. What did I know about bears? As the hours wore on, I prayed aloud.

My prayers were answered when the men arrived back with the horses, who had stopped at a hot creek and, reluctant to cross it, tore at the grass rather than heading on home. But instead of us now returning to get out of the storm, the men decided that since we were so close to the falls, just five miles, we couldn't turn back, now could we? I would not complain and be known as the first white woman to deprive men of their Yellowstone adventures.

It was decided Mr. Marshall and I remain behind, and Colonel Norris and Pard rode on to see the falls.

Now, that decision smoldered my thinking. After all this sitting and freezing, I should be deprived of being the pioneering woman to visit the falls? No. It took me awhile to decide what to do about that—and I then asked Mr. Marshall to saddle my horse. We argued—I was very ladylike—telling him if he didn't saddle my mount, I'd head out on foot and follow the horse's tracks. He finally saddled both our mounts and we started off, but he muttered about bears getting our camp box so I told him, "You head back. Look after things, pack up. When we return, we can leave straightaway. Go on." My gloved hands shooed him like he was a gaggle of geese. He finally agreed, but I suspect he watched me until I was out of sight.

I had much less fear being alone between Mr. Marshall and Pard and the colonel than when I'd sat and waited for those same men as they searched for horses in bear country. Having a direction, knowing I was headed somewhere with a trail to follow, invigorated me. Plus, I began to sing. Oh, what a glorious time to hear my voice pressing against the low clouds, the dense timber, the snow-filled trail. My horse kept up a steady pace.

I met Pard and the colonel coming back. "I'm glad you decided to come," Robert said. "I should have let you in the first place." He reached out to pat my shoulder as he brought his horse up beside mine. "It is truly magnificent. I wish you could have seen it."

"And why can't I? I've come this far."

"Let's hurry on now, Strahorn, Missus." The colonel tipped his hat at me, wore a worried face.

"I deserve to see the falls, don't I?"

Robert frowned, then to the colonel, "You go

ahead to Marshall's camp. I'm taking her on up. She's come this far. She deserves to see it all."

"It looks like more weather rolling in. It's not a good idea."

"I see that."

I'd rarely seen Robert stand up to a colonel, but he did this time. Maybe he shouldn't have. Off we rode to that magnificent canyon to see those breath-arresting falls. Robert and I lingered longer than we should have, even lying on our bellies in the snow to look over the side of the canyon to that marvel of color and depth. My fingers felt numb inside my gloves; my feet felt frozen. But I'd seen the magnificent artistry of God's very hand and I was in awe.

"We'd better get going now," Robert said. His eyes searched the lowering sky.

"I'm ready." We let our ponies take us back, the animals seemingly aware that we headed now toward home.

The weather didn't cooperate. Snow, sleet, misery, but we caught up with the colonel, who had sent Mr. Marshall on ahead to make our next camp—forty miles forward at that unfinished log house.

It was a long, quiet ride as the cold seeped through my bones, and I did have a moment of wondering if my blustering toward adventure, not wanting to be left out, might have a cost greater than anticipated. Frostbite was nothing to laugh at.

Robert said to me, "What is there worth having that one does not have to strive for?"

"I'll feel better about philosophy when I'm in front of a stove," I told him.

We kept a steady pace, but in snow, well, we had magnificent animals. I felt guilty for asking them to do what they did. The pale light of the cabin pierced the darkness, a beacon. The horses hurried up, then stopped at the hitching post, heads hung low. Robert dismounted. He reached up to help me down.

"I can't move."

I couldn't.

All three men had to lift me, nearly frozen, from the saddle and carried me into the cabin. Robert clucked over me and hung a blanket for privacy so he could help me strip the frozen garments, wrapped a blanket around me, then set me before the small stove. Here I offer statistics as it seems relevant: I had ridden eighty-five miles in two days, one hundred twenty-five miles in three days, all in a man's saddle splitting my hips, in horrible weather. I felt like a wishbone already pulled apart.

I could barely move the next day, but we had to leave. The men created a platform so I could slide into the saddle, and I rode with them another twenty-five miles, eating my lunch of bacon and bread atop the horse for fear I would not be able to get back on if I slipped off. My knees ached in places never known to me; my hips were stones that nevertheless felt pain. And we were getting low on beans, bacon, and bread.

Pard did shoot a fine elk later that next day, which helped. It had seven prongs. Colonel Norris insisted he would ship the head back for mounting so it could hang in Pard's office. "People see that and they'll flock to Yellowstone." He sent other specimens of plants and rocks that Robert had packed into our saddlebags, too, so many that later in his career, all that we'd brought back became an exhibit at a special showing in Denver.

I did not tell Pard of my continuing discomfort in my knees and hips. I hoped that if I put distance between the four hundred miles on horseback that we'd ridden during our weeks in the park, my body would heal up. But he must have noticed. I hope he noticed just a little.

We were back at Virginia City (where I'd bought those boots), staying at the Rodgers House recuperating, when Pard said, "I think we'll stick to a few more populated places in the next year and then, maybe find an alternative way for us to make a living." He rubbed my feet, his good strong hands felt heavenly against my arches and toes.

"Give up the railroad writing?"

"No. Well, maybe do a bit of a side line with the UP's permission. They want an Idaho book and a Pacific book and after that, we'll see. The truth is, I never want to see you as you were the night it took three of us to get you off that horse. Golly, I felt responsible for that." He shook his head. "I meant to expose you to amazing things but not to bring you physical pain like that. The colonel was right, we should have headed back."

"And miss the most glorious moment of lying on our bellies looking into that canyon, together as partners? Oh, Robert, no. Please don't decide on what to do next based on that one painful day. I found out I could endure more physical discomfort than I ever imagined. I don't know if you heard me, but I sang Handel's 'Hallelujah Chorus' in German riding through that landscape alone, tracking you down. It was one of the most magnificent moments of my life. And I have you to thank for that."

"I didn't hear you. That would have been grand." He kissed my toes.

"Besides, we must strive for things that matter."

"If you say so, Mrs. Strahorn."

"I do."

From *Fifteen Thousand Miles by Stage,* vol. 1, by Carrie Adell Strahorn (page 187)

Robert Strahorn: "But what is there worth having that one does not have to strive for?"

19

Stepping In

I've fallen in love with Walla Walla,
Washington. A perfect little Pacific town.
I know Robert loves the travel and his
writing is so well-received because he
makes real in his words the grandeur and
promise of the West. I fear we aren't going
to make it back to Marengo in time for
Christmas this year though. Robert wants
to race down the Columbia, head to Los
Angeles, and return to Omaha by train. I
just want a home. Walla Walla would be
the perfect place to settle.

December 1, 1880

We hadn't been idle after we left Yellowstone.
We traveled to Virginia City, back to Helena
and Butte, other places where the railroad and
Robert's books had brought bustling commerce
since we'd been there two years before. I had
written in letter form articles for the Helena
Weekly Herald that were well-received. They
were letters from "A. Stray," written as though
an eastern lady wrote to her mother of her tourist
experiences in the West. I wondered how many

readers didn't realize who A. Stray really was. Robert approved and I found that the writing made my evenings a little less lonely, as I had a task and didn't just watch Robert work at his.

We visited Baker City, in the state of Oregon. It boasted a boys' college and a fine public school, too. I liked the idea that the state had helped build the Academy and there seemed a high commitment to education. It was the sign of progress when schools flourished, especially in the vast west where indoor education had to compete with the mountains, rivers, and verdant grasses.

Robert worked on his book in between our stops and stays at places like La Grand and Pendleton. In the evenings, I'd help edit Robert's book about Idaho: *The Resources and Attractions of Idaho Territory, for the Homeseeker, Capitalist and Tourist.* A bit of a stuffy title, but then a title is meant to tell a reader what's inside and it surely did that. I do think it's why I love to read novels, though, because the titles are meant to intrigue, perhaps be a double entendre. No guessing about Pard's books.

The Idaho legislature had paid for the work, but the Union Pacific, unbeknownst to the legislature, had backed its publication. I wasn't sure why Robert didn't tell those politicians. Maybe he thought they'd be suspicious of his words if the railroad gained as much as their territory did. But surely, they could figure out that we couldn't make all those forays into the wilds of the unknown by stage and horseback without financial backing. Perhaps they wanted to believe that the book was written to celebrate the natural attraction of the mountains, valleys, and people without a whiff of railroad self-promotion.

Another of Robert's brothers had moved west and taken employment with the railroad as a ticket agent. At least Pard could write that his own family listened to his words and no one would want to lead one's family *a stray,* no pun intended.

"We're so far away from home," I told him as we looked out upon the streets of that little settlement of Walla Walla. Perhaps it was the well-built two-story houses and mature trees and a little creek that gurgled through the town and into people's gardens, linking them as neighbors and, yes, pioneers all stitched together like a homey quilt. I felt the wanting of a home base. "Traveling down the Columbia and on to California means we'll be even farther away from Marengo. It's been forever since I've seen Christina or Hattie. She has her own practice now."

"Don't think of the longing." He sat beside me on the hotel bed. I tossed my ore from hand to hand, one of my precious things. "Where are your writing materials?" He made a show of looking around.

"I'm out." I set the ore down, crossed my arms over my chest, pouted.

"I'll get you more," and without a hitch he grabbed his hat and headed out the door.

"Robert—"

I wasn't sure where he'd find writing materials. I picked up a novel. Couldn't get back into the words. I sang and hummed. Even that failed to revive my usual good humor. What was Robert really up to?

He returned, paper and lead in hand, a good hour later. He'd located the newspaper office and bought a few sheets of paper, returning to our rooms with the scent of ink on his jacket. "Now, carry on." He handed me his stash, totally ignored my pout. "Another letter for publication."

But I was forlorn and that trip ahead down the Columbia seemed more tedious than treasured.

So, of course, Pard came up with another plan. We would head east, not west, first to Lewiston and Spokane Falls before making our Columbia River ride.

"What if we get iced in here and never make it back to Illinois by Christmas?"

"We won't." He held up one of his jackets for scrutiny. "Did you spot clean this, Dell?"

We won't be home for Christmas or we won't get iced in? "No, I did not spot clean it."

"I'll send it out then." He swatted the tweed. "They'll have it back within the hour, I suspect."

I couldn't even annoy him with my failure at wifely duties. "Come along, old girl." He swatted at my stocking feet. "It's a five-hundred-mile round-trip by stage and by horse. We'd best get packing for tomorrow."

I didn't move.

"Dell . . ."

"And what is there to see in this Lewiston?"

"Wheat country. I need to assess the long-term sustainability. West coasters seem to think theirs is the only coast, but I need to see more of what they think makes this half of the country so great."

"It's because their stories of survival are so fresh. Unlike Bostonians who now have all their pioneering stories as second and third generations, this place is a firsthand land. Of course they think higher of what is than what once was."

"A firsthand land. You may have something there, Dell." He lifted another jacket of his, then held up one of mine as well. "You could use a new frock or two. Spokane Falls is said to be at the heart of this great wheatland where the black soil is fifty feet deep and can grow anything as long as water gets to it. And they've quite a commercial center. A few new ear bobs might make the journey worth it. We'll go there after Lewiston."

"Robert. Do I strike you as someone motivated by ear bobs?"

He sat on the bed beside me. "I just need to see this landscape said to be so different from any we've seen thus far. You know, to want something very much is half the effort of achieving it. Desire pulls us toward a goal better than a fine Concord stage pulled by the best horses. These people out here, these 'westerners,' they're drawn by something bigger and I'm not exactly sure what it is. But I think the landscape will tell me."

"Perhaps the fact that they're required to change, forced to deal with the vagaries, face unknown challenges each day. They're being carved by the very land they've come to conquer." I paused. "Maybe that's the very thing I'm missing, Robert."

"What?"

"We leave no mark on this country. We're merely observers riding through it. Your pencils lure people here and their lives are changed forever. We pack our pens and ride on to the next bluff or valley, taking in the grandeur and perhaps being filled up by God's great creation, penning a word or two about it, but then what? What is our desire? Your desire, Robert?"

I hoped he wouldn't ask me mine. I wasn't sure I could articulate it.

"Too deep for my taste, Mrs. Strahorn. My desire now is to get you up and going so we can catch that stage to Lewiston, ride the steamer on the Snake, then head on north to Spokane Falls.

Chop-chop." He clapped his hands as though I was one of the Chinese waiters.

And I chop-chopped. Well, what else was there for me to do?

Lewiston Bluffs were nearly a half-mile high, a marvel to the traveler. The hillsides were bare as a baby's bottom, while wheat grew on top. Wooden chutes carried grain to the ships waiting on the Snake. I'm quite sure Robert saw railroad grades wherever he looked, tracks to compete with the ships or service them.

I experienced the dry heat of early November and removed my jacket, fanning myself, while Pard did his notetaking and chatting with local dignitaries who gave us the tour on a ferry that offered greater ease of travel compared to our stagecoach.

I was pleased later to make Spokane Falls, though. It was a jewel in the crown of the West, perhaps made the more joyful because we'd survived a few swollen streams by horseback and an encounter with a band of Spokane Indians that wasn't pleasant and served us right for deliberately slipping away from our guide. Still, my stomach powders saved the day when I offered them up to a suffering Spokane Indian woman—at the insistence of her rather intimidating spouse.

Then there was this encounter between Pard and the apparently now happy husband (after I assisted his wife) about "trading some horses for me." I've often read of accounts since then of Indians offering ponies for a white woman's hand. It really happened to me, but honestly, the repeat of that story by other pens is a demeaning statement about that race's interest in "white women." What would they do with the likes of us? Would there really be status in having a second wife with few survival skills? Or perhaps they could trade us away for a better horse at some point in the future—we might be worth that.

Personally, I think Pard misunderstood or preferred to tease me about that grateful brave coming into Spokane Falls the next day to finish the barter and take me away. I might have been losing my sense of humor, but it bothered me that a woman, even in jest, could be chattel to be traded away. How could a region as progressive as Wyoming, giving women the vote, or Oregon, allowing women to own land in their own name, also be the home of bartering a woman? Perhaps it was that "anything goes" attitude of a mining town before women arrived to civilize it that ruled this West.

At any point, Spokane Falls was more than a bit of civilization. It was a spectacular city that I was sure my mother would never believe could exist so far from Chicago. It had the hustle and bustle of Boston without the harbor. Its streets sported a mix of friendly Indians, Chinese, Mexicans, Italians, and a dozen languages of Europe and Scandinavia heard as I strolled the boardwalks and entered the lush shops selling furs and gowns. No, I wasn't motivated by ear bobs, but I did love the finery offered and bought myself a silk dress (silk takes up little trunk space) that I wore to a reception the mayor organized for us. It was a city I could have spent a few more days in. I told Robert that and he nodded. "We'll return," he said.

But once back in Walla Walla before we boarded our steamer to take us down the Columbia, I took one last stroll through its streets and paused before a lovely two-story house on Cherry Street as the woman decorated the porch with Christmas greens tied with big red bows. How I longed to remain, to plant my feet in such a place. Lacking that option and tired of feeling sorry for myself, I walked up and introduced myself to the woman, who said her name was Mrs. Crislip. I was soon helping her make streamers to link the greens around the lovely glass insert in the oak door.

"Join me for tea?" she offered when we finished. Robert waited for me I knew, but when she invited me inside, I accepted and found the Christmas memory I'd been longing for: a home where greens lined the staircase and a finely stitched quilt graced the chair beneath the mirror. A Christmas tree yet untrimmed stood in the parlor. The scent of fresh-baked goods wafted toward the door. It reminded me of Marengo, of home.

I was pleased I took the time to make a fleeting friend. After all, the best way to brush aside longing is to step into something whole-heartedly. So I made a new friend—a pioneer—on Cherry Street. It made our inability to cele-brate Christmas in Illinois bearable.

From *Fifteen Thousand Miles by Stage*, vol. 1, by Carrie Adell Strahorn (page 297)

The hardships we had endured would only make our joy the greater.

20

A Remarkable Journey

Cleopatra's journey down the Nile was remarkable. Mary's journey to Bethlehem was remarkable. I'd venture to say that Tabitha Moffat Brown, who wrote of her journey by wagon across the continent from Missouri to start a university in Oregon, was a more remarkable traveler than me, but the eastern papers commented on our previous year of so much travel. Frankly, exploring in different conveyances while hoping to remain friends with your husband, well, that might be the most remarkable challenge in any woman's history. The eastern papers never wrote about that.

December 15, 1880

I did my best to enjoy the moments on the Columbia River as they presented themselves to me. *I'm building memories,* I told myself. I did notice that my memories were starting to incorporate a lot more statistics and data than I had ever intended. But it was easier, less painful to write of "twenty-five thousand miles" somewhere than of what was really happening.

Fog greeted us on that Columbia River steamboat as we headed to Los Angeles, leaving sweet Walla Walla behind. The rapids and falls on the river required numerous portages around places like Celilo Falls, where chubby Indians standing on platforms brought up big fish called sturgeon and salmon, while our portage line proved to be a cart and a mule on the Washington side of the river. In my memoir, if I write it, I will neglect to mention that cart and the taciturn man who had managed to claim the portage line, as he referred to it.

I'd tell you about the small towns like Dallas City, but I was looking at them and the terrain as Robert might have, because he was taken to our cabin by seasickness. My notes were not of what intrigued me but meant to cover what he was missing, suffering in that chilly room even with the little stove popping itself out to give us heat. I suffered too. Everyone was gracious when I joined them at the dining table without my husband in the evenings, but I felt false having to make small talk, smile, and ask questions of others to keep them talking so I didn't have to speak about anything that really mattered. But Robert's reputation meant everyone wanted a few minutes with him or his "remarkable" proxy, me, seeking information they thought we had about the railroad's interests, commerce, migration, economics, politics, et cetera, et cetera. It was fatiguing.

"What were they asking?" Robert queried when I returned to our room after a lengthy dinner during which I regaled the other passengers with my stories, making them laugh and think me the finest of table hostesses. I was tired, cranky as a hungry baby, even though I'd eaten more than my share of roast pork at the Umatilla where we'd pulled up for the night and checked in, hoping to sleep before resuming our steamboat cruise. I wasn't hungry for food.

"The usual. They want to know what you know." I set the tray down and unhooked my throat brooch, put it in my precious box along with my rings. Robert looked peaked, but he wasn't vomiting anymore, which was good. "I brought you a cracker and some weak tea. Do you think you can drink it?"

"I'm miserable, Dell. I don't think I should try. I'll just heave it up."

The lavender sachets I'd put around the room helped but clearly not enough. "You've got to keep fluids in you. My father always insisted that the sick suffered more from dehydration than from whatever might ail them. Should I call for a doctor?"

"What good would he do?"

"He might have powders to settle your stomach." *And it would be someone else to tell your troubles to and not follow his advice, as you don't follow mine.* Yes, I was sarcastic and petty in my nursing role, but at least I didn't say those things out loud to him. After all, I was on a remarkable journey.

"Not worth the effort. I feel miserable."

"I know, poor baby." I patted his hand. It felt chilly, but then the room was. It was nearly January. Of course, the room felt cold. "Try the tea. I brought some sugar."

"No. Nothing." He sighed. "Read to me."

"In a minute."

I don't know why, but his tone caused my own stomach to tense. I slipped behind the painted screen, peeling off the layers of clothing down to my nakedness, donned a linen nightdress, then squatted over the chamber pot. At the washstand, I poured water in the basin to rinse out my under-drawers that I twisted, then hung to dry, when my dear Pard said in a voice no louder than a kitten's mew, "Alright, Dellie. Go ahead and call for the doctor. Maybe he could help me."

"Won't you try the tea and crackers?" I spoke with my back to him, wet hands holding sopping unmentionables.

"No, you're right. I should talk to the doctor."

I slapped my underthings into the bowl, stomped behind the screen, tore off the linen, yanked on my underdrawers that I had to dig through the trunk to get, donned the still warm chemise, loosely laced my corset, pillowed my dress over my head. I did not re-pin the brooch. I decided to just wear my slippers and not take the time to re-hook my shoes.

"I'll only be—"

He snored.

I left our room, seeking out the doctor for anti-anxiety powders. For myself.

We both survived the night, though Pard barely.

Thank goodness, the little coastal town of Astoria proved a fine respite from the rainy December weather, the rocking of the steamboat, and Robert's stomach upset. We had not yet embarked on the ocean journey, which was said to have its trials. But the three days we waited in Astoria were godsent. Robert felt better and his mewing ceased. He was his jovial self at the dining table and I could once again watch and listen. More importantly, we walked on Clatsop Beach and heard it attracted honeymooners. I could see why.

Seagulls swooped over us and I did for a little while have that sense of what a "remarkable" journey we were on.

"We never took a honeymoon like others," I commented. We walked arm in arm, bundled up in our robes and wraps, basking in sea air so crisp and a sky so blue. A look toward the horizon brought the vast ocean rolling almost as though the two were one.

"We'll never do anything the way others do, Dell. That's part of the marriage contract."

"Is it? I guess I didn't realize that when I said 'I do.' "

"I'm sure I promised you a journey unlike any other." He maneuvered me around a driftwood log and we continued our stroll.

"And the cowcatcher ride certainly qualifies."

Robert laughed. "I do have other plans, you know, for thrilling adventures you can tell your grandchildren about." I must have stiffened because he stopped. He stuttered, "I . . . I didn't mean—"

"It's a great line to lure the adventurer west, speaking of legacy." I kept my voice light. "You'll have to remember who you're talking to, though."

"Forgive me. That was thoughtless."

It was a moment I might have broached a discussion about taking on an orphan—there were plenty in the West. Or perhaps seeking agreement about talking to a doctor once we reached Los Angeles. My sister said there were specialists there working on issues of infertility. But in that brief moment, Robert's developer-self had slipped into his husband-self and I had trouble sorting out my own feelings about which one I was truly married to. I let the opportunity slip by. He spoke then of the complexity of laying tracks in remote places, of his own wish to one day build his own railroad. "It's a license to make money, Dell." He prattled on about wealth in money, not in relationships.

Robert's sickness continued once we "crossed the bar," as they referred to the ocean-meeting-river place. We had to wait out a storm, and the sea that had been so much a part of the horizon now roiled and boiled often beneath a cloud of fog and rain. I did much nursing during that voyage, and as I look back, I can see how my role began to change. He was a different man when he was ill, more . . . needy. The effects of tuberculosis persisted long past the original disease. I wondered if his illness during the Sioux siege came back to him when his body didn't respond in the way he willed it to. And was that why he pushed his body so when we were on dry land?

⫷ ⫸

The trip south took three days longer than scheduled because of the severe weather, and our captain had taken us farther out to sea, so when we finally came to dock, there was much ado as people had thought we were lost. There was quite a write-up in the paper about our "resurrection" when we hadn't even known of our demise. I hoped my mother hadn't seen it.

Robert recovered and we explored Los Angeles.

I thought we'd then go back to San Francisco and take the transatlantic back to Omaha. But no, we took a southern rail to Yuma, my first real exposure to desert land. *Barren* was the word that came to mind and I said as much.

"I don't see it as that. Wait until we spend the night here. You've never seen stars as you'll see them from a desert perch."

"There's a perch there?" It all looked like a squashed straw hat brim, colorless to me.

"The stars at night are pluckable," Robert said. "You'll see."

And there in our hotel, he gave me my Christmas present. A diamond bracelet.

"It's . . . fabulous. Where did you . . . ?"

"You can get anything in Los Angeles."

"But can we afford this?"

"We can. And I hope you'll think of the desert night sky when you look at that bracelet. The stars sparkle like those stones."

"You're a hopeless romantic, Robert Strahorn." I used my most affectionate name for him, then kissed him. I loved the bracelet.

"I have a new romantic adventure planned for us."

"Should I pack my boots?"

"Maybe. We're going to make a town." He said it like a man might say to his wife, "We're going to make a baby!" He continued: "Our writing work"—I was glad he included me—"has paid off and people are arriving with no place for them to unload or for the tracks to end. The UP has a new route for us, to not only assess what's possible, but also to make it happen." I looked confused, I guess, because he sat me down. "This is what we worked for, Dell. City building." He was a child in a toy shop, with visions of the future where he'd not only get all the toys inside but he'd own the shop itself. "And you'll get a diamond or another precious stone for every town we build."

I would have preferred a child.

His boyish joy was bittersweet. I wanted to see that look in his eye not just on town building but on our lives. But I would have to set aside my hopes for that and be grateful that he loved me in his way, looked after me, gave me diamonds in lieu of babes.

We didn't make Omaha for Christmas, of course. And early in 1881 we returned to Idaho, and before long, Pard and others formed the Idaho and Oregon Land Improvement Company. Here I must digress because our dear federal government, in an effort to advance the cause of expansion in the West, gave the Union Pacific sixty million acres of western landscape from Lake Superior west to Puget Sound. An 1862 act granted ten square miles in alternate sections on either side of the railroad right-of-way for each mile of track laid. The railroads could sell that property or develop it. (It's true that in later years the UP had to give back twenty million dollars because they didn't live up to the contract, but it was still more land than any other railroad received.) Robert's development company then purchased some of those lands for resale for future townsites and to sell to merchants and even homesteaders who might not qualify for free land, all with the intent to lure people west. The railroad, investors, and Robert's partnership would make money—after a time. The country would expand.

I found myself intrigued by all the court doings, the trips hither and yon settling deeds and registrations and boundary lines and forming new counties. Pard was in meeting after meeting about how to fund needed public things, like getting water to a potential townsite because parts of Idaho resembled Yuma, Arizona, if one was honest. And there was politics galore, the most significant being where a town would grow up and then whether it would be the county seat or not. These negotiations, Pard assured me, were all part of our remarkable journey.

Hailey, Idaho, became Pard and his partners' firstborn. It was a mining town with few structures to recommend it, but it was for sale.

It became the coveted county seat of the new Blaine County where, when the election for county seat was over with, Hailey earned fourteen more votes than Bellevue and fourteen more votes than all the registered voters in the county, imagine that.

Then the voting boxes were stolen.

A new count gave the win to Bellevue, but Hailey supporters hired their lawyers, and it was determined by the court six months later that Hailey it was! Of course, all that was there to start the town was a tent mercantile and the promise of a railroad stop. Soon a newspaper was started, the *Hailey Miner.* I wrote a piece or two for it under my own name, Dell Strahorn.

It was Robert's choice, Hailey. Or rather, the company's choice. The railroad would lay its tracks and Robert's status as a town builder took off.

"We could settle here, Dell. Build a house. You could write your letters about a town forming out of nothing but goodwill and effort."

"And the government giving millions of acres of land to the railroad." I'd had forty-five of my letters printed in the Omaha *Republican* that summer, and I was enamored with Hailey's landscape nestled inside mountainous country along the rushing Wood River. It was high and dry—Pard said almost a mile high like Denver. It got lots of snow in the winter. We walked beside the river in the spring. But Pard would still be traveling on to start the next town, and there I'd be, left behind. Maybe in a makeshift house, but worse of all, driftless without him, without a family, without a direction.

"And what if you get sick again while you travel hither and yon? Who will look after you?"

"I'm hardy as a horse in this country. It's an ocean that does me in." He'd forgotten Omaha. "You could entertain the senators and mayors who will come and explore the West. And when I'm home, we'll have a happy little love nest. You won't have to pack and unpack ever again. And there are hot springs here, good for TB patients and others. A healing place."

I imagined myself with pioneering tables and stumps for chairs. "No. Let's not make Hailey our permanent home, but we could build a little cottage."

Hailey became the beginning of a separation with the railroad, even while Pard's prospects improved because of the UP. Those lengthy railroad tracks scratched westward like a two-clawed sloth inching its way to change what had been wilderness. And it changed our lives once again. We'd no longer be traveling wide stretches of the West. But neither would we be settled into one place for a very long time. We were indeed on a remarkable journey.

From *Fifteen Thousand Miles by Stage*, vol. 2, by Carrie Adell Strahorn (page 37)

As we neared the City of Angels we summed up our travels since breaking up our Omaha home on June first, six months previous, and the results were somewhat startling. It was more than twenty-five thousand miles by steamboat, rail, and horseback, and three thousand miles by stage. Some Eastern papers commented on the trip as being the most remarkable one in any woman's history, and the end was not yet.

21

Tales to Tell

By the time Pard began our separation from the Union Pacific and moved full bore into land development, I wrote to my mother and sisters with pride that I'd had several more letters published. Robert now penned and printed a monthly paper called The North West Illustrated, an expansion of his New West Illustrated. He'd completed revisions of his Wyoming book, and worked on another title integrating pieces of former articles he called "Where Rolls the Oregon." He sought my editing advice and usually took it and incorporated some of my writing into his compilation without credit. Nothing has changed, but then I haven't told him that his conscription of my words bothers me either.

March 20, 1881

My writings were autumn leaves, bright and beautiful and flashy but unmoored from their larger, more imposing hosts, simply dropped to the forest floor to be trampled upon and turned into humus for an acorn to grow one day into a mighty oak. But who remembered the leaves that mulched and gave the nutrient? It's the oak we admire.

My investment in my mining town real estate had gone nowhere. I paid my taxes on the commercial property, but otherwise, it sat. I guess that's what happens when one speculates in land acquisitions. It's risky. I thought I had an inside track, pun intended, with Robert's having discussed with city fathers that the railroad might well come their way.

We rented a small house in Hailey. Pard's company hoped to buy up the silver mining town that nestled in the Wood River Valley, build a hotel near the hot springs, market it as a healing resort. We only spent the summers there. It was a respite from boardinghouses and stage stops and we often had visitors. Pard's father came for a few weeks. Like Robert, he was tall and slender and a gentleman toward me. After a few days, he would share little worries he had, and I'd give him suggestions for his foot that sometimes ached, or he'd describe a discomfort in a letter from one of his sons and ask how to address it. Apparently, I had "I listen" tattooed on my forehead, and I was glad for that. It gave us a way to relate when we had but few days together before he headed out to visit his son in Denver.

He was a more revealing man than Robert. Perhaps that comes with age. One afternoon while we sat on the porch beneath that Idaho sun, he spoke of Robert's growing up, how he hated to have Robert leave school when he was ten to help him on the farm, then Robert took that job working in a printer's shop. "He was a little tyke, but with his mama gone and younger ones at home, what could I do?"

"It must have been a very difficult time for you."

He nodded. "I didn't need to ask the boy. He offered. He's that kind of generous."

"He had a good model."

He spoke then of the death of his wife and two children in their toddler years. The grief was still raw in his voice, and I wondered how a soul went on after the loss of one's flesh and blood. Having no children at nearly thirty, and no prospects in sight, I'd be spared of so great an absence as that.

Robert's father was not the only one who brought small worries to my door, and I found that my "I listen" stature could bring a comfort to others that in a small way brought comfort to myself.

❧❧❦

My sister, now Dr. Harriet E. Green of Chicago, arrived that summer in Hailey. She traveled with Alexander Caldwell, a former Kansas senator, who was the president of Pard's land development company, and his wife, Pace. With them came a Pittsburgh banker, Mr. Mellon. The senator came with a bit of corruption behind his name, having bribed other candidates with cash to get out of the race so he would win. When the subterfuge was discovered, Caldwell resigned and went into banking. Past history was simply overlooked in the West, where criminals of a more violent nature tended to follow the railroad, attempting to overtake a town, while those committing crimes in their suits moved into acceptance, a fresh "den" even if they didn't always change their stripes. I think Caldwell did, but I write this as a reminder that these were the sorts my husband teamed up with. Shaving the icy edges of ethics.

Robert and I took Hattie and the rest of that party around, showing off the vistas, traveling to Shoshone Falls, a primitive stage stop that Pard and Caldwell believed would make a good railroad depot and which Pard had touted as the Niagara of the West in his book. The falls were 212 feet higher than Niagara's. Pard could see a hotel near the springs in Hailey and a lovely inn near Shoshone Falls for tourists to gaze agog.

"This is fabulous," Hattie told me. Well, she had to shout it to me over the roar of the falls. We sat beside them, having made a precarious move down slick lava rocks while the great Snake River surged over smooth boulders, forming rainbows as it plunged into pools and rock cauldrons below. I could feel the thundering at my feet. Cool mist proved a pleasant wisping on our July-hot faces. Later when the two of us walked back in front of the others toward the small boardinghouse that Pard imagined a hotel site one day, my sister said, "Have you written of this place?"

"This one's Robert's venue," I said. "But I did get a lovely review of my work in the Helena *Herald*. The editor said, 'Montana's scenic grandeurs were the charms that broke the chrysalis from Mrs. Strahorn's embryonic literary talent and developed its charming colorings.' Quite impressive, wouldn't you say?"

"It's a bit over the top, though, don't you think?"

I felt my face grow warm because I had liked the praise despite its cloying flower. "I write effusively sometimes and I think the editor was matching my style. It might have been a tiny bit lavish." A thought occurred to me: "You don't think he was mocking me."

She shook her head no, but I wondered. Hattie asked, "How did he know it was your work?"

"I've written a few stories for the *Herald* under my own name, with Robert's approval, of course. Now that we're in a different relationship with the railroad, there doesn't seem to be a problem with my expounding as someone other than Emerald Green or A. Stray."

"I always thought that a funny nom de plume."

"You got the pun."

"Sadly, yes. I worry about you." My sister put her arm around me and hugged me to her.

"No need." I chirped, so far from any intimate discussion of my mental being did I want Hattie to travel. "I'm fine."

Back at the hotel, Pace Caldwell, the senator's wife, joined us. Hattie told her of my nom de plume. It annoyed me a little, her mentioning them.

"Why do women write under those?" Pace asked. She was a tiny woman, birdlike, more with my sister Hattie's frame than my fuller form. Her bottom barely took up the pillow on the cane rocker. One could see the cross-stitch edges, whereas my chair pillow was drowned by my linen skirt—among other things. I had given up a few of my petticoats though. Travel was cooler that way and thank goodness fashion had given the death knoll to the steel forms for hoops, making way for the flouncy peplum that emphasized my narrow waist over my rounded hips. This heat of Idaho called for a simple summer frock. "I would have read *Jane Eyre* if Charlotte Brontë had used her real name," Pace added.

"Charlotte Brontë wouldn't have gotten it published with her real name," I said. "Men make those publishing decisions even today. I used A. Stray for a variety of reasons, but one was that I hoped an editor and eventually readers might at least read what I wrote. If it had come from Adell Stray, a woman, I have my doubts."

"Surely the name Strahorn would have gotten you published." Pace blinked when she talked. Frequently. Perhaps the western sun was too bright for her pale blue eyes. She didn't wear a hat as we sat on the porch.

"It did, I'm sure. But I wanted to see if without Robert's influence, would someone other than my mother like my work enough to print it for general consumption. And they did a few times."

"Did you write an essay or a feature story, the way Mary got her article picked up?" Hattie asked.

"It was a humorous piece about travel in the West. It was an honest rendition of the conditions, but I think it made people laugh. I didn't want to discourage them from coming west, of course."

I went inside and requested a tray of iced tea. We could get ice, with the snowcapped mountains close.

"We women ought to read some books together," Pace said when I returned. "We could write to each other about them, how they affected us or what we thought was missing, maybe how the story spoke to our hearts in some way. Or didn't. I'm a terrible letter writer and can rarely find a thing to say so I don't, but then I lose contact with people. I'd never think to write about the senator's travels the way you do, Carrie."

"That's a great idea." My sister cooled her face with the boardinghouse's advertising fan, featuring a drawing of the falls on it. Guests could take the fans with them when they left. That had been Pard's idea. Commerce mustn't miss a beat. "I love your letters, Carrie, but you seldom let us know what's really going on. Your words about Robert are always so sweet, but I have married patients and they let me know that life isn't always sugared." She raised one eyebrow at me.

"That's for certain," Pace said, "though you and your Pard are such lovebirds."

"He's my best friend."

"Even friends have disturbances. That's what *Pride and Prejudice* is all about, really."

"Jane Austen wrote with a pen name too but gave away her gender, writing as 'A Lady.' That was quite nervy for her time," I said. "It took courage to pursue her passion that way."

"Courage marks what you're doing too," Pace said. "I admire your vagabond life. I could never get comfortable not having a home base."

I considered what to say. "Riding the stage or horses into unknown places isn't courageous. I'm rarely alone." I hadn't told either of the women about my time waiting in Yellowstone with rifle in hand to fend off a grizzly bear while the men chased after our horses. I sat quite alone then. "I'm more inclined to think of the true pioneering women as courageous. There was a mother we encountered on Inspiration Pass one winter, nursing a baby in a high snowstorm, wind blowing, kids sent off with freezing hands to hold horses pawing for sparse grass. It was chilling to think they'd left the green fields of Missouri for that unwelcoming place." I also didn't share how she'd blamed Robert for their misfortune on the mountain nor the guilt I felt about my part in that.

"See, we could have quite a conversation sending the letter around, adding to it and posting it on to the next. I bet Mary would join in too. We could let the novels help us think about things like courage and overcoming fears." Hattie warmed to the idea.

"And keeping marriages alive during strained times." Pace added that last. Having a husband resign his Senate post because of corruption charges had to be one of those times.

"We could do that. Oh, did you see that deer bound over there?" All eyes squinted toward the rocky landscape close to the falls.

And I successfully diverted the conversation, not committing to the round-robin book letter. The idea of sharing my feelings with people— even those I loved, even about a book—gave me pause. It's easier to move into what I call my "happy lane." I'd likely never write about a night we spent next to those falls waiting for the ferryman to rouse and bring us across. We shivered together, the senator and Pace, Mr. Mellon and Hattie and Pard and me without blankets above the falls, hoping the rocks would keep us warm but knowing also that rattlers liked warm rocks too. We used our luggage for pillows, and I confess that though there were stars above us as bright as diamonds, I was so disgusted with our plight that I failed to enjoy them. Now that's a sin, surely. But writing of that? No. What would my mother say if I had to tell her of Hattie's demise by a rattlesnake or because of exposure to the elements beside the wild Snake River?

Truthfully, I hated Hattie seeing the primitive nature of our life in the West, one adventure at a time, going back and forth as it were, getting nowhere really, except in and out of the boat, that rowboat a metaphor for my life then. And I was embarrassed, wanting my West to show a bigger heart than the ferryman's who had neglected us.

From *Fifteen Thousand Miles by Stage*, vol. 2, by Carrie Adell Strahorn (page 45)

We spent some weeks on Wood River gathering statistics which Pard wove into an entertaining narrative, clothing it in attractive garb that it might coquette with restless spirits in the far East who were waiting for an enchantress to lure them to the great mysterious West.

The manuscript from my own pen flowed more in a humorous vein, showing a search for romantic history, social status, pastimes, and conditions of the people already in the new land, weaving together the ludicrous and amusing episodes, and describing the grandeur of the scenery; mine to be soon forgotten by those who read to be amused, and Pard's to live always in the great sea of commercial figures.

22

A Dog beneath the Maple Tree

Robert has promised me a different way of life now. We're to put down roots, build a home, have neighbors to serve, friends for supper. A garden I'll tend and maybe, a dog! We head today to this place of promise. My delight knows no heights!

July 15, 1883

A desert is the only way to describe the townsite that Pard staked out. I could hardly hold back the tears while my promoting husband waxed eloquently on.

I struggled with being trustworthy as we lured people to landscapes such as Pard wrote of, not speaking of the reality of the alkali flat I stared at that day, but instead, of all he envisioned. He didn't lie about it exactly. But it wasn't the whole truth either. As with Emily Dickinson, he was telling it "slant."

Caldwell was the company's choice for the railroad terminal to be built in Idaho Territory, much to the chagrin of Boise City, thirty miles away. Already thriving, those Boise founders knew they'd grow bigger if the railroad came their way. They were not silent about their dislike for my dear husband. But Robert in his wisdom thought starting a town from scratch on a flat would be a cheaper build for Union Pacific and get the tracks that much closer, linking to those that would take passengers one day all the way through to Portland and Puget Sound.

I nodded, mute as he described his dream.

"We'll site a mercantile over there. I've got a load of lumber ordered. We'll post it there." He pointed to stakes ankle deep in white dust. "See, I've laid the streets out. You can help name them, Dell."

"Quite a lot of them."

"It'll be a big town. The center of this growing region, and it'll serve people outlying maybe two hundred miles. There's nothing else to reach them. Look over here." He pointed to a place beyond the horses we'd tied to the back of the wagon, where they munched on their oats. "We'll have a livery there. That'll be a park." He gestured toward a sagebrush. "We'll have barbershops and a doodad store or two for the ladies. Real estate offices, tinsmiths, the necessary saloons. Here, walk with me."

It was like pushing through snow as the dirt rolled like powder and whitened our shoes, stockings, my skirt bottom, Robert's pants and boots. The dust rose to stink up our faces and sting the backs of our hands. It was hot, so I'd taken off my gloves but put them back on after that "stroll" through the "downtown." Sagebrush and greasewood grew over our heads—and were the only welcome shade—but Pard assured me that wherever sagebrush grew, it meant that with water, the soil could nurture any crop.

"Where is the water?"

"Snake River is full of water. So is the Boise River, which is closer, and there are creeks. We just have to get it across the flat to here. That'll come in time. First, we get lumber and we build."

"School? Churches?"

"Of course." He scanned the landscape. "I can see them. Can't you?"

"I lack the imagination."

He chuckled at that. "Not a true statement, Mrs. Strahorn. I know you."

I smiled. "I need a little time. I had visions of shade trees and grasses, not tumbling weeds."

"We'll make those things happen. Are you crying?"

"Dust in my eyes."

"Rest in the wagon shade, then. Read your book. I've got a little more surveying to do."

I watched my husband move with the joy of a child seeing newness and possibility everywhere. The stillness felt heavy to me, but to Robert, it opened a whole new world. *Can I come to love this desert?* In my mind's eyes, I tried to imagine women arriving, anticipating. Instead, I saw a woman blinking back tears, a pudgy child's hand in hers, sinking into the poison dust so white it matched the snowcaps on the mountains far, far beyond. What would they say to their husbands? What would I say to them as I greeted them in this heat, with memories of shady oak and elm still fresh in their hearts? How could I tout Robert's promotional writing and still be a trustworthy steward of the truth?

I saw no birds. Heard no sounds but the horses munching. There must be beetles and bugs out there. I knew there were snakes, though that day I saw none. Had this landscape once been lush or had it always been flat, abandoned, a place where people, if they ever came here, moved quickly on through? Robert saw it as a destination, a place to call home. It would be my home.

The only way I could think to congeal the reality I saw with the vision my Pard imagined was to plunge into the effort, to show those arriving women that making a home and life in this barrenness could be done. There'd be no showing up in the summer to rent a little cottage, as with Hailey, nor helping a house get built with supplies close by, as in Omaha. In fact, a house would be one of the last things to construct in this landscape. A train depot and freight yard and commercial enterprises would come first. There'd be no overnight riches as in a mining town. Money here would be hard earned. Yet with water—

yes, water—life could flourish on this flat.

We would have to live on-site without irrigation until it arrived. I let my eyes scan the sagebrush. I saw the wheat-colored shirt my husband wore as he stepped off distances to place yet another stake, wondering if that would be my backyard. I took heart from his enthusiasm as I watched him, smelled the sagebrush, let the silence fall around me like a warming cloak. Maybe this was where I was set to bloom. How ironic, one's blooming in the desert.

And so that day in 1883 I chose to become the mistress of Caldwell. My heart moved into my throat then, and I had trouble swallowing, but I was sure it was from the choking alkali dust and not from my understanding of the commitment I'd just made. The lyrical poet Von Goethe wrote that once a commitment is made, Providence moves. I was counting on that.

When his surveying was finished, I gave Robert jerked venison and cheese along with bread now dry as a bone. We washed everything down with water from our canteens, savoring each precious drop. I'd spread a blanket at the side of the wagon to catch a little shade. The horses switched their tails at flies. A jackrabbit hopped beneath a greasewood, stared at us, and moved on. I'd learn to fix a rabbit stew.

"Now that I think about it more, Dell, there's no need for you to risk this desert while we're building," Robert told me. "Just stay in Hailey. Or go back to Denver. Or maybe west to Walla Walla. You liked that little city."

"I did, but I envisioned you there with me."

He was thinking out loud. "Boise won't be a place to stay. They're boiled about my wanting to create Caldwell. This . . . building is going to be a hardship for a time. You can see that."

"What would I do in Denver with you up here?" I'd accepted his invitation to make Caldwell our home and he then decided I might not be all that helpful. "I need to be able to look at those arriving men and women and children and assure them that it can be done by a woman, even an eastern woman with as few survival skills as a frog out of water."

"You have good common sense and persistence, Mrs. Strahorn. Those are prerequisites for survival in any circumstance."

"Maybe I'll have to be the shoulder they lean on, dealing with their own visionary mates bringing them to—this—until they find their own dream here." I would have to make his promised land mine.

He took a drink. The horses shifted their stance. We'd need to water them before we slipped back into Boise. "It would be good to have you here, but I fear your mother would have my throat if she knew the conditions."

"I can be elusive about the . . . setting. She

doesn't have to know Caldwell is right now nothing more than a twinkle in your eye."

"It won't be easy, Dell." He took my hand. "It's probably not fair to have asked you in the first place."

"I'm willing. I want to see what it's like to settle down."

"It'll be much harder than adjusting to a strange stage stop each night and certainly more demanding than directing those house builders in Omaha."

"What a good idea. Could we get them to come here?" He knew I jested.

"I don't think they'd come within a hundred miles of this site, at least not until we have a thriving town. And we will, Dell. And I will build you a fine, fine home here. It'll be our base from now on. It would be easier with you here, if you can tolerate the heat and later the cold."

"If I set my mind to it. We're in this together."

"I, uh, should tell you that trying to get the Oregon Short Line to come to Caldwell is not a sure thing. We're kind of doing this as a speculation, Caldwell and Mellon and me."

"Us."

"Yes. Us. But what I mean is, I'm no longer working for Union Pacific. I had to sever ties with them to create the development company, remember that. So, the UP could change their minds about where to bring the line."

"But they trust your surveying, all the work you've done for them."

Robert nodded. "They agree to the likelihood of where tracks will be laid next, including Caldwell. But things can happen. Politics. Boise City really wants the short line there, and it could be they have deep pockets enough to get the railroad to switch tracks on us. We'll be investing our own money in this venture, not the railroad's. You understand that."

"Even more reason for me to live and work here, where Caldwell is." I said it with certainty, giving myself a little time to absorb what he'd told me about severing *all* ties with the UP. "Does that mean our passes are now invalid?"

"No, no. I managed to keep those." He laughed. "But I need you to know that there is some risk. There won't be a monthly salary from the railroad but from the Land company, and it'll be much less, as the company has taken out loans to invest in this venture and that's where that money must go right now. We'll see the return when we sell commercial and home lots and outlying land to newcomers. And rights of way to the railroad. It'll take time."

"A little late to tell me now, isn't it?" My retort held more bite than I intended to show at that moment, but perhaps again, my heart knew something my head hadn't yet grasped.

"I should have included you in the negotiations, or at least kept you apprised, but Caldwell and

Mellon are the bankers and they gave it thumbs up even with that miserable night at Shoshone Falls. And the senator didn't include Pace in all of this, so I didn't involve you either."

"Since when does what other men do with their wives direct what you do? We're 'pardners,' or so I thought."

"Of course we are." He leaned over to kiss my alkali-dusted nose.

I sighed. "I need to be here while we undertake this town building. Will the senator be on-site? Pace?"

"They'll visit. We can stay with them when we go back east. You and Pace get along?" I nodded. "They say Kansas is beautiful country."

"Pace speaks fondly of all the trees they've planted." That spurred my thoughts. "Trees, Robert. We need to plant sheltering trees, which brings me back to water."

"We already have plans under way. Our company will pay for the canals. But meanwhile, we'll haul water by wagon and eventually by rail until the ditches are dug. A cooper will make good money here. Water'll be scarce, so I'm not sure about trees as a top priority."

"Oh, I'll plant trees," I said. "And give up my tea for the cause." I tried to imagine where our own home might be and wondered if maple trees would grow in this heat. "Do you have our house site marked out?"

"I do. But before I show you, know that for now, development won't be in the residential sections. We'll set up a tent close to where the terminal tracks will come, when they come."

"Tent living. Well, we've done that before for a short time. I'm sure I can figure out how to extend it. But give me the home tour." I stood, brushed my skirts of bread crumbs, reset my hat as a warm breeze had stirred itself up. I pulled him up. Robert pooched out his elbow for me to take it as we made a promenade toward a cluster of sagebrush well beyond the horses, our boots puffing up white dust as we walked. High above I saw a bird, soaring. A good sign. I don't think it was a vulture.

I soon stood in the middle of my house, swirled around, slowly so as not to add to the dust bowl rising at my skirts. Both of us coughed, the sound like a knife cutting the vast stillness. "We'll have a spectacular view, as far as the eye can see."

"That we will."

I kept turning, stopping at each directional point: east, north, west, south. "I think I see the picket fence."

He laughed, then kissed me beneath a sky so blue it put a morning glory pool of the Yellowstone to shame.

"Chickens are scratching. There's the garden." I pointed. "And I see a dog lounging beneath a maple tree."

"I love you, Dell Strahorn." He kissed me again.

"I have to be able to see it to be a trustworthy reporter to all those souls you've enchanted west."

"We'd best get started, then," he said. And so we did.

From *Fifteen Thousand Miles by Stage*, vol. 2, by Carrie Adell Strahorn (pages 120–21)

To plump one's self down in an alkali flat, with railroad survey stakes for company, and expect an Aladdin's lamp to throw pictures of a thriving city, invites feelings of sobbing and laughter so closely allied that one can hardly tell which is which, or which will dominate. It means success or failure and only laughter must go echoing through the air, to be caught up and passed along the road of success to cheer and encourage all who hear it. The sobbing must be hidden so deep that one's own sweetheart will not know it is there. Work and courage are the essential attributes for the pioneer.

23

Buckets from the Boise

I find myself struggling with what to write here. The task ahead is overwhelming. And if I write of the hardships, will that bring me down at a time when I must maintain a stalwart stand? I'll try to be honest so I may draw on what I was feeling if later I write that memoir. But who wants to read of everything going well when within our own lives things usually aren't chugging along without a break in the tracks? It will take my greatest effort to imagine what Pard sees and to not be discouraged by the day-to-day plodding through alkali desert toward success. Perhaps I will write less until I can bring in the light that makes things grow.

August 7, 1883 in Caldwell

What I hadn't realized then—and that Caldwell helped teach me—is that it's how we respond to the broken tracks that matters, because there will always be brokenness. It's what we do with the punches we take, the heart-stopping moments, those are the knives that carve out who we are. I came to believe that people born with silver spoons in their mouths never get the real nourishment they need to grow to their full height unless the spoon tarnishes or the food drops off now and then and they have to find a way to pick it up themselves. They're really deprived, which may be why we call them "spoiled," like meat left out in the sun.

I was one of those spoiled children until Robert and stagecoaches and Caldwell. Wealthy parents, matriculating at the University of Michigan, a European voice tour and instruction, marrying a popular writer and adventurer, diamonds on my wrist and ears, never lacking for anything. Yes, when Pard gets ill, his needs carve something of my character in how I respond, but any woman wearing diamonds cannot complain loudly, or ought not to.

≫※≪

Pard got the load of lumber ordered in first off and had spoken with a man about setting up a mercantile to handle the lumber sales. They sat on those boards while Pard did his best pitch.

"You're sure the railroad is coming here? I want to see some side rails before I buy property and start to build." He was a man after my own heart, that lumberman.

Pard had barely opened his mouth to assure him yet again when we heard the train whistle, and a work crew coming from afar arrived ready to lay the rails. It was what I called "divine intervention" and needed as, until then, our tent was but a lonely dot in that town-building sentence.

We moved full steam ahead and then that lumberman stuck Pard with the bill. Scoundrels abound in a growing town, I came to discover. I worked at not letting that fact discourage.

Then came the death threats. Boise people were truly distressed by Robert's starting a new city rather than urging the railroad to go where one already was. And I was worried sick each time he had to go to Boise, where once we'd enjoyed ourselves in that bustling place.

"Don't think about it," Robert said. We were huddled in our tent home. I swept the canvas floor of what dirt I could, the action serving as a snake patrol too. "I understand why they're upset. They worked hard to build a town that would do even better with the railroad."

"Those threats and rumors make my blood boil."

"Very few people act on their outrage, Dell. As long as they're making threats, there's a greater likelihood they won't manifest it."

"I'm not sure my doctor sister would agree with your assessment. Threats ought to be taken seriously." I brushed the dust from my shoes on the back of my calves, one at a time.

"Every time I go into Boise where a bunch of men stand around, and I hear them saying my name before I enter, grousing about me, threatening to run me out on a rail, I greet them with a hearty, 'Hello, gents. Great to see you.' They always turn with a scowl that fades into a smile, and they greet me with a handshake. It's blowing off steam, the complaints, Dell. Don't worry over it. Fear's an elixir that feeds anxiety and drains common sense."

"I won't try to talk you out of going there, but be careful." I wiped my hands on my apron.

"I will."

Robert could lessen my worries with his confidence. Still, I said, "Shouldn't we try to get a sheriff here?"

"There's a county sheriff. He covers Caldwell too."

"And would take hours to reach us after sending a runner." I put aside the broom, sat on one of the leather folding stools that traveled well in wagons and now helped furnish our home.

Robert took my hand. "Every venture forward carries risk with it. We can't be deterred by that."

"I know, but—"

"No buts." He patted my hand. "I'll be careful. I've calmed many a soldier riled up beyond where he should be. I can simmer down those Boise boys. Don't let your worries drag you down, Dell. Put that fuel somewhere else."

Don't let your worries drag you down, Dell. Doesn't that sound like a song lyric? Phrases from other people's mouths would get stuck in a rhythm in my head. *Don't let your worries drag you down, Dell. Fear's an elixir that drains our common sense.* I hummed those mantras whenever I began to hear a dissonant note.

We platted the townsite in August of 1883, and within four months, forty businesses had set up shop. One hundred fifty dwellings grew out of the desert almost overnight, though mostly they began as tents and shacks.

Pard built a frame office to work out of, to meet various investors, to charm and cajole a banker to come, druggist, hardware shopkeeper, and of course there was the necessary saloon operator, though I was grateful Robert hadn't sought after that commercial establishment. The Fahey brothers came on their own.

We lived upstairs of the Land company's offices. Not a house. Not even a cottage. I cooked for workers, until Pard and I began taking meals in a freight car, which served as the boardinghouse for the town. That was fine with me. Cooking over an open fire was not my idea of time well spent, but the arrival of cookstoves would have to wait for the train to bring them or to be hauled in with some enterprising freighter leading his sturdy pack mule. Still, a framed house would have been nice.

A tent mercantile opened within those first weeks, operated by Montie B. Gwinn—of Boise, no less—and his wife, Delia. He was the son of the Methodist minister in Boise and he had a sister too. The merchant Gwinns lived in the back of the tent. I looked forward to having another woman in the vicinity.

"Your husband could have convinced the Union Pacific to come through Boise and saved all this mess here. What were you thinking letting him talk you into coming to this jackrabbit-and-badger resort?" Delia had quoted that description from the Boise paper. I'd read it in there myself. She swung her arm to take in the tents and grease-wood, the flesh of her arm still swinging long after she'd lowered her hands and her gaze at me.

"Welcome to you as well," I said. She hadn't even given me a chance to introduce myself, but I guess I didn't need to. "The Union Pacific has its own ways, I'm afraid. It's run by men, after all. And a good many of them take no quarter from a woman."

She harrumphed but nodded. "It's just such an effort to start anew, isn't it? I grew up in Portland and this is quite the change. We're trying to keep the Boise store going while we're here and putting up with people not too happy that we've gone over to the enemy in the first place."

The enemy? Was it as serious as that?

"You'll find the people here quite accommodating. There's almost a festive mood in the air, a little like mining town eruptions."

"Oh, we've packed into our share of those. At least we're on flat ground here. And there is the promise it'll get better once the short line is finished. It will get finished, won't it? I don't want to get a supply line all put together only to have it peter out like mines sometimes do." She had intense green eyes.

"If Robert Strahorn has anything to say about it, you'll hear the whistle by spring. Meanwhile, can I help you unpack? I've got some spare time."

"Aren't you building your own stick house?"

"In time. Mr. Strahorn believes the commercial establishments like yours are the most important. People need to know when they get here that they won't starve to death. Your being here with your husband is significant."

"Too bad we can't eat dust. We'd all be fat as pigs." She laughed. "Well, I am anyway. I like my baked goods too much." She patted her ample stomach. "I'm hoping the master of the freight-car boardinghouse will let me use his cookstove to make a batch or two of my croissants until we get the stove here. Nothing better than a croissant on the desert. You like croissants?"

"I do. I ate them in France and Italy. Quite different in texture but both quite tasty."

"I make the French kind with lots of butter." I'd begun helping her take pots and pans out of

245

wooden boxes and set them on the tables that had been made with two wide boards and legs pegged into the four corners. "Which is another thing. Are there any cows around here? You won't get families with kids to settle without a few milk cows or goats to serve them. Kids tire of condensed milk. But then, what'll the cows eat? We'll have to haul in oats and whatnot. I better get animal grains on the list. At least until there's water for planting crops. What's happening with the water? It gets old hauling our buckets from the Boise."

Something in the way she said those words—hauling our buckets from the Boise—made me smile. I could almost hear a tune in my head to go with them.

"Mr. Strahorn's working on that this very afternoon, trying to hire engineers and shovelers and mules enough to start that big ditch. Where would you like this spider?"

"Oh, put it over there for now." She pointed toward a box turned upside down sporting several other frying pans. She'd be cooking over an open fire, bless her. "Sorry I barked at you."

"Understandable. We women keep following them, don't we, through high water and snow-drifts too."

"Montie always did have big ideas. Your Mr. Strahorn's like that too. I guess if they weren't of that kind we wouldn't be happy either. There's something invigorating about a dreamer, isn't there?"

She was right about that.

"Got any kids out here catching the dust?" She looked around.

"No children."

She hesitated, then said, "We're childless as well. I imagined one day having children to take care of me and their father. Not to be. Maybe we'll elicit nieces and nephews if Montie's sister ever marries." We worked awhile and then she motioned for us to sit on a camp box and rest a minute. "At least I hope we've learned a little along the way and don't repeat the same pitiful mistakes made when we started out in Boise. My question is, what are you doing here, a lady like you? This isn't a place for such as you."

"You're a lady and you're here."

She guffawed at that, a big noisy sound like a French horn blasting from a beginner.

"You are," I insisted. "Well-mannered, practical, able to adapt as needed, loyal to your husband, with a good business head on your shoulders too. What more is there to a lady than that?"

"Probably a higher quality of the English language than what I speak. Neither Montie nor I ever went to school beyond a few grades."

"You've both done well. Maybe one day we'll have a college right here in Caldwell."

"Where we can put out finished ladies." She

held her little finger out with a pretend cup of tea.

"Oh, I imagine more a real educational institution with science and music and sports teams. For both young men and women."

She guffawed again. "If we ever have children, I'll send them to it."

"We both will," I said.

She stood, put her hands on her hips, elbows out and said, "You'll do, Mrs. Strahorn. You'll do."

"Call me Dell. Mr. Strahorn does."

"Oh, Della is my real name but Delia got into the mix somehow."

"My real name is Carrie."

"My sister-in-law's name. You'll like her. She's coming to visit before long. I hope to marry her off to a young Idaho man so I can spoil a niece or nephew."

Having made short work of the unpacking for the day, she said, "Do you have any errands pressing I can help you with? Turnabout's fair trade, you know."

"Now that you mention it, I do. You see that tiny speck of green, way over that way?" I pointed to our plot of ground that would one day sprout a house. "I've planted a couple of trees there and I need to do my daily water haul to keep them thriving."

"Well, let's get at it, Mrs—I mean Dell. I got a wooden bucket and it's easier to carry two at a time. Keeps me balanced, though my dear

Montie thinks nuthin' will keep my brain from being unbalanced." She laughed her French horn laugh again. "No better way to spend a day than hauling buckets from the Boise, bringing green to the desert and shade for the soul. 'Course we'll have to wait a few years for the shade part."

Caldwell's population was six hundred by Christmas. I was stunned. We had a school where we gathered for Sunday services minus a pastor, boasted a telephone exchange and, yes, a newspaper. I was given the first issue of the *Caldwell Tribune* published December 9, 1883. Editor Cuddy handed me the publication himself and I have it still, a treasure among my papers. Before long there was a competing newspaper, the true sign of a thriving town, where people took their buckets to the Boise, finding shade for their souls. I didn't have a house yet, but I felt I'd found a home.

From *Fifteen Thousand Miles by Stage*, vol. 2, by Carrie Adell Strahorn (page 133)

There is charm in building up a town that one cannot put into song, for there would be a sad accompaniment of disappointments that would not catch the public favor, but a pen picture of its ultimate success, with some of its grotesque features and the devious ways to such a pinnacle, will always be hung in a strong light.

24

Mining Emotions

I want more time with Robert, when I'm not sharing him with investors and bankers and newcomers. He tells me to seek out women friends. And I have, but I also find the presence of other women on a daily basis both vexing and a blessing. I like silence and being alone. I haven't found a gracious way to leave my talkative neighbors without offense. Perhaps it's the difference between pioneering and settling. Different skills required. Friendships take adapting. I have also come to suspicion that Pard prefers pioneering. He is off starting other towns like Ontario and Lower Weizer, leaving me here. But I hope to make his moving boots find stillness beneath a table inside a sturdy house. Soon.

March 21, 1884, Caldwell

We'd finally undertaken the building of our own home. It was slow, as Pard was constantly called off for some deed issue or complication with plots in Hailey or Lower Weizer, another town he nudged from the wilderness. The hotel he wanted built at Shoshone Falls called to him. Once, when our house was but a frame structure and we returned from a Hailey visit, we arrived back to witness a horse race going on for entertainment with our unfinished house set up for the gambling pool to meet. He wasn't a man to keep his feet beneath one bed in one town for very long, and he didn't seem too distressed that he had no bed inside a Caldwell house.

Surprisingly, I took my greatest pleasure in those early days from watering my trees. I grew to like the silence of the work done early in the morning to avoid the rising heat. I'd planted six little elm trees initially, but a windstorm one day cut three of them off as though a rabbit had chewed them halfway to the desert floor. In the Idaho wind, the alkali sand cuts like a metal file. Then a rabbit took the rest of them. From Hailey, I brought another ten trees, and this time made a fence out of wooden boxes that surrounded the sprouts, keeping them in one place until they were larger and I could plant them at the corner of the house when it was finished. The barrier helped and I had my little nursery in the desert.

Delia agreed to water them when we traveled, and the hardware store owner had a boy and girl who responded to my offer of their help in return for a few coins to spend at Delia's store. The trees' progress became something for me to talk with my neighbors about. That proved helpful, because as more families did come to Caldwell, there seemed to be this distance between the women and me, as though being the wife of the developer put me into a different category. I wasn't sure how to bridge that gap, especially as I struggled to know who I really was: Robert's wife, my mother's spoiled daughter, my smart sister's sister, a kind of friend to Pace when the senator brought her to visit, and a sort of friend to Delia. But the "lady-ness" she ascribed to me kept me at a distance.

Delia and I shared conversations about the coyotes howling at night, how eerie they sounded when they called to each other in the dark. But as a group, circling the house, their voices intimidated, threatening danger and keeping me from reading my book. Robert thought to shoot them, but they'd only return or move on to the next house, so we all agreed to put up with them. I delayed getting an English bulldog pup for fear I'd lose it to those scavengers and looked instead for a grown dog, one who I hoped would not mind going from house to house, as we kept the Hailey house and one rented in Denver—and we had rooms set up for us at the hotel in Shoshone Falls. All were connected then by a train. A dog would have to adapt.

So would Robert. He didn't really want me to have a dog.

I thought with our moving into the finished house in Caldwell and my struggle to have a garden as other women did, that things might change between me and my neighbors. But we Strahorns were of another ilk with all our houses and travel and whatnot. We were famous, spending our time with lawyers and legislators, making trips to Washington, DC, entertaining former senators, keeping busy, still writing Pard's monthly *Illustrated*, replacing servants in Denver when they left to marry, working on the hotel for Hailey at the springs. All those doings set us apart. Set me apart. I was famous by association with my husband, not for anything I did. My writing wasn't enough to bring much attention but maybe enough to keep me from having real women friends. It was difficult to have those thoughts and interchanges, though they led me toward a strengthening of the soul as I asked, "What is it I'm to do?"

❧❧

With the completion of the Oregon Short Line, a Pullman car was added so one could travel with a little more comfort from Wyoming all the way to Portland. At the Willamette River, it required a ferry to Portland, but the time between that city and Omaha was now cut by thirty hours. We held a celebration, of course, when the railroad sent their first car all the way from Pocatello to Payette, rolling through Caldwell as we always hoped. A group from Ogden rode on that train, and we met them to travel with them from Pocatello on.

It was a grand day and the railroad offered free short rides into Payette and back to Caldwell. All sorts of cars were put into place, including the caboose, and people walked from car to car while the train moved, not realizing how dangerous that could be. But everyone survived and we gathered at the end of the day for an evening dance.

My dear Pard is not a terpsichorean. He hates dancing. He handed me off to the sheriff to spin me while his spurs clanked on the wood floor of the depot. We made the square, my "partner" loaded with his own pistols and handcuffs and a club, none of which halted him in the least from swinging me around, making me laugh and feel light as a feather, even though I knew I wasn't, and sashaying me out the door into the cool night air at the last call.

"You're quite a dancer, Mrs. S." The sheriff bowed. Someone handed him his hat he'd removed for the dance. His forehead had a sheen of sweat.

"As are you, Sheriff Wells."

"Thanks for returning her in good condition,"

Robert said, leaving a group of men, the Pullman behind them black as night. Our presence broke up the conversation but not the cigar smoke.

"Easiest arrest I ever made."

"Me too," Robert said and took my arm. "Let's head home." We walked arm in arm. "You're quite the arresting woman, Mrs. Strahorn." He leaned to kiss my head and pulled me to him.

I felt so fortunate to have this man beside me whom I loved and who was also my best friend. One can put up with a lot of wind and dust when there's warm strength to lean into.

It did concern me now and then that I was more attuned to the men than to women. More aware of what the men talked about, offering my thoughts that were sometimes listened to, and even wishing I'd been out there with Pard rather than high-footing it with the terpsichorean sheriff.

❧❦

Caldwell grew over the next years. My sister Hattie had married and we'd gone to the wedding and were back from Chicago after a longer than usual absence. Something about the service had made me wistful, longing for that new beginning that Hattie and her William looked forward to. She'd return to her medical practice. She had a direction.

Delia stopped by to assess my suffering garden.

Travel does bad things to greenery, but so did the high heat of Caldwell. We spoke of this and that and then in a moment of unguardedness I made a comment about not being all that good at making women friends.

"We don't want to bother you. You're busy and when you're home we expect you want to rest, look over your trees. I think the Oakley boys are keeping them watered good. The heat wilts the lettuce."

"I guess once we talk about the state of our home sites there isn't much to share, is there?"

"Oh, there would be. But friends must be . . . available when things get tough, and that's hard to do when one is miles away. Letters work then, 'course, but by the time there's a response, the crisis has passed."

"There's the phone now."

"Too expensive for our taste, I'm afraid. Only for emergencies. We appreciate your husband letting us use that one in the office." We lived too far out for phone service. "I'm glad you're back. Got that dog yet?" I shook my head. "They make great pals if you can keep them from chasing the rabbits. Might have to build a fence that goes all the way around your house and not just halfway to hold your climbing roses. It looks really pretty, Dell, but what good is a fence that won't hold a dog in?"

The half fence had been my creative effort.

Clearly, I needed more. "Sometimes I feel like a visitor in my own town."

Delia lowered her eyes. "You're not really a part of what goes on here. I don't mean to be hurtful in any way, but you have another life. It's not in Caldwell."

I didn't have the words then nor the self-reflection needed to respond to Delia. I felt defensive, wanted to say, "I helped start this town." But like any birthing, as the child grows, it takes on its own goal and direction. Its parents are forced to watch it teethe and tumble as a toddler, then pick up speed and height and soon it has a life separate from its parents and they must find a full life without a child's needs directing them.

"I'd like to have a life in Caldwell," I said. I twisted my diamond wedding ring on my finger.

"If it's what you want, you'll find a way. A woman does."

She patted my shoulder and headed back down the road a mile or more to that growing metropolis. Even our home site spoke of our isolation: Robert had staked a site quite a distance from the town center, he said to avoid the noise. But it also meant people had to make a trek to stop by. We were more of a destination than a place to take a pause on a hot day. The town folks even named where we were the Sunnyside district.

Reading books and Scripture, writing letters home, even my articles from my happy lane, didn't really appease what I know now was spiritual drift, pure and simple. My diary focused on the happy lane rather than mining the depths of those isolating, purposeless emotions.

By early 1886, the work Robert did with the Land company had made progress on the irrigation system. He and his investors had formed the Caldwell Canal, and the diggers with their mules and land scrapers and hand shovels watched as water from the river made its way into the lower canal. A high line would come later to serve even more land. The nourishment of that water transformed the desert that season and for years to come. But that year, after we'd gone off to Denver for a time and returned seeing green instead of white dust, tweaked something in me.

Where was my nourishment? I needed exhilaration but a cowcatcher ride didn't rise to the expectation.

"I'm going to stay here more often," I told Robert that next day.

He sat at his desk and didn't turn around. "Whatever you think, Dell."

"I want to do more of what other women do here."

"What do they do that you don't?" He shook his head. "Labor costs for the canal are astronomical."

"Preserve fruit. Make pickles. Boil jellies. Bottle conserves, label them and serve them for supper to young men who would like a home-cooked meal rather than visit the saloons. And I want that dog."

"Well, get one. Pick one that's not too pretty, to turn the tramps away that'll come by once they hear about your fine viands being served on the front porch."

"Without a cook, I'm not sure how fine a table I'll prepare, but you've survived."

"You're a fine cook, Dell. Have you seen my good pen?" He patted his vest.

"In your jacket, the one that needed the sleeve repaired. I mended it."

"Good girl."

He returned to his papers, prompting me to say, "And I think I've found a passion of my own. I want to get a group of women together and start a Presbyterian church."

"Doesn't the church bureaucracy have to initiate a church? Send a missionary out first or something?"

I wanted him to honor my desire. "In the West, we do things differently. To begin, I'd like the Idaho and Oregon Land Improvement Company to make the first donation to the First

Presbyterian Church of Caldwell." Saying those words felt empowering. I could be a promoter in the interchange of thoughts and experiences. That was what Robert did and so could I. My spiritual drift began to find direction.

From *Fifteen Thousand Miles by Stage*, vol. 2, by Carrie Adell Strahorn (page 135)

It is through speech and association that souls are revealed to one another, and banding women together in active Christian service was not only for the good they might do for the town, but for an individual help in the interchange of thoughts and experiences.

25

Hallelujah

Now that I've said out loud my intention, I can no longer lay blame to Pard or anyone else for my homesickness nor loneliness nor spiritual drift. I have made a commitment and must now make frequent deposits toward that goal.

May 6, 1886

We, that is me, wanted to see a church with a real pastor in Caldwell and not wait for years to bring a missionary out first. It would mark the true distinction of a city that could build and sustain a remain-in-town pastor rather than rely on the sporadic visits of an itinerant reverend or a missionary sent to win souls as Delia's father-in-law was.

It was my studied view that our souls had been won and what we needed now was a way to sustain our passion for the faith and to encourage our service. It was always my belief that our lives are the stories others read first. And I wanted my life story to say something besides "She was famous for traveling around the West with her husband." Besides, making things happen was something I was certain I could do, though I hadn't yet done anything more admirable than cook for my husband and write a few words for the entertainment of others.

Our purpose was, yes, to raise a church. But when we wrote up the formal organization—Presbyterians are known for their formality, sometimes to a fault—we added that, in addition to the formation of a church, the Presbyterian Society also existed in Caldwell to "encourage social intercourse, to preserve harmony, and create a more homelike feeling among the ladies." To me, this is the message our lives ought to carry.

I had begun to think that perhaps my listening, serving food and offering shelter to young men to keep them from saloons, and welcoming men and women to a new community were acts of service, acts I had somewhat diminished because they weren't healing the sick as my sister Hattie did and they weren't raising a family up as my sister Mary was.

That first gathering was memorable. Bessie Donaldson left the meeting not long after it started because she said it wasn't possible for our little Caldwell to make a go of raising such funds to build and operate a church, and she didn't want to have the weight of a failing religious institution on her back. "I'm too old to carry a church around."

After Bessie left, and tea and little cakes and croissants with cheese melted inside had been served, the first order of business was to elect officers. I was chosen as president though I did not seek it. Mrs. George Little—we always used our formal names—vice president; Mrs. Gibson, a widow, secretary; and Mrs. Meacham, treasurer, also a widow, whose husband had died after he and his brother founded the town of Encampment on the stage line in Eastern Oregon. She'd come to Caldwell because she couldn't stand the winters anymore in that mountainous little village. She might have been lonely too. Mrs. Brown—Hester—also joined our group. Her husband operated the livery, always a good person to have on board.

The second order of business was apparently deciding where to meet next and when.

"After today, I think we should meet closer to town," Mrs. Meacham said. "Your home is lovely, Mrs. Strahorn, out here in Sunnyside, but it's so far out. My hips are of an age." She walked with a crooked stick for a cane.

"Mine too," Mrs. Gibson said. "Though taking the wagon isn't so bad. And Mrs. Strahorn does have the softest divan and she gets Mrs. Gwinn to make those astonishing croissants. Or did you make them yourself, Mrs. Strahorn?"

"I like to support the local establishments."

"Where does she get the butter?" Mrs. Little

asked. Her husband was the probate judge and superintendent of Public Instruction.

"They've brought in a few neat cows," Mrs. Gibson said. She had a missing front tooth so she rarely smiled, but something about the cows made her, just before she covered her mouth with her hand.

"It's about time," Mrs. Meacham said. "Mrs. Strahorn, didn't you lose a pedigreed shorthorn the other night?"

"Yes. The evening my husband joined the Odd Fellows Lodge. He came home a little late."

"Those men and their odd fellows. I suspect they do a little more than public service," Mrs. Brown said.

"I've a funny story to tell about that . . . ," I began, but thought better of it with Mrs. Brown's raised eyebrow. "Some other time." I could see how easily we could get off track. "Let's meet here next week again, and meanwhile I'll see if we can use our old quarters above the Land office. Can you make the stairs, Mrs. Meacham?"

"I can. I have a few to climb to my loft at night."

A mouse ran behind the divan and out toward the kitchen. No one saw it but me. They were a constant nuisance. I needed a cat. And a dog.

"That's settled if we can agree on a date."

"Let's set Tuesday afternoons as our regular day at 2:00 p.m." Mrs. Brown was a problem-solver. That was one reason I'd invited her.

"That worked this week, but usually I have my knitting group at that time." Mrs. Little clicked knitting needles on her lap. She'd not taken a croissant. "Mavis Kline had to visit her sister in Hailey," she continued. "She wouldn't be there and we meet at her house. Thus, knitting was cancelled."

"There'll be many conflicts, I suspect. And we travel some."

"Some?" Mrs. Gibson giggled at that.

My face grew warm. "Yes, some. But I am committed to remaining closer to home to launch this enterprise. I've already gotten a commitment from the Land company for twenty-five dollars."

"A fine start," Mrs. Brown announced. "Money is hard to come by here." She had started a millinery. "No overnight millionaires like at Bonanza City or Yellowjacket. Miners are generous with their fast successes."

"Giving is a gift," I said. "We're offering people a chance to be generous and to feel good about it. But first, is there an alternate date we can agree on?"

Mrs. Meacham piped up. "I think church business ought to come before knitting, Mrs. Little. And as vice president you really ought to be willing to forgo that commitment for this one."

"We'll all have conflicts," Mrs. Gibson said. "Let's decide now to forgive each other when we have to miss and instead send a new person along, so that we expand our group."

"An excellent idea. We'll have proxies." I did think it a good idea.

"Proxy?" Mrs. Gibson said. "But will they be . . . of a good . . . nature? A good reputation."

"Would we know anyone who wasn't?" Mrs. Little said.

"Let's patch that quilt when winter comes." I wanted this group to include all sorts of women, not just the pillars of the community. We'd already lost one of those who thought the effort would be too demanding. Younger women would be important to engage. "An alternate day, ladies?"

"Sunday afternoon."

"That's the only time I have to be with my husband." Mrs. Little again. He and Henry Blatchley had a druggist business. Very busy men.

"Be with him on Tuesday afternoons after our meeting." Mrs. Meacham sounded testy and I knew we had to move on to important things. We were bogged down in insignificant issues of when to meet. We'd never get a church funded. Maybe Mrs. Donaldson was right!

"Please. What about Monday afternoon? I know we usually do our wash then, but perhaps later in the day, while the sheets and pillowcases are drying in the wind we could meet here. Next Monday?"

"That would work if I can bring my laundered items to hang on your lines, Mrs. Strahorn."

"Certainly. All of you are welcome to do that." I'd get Robert to sink another two posts and string more lines. "And Mrs. Gibson, would you be willing to pick up Mrs. Meacham and we'll have our meetings here instead?"

"Why, of course," she said. Mrs. Meacham looked quite pleased.

"That way we can also avoid the stairs at the Land office. We're agreed, then?" Heads nodded. "Good. You have that in your notes, Mrs. Gibson?"

"How do you spell proxy? With an *i* or a *y*?"

"Put the day and time down for now. The first order of the day is that we publicize our beginning efforts. Who would like to write up a little article for Editor Cuddy?"

Mrs. Brown spoke up. "You do that well, Mrs. Strahorn."

"You write it up and I'll deliver it. I'll be sure to limp with my trusty cane and appeal to his sympathy to publish it." Mrs. Meacham shook her cane for us.

"Excellent. And while you're there, perhaps you might ask how the paper plans to support our endeavors."

"Won't they have to be neutral as a member of the press?" Mrs. Gibson licked her fingers of the sugar-dusted cake, then shook sugar from her paper where she was taking notes, I hoped. "There are other churches in town. The Baptists. And Mr. Gwinn's a Methodist." She whispered that last.

"Caldwell needs a Presbyterian church," Mrs. Meacham reminded her. "When we meet at the school, any number of men rise to read the Scripture and pontificate with a dozen different theological views coming our way. None of them are pastors. Well, the itinerant ones we sometimes get from the Episcopal Diocese and the Methodists, they're fine enough. But not steeped in issues of discerning God's direction until we know 'the way to be clear,' as Presbyterians must."

"I wish we could sit with our husbands," Mrs. Brown said.

"Yes. This is the West, for goodness' sake." Mrs. Little's voice carried passion. "Women work side by side with their husbands or brothers in the fields and stores and then have to sit separately in the schoolhouse church?"

"When you say, 'for goodness' sake,' you're taking the Lord's name in vain." Mrs. Meacham chastised Mrs. Little. " 'Goodness' is a perversion of the word *God*. We aren't going to go down that road, are we, ladies?"

"Oh, for heaven's sake!" Mrs. Little said.

"That also borders on cursing."

"Well, not—"

"Ladies, ladies. Please," I said. "Let's first talk about a goal that we are reaching toward. Yes, to form a Presbyterian church, but at what amount of money raised would we feel secure in seeking a pastor? Ideas? We aren't building a structure, we are building a congregation that will need an ordained pastor."

"If we can get donations as your husband gave of $25, we'll only need twenty more subscribers for $500. I think that would be enough." Mrs. Little seemed relieved for the change of subject from her theologically impaired language choices.

"Five hundred is a fine goal." I almost said, "Goodness, what a good idea," but let that fade away. "Are we agreed on that?" Heads nodded again.

"Is that enough to build a church and call a pastor?" Mrs. Brown asked.

I looked to the faces before me. *Would it be?* I could ask Robert. He was better with numbers than I was. "We can always increase it as we move along."

"Should we have a date by which, if we haven't reached the goal, we would end the plan and return the money?" Mrs. Little again. "And would it be enough to get a choir director too? One can hardly offer a pastor just a building. He'll want a choir director."

"Maybe he can do that himself, get someone who has musical abilities. What should I put as our end goal then, Mrs. Strahorn? Five hundred dollars?"

"Let's take a vote. All in favor of five hundred dollars, please raise your hand."

All went up except Mrs. Meacham's, our

treasurer. "I don't know how I'll keep track of small donations enough to hold them so if we have to give them back we can. It'll be too much for me. I'm an old woman."

We're losing our treasurer at the first meeting too?

"I'll help you, Elizabeth." Mrs. Brown not only offered to help but put us on a first-name basis.

"Thank you, Hester," I said. "Right now, we're voting on a goal. We can talk next about what happens if we don't reach our goal, how we'd keep track of the funds, where we might divert them if we disband our efforts toward the church and pastor." I was already tired myself. I sighed. "What I do know, ladies, is that making a commitment to something changes everything. A writer I know of, Von Goethe, a German, wrote that 'Knowing is not enough. We must apply. Willing is not enough, we must do.' We know what we're about. Now, we must begin to do. Let each of us approach one other person to join our cause and bring them here next Monday when we'll hang our wash and then put our heads together for how to build a church. Agreed?" Even Mrs. Meacham agreed. "All in favor say aye?" All said the word. "Opposed, nay? The ayes have it. Hallelujah!"

"There's no need to ask for the nays if everyone here has said aye," Mrs. Little said.

"A very good point. I'll remember that in the

future and hopefully next week, there'll be eight of us to say aye."

Mrs. Little spoke up again. "Hallelujah in Hebrew means 'Praise ye Yahweh' or 'Praise ye the Lord.' It should be reserved for more sacred occasions."

"Meeting adjourned until next Monday," I said. "Bring your laundry. And bring a friend."

"There is something sacred in everyday things," Hester added.

Goodness, it had been a long afternoon. Hallelujah, it was over.

From *Fifteen Thousand Miles by Stage*, vol. 2, by Carrie Adell Strahorn (page 136)

Homesickness is one of the most formidable of diseases to contend against, and only the hope of bettering one's worldly condition could make such a life even tolerable. . . . It may have been that pathetic need of sympathy that drew the women of Caldwell together so easily into the Presbyterian organization, for it was soon composed of representatives of widely diversified beliefs, but with the will to work that became the envy of many an established church in other towns.

26

Offerings

Sometimes, while exploring for gold, one finds diamonds instead. I discovered this while devoting my time and energy to the church building and finding—in addition—friends, a deeper understanding of my own desires, and the true pleasure of hospitality. Diamonds don't always sparkle when they're found, I've heard. They are like clear agate, transparent, with the promise of their beauty, a beauty often overlooked by the uninitiated.

July 19, 1886

My parents decided to visit us at last. I could share my finished home that had become a happy place on our Monday gatherings and afterward. Happy that my parents made the effort, I also knew it couldn't have happened at a more intensive time. The Presbyterian group— we shortened our name to First Pres in our meetings—planned a major fund-raising fair with kissing booths; dunking sites; bobbing for apples with a dollar amount carved into the side, telling what coins they'd have to donate if they bit into that fruit. Hester worried they'd bite at the amount and deliberately try to eat the evidence, but they'd get charged twenty-five cents as a minimum if we couldn't see the price.

There'd be three-legged sack races with a small entry fee and donated prizes for the winners. For weeks, we'd been collecting bayberry candles, penny whistles, a new hammer, and a black-and-white spotted roasting pan as donations from local merchants, and this was to be our big fund-raiser for the summer. Robert had secured an ice source and we needed to go into the mountains to get it packed in straw to keep it from melting. Timing was everything with that addition, but we'd have ice cream, a real treat, and could charge ten cents a scoop.

Into this, my parents traveled west and we were to meet them in Ogden and ride back on the train with them from there. I'd left the planning in the care of the committee, Hester at the helm.

❧❧❧

"How was your trip? Have you eaten?" We offered both traveling questions to my parents when we met them at Ogden. I hugged my mother, bending my head to maneuver around the wide-brimmed hat she wore, feathers bobbing between the flowers made of dyed straw. I wore a tall, red felt hat with little trim, a wide brim in the front and cut out in the back to make room for the bun twisted at my neck.

"Used the last of the cheese and meats out of your mother's hamper just before Ogden. Worked fine. The Pullman car is luxury, isn't it, Mother?"

"It was fine. What happened to your face, Carrie?"

"I got careless." I touched my cheek. My makeup hadn't hidden my bruise. "I was shooting jackrabbits from the porch with my pistol on my knee and it backfired, breaking my glasses and cutting my cheeks. So careless of me."

"I told her she must have used her game eye because she got the rabbit. Had it for supper that night." Robert sounded proud.

Robert, my father, and I laughed at that. My mother tsked.

"Facial cuts always bleed profusely." My doctor-father eyed my face, then kissed each cheek. "Healing well."

"Yes, it is, Daddy. I had two black eyes, which caused quite a stir at the First Pres gathering."

"You wouldn't believe the rumors that ran through town after that," Robert said.

"Oh, my heavens." My mother patted my arm. "Poor Carrie."

"Rumors about my poor shooting, Mama, not that Robert was the cause of my facial distress." I pointed toward the mountains. "Look at that view." I'd developed diversion to a fine art. The

Wasatch peaks rose up like cathedrals to the sky.

Of course, Pard had to show them the Mormon Square when we reached Salt Lake, which was a good idea with its grand Gothic-like temple, fruit orchards, and streets tidy as a new wife's kitchen the day her in-laws come for dinner. Caldwell wasn't quite so grand. "Our little babies like Hailey and Caldwell are still at the primary age," Robert told my father, "but this is what it could be one day."

"You've a big lake near Caldwell, do you?" my father asked.

"No. But rivers and streams, and they are even now bringing water to the wasteland. You'll see."

Caldwell lacked the grandeur of those snow-capped peaks and the diligence of an all-powerful authority making decisions as the Mormons had. I'd become sensitive to how hard it was to get a committee to agree on anything. Our own church committee had grown, but Mrs. Meacham had declined to be our treasurer after the first fund-raiser, so we'd had to find another. Carrie Gwinn, Delia's sister-in-law, arrived to save our day, and along with the others, Mrs. Mattie Meacham continued to bring her ideas and her laundry on Mondays. At least we'd managed to get to first names in our meetings, and my hope that a church would allow for social interaction and a homelike gathering for women was proving true. I knew my mother would pitch in but worried a little over how she'd find Caldwell.

When we finally arrived home with my parents, we had a mess to contend with. Badgers had dug through the canal as they sometimes did and flooded the area around our house, soaking the five hundred trees Pard had planted. Most of the water had receded, leaving shiny wet mud to welcome us.

"I thought you said you had no lake," my father jested.

"Goodness me," my mother said. "Carrie, how will we—"

"The head gate's been closed until the badgers' work is patched, I'm sure," I told her. "A little adventure here in the West." I was in my happy lane.

Pard added, "They'll check for other holes along the canal. Meanwhile, we'll spend the night at the hotel and after breakfast walk the boardwalk to our sunny home. Just one of the vagaries of desert living."

It was the great light of the morning desert that won my mother over, I think. The sun rolled up out of the horizon like a lazy boy slowly getting out of bed, then shone with brilliance that warmed the land as far as the eye could see. I'd walked onto the porch outside our room that faced the desert flat and noticed my mother had stepped outside her room too.

"It's quite dramatic, isn't it?" We faced east.

My mother nodded agreement. "I didn't expect the light to be so . . . expansive, so . . . brilliant and yet not blazing bright. It's quite extra ordinary."

"I've planted sunflowers at the house. I love the way their heads turn toward the sunlight and open their faces to the morning." I wanted her to know that I was happy. "I have found peace here, Mama."

"Dell! Can you come here, please?" Robert called from behind me.

"Though not a steady peace." I smiled. "Enjoy for as long as you like. We'll see you in the dining room."

It was a rare, uncontested moment with my mother, and I wish now I had let Robert wait. All he needed me for was to find his tie clip. I gave up a miraculous moment for that.

We took breakfast at the hotel with Delia's croissants, a regular at that cook's table too.

"These are exceptional. So flaky and light." My mother rarely complimented anyone else's baking. "I don't think I've eaten better, even in France."

"Delia Gwinn makes them. She used to bake them at the freight car we used for a boarding-house when we first arrived."

We stepped out onto the boardwalk while Robert got the wagon from the livery. The sun was up by then. "I can show you Robert's office. We lived above it before we built the house."

"I'm sure we'll get the tour, but meanwhile,

278

I'm anxious to see your home as more than an island unto itself."

" 'Every man is a piece of the continent, a part of the main.' " I straightened her quote of John Donne's poem. " 'If a clod be washed away by the sea—' "

"We can hope a few clods got washed away and left your home behind," my mother said.

"It'll be fine. Robert's likely already gotten men there to help clean up. The water soaks in and feeds the lawn and nourishes some of the thousand trees we had planted between our home and Caldwell proper. You'll see as we ride on home."

She did appear to be impressed and the walkway, while still wet, had been swept of its mud. I tried to see it as my mother might, for the first time. It wasn't the grand home like the one I'd grown up in nor like any of the Chicago homes that graced the lakeside. But it was well-built, with a sweeping porch around the front and sides, and on that morning with the sun not yet blazing hot, the crisp air, and cry of a hawk catching a current, I thought it a homey place. That's what my mother called it, "homey," and in all honesty the three months they spent with us were the homiest of times.

❧❀❧

They were both girls, chubby, hair the color of good earth, one with blue eyes, the other with brown. Maybe three months old. Each wore simple homespun dresses carefully stitched, cleaned, and ironed. Kate and Kambree, their mother called them.

"Kate's got blue eyes; Kambree's brown."

"Aren't they precious," I said.

We were at the fair and the mother handed the twins to me as I brought change to Carrie Gwinn as the cashier for all the fair events. The Presbyterian committee had a booth to raise funds and inform, and to that booth had come Mrs. Bunting and her twins. "But you can change the names if you'd like." Their mother was thin as a railroad tie and one could see all the nutrition she got she gave to those twins.

"Pardon me?"

"You could change their names. They don't know them yet. They was pretty sounding to me. Kate's a family name. Kambree's what a sister called her when she tried to say 'candy.' "

"Those are lovely names," I said.

I held Kambree as her mother pushed Kate into my other arm. I wasn't getting the mother's intent. I held sweet babies at a fair, that was all. Several dozen people milled about on that Saturday church fund-raiser: an agent auctioned off a donated milk cow, a cake-walk with music played on behind me. My parents had wandered off to the booth where for a nickel one could toss a ring over a bottle and win a penny prize, and Robert was at another booth hawking tickets to win a Pullman ride for eight to Omaha. He'd arranged it with his friends at Union Pacific and our own Land Development Company. All that rolled on around us as I held those bouncing babes.

"They're beautiful, Missus—"

"Bunting. Rose Bunting. Wife of Harold Bunting and mother of eleven other Buntings. The twins are numbers twelve and thirteen."

"Congratulations are in order."

"Not really. The sad truth of it, Mrs. Strahorn, is that I'm peel—as we Irish say—broken, and with child yet again. I . . ." Tears formed in her eyes. "I can't care for them as a mother must and I know ye and your fine husband have no *babbies*. Me and Mr. Bunting talked about it and we felt ye'd be best to care for 'em. We'd make it legal and all. I wouldn't try to come back later and rob ye of 'em." She wiggled her fingers before them and both either burped or smiled, I couldn't tell.

"Oh my goodness. No . . . I . . . we . . . couldn't. I mean, you're most kind to think of us but we aren't prepared—"

"No one's ever ready. Take some time. We live out a way, have a homestead claim we're working. I've five other girls and six sons, my first set of twins, a boy and girl that we didn't have to look at their eye color to keep track of." She smiled, a sad, tired, exhausted smile.

"Dell?" Carrie had joined us. "Do you have the change for me?"

"Oh, yes. It's in my reticule. Here." I handed Kate back to her mother, put Kambree into Carrie's arms, and slipped the reticule from my wrist. "Here you go." The exchange made, I took Kambree back. She was the most beautiful weight. Those brown eyes big as biscuits stared at me, sober, thoughtful. *Pleading?*

"She looks a bit like you," Mrs. Bunting said. "We're hard workers if ye wonder. Come from good Irish stock. Our parents fled the famine and came here in the '40s. To Wisconsin, first. Then we read your husband's books and went to Montana and now, here we are. It was tough until the water came, but we've a good wheat crop this year."

"I'm glad for you."

"But it's too many mouths. And with a new *babby* growing within me, I don't think I'll have enough for three so close together. You . . . you'd be saving lives to take them as your own."

She pushed Kate back to me. The larger of the two, her hair was slightly less dark and might turn to blonde as she grew older. Once again I had the weight of both babies in my arms. It felt good, very good. And didn't people often ask an aunt or uncle to raise a child? Wasn't that a code of the West to give orphans a chance for family? I knew that orphanages often served children with a parent still living but who couldn't afford to tend to them and earn money enough to survive themselves, let alone keep a child alive. What she asked was of great sacrifice to save her children. Perhaps other of her children as well. If one got sick . . .

As though she read my mind, she said, "The others are healthy too. My body gave them good starts, all. There's no sickness runs through our line. All survived, so ye can see they come from sturdy stock." Sturdy was not the word I would have put to her, frail and pale as she was. I wondered where her husband was and what he looked like. She had good bone structure in her face, emphasized by how thin it was. They'd be attractive young girls. What fun it would be to help them grow up.

Stop it!

I handed both babies back. "I have some things to take care of, Mrs. Bunting. It's been a pleasure to meet you and you too, Kambree and Kate. Which one is Kambree again?"

She tapped a brown ribbon on Kambree's chubby wrist. "You wouldn't want to separate them."

"No, I . . . must say goodbye now."

She jostled her babies. "I'll come by your house later."

"No. Please. It's not possible." I stepped back. The grass was still squishy from where the church lot we'd chosen (that didn't have a building on it yet) had also been the victim of a badger brigade.

"Talk to your mister. I'll come by with the girls so Mr. Strahorn can meet them. I know where ye live. Well, don't everyone know that." She attempted another smile. "Here. Take Kate. For the afternoon."

"No—I've got to go now. Goodbye, Mrs. Bunting. It was lovely meeting you."

I turned my back on them. My heart beat like a metronome. Such beautiful children. Such a horrific choice this mother and father had come to, to give away your children to keep them alive. This pioneering, such courage, to do the right thing, to do the best thing. Had they stayed in Wisconsin, would that fertile land have served them better? And Montana. I loved Montana but it could be a harsh land too. Here, with the canal, water promised greater ease, but not when one had thirteen children and another on the way. My sister Hattie said there were ways women used to keep from becoming pregnant. I wondered if this woman knew of them—or was of a faith that prohibited such intervention in the natural order of progeny.

The irony wasn't lost on me. I longed to give birth and had nothing to show for it, while Rose Bunting had thirteen and no end in sight.

≫≪

"The strangest thing happened at the fair today," I told my dear husband and parents as we sat at the supper table. I'd hired a cook some months before, and she came in the mornings, prepared lunch and supper meals so we could spend our days together visiting sites, taking the train to Hailey, fishing at that town's nearby lakes, lounging in the hot springs. Robert kept our shorthorn herd at Hailey. We walked the fields to check on them. We owned the Alturas Hotel there, and sometimes there were management issues he had to tend to in Hailey.

"That's what fairs are for, aren't they? Strange happenings?" Robert chewed on a piece of sage grouse deep fried with a milk and flour batter. It was as tasty as chicken ever was.

"You have that strange man who comes by nearly every morning, cursing away, looking disheveled and forlorn. Something really should be done about him." My mother spoke behind a napkin.

"He's harmless, Mama, though I do worry about him in the winter."

"Mentally impaired, is he?" said my father.

"I've offered him food now and then, but he scowls and curses, shaking his fist at the sky. Not at me, so I haven't been worried."

"I suspect that pistol you carry frightens him off. A good dog could help, Daughter."

"I doubt he can tell I have a firearm unless he's heard me shoot rabbits, Papa. He lives in another world where everything is strange, I suspect."

"What was the strangeness you saw at the fair, Dell?"

"A woman, a Mrs. Bunting, offered us her . . . babies. Her twins, Kate and Kambree—though she said we could change their names if we wished."

Robert stopped chewing, interested now. "You mean she *offered,* as in giving them to you for more than just holding?"

"Yes. She said they'd do it legally, that they'd never ask for them back."

My mother frowned. "Odd names."

"Not Kate, but Kambree is unusual. It has a lovely ring to it, the two together especially. Musical almost. Kate and Kambree Bunting."

"Bunting. Yes, I know of them. Big family," Robert said. "Hard workers."

"She's apparently with child, again."

"Such intimacies to share with a stranger." My mother shook her head.

"I don't think she saw me as a stranger, Mama. She knew about us. Well, that's not hard, I suspect. But it was a plaintive cry that pressed through every word she spoke." My heart ached thinking about it. Beautiful girls. My fork made a hole in the mashed potatoes.

"Dell." Robert cleared his throat. "It isn't possible, you know. We travel so much."

"Yes, we do that. But—"

"They're hardy people, those Buntings. The girls will do as well there as anywhere."

"I wish you could have seen them though. Round little faces."

"How many siblings?" my father asked. I told him. "They're doing something right to bring so many into the world and keep them alive."

The knock on the door interrupted. "She said she would come by."

"Oh, no, Carrie, surely not." My mother gasped. Robert's eyes were large. My father cleared his throat.

"Best you see to the door, Dell."

"Why don't you, Robert. Pard?"

From *Fifteen Thousand Miles by Stage*, vol. 2 by Carrie Adell Strahorn (page 151)

But there was one man and wife at our church fair who, if they did not live in a shoe, had more children than they knew what to do with, the latest being a pair of healthy twins which they insisted that we must take.

27

Desire

Pard took a long, slow walk to the front door. Enough time for me to remember a day in my philosophy class at Ann Arbor, where we entered a discussion about desire, how humans have longings but that we are often better able to describe what our spouses desire, our kitchen staffs, our children or even parents, than we are our own hopes and dreams. Perhaps it's lack of practice, I remember one student suggesting. Another said it was because once a desire was named, it was more diffi-cult to blame someone else for its not being fulfilled. "Women are notorious for such as that," expounded the male student who, mercifully, was allowed to live only because what he said carried the tiniest bit of truth. If we never express a desire, we don't have to be overtly disappointed. How much easier it is to never say "I will write a memoir" than to say it and then lament that one never followed through. Or worse, to never name the thing we want and then suggest we couldn't have done it anyway because of this or that. Could I say to myself and to Robert, "I desire to keep those two children"? Because I did, so very much.

July 20, 1886

I hoped when Pard went to the door and he saw those babies that he'd make the decision that I so wanted.

But it wasn't Mrs. Bunting after all. It was a tramp asking for a scrap, which Robert gave him while my mother chastised afterward, "They'll only keep coming back. You need a dog to bark, one that doesn't like tramps, of course."

"They do no harm," Robert said. "They follow the railroad and are better to deal with than the scalawags who set up brothels and gambling houses for the workers. The Chinese are better railroad builders. They keep to themselves and send all their money back to their families."

"You still need a dog," my father said. "A big, brawny brute."

"I'd prefer a bulldog," I said.

"They don't like to exercise. A big dog will get you out, Carrie." My father's desire was that I be healthier and have a dog lead me to it?

There was no more mention of Kate and Kambree.

But that evening as we prepared for bed, Robert and I talked about the twins, about how he felt when he thought it was Mrs. Bunting at the door.

"What would you have done?" I brushed my

hair draped over my shoulder, sprinkled rose water on the tips, then began to braid.

"Invite them in, offer them cookies and coffee, I suppose." He removed his suspenders, his detached collar. He sat on the edge of the bed, didn't look at me as he talked, removing things from his pockets, slipping off his bleached white shirt.

"The babies look well fed. They're beautiful children, Robert. And their mother—she's desperate."

"Tell them we'll get them a cow or something." His voice was soft.

"You can't throw money at everything." I watched him in the mirror. "Do you have no interest at all in having a family?" I was thirty-two but had never really asked that question of my husband. Strange for a woman leaving "obey" out of her marriage vows.

"You've always talked about our towns being our children," he said. "Remember when I picked up a plastic baby nipple on that trip to Denver on the train and didn't recognize what it was? You told me to give it to Caldwell as 'that town is teething.' That made me laugh and I thought then that you'd settled on our life with an unusual array of offspring. You're an important part in my town building."

"'My town building.' Therein lies the truth. I'm a helper but not one of the creators."

"Taking on another woman's children isn't creative either."

His words stung more than I'd thought they could. "I think it is. I watch your brothers grow their families. I see the joy in my sister's face when she speaks of Christina, of George. I—I miss that. And I always thought we'd, you know, one day have children or take in an orphan. There's nothing wrong with raising another's child. It's a gift we can give. You're generous. I don't understand why we don't?"

"I'm selfish about that, I guess you could say. I don't want to share you with a child. Or two." He smiled at me.

A fury rose inside me. "Don't want to share me with a child? You share me with publishers. You share me with the railroad, with the land company, with the canal company, the shorthorns, with the towns we—"

He stood and pressed his hands to my shoulders. "Carrie."

But the tears came and he took the brush from my hands, pulled me to him. "You're creating a church. That'll be your offspring."

"But I see the way clear . . . to having children. It's my greatest desire."

"I don't see my way clear. That's the difference. I promised you a full life, Dell. And if we have a child of our own, fully of the two of us, I will love that child, you know that. But not of another's loins. I offer you something different."

"But what if I want this?"

"We can't have everything we want. Desires aren't a right. And when they conflict, well . . ." He shrugged. "One has to give in."

And pray that the one who gives in does not carry a stage-load full of animosity while dealing with her grief.

❧❦

In the morning, Mrs. Bunting with her *babbies* and two other children waited outside our gate in a wagon. My mother was up early and she invited them forward and they stood on the porch when Delia delivered her croissants. She gave a few to the Buntings' older children. They ate quietly to the *swish-swish-swish* of the windmill bringing up water for the tank that nurtured our trees.

"I brought the older ones, to witness," Mrs. Bunting said to me when I came out onto the porch. Robert stood behind me but he did not touch me nor offer physical support of any kind. "So's they'll know where they little sisters live."

"Mrs. Bunting," Robert said. "They are beautiful girls. But we cannot take them from you. Children thrive when they are with their parents who meet their needs, the parents from whom they were birthed. Mrs. Strahorn and I appreciate your offerings, your kindnesses in imagining that we could raise your daughters better than you and your husband can."

She pushed Kate at me and I took her, the warmth sinking into my arms, the smell of her sweet as roses. Those big blue eyes, staring. I imagined myself reading to her, watching her grow up to be a kind, loving child.

"Dell—"

I made mouth sounds that brought a hesitant smile on the child's face.

Robert paused. "They'd only have each other with us and always feel left out of your large and loving family. We couldn't do that to them. We couldn't."

She looked not at him but at me—their mother, searching for the best way for them. I handed the baby back, the scent of her powder lingered on my bodice ruffles.

Mrs. Bunting said nothing and left.

But she was back every single morning. For a week. Robert gave the same speech, adding once that he had dispatched a cow to their farm and arranged for canal fees for a year to be covered for their crops. I suppose he thought money was the best offering.

On the last morning, she and her witnesses came later, after Robert had left. I stepped out onto the porch, arms clasped around me as though I felt cold. "You can see that I would . . . but my husband. I'm so sorry. Please, stop coming. It—it hurts too much."

She sighed. "Aye. I know. We women surrender, don't we?"

I wondered at that moment if her morning visits had been a yielding to her husband and not a desire of her own at all. "Yes, we surrender. We try to find the heart in what they want and let go of what we want, hoping not to carry sadness too long nor deep."

"If ye went against him, would he forgive ye in time?"

I reached out to fondle Kambree's fingers, slender as new carrots. She would play the violin one day if allowed lessons. "I honestly don't know," I said. I lacked the courage to find out.

⫸⫷

The next morning, without seeing them, felt like dying to me. The hot morning air suffocated and even the birdsong didn't lift my spirits. I admired Mrs. Bunting for being willing to give up her flesh and blood because she thought it would better their lives and those of her remaining children. Her husband never joined her. His pride? Who knew?

I imagined in their later years, Kate and Kambree would hear the story of how their parents almost left them with a couple who had no children. The story would be more vivid with the witnesses' recall. Kate might remember that they were going to leave Kambree; and Kambree's story would be that it was Kate who was almost left behind. Neither would imagine *they* would be the child chosen to live with the pain of knowing she'd been given away.

"Your enthusiasm falters." It was after the concert fund-raiser and Hester Brown was sensitive to my mood. We hung our Monday-morning laundry. "I'm so sorry." She stopped her work and held me as I wiped my eyes.

Yes, I shared my sorrow with a friend. All those founding Presbyterian women.

"Oh, Adell." Mattie Meacham had taken to calling me that rather than plain Dell. I didn't correct her. "How very hard for you. I remember how I ached when my Harvey died and I knew I'd never marry again. Nor have a baby of my own."

The others patted my shoulder. I felt awkward receiving sympathy, having rarely exposed my sadness to these women or anyone outside my family. I was surprised at their compassion. I'm not sure why I should have been. Women have a way of knowing what another needs. Some of us struggle with receiving kindness.

"You could decide on your own. Sometimes Mr. Little puffs all up about a thing, and when I do it anyway, he comes along."

"The addition of two children . . ." Marvel shook her head. "My Mr. Gibson would leave me if I'd done that."

"I doubt Robert would go away," I said.

"But are you leaving him, in your spirit?" Carrie Gwinn took my hand in hers. I'd come to appreciate the young woman. "To deny so great a desire, I fear it will leave a hole in your heart."

"You'll have to be careful and not allow your grief to build a fence around yourself," Flora Little offered. "When your husband won't allow you the one thing you want more than anything else . . . a child . . . we can become unwitting punishers."

"And that's not like you, Dell. You're too generous, too forgiving for that," Mrs. Meacham said.

Was I generous? Forgiving? I looked around the room at these women. Courageous pioneers who lived with accommodation daily. Was I giving up the one thing I truly wanted in life? Was being a mother what I desired more than anything else? At the price of straining my marriage?

Apparently not. Because I did not take the risk of a lifetime and bring those babies home with me and tell Robert he must simply adjust. I could have done it. I have always wondered why I didn't.

From *Fifteen Thousand Miles by Stage*, vol. 2, by Carrie Adell Strahorn (page 151)

And surely parents never tried more persistently to dispose of their offspring, in a week of untiring effort.

28

The Way Be Clear

The church became the child I longed for, and the ups and downs of those final days of either having one or letting it go—as a mother must her child—proved the keeping of my sanity that following year. That and Argos and the stage and railroad pass that could take me anywhere I wanted to escape to.

September 12, 1887

I invited my sister Hattie to come out, and off we traveled with those railroad passes, for a day trip or a fortnight. Yet it always improved my spirits to return to the work I felt called to do in Caldwell—building up that church. I didn't want to think about what would happen when that task was accomplished—nor if we failed.

Besides, I missed Argos when Hattie and I traveled. Yes, I now had a dog. My father had sent the pedigreed wolfhound to me. Not a bulldog.

Argos arrived by train and must have been nurtured along the way by a tramp or two riding in the freight car, because he loved tramps! Maybe the smell of them was more interesting than the men in suits and uniforms that he growled at, taking him a time to warm up to Robert, which secretly tickled me before I sought forgiveness.

Argos loved me at first sight and I him. Dark, long, silky fur, firm shoulders, he stood tall for a year-old dog. I could touch his head when he leaned into my legs and I never feared a knock on the door after Argos came. And as with Homer's Argos in the *Odyssey*, he always recognized me no matter how long I'd been away.

"B-flat." I taught him that command to lie down.

"Shouldn't it be 'Down'? I think that's the preferred dog command." Pard added his point of view.

"I'm a musician," I reminded him. "B-flat works fine."

I was pleased my father took it upon himself to have the dog delivered, already house-trained and wanting to learn new commands. But I would have preferred my breed of choice. The men in my life simply refused to hear what it was I preferred. And I let them.

❧❧❧

The church work kept me sane that fall and winter. I threw myself into fund-raising after my parents and the Bunting twins were no longer daily greetings. I did listen for snippets of the twins' family stories. Mostly, hard work was what I heard about and that Mrs. Bunting's last delivery had gone well. I sent money and a little knitted jacket I asked Hester to make or find through her millinery contacts. Like Robert, I'd succumbed to cash and a little treasure to salve my guilt for not doing more.

Our small committee grew; we had grand support from merchants. A glitch or two threatened to take us off our rails. Another pastor had come to Caldwell, a Methodist who was Delia Gwinn's father-in-law, Carrie's father. He operated a house of worship in Caldwell with a different tradition than the Presbyterians. Montie, his son, and Carrie, his daughter, were active in our Presbyterian activities and he was not happy. One can understand why a father would want his own offspring to work in *his* church and not for another's. But Carrie loved to sing and had a voice like an angel at our concerts we put on, which proved our biggest fund-raiser. And Montie, that early merchant in Caldwell, offered prizes of different values, from washboards to baby carriages, for our numerous raffles and cake-walk events.

I was sensitive to a family spat and didn't want to add to that minister's distress, but I was driven at that time in my life, driven to get that church funded and built so we could at last seek a pastor. Work, I found, is a good healer.

Carrie represented how young people added not only hands to our efforts but a joyousness that cannot be replaced by any other elixir than basking in the vitality and passion of youth. I vowed that summer that I would always find a way to be around children and young men and women, even if none ever called me mother. If I could claim none as my own, I would claim all as mine, so in addition to the church, I began paying attention to public instruction. Those years of the second half of the 1880s, I also spent time watching young sporting teams that Pard sponsored. And I invited my nieces and nephews for extended visits and spoiled them rotten when they came.

But it was the work that kept me on the straight and narrow. Work raising funds. Work singing, putting on concerts. And I always knew I could disappear with those railroad passes. Having an escape, though perhaps a sign of not being fully committed, is also a balm to a broken heart.

⁂

Within two years, Carrie Gwinn had married Henry Blatchley, a Presbyterian to the core, though they'd married in the Methodist church in Boise. Her father officiated. Henry was a great contributor to the cause—and we finally had $500 in the bank and enough to let the contract for the building. "Let's build until the money runs out," Hester Brown suggested. And that's what the committee of women decided.

What a great day that was when we broke ground. We held a party and served food and children ate ice cream, their faces messed with glee.

With the building under construction, we felt that we could approach the Home Mission Society of New York for assistance now and to seek a pastor.

"I wonder if we shouldn't wait until the building is up before asking?" Marvel Gibson looked up from her copious notes and adjusted her glasses. It was at one of our Monday meetings. "What if they happen to have a young minister ready and then he arrives and sees what little we have to show? Just the bones of a structure. He might get right back on that train."

"We agreed we'd make the request when we started to build," Mattie Meacham said. I always admired that she knew her limits and let another take over as treasurer without regret. She knitted enough shawls for sale at the fair to more than make up for her disappearance as a board officer.

"But we have new information now," Marvel continued. "It's alright to change our route if we get new facts to better set our course."

Carrie opined that a young pastor might like to have a say in how his new church building was framed.

"All Presbyterian churches are built alike," I said. "They have acceptable plans everyone follows." Argos moaned beneath the table.

"Is that a commentary by your dog?" Hester said. We laughed.

"It could be. There are some polity issues with the Presbyterians that can be quite irksome about doing anything truly inventive. We'll have to put our creativity into the furnishings, considering the new pastor's wishes, of course. B-flat," I told Argos when he started to get up.

"Maybe he'll be single." Ida Waters teased. She was a new recruit. "And wanting the advice of a young congregant."

"Aren't you spoken for?" Carrie's blonde curls bobbed on her cheeks.

"Who is the lucky fellow?" Hester asked.

"Jacob Wilson, the blacksmith on Cedar Street."

"Ah. That handsome young man with the massive arms." Flora Little winked.

"Have you been ogling youth, Mrs. Little?" Carrie teased.

"Nothing wrong with eye-grazing. I love looking at lively young men. Carrie does too, I can tell."

"We have work to do ladies." I sang out my directive.

"Will there be a wedding soon, Ida?"

"After we get a pastor."

"Let's hurry that along then," I said. "Now, is it agreed we'll send the letter to the Home Mission

Society of New York? Do I have a motion to that effect?" I got it, a second, no more discussion, and the motion was passed. Marvel Gibson recorded the decision. I drafted the letter that we sent out the following week.

Hammering could be heard as the building rose from the desert land. Another contractor dug a well, not too deep, and the workmen had a hand pump then for refreshment and to ease their thirst. We women had water for our plantings that we put out as soon as we knew the layout of the structure. We'd show the new pastor how we cared for this church from the first moment he stepped from the train. We were imagining something into being. That's quite an achievement.

❄❄

Life went on while we awaited word, believing we had plenty of time to finish the building and keep raising funds. Faith institutions could move as slowly as sloths.

The structure was nearly completed (though not yet painted) and windows were ordered (but the openings boarded over). Nothing was finished inside when we received a letter stating that William Judson Boone, a recent graduate of Pittsburgh Theological Seminary, and his young bride would come out to see if they would accept the call.

Oh, what joy we shared with that announcement. Even Argos howled his delight as I danced around Pard, the letter in hand.

"When does he get here, Dell?" Pard asked.

"It says within the week. We won't be ready. Whoever knew the Presbyterians to act so swiftly?" I looked out our window toward the direction of our unfinished structure. I couldn't see it from our home, but I saw it in my mind's eye. Building only on weekends took time.

"Maybe we can gather up a few extra men," Robert said. "Try to get it painted." He hadn't lifted a hammer himself, but he had garnered financial support for our cause and was a vocal supporter.

"He'll be answering God's call, not ours. He'll have to see that 'the way be clear' for him to stay. Oh." I read further. "Oh no. They're going to spend the first night with Reverend Barton. In Boise. 'To consult.'"

"If Boise gets a hold of him, they'll warp that young man's mind about our Caldwell," Robert said.

Robert wasn't pained by the death threats of Boise enthusiasts, but he did see city-to-city competition for what it was and how devastating it could be. I still smarted from those numerous threats years before. Steam from the fuming Boise fathers could still be seen for miles after the railroad bypassed them, and now they'd have the new pastor in their clutches and might well pay us back in a most painful way.

Our new, fresh, young, innocent recruit would take his bride for a night or two in Boise. I could only pray that the Holy Spirit would speak to Reverend Barton and bid him break with the animosity between towns. The Reverend's constant harping that our efforts would amount to nothing, that no church should grow from the people upward but must come from the holy presbytery down, when the "way be clear" had been a constant complaint throughout our fund-raising efforts. I so wanted him to give Caldwell and especially our committee's efforts a fair hearing.

After two days of hearing nothing, I telegraphed Reverend Barton, asking when young Mr. Boone and his lovely wife would be arriving in Caldwell, as we planned a reception for them and did want to be amply prepared. He wrote back that he would telegraph in a few days, as the two needed time to acclimate to this western climate.

"He can acclimate in Caldwell." Argos heard my tone of voice and lifted his head from his paws. He had a way of cocking his handsome face, looking so engaged that I often thought he would start to talk. "I hope that young pastor is his own man. We'll rehearse more for our welcoming concert." I had to be careful with too much rehearsal, as my choir could get testy coming together as often as I wanted them to.

I nearly used my stage pass and rode to Boise to snatch the couple up, but Pard—the wise negotiator—said that would be a mistake and he was right, of course. "Let the man hear what he's going to hear up front, and if he takes the position after Barton's bantering us about"—I was pleased he said "us"—"then we'll know he was following God's lead and coming here as he should." I'd brought the telegram and Argos to Robert's office. "Let's get a cup of coffee at the café. Calm you down."

"Coffee won't calm me down. Only seeing that young pastor in this town will do that. But I'll take tea with you. And one of Delia's croissants." Food has always been my best medicine; music soothing the wild beast was second best. And I had need of both. We'd rehearsed for that concert and would have a large feast when they finally reached Caldwell.

It took two more days, but the telegram finally arrived saying young Boone and his bride would arrive on the afternoon train.

"It'll be alright, Dell, it will. You've done all you could. It's out of our hands now."

Oh, such bustling then! This was the work to keep me from homesickness and lonesomeness. It was the work that I didn't know I needed to do when riding those dusty stagecoach miles, crafting homes out of deserts, mining towns, flat plains, and mountains, saying no to generous mothers. Our building of little offsprings—Ontario, Mountain Home, Shoshone Falls, New Weizer—held nothing in my mind to that of building that church up. I'm still not sure why it meant so much. But I could say I was no longer suffering from spiritual drift. I knew exactly where I was headed.

❧❧

Young Boone and his wife slipped into Caldwell on the 5:45 a.m. stage and went immediately to the Pacific Hotel. We learned of this later, knowing that he had likely seen our unpainted, window-boarded-up church without the benefit of our enthusiastic story-telling of its existence.

We first saw our hoped-for pastor when the three arrived at our little cottage in Sunnyside later that morning.

Yes, behind them, coming into our home, was Reverend Barton.

Mr. Boone was not the quavering leaf of a man I had come to expect of a pastor. No, he was over six feet tall with a boxer's shoulders (it was said he boxed in college). Descended from the famous Daniel Boone, he had a rugged, western look, but when he lifted a violin to play it at our welcoming concert, his eyes softened like a baby's. It was Annie Boone, married just a week, who was delicate as rice grass that flourished in the desert through its drought-resistant nature.

We did everything right, or so we thought. We told them of the little manse we'd chosen for them to live in and furnished it fully, including an entry hall tree with a mirror, marble-topped bench, and flowered carvings, as fine as any had ever seen.

Barton scoffed.

Pard suggested driving them around Caldwell, which we did. They saw the dam, the bridge across the Boise that Pard's company had built. He spoke of how the irrigation company had allowed for farming, sheep, and cattle to bring more people west. He noted the advances of telephone lines, telegraph lines, the bustling business district. And of course, the railroad. Barton cleared his throat and mentioned the problems with the canals, including the "lack of oversight by the owner, Mr. Strahorn's Land Development Company." The man had an opinion on everything.

The committee met with him next. We served tea in the unfurnished building made festive nonetheless with colorful quilts tacked to the walls and a cross Hester's husband had carved. They all loved the young couple.

Back at our home, Barton continued his harangue. "You women began an enterprise before having your faith tested by the male elders of a Session and you started this so-called church without benefit of Presbytery direction. Therefore, I have opposed it. It cannot flourish under these circumstances, and it's why I have recommended to Pastor Boone that he turn aside this ridiculous example of a call."

"It didn't actually grow from a group of women," I said. We were seated in our living room and I'd served a small dessert before Robert would drive them back to the hotel. "It grew from a community's wish to have a Presbyterian church even without a missionary arriving first. It grew out of our faith."

"Reverend Barton suggests that your Ladies Aid Society was formed out of your dismissal by another Presbyterian church, for 'moral lapses,' he said." Reverend Boone posed that question.

"What? I never. We never." Argos stood up and barked, causing my guests to blink. "Why would you say such a thing? That's—that's slanderous to suggest that we are anything other than the dedicated Ladies Aid Society that we are." I lowered my voice.

"Yes," I said, "some of us listened to an itinerant Presbyterian pastor and objected to his insistence that women must sit on one side while men sat on the other. But that's hardly a 'moral lapse.' The Methodist minister has objected to our efforts, but I think mostly because his daughter and son have chosen us. We have listened to various voices in the Baptist church, but they never had a pastor, so I can't imagine that they think we've had a moral lapse." I stopped to take a drink of water. My heart pounded, preparing for yet another loss.

"Perhaps he was mistaken," Annie Boone said. She was a soothing force to my outrage. Argos settled back down and sighed.

"It is true that if I accept this pastorate—or anyone does—that it will be the only Presbyterian church in the history of the church to be formed by women."

"Is that such a terrible distinction?" I hadn't ever thought of it that way before.

"I note it for the record." Boone had a baritone voice, deep and rich, with kind brown eyes and a workman's hands.

I liked him very much. Everyone on the committee liked him and Annie; all the men felt he'd be a grand asset to Caldwell and surrounding areas where he'd also be asked to serve as an itinerant at times. I was certain he was our man so was incredibly disappointed by his next words.

"I—I must tell you, Mrs. Strahorn."

"Call me Dell, please."

"Dell. Mrs. Strahorn." He took a deep breath. "I do not feel I have the courage nor will that I see in you pioneering women to undertake this cause. And it will take such effort to build resources to finish and sustain the church building, let alone form a congregation." Annie smoothed her skirts over her slender knees. She didn't look at us. "And it is of our opinion that this is not the place for us now. We've asked the Lord to make the way clear for us and God has not done so."

Reverend Barton sighed deeply, a satisfactory grin upon his face.

You could have knocked me over with a fragile seed of rice grass. Our railroad pass to disappear to somewhere far away looked ever more inviting. But I could not run from this grave disappointment.

"Not made the way clear for you? But he's done so for us."

"I believe that. I truly do. And I find no fault with the efforts of women moving the faith forward, whether for commercial enterprise to help the community or to save men's and women's souls. It's *my* lack that makes this decision." He cleared his throat. "I'm not sure I'm up to the cause."

For a moment I had a flash of understanding why some hardworking men and women find fault with those educated men who, like Boone, held advanced degrees in theology and botany but who had never lifted a board to build a thing.

Robert reached for my hand, patted it. I was never more grateful that he understood the great pain this loss pressed against my heart. Even greater than those twins no longer weighing in my arms.

But an inner voice pushed me past my grief, and I found words I hadn't rehearsed. This Boone was the perfect man for our Caldwell. I felt it to my bones. He would expand our minds as well as our church. As we'd interviewed him, he found no dissonance between Darwin and Deuteronomy, didn't object to the advancement of women in the faith. Annie Boone already expressed interest in the Chautauqua courses to deepen our education. They had to be the right people.

"If that is your choice, Reverend Boone," I said at last, "then I will simply state that the work we have done thus far stops here. We will have that building up for sale in the morning. It will be a sheep-shearing shed or perhaps a saloon, though windows will discourage that latter enterprise. We'll return the money raised upon the sale and all the twenty-five-cent meals we've served, the quilts we've pieced, the reduced freight rates we negotiated with the railroad, all that will be for naught. It is ended with your no." Then I added, this time with tears in my eyes, though they were of frustration as much as sorrow, "If you have not the moral courage to take up what a few women without missionary help have put together thus far, then we will surrender to Reverend Barton, who has ever discouraged this enterprise." I nodded to the old pastor, conceding his win.

In truth, I suppose I wanted to give Boone a cause. Men need a cause *for* something and not just *against*. This was the strength of our argument that Reverend Barton could not compete with.

The spirit moved in that room. Quiet became a note before the symphony began. The *swish-swish* of the windmill filled the silence. A breeze drifted jasmine through the window. Then he glanced at his new wife, who nodded ever so slightly. Boone reached for my hand, putting both of his over mine, and said, "Mrs. Strahorn, I will remain and take up this work."

"You . . . you will?"

"But—but—" Barton sputtered.

"I will. We will. I can see the way be clear."

It turns out, Reverend Boone was his own man. But it also turns out we women had done a good thing in bringing a community along with us to have a church. We had not done it for our own aggrandizement but because we'd felt called to pursue a cause that truly mattered. How I'd needed that work and would always remember that moment as both the proudest and most humbling of my life.

There was still more work ahead, of course. To raise money to finish the building. Form an official congregation which, of course, did not have any women elders. But by February of 1888, Reverend Barton of Boise was named a founding elder—yes, the upsetting reverend was brought on to keep us from any moral lapse, I suppose, or

313

to keep one's enemies close. Robert Henderson, and George Little were ordained as elders as well with Robert and George Little as trustees for the First Presbyterian Church of Caldwell. To them we added charter members: Mrs. Steunneberg, Mrs. Mattie Meacham, George Little, Flora Little, Robert Henderson (who ran the ferry across the Snake), Hester and Peter Brown, and Annie J. Boone. The charter members and trustees met in the Baptist church on Chicago Street for the official votes and registrations. Reverend Boone preached his first sermon in the Baptists' building—to a full house. They'd finish our church building in due time. I did not put my name in for consideration of a charter member. I could have. But by then, I knew: we'd not be long in Caldwell.

From *Fifteen Thousand Miles by Stage*, vol. 2, by Carrie Adell Strahorn (page 162), from a letter to her mother

I do not think you will wonder any more why I do not get lonesome and homesick myself with three such very good reasons: first of all, my good husband; second, work without ceasing; and third, the annual pass in my pocket that will take me away whenever I want to go.

29

Lingering on the Dark Side

Robert has not shared all with me: complaints about maintenance of the canals, the lack of capital for the Hailey resort, cattle sales not going as well as before and his over-extension of those things that can make a man look prosperous while he sheds money like oaks their leaves in the fall.

February 1, 1888

Pard, while excellent at building things up, was not grand at keeping things going—maintenance, I called it; and I suppose I discovered that about myself as well. For example, the College of Idaho was only an idea when we left Caldwell, one that Reverend Boone took hold of after a few years while building up the Presbyterian congregation. But Boone soon became the president of that institution and carried it forth for all these many years since. We, however, were leaving our investments in Caldwell behind.

"It's business." Pard snapped the newspaper he read. "The railroads have overbuilt, banks overlent. We're overextended." He put the paper down. "That's why we're leaving. We're broke, Dell. That's the truth of it."

"Broke?" It was not long after Boone had preached his first sermon. We were at home, Argos lying at my feet. I knitted, the yarn itchy that day. "How can we be broke?"

"After we sell everything, we'll meet our debts, but we'll have to start over. It's business."

Pard's big ideas, his promotions, all his grandstanding, days and nights on the road, gaining investors, and now we were penniless? I lay awake that night feeling humiliated and embarrassed too that Pard didn't seem to have regrets. Could the financial fortunes of people not be related to choices made but only to the vagaries of markets?

It was beyond me. I didn't know what I'd say to our friends. Maybe they were in the same boat.

We came back for the dedication of that little church in 1889, a glorious day and one where I felt that for all the work I'd put into taking an idea and making it real, I understood I no longer belonged to it. It was a child of mine that I had to let go. I looked for the Buntings that day but didn't see a one of them and learned that they'd moved on to different climes too. Those twins . . . how I missed them.

True pioneering requires staying through the hard times, not just flourishing through the joy of new beginnings. It's thriving during the muddle in the middle that marks a strong character. And we had stepped away.

Pard sold the canal company to others more adept at maintaining the waterways and the roads and bridges that crossed them. He took a loss, as cities and counties had little tax money with which to buy up public workings when the national economy slowed. That was the word they used, *slowed*. Private buyers urged a harder bargain. Pard dissolved the partnership of the Oregon Land Development Company, which at the time I thought was because he was tired of the effort of town building but later learned it was because we needed the money. Doing anything solely for money has its dark side.

We headed to Hailey first, where at the behest of the railroad, it was suggested we develop the area's hot springs into a resort. I never did find out if Pard suggested the idea or if Jay Gould, head of the Union Pacific, thought it a grand idea. But Pard formed another partnership to do it.

We kept the shorthorn herd at Hailey and sold bulls and had breeding fees and lived the summer in our little Hailey house. At least I had a horse close by to ride. We left before the snows fell, spending happy months at my parents' home, never mentioning our financial affairs.

The next summer, we built up a grand Hot Springs Resort outside of Hailey that was a huge success. Robert's health improved from use of the hot springs too. I'd had a fair amount of fun as we bought all the furnishings in Chicago for the new hotel (with the railroad's money), and I had the joy of creating designs and using paint and wallpaper to form a festive retreat. But it wasn't long before Pard dissolved that company too, and I learned that our indebtedness had increased. Then the hotel burned down.

To make ends meet, Pard took on a huge writing task for money, from the railroad, creating six one-hundred-page pamphlets on Oregon, Washington, Idaho Territory, Montana, Wyoming, and Colorado. They were all due in ninety days. I told him it was a crazy contract, which was when he reminded me of how very desperate we were for money.

"But the sale from the canal company, the Caldwell house, from the cattle, from dissolving the Hailey partnership. I . . . I don't understand—"

"Putting it into pretty words won't change the fact, Dell." We were staying at a small hotel down the street from the Brown Palace in Denver, compliments of the railroad, while Pard worked on this writing project. "We invested our own money and it didn't always have the return I hoped for."

"I should sell my little real estate at Crested Butte."

He snorted. "A real estate company has moved onto your property like it's theirs. They're squatting and they don't want to buy it. Crested Butte isn't exactly booming."

"You've been in touch with them? You offered to sell it without talking to me about it?"

He looked like a lost sheep. Argos came over to him and put his head on Robert's thigh.

"Well. I won't pay the taxes anymore then. Let those squatters."

I was too tired and chagrined and could see Robert's dismay about the entire situation so chose not to get into an argument with him about my being blocked out of my own trans-actions. I was angry with myself that I hadn't engaged more in our financial affairs. I'd let him who was wiser do that, but I was beginning to see there were problems in that kind of arrangement.

"Then I guess the writing project is our saving grace," I said cheerily. That's what I'm known for, being cheery in times of trial. Looking back, I wonder if the railroad had taken pity on us for all Pard's years of service and that was why they gave him the contract for the six books.

Robert had all the materials to write the pamphlets, most of it in his head. I couldn't help much, just edit as he finished sections. While he wrote, I submitted a few stories to newspapers back east as "Emerald Green" (in honor of my maiden name) that were light and funny. My mother kept all my letters and I got a few back from her and used them to trigger memories I thought others might enjoy reading about. It was the only way I could see to contribute except to sell some of the jewelry—which I did, quietly in Denver without Robert having to know.

❧❦

Robert completed all six pamphlets, all six hundred pages within the timeline, but at great personal cost. My Pard was on the verge of collapse when he finished, the high Denver altitude not good for his TB-affected lungs. He shook, kept to his bed, had night sweats though no fever. I couldn't get him to drink even water. I called for the hotel doctor, then spoke with my father about Robert's condition after the hotel doctor said his heart was impaired and that he was fading away.

"Fading away, Daddy. That's what they said. He's dying." I sobbed into the phone.

"Shush, now, that won't help, Carrie. Even Argos is upset by your upset." He could hear Argos whining in the background. "Get him to the sea. New Orleans. Mississippi. Somewhere that his heart doesn't have to work so hard. Can he make the trip? We'll come out and help you."

"No. No. I'll get us there."

"Maybe one of your friends can assist?"

We had friends to call on, didn't we? Our Caldwell pals?

No, all our friends were business connected

and I didn't feel I could ask Jay Gould of the UP. I thought of Carrie Blatchley, of Hester Brown, my Presbyterian women, and wished we were still in Caldwell. I wondered if I ought to find a place for Argos to stay. Caring for dear Robert and managing Argos could be a strain while traveling; but the dog gave me moments of joy that I found nowhere else. And I didn't want to rely on my sisters. Again. "I'll be alright. We'll go south. Good idea. That'll help."

And it did, though by the time the next months were over and I'd nursed Pard back to good health in Mississippi, I was exhausted. "I need a respite, Robert. Could you see your way to looking after me for a week or two?" We were in yet another hotel on the delta. My fan barely cooled my face.

"Send for your sister. She can bring Christina." He straightened his red cravat. The color brought out his dark eyes. "You can have a girls' week or two before your niece gets married." He packed his bag while I curled in a ball on the bed.

"You couldn't fix me tea, plump my pillow?"

He sat on the side of the bed then, patted my shoulder. "I've got a job, Dell. I've lost a lot of time being ill. I'm going to Washington on railroad business."

"I thought the railroads overextended."

"Union Pacific is in bankruptcy, yes. And a few others. But not the Great Northern. Take a few weeks, a month or more. Then join me."

"Will you miss me?" I didn't want to complain. Life is too short to whine. He didn't answer. Perhaps he didn't hear me.

※※

We three "girls" took a vacation on the Clatsop Beach in Oregon while Pard headed to Bellingham Bay in Washington where he anticipated getting another railroad—this time The Great Northern—to make a hopeful town a potential terminus site, an area called Fairhaven. James J. Hill of Minneapolis was at the helm, a truly self-made railroad man who took no free land from the government, owed no banks. A different type of tycoon, Robert called him.

Pard did what he always did there, I learned later: borrowed money, formed a company, sold property, invested to build up the area with no guarantee that Hill would bring the railroad there. But his interest and his reputation got others to invest in Fairhaven. Even a few of our Wood River friends from Caldwell put money into the projects.

"He's always going to go up and down," my sister Mary said as we dug for clams on the beach. I shared Pard's letters with her. "It disturbs me that you're always there for him, but he finds a way to be somewhere else when you need a little tender loving care."

"You give great tender loving care." Argos

322

chased after foam, barking his delight. He trotted over to us. Why do dogs always shake themselves of the wet nearest their masters? A subtle effort at control?

"And I'm happy to come take care of you, Carrie, but—"

"Oh, please don't not love him because I complain." I brushed off Argos's shower. "I need for you to be a safe person who I can grouse to about my spouse without fear that you'll love him less."

"How a couple lives their lives is no business of others."

"That's right. And I won't think less of your Willie even though he thinks if you put food in the cold fridge in a glass jar that it will keep for three weeks and still be good. It won't."

"And I won't think badly of your Pard that, though he is a man of science, he believes that adding beans to any food makes it a complete meal. It doesn't."

We laughed. "This is what you have to look forward to when you and your Quinard marry," Mary told her daughter.

"Strange challenges to science and botulism?" My niece laughed and we joined her.

I let the seagulls serenade us, added a clam to the bucket, and pulled my gloves off, shaking them of sand. A wind gust threatened to take my straw hat, but I rescued it. "It's that we're wrapped up in the railroad and they are corporations. Railroads can do good things and they can dump you in a moment. I worry that we're back in their clutches."

"Maybe Robert's next book will be a bestseller and you can find a place to settle in and stay. Where would that be, Aunt Carrie?"

I thought of all the spots where we'd put our slippers beneath a bed. *Walla Walla? Santa Fe? Bend? Astoria?*

"Spokane Falls." I surprised myself with that. "I love the climate, the landscape, the mix of people. It's the most European of any city I know in the West. Grand yet friendly, not full of itself as Denver can be. Or San Francisco."

"Something to seek then." My sister hugged me with one arm. We swung the bucket and decided we had enough clams and headed back to our rooms.

❧❧❧

We lolled at our Single Occupancy Hotel, read books, visited the salt works supposedly established by Lewis and Clark. I wrote letters and we even took a trip to San Francisco. But I missed my Pard and I suspect Argos did too, though he'd loved bounding at the beach, chasing waves. I put Mary and Christina on the train back to Chicago, said goodbye to family, and I headed north to our new venture, Fairhaven, where Pard had written that he had an idea for a new book and if I felt better, to please join him.

It was a fine reunion in that mild climate off Bellingham Bay. "You look well, Dell. I've missed you." He pecked me on my cheek, a big smile on his face. He needed a haircut.

"I imagine you have, though the hotel's chef must be to your liking. It's good to see a little weight on you." It wasn't much weight and he looked pale, but I didn't want to mention that. Only staying in my happy tracks.

"I eat mostly at the tavern. The hotel dining room isn't quite finished, but it will be soon."

Robert had been welcomed in that region, and as he'd done in Idaho, he began building up Fairhaven, getting a hotel constructed, investing in the electric plant, urging city fathers to agree to give a piece of prime property to the railroad if they built its depot and terminus there. He met the Larrabees, founders of Fairhaven. I spent pleasant afternoons with Frances in her lovely home while we watched the fog lift.

"It would be the perfect climate without the fog," Frances said once.

"Yes, but then there'd be less reason to build a fire in the fireplace. I always love a fireplace," I said.

"Oh, me too. We only have five in this house. When the railroad comes, Charles has promised me a mansion." She smiled. "But if it doesn't, this

325

will do." It was a marvelous place to dream of a metropolis, with tall timber, mining, honeybees, and lush green growth right up to the beautiful deep harbor on Puget Sound. A perfect place for a railroad terminus. It even boasted of less winter rainfall than areas farther south. And the Larrabees were people who could weather a storm if the railroad didn't come. After all, he owned the bank.

Pard had been buying property he hoped to sell to the railroad when it came through, but meanwhile said he needed it for electric and water rights-of-way for his generating company. He planned to later sell those rights for a tidy profit to the railroad. Frances had told me that Pard and her husband and other investors had instituted condemnation proceedings on land that people didn't want to sell just to get those electric and water lines.

"We pay them," Pard defended when I brought up the issue.

"But they don't want to leave their homes," I said. "That's reasonable."

"Stands in the way of progress. They'll get over it."

I didn't like his crass view. "People put down roots and forcing them to dig them up is like—" I tried to think of the words. "It's like an amputation. They're cut off and have to leave a part of themselves there and progress runs right over them."

"It's what has to happen for the railroad to come."

"But if it doesn't come. Then all that disruption—"

"It's part of commerce, yes, it's part of commerce."

"Is the railroad going to come here? I notice other little towns are sprucing up too. They're cutting trees, those beautiful trees. Are they hoping they'll be the terminus for the Great Northern?" We were in the Fairhaven hotel and Pard was finishing up that book he'd been buried in when he wasn't co-opting property. He'd gotten use of a "literary den," as I called it, a room where he kept his notes and statistics and typewriter. That way, our hotel rooms proved less a worksite than a suite where we could entertain guests, all railroad or commerce related, I'm sad to say.

"They're looking at a number of areas, as they always do. Hill's a little harder to read than Gould. But this bay has much to commend it."

"People think because *we're* here that the railroad will come here."

"That's what the railroad wants. Get that interest up and commerce takes over and is bustling before the tracks arrive. And we'll make a killing when they have to buy what we own to make their tracks go where they need to."

"They'll be terribly disappointed if the tracks go elsewhere, like the Boise people were. And

Weizer, when we started New Weizer just a mile away." If people had been forced to sell, receiving less-than-desired compensation, and the railroad *didn't* come . . . well, I could imagine the disappointments. And the outrage, not to mention our personal losses if the railroad went another way.

"It's a part of life, Dell. Investment, disappointment. And recovery."

He didn't look at me while we talked; he was always busy with his writing.

"Look, let's take breakfast out of our rooms, celebrate," I said. "You're almost finished with the book, aren't you?"

"Checking footnotes."

"If you become ill again . . . I'll beat you with a stick. We need to celebrate being together. And your book. Celebration means to fill up, to give fuel for the next book, the next project. You didn't pace yourself with those six, and this time, you must, Robert. I'm not sure I could nurse you back to health by myself again."

He ran his hands through his hair, the light hitting tiny hints of gray at the temples. "Why don't you order something in for us?"

"No. You've worked all night. We're going out, taking a short walk, and then we'll have breakfast at your tavern. Come on. Argos is tired of me holding the leash. He needs to feel your hand on it." The dog lifted his head at the sound of his name, sat and scratched his ear.

Robert stared. *How can what he loves to do take so much from him?* Argos trotted over to him. He patted the dog's head. "All right." He put the manuscript on the floor, what he always did when he finished and before I took the pages to the printer. Stacks of statistics, notes, graphs, and maps looked like detritus on his desk. He always seemed to know where a certain note about the climate or number of board feet of timber in a Wyoming stand could be grabbed from the stacks of paper. At least now he used a typewriter, which made editing easier.

We dressed and Argos hopped around in happiness that all of us were heading out. The air felt damp from the morning fog. I confess, I did not like the fog. We heard hammering, dogs barking, children's patting on the boardwalk near the wharf as they headed to school. The *clunk* of a boat hitting a dock caused my head to turn. It was a pretty town when the fog stayed away.

We dropped Argos back in our hotel room before heading for Joe Morell's little tavern on the wharf where he refused to serve baked potatoes because he said people used too much butter on them that he couldn't afford. We chatted like old friends, Pard and I, over a hot breakfast of pancakes with a poached egg on top, served on heavy white plates, with our coffee delivered in big mugs. I inhaled the steam.

"You were right, Dell. This is good to be here. I

guess I get engrossed in the work and can't let it go, even for a little refreshment."

I took his hand across the wooden table marked by the nicks of steins and forks. "You're a true writer, Robert. Losing sight of time and rations. We'll get through this. Just don't become ill over it. Argos and I need you."

He smiled, squeezed my fingers. We walked slowly back to our hotel, my arm through his, and watched while a boat docked and unloaded baskets of fish that men hoisted onto their shoulders. It was that little delay, I suppose, that allowed for the disaster.

※

We reached the room, heard Argos whining on the other side of the door that Robert opened. Everything looked fine. The maid had been in and tidied up the bed. Then Robert went to his literary den.

I heard his wail from the end of the hall.

"The manuscript! It's gone! Everything, it's gone." The maid had been there too.

"No, surely not." That sinking feeling clutched at my stomach. "It's got to be here. She wouldn't have thrown it out."

Robert groaned. "It was trash to her." The room was picked clean except for the typewriter. That detritus on the desk was neatly stacked.

"I'll check with the manager. The manuscript must be in the garbage. We'll get it back. It might have eggs and bacon on it, but it'll be alright. You look around here while I check with the desk."

I raced down the stairs, pounded the little bell that brought the manager out. "What is it, Mrs. Strahorn? What's wrong?"

"We think the maid tossed out Robert's book by mistake. Can you find her, see what she did with it?"

"Our maids are very reliable."

"I know. Yes. How long ago did she clean our room?"

He looked at a page, ran his finger down a list. "First thing. You're usually there in the room, I believe. She might have taken extra time with the dog and you out."

"She's never cleaned Robert's writing room."

"She's new." He didn't look at me. "She would only toss what was on that floor."

I swallowed. "What would she do with the trash?"

"Oh, that goes immediately to the incinerator in the furnace room. And that floor has been . . ." He looked at the clock. "Completed fifteen minutes ago."

"Can you take me to the furnace room? Please."

"I can't leave my post. But it's down those steps." He pointed. "You can check with the custodian to see if there's anything left to burn. I'm so sorry."

"It's wasteful to burn so many papers when one

could write on the back side of the discard." The furnace man carried chastisement in his voice. I had a moment of hope until he added that it was policy to not take anything from the hotel that guests might leave behind, so in it went. The manuscript was ash.

To his credit, Pard did not blame me nor the maid. He blamed himself, which was worse. It deepened his moroseness as he tried to recapture what he'd written, a hopeless effort as any writer who has lost a manuscript will tell you. What's lost is always better than the recovery.

He never did attempt to write of Fairhaven again.

❧❦

Pard woke me in the dead of night. "We have to leave. Now. Quietly."

"What—?"

"I'll explain later."

I only had time to grab a bag and Argos and my chunk of ore as a reminder of what I could overcome if I had to.

From *Fifteen Thousand Miles by Stage*, vol. 2, by Carrie Adell Strahorn (pages 157, 179)

Leaving the town of Caldwell in 1888 was a most pathetic incident in our frontier lives. The friends who had struggled for the upbuilding of the town and the opening of the College of Idaho had woven themselves into our affections as only people do who suffer and endure the hardships of pioneering together. . . . [T]o record the heartaches and discouragements threading through the pioneer days would deprive these pages of the romance of the experience, and the reader might lose sight of the marrow of joy that always accompanies a life of useful work. . . . I am not prone to linger on the dark side of life, for I love the sunshine and gladness, and keep myself in it whenever possible.

30

Bonds

Leaving. Always leaving. The idea of a stagecoach and railroad life had held the promise of adventure, discovering the new. But every new turns into old and must be left, it seems. At least that is my life now. I can hardly write of leaving Bellingham Bay. I might not. It hurts too much—the leaving and what followed.

October 22, 1890

We left Bellingham Bay in the dark of dawn after Pard received word of where James J. Hill would take his railroad. It wasn't Fairhaven. It was Tacoma. At least they had the courtesy to tell Pard by telegram before the news broke region-wide. We tiptoed past the hotel manager's desk and scurried to the wharf where, with what little cash we had, we hired a wooden boat and oar man to row us across the sound, catching the morning tide. The thump of oars in the rings and the *swish* of the water against the boat couldn't drown out my soft cries. On shore, Pard borrowed money from a tavern owner who had yet to get the bad news—and who figured Pard would be good for it. "Left my wallet at the hotel," he said. It wasn't a lie. He had left it . . . but there was nothing in it anyway.

"Maybe if I'd gotten that Fairhaven book published, they would have chosen it," Pard said. He leaned his head back against the leather padding of the stage as the morning fog settled around us and we escaped the town.

"Oh, yes, blame yourself—or worse, assume you're that influential over the railroad's inconsistencies." The stage rolled us on the seats as we faced each other. "They chose where they thought they could get the most gain. Tacoma has greater potential than the bay area. And Tacoma's not as far from Portland as Bellingham is." I patted the seat next to me and Argos hopped up onto it. "B-flat." I hugged him to me. We were the only passengers that morning and I was grateful I didn't have to be cheery to preening women or loathsome men. "Don't even think that you didn't do enough to raise Fairhaven to the heights of Tacoma. Or that you haven't done enough to serve railroads in all these years."

I didn't want to mention those people who had sold their property or remind him of the days the sheriff had taken condemnation notices to hardy pioneers who were left with a pittance and for what? What Pard had done wasn't illegal, but ethically? My stomach hurt thinking of it. Yet I defended him.

"Railroads have been our greatest source of income through the years, not to mention our world of adventures." He closed his eyes. "Remember Cuba?"

"Yes, we almost died of food poisoning."

"And British Columbia."

"Five hundred miles of canoeing." I was crabby.

"We've had an astonishing life because of the railroad, Dell. You even got to go to Alaska while I headed back to DC that time, remember?"

"I recovered in Clatsop Beach with my sister after taking care of you when you nearly died writing those pamphlets. Truly, Robert, let me be annoyed and outraged at those people for a little while before you begin singing their praises. I'll get there. Just give me pause." I didn't add that I needed time to lessen my outrage at him.

"Take all the time you need."

"If I might ask, where are we going?"

"I was going to talk with you about that." He removed his hat, placed it on the seat next to him, crown down. "We're about to go into an economic depression." I snorted. "I mean all of us. The West has been in it already with the collapse of the silver market in '88. Currency is tight out here. People aren't paying their taxes, so cities are struggling."

"I wasn't aware."

"Not many are. But banks have started lending warrants and bonds to tax entities who agree to pay it back with interest—lucrative interest rates. Six to ten percent."

"I'm not sure I know what that means, Robert." My poor brain could barely manage this talk of finances in the early morning as we made our escape.

He leaned forward, forearms on his thighs. "It means that a good banker can buy up those warrants at a discount and resell them. The buyer will—in time—get paid when things pick up again. These are tax entities who will collect the money eventually, if only by selling property for nonpayment of back taxes. And meanwhile, those who hold the warrants can resell them at a profit and do quite nicely. One heads to places where there is still money available for investment purposes. I'll get money, then buy up warrants and resell them."

"And how will you get the money? We had to borrow stage fare."

"New England. Boston, to be exact. Pretty city, I'm told. Mellon says it's a banking mecca and cultural realm. You'll like it. A great place to begin the new decade. I had an out for us, Dell. If needed."

An out. One filled with shame and regret.

We caught the train, rode through Spokane Falls again. On Hill's Great Northern we used our passes, stopping in Billings when Pard became ill and I thought I'd lose him again. We were there weeks during a flu epidemic. I stayed strong as a horse. I eventually wrote and asked my parents for money, though. I told them something like, "We left before the bank opened, silly us," or some such thing. My mother sent us cash. Except for paying for our rooms, meals, and medicine, I hung onto those dollars, made them go as far as I could. From Billings, when Pard recovered, we pressed our passes onto the ticket masters' hands, then headed to Minneapolis, home of James J. Hill, head of the Great Northern Railroad, the titan who had forced our escape from Fairhaven.

Minneapolis. The city was hot and humid like Marengo in the summer.

"Why are we stopping here? Do you think you can get Hill to change his mind about Tacoma?"

"I just want to make personal contact with him, let him know there are no hard feelings and I'd be happy to advance for him again."

"No hard feelings? Really, Robert." I wondered if my dear Pard was demented.

The Single Occupancy Room we had in the Minneapolis hotel stretched our final dollars, and I told Robert that we simply had to find a way to make ends meet. "I'll sing for my supper if I have to. Remember when Mama said that I could always do that, when we got married?"

"I'll write articles. That'll help. Yes, it'll help."

I auditioned for paid solo work and Pard wrote an article for the Omaha paper while Hill declined to invest in warrants nor to hire Pard to advance anywhere else. Finally, we went home to Marengo where my dear father wasn't looking so well himself.

"What'll you do now?" my mother asked. She brewed tea for my father.

"Oh, we'll be up for new adventure," I chirped. "Don't you like seeing Argos as a mature dog? Did you imagine he'd get so tall when you shipped him west?"

I am so good at diversion. The worry, of course, was that I was diverting myself from facing the pain of all the losses and disappointments and entering an era of yet more risk in the relationship with my husband.

"Your father did the choosing and the shipping."

"I love that dog."

"Will he go with you to wherever it is you're going?"

"Pard has secured rooms for us in Boston."

"Boston. Oh, my heavens!"

"I've never been there. I'm looking forward to it."

But of course, I wasn't. Is it a greater sin to lie to your mother than to anyone else? We diverted to New York, where Pard conferred again with Jay Gould of the Union Pacific, and they discussed the warrants and bonds and I think he got a loan from Gould. I never knew.

But it was in my nature to make the best of things and learn something in the process.

We arrived in Boston, to a modest . . . no, it was a dump of a hotel. But there we stayed, strangers to Boston and in ways to each other.

❧❦

People in New England don't know how to deal with strangers. Bostonians, especially, come from long lines of ancestors and webs of relatives. Everyone knows everyone in those circles and what lineage they've descended from. Old money speaks the loudest. Strangers are anomalies. It was alright with me that they didn't know how to deal with a westerner, as I didn't want to spend time with most of them anyway. I heard pity in their voices with the limited image many held of the West. "Do you have stoves to heat your tents?" "Do you haul water from the river?" I had chatty comments to these and more that made people laugh and, frankly, kept any real questions of life in the West—my life in the West—at a distance.

What I had was a purpose: to bind the wounds of humiliation. If I write my memoir, I won't be too specific about anything in Boston. A good story always has a little mystery. But I wanted to know about business, about how things worked in the financial world, build a defense against the humiliation of our late-night departure, leaving friends holding worthless deeds. I wanted us to have a life together that was not infused with railroad talk or its torture. Yes, torture. But I didn't let go of my pass.

I was bitter in Boston. Bitter about the losses we'd sustained in Caldwell and Hailey and Fairhaven. Bitter about the betrayals within the partnerships we'd had. And honestly? I was bitter about those twins I hadn't been allowed to mother. Pard had his passion, his way of recovering from a fall; me, I propped him up. I didn't have anyone but our Lord lifting me, and sometimes I couldn't feel his arms.

When Gould of the UP died and Robert's golden goose was no longer laying eggs, I said to him, "I'd like to know about the financial transactions we're undertaking." We stood in his office he'd rented in the Massachusetts First National Bank building in Boston. *He can afford this, how?*

"Let me handle this, Dell. I was already buying up warrants before the Fairhaven decision was made. Both Mellon and Gould, too, saw the merit. We're on good ground here. You find projects in between when I need you to charm those buyers with your dinner conversation and entertaining wit. We're pardners, remember?" He patted his knee and Argos left me for his side.

I suppose I could have insisted he tell me more, but the truth is, I didn't really understand all this business about warrants and bonds and interest and silver markets. Reading about it flummoxed my mind. I never did have confidence knowing enough to make suggestions and perhaps I lacked the courage to offer advice—even if I did understand decimals and dollar signs. And Robert could be vague. It was easier, before long, to hide behind the Victorian woman who simply depended on her husband and didn't bother her pretty little brain with finance.

I still held images of those families who came west at our "partnership" writings, though, urging them to leave lush and productive only to find alkali dust and desert. I felt badly for our Wood River friends stuck with worthless land in Fairhaven, but I wasn't sure that if I'd known about economics, I'd have had the courage to disagree with Robert.

So, while Pard was banking and buying and schmoozing investors, I made small commitments, found small purposes. I located a voice instructor and took lessons. I made no new friends, only acquaintances: the butcher down the street who saved cheap cuts of meat for me and bones for Argos; the organist at Old South Presbyterian Church with the bell made by Paul Revere. I didn't want to befriend anyone whom Robert might involve in his financial schemes. At Robert's request, I planned dinner gatherings for his clients, hand-designed the invitations, bought candles by the dozens to give that luxury feeling while keeping the dank corners of our rooms in the dark. I took Chautauqua courses and attended lectures, alone. I auditioned for the choir, grateful to be accepted and to lose myself in choral therapy. I found a stable and rode, forgetting for a moment the pain of loss while I inhaled the equine scent and rubbed the velvet nose of my mount. A few suffrage meetings drew me in, but I didn't let myself engage in public marches; Robert's associates might not approve. Above all, it was my job to charm potential investors, tell bracing stories of the West, be a one-woman performer wearing silk instead of homespun.

In my happy lane, I noted that it was easier to visit my family in Marengo. We attended my niece Christina's wedding. I joined my sisters to celebrate my mother's birthday, my parents' anniversary. As Robert's fortunes began to improve, I indulged my nieces and nephews, setting aside small portions of my allowance for gifts. When my father became ill in '93, I used my pass to head to Marengo and was there for his dying. Argos rode the train with me. Robert remained behind, tied up with business.

≫✺≪

I was grateful my father did not live to see the Panic of '93, as investors called it. Banks called in notes; closed. Several railroads went bankrupt. The steel workers labor action against Carnegie and a Pullman strike in Chicago left unemployment in those places as high as 25 percent. Those next years, our little rooms in Boston looked prosperous compared to people living on the streets.

In the New York *Herald* of 1896, I read of a Norwegian emigrant mother and daughter who were leaving from Spokane—it no longer had *Falls* attached to the name. The women were walking, yes, walking, from that western city, earning their way across the country to arrive in New York that fall. They were doing it to show how strong women were, to advertise new, looser clothing worn without corsets. And if they made it, they would earn a sum of money to help pay family debts. I applauded their boldness in showing how the economy affected families and what women were willing to do to help. It was an extraordinary adventure, inspiring really, for what a woman's body was capable of. I thought too of how grand it would be to spend months with one's daughter, sharing experiences, building a bond of family. The women's route, it was said, would take them across the Dale Creek Canyon where Pard and I had crossed on that cowcatcher.

Their journey spoke of desperation, women finding ways to support and save their families, and I wondered if another depression was on its way while we still struggled with the repercussions of the Panic of '93. I often felt hollowed out those Boston years, like a Ponderosa pine toppled by the western winds.

In 1898, Robert sold all his bonds and warrants and closed his business. We were wealthier, financially, than we'd ever been, Robert told me. "We rival the bankers and maybe even the railroad barons. At least a few of the short line owners." I suspected he exaggerated. He let me look at the accounts, but I confess, I didn't understand them. He said another economic depression was coming but that we were cushioned, whatever that meant. I believed him.

Wealth didn't make me deliriously happy. We'd been here before. I was a Victorian lady, "at home" as the census-taker noted. Being "taken care of." There was no grand calling like those Norwegian women had who walked across a continent.

"Where do you want to go?" Robert asked me after giving me diamond earrings at Thanksgiving.

The two of us occupied our rooms. I'd done my best to live frugally those Boston years, but I do love diamonds. Does that make me a bad person? "We should be saving, not be extravagant."

"Come on, Dell. Looking wealthy attracts wealth. And you deserve diamonds."

He didn't really understand what I longed for.

"Don't spend any more for Christmas or my birth-

345

day. Save it for the West. I want to go west again."

"Of course, but where? Denver? Omaha, San Francisco?"

I thought of places that had drawn me. "Walla Walla."

"Too small."

I wanted to say, *Don't ask me without giving me parameters*. "Where do you want to go?"

"Spokane."

I had liked the beautiful falls and the cosmopolitan feel, all the different languages spoken on the streets. It was the town I'd named when my niece had asked years ago.

"My thoughts exactly." I clapped my hands and Argos barked. The dog wore a red ribbon around his neck for the holidays. He was already eleven. I didn't want to think about him growing older. "Is it the climate of Spokane that's such a draw for you?" I didn't look at Pard as I put the posts of my new earrings through my pierced ears, twisted my head in the mirror. They sparkled like starlight.

"It could be the biggest railroad terminus in the West, Dell. The Northern Pacific, Great Northern, and Union Pacific should all be vying for that inland market. Those Palouse wheat field harvests need transport out, tracks'll bring immigrants in. I want to build the North Coast Railroad, Dell. Link Spokane and Walla Walla to Portland and Seattle."

"You want to build a railroad?" I swallowed.

"But that's thousands and thousands of dollars. And you said railroads have overextended and many short lines have gone under. Why would you risk it?"

"Why not? What's money for if not to invest and make more?"

There was the crux of the matter: what I wanted in my life wasn't available through money. I wanted to feel useful. I wanted to do something good for children whom I could call my own. I wanted to put down roots.

"I think my family hoped we'd settle in Chicago when we leave Boston."

"You love the West, don't you, Dell?"

I nodded. It was a landscape that fed my soul.

"It's better for my own health too."

"It'll be twenty below in Spokane this time of year."

He laughed. "You're right. After New Year's we'll take on Spokane. Hawaii first, then head to Washington in the spring."

I agreed and made myself get into that happy lane of looking forward.

⊰≫✕≪⊱

We took the train to Marengo, loaded with presents for my family. My earrings sparkled and I heard music in the train wheels clicking on the tracks.

But the mood turned somber when my mother

developed a chest cough Christmas morning. Wheezing and then pneumonia came on quickly. She died eleven days after my forty-fifth birthday. My confidant, my correspondent, my letter-listener, was gone. That bond of mother and child, severed from this earth. I sang at her funeral. I stopped writing letters after that—and singing—for a very long time.

I remained in Marengo to help handle my mother's estate while Robert went back to Boston to close things up. We traveled back and forth but managing my parents' affairs took longer than I'd thought, and Robert was engaged in his newfound wealth-making plans. For the first time I considered how it was good to not have children in our lives; taking them from schools, moving about, living in hotels would have been a strain on them. Perhaps I was being nostalgic spending so much time in my childhood home where I'd felt loved, safe, and had a platform of hopefulness that never wavered. I knew Pard loved me as he could, but Boston and all that got us there had burned me. I had yet to heal the inner wounds of disappointment.

From *Fifteen Thousand Miles by Stage*, vol. 2, by Carrie Adell Strahorn (page 297)

My own heart was more bitterly sealed against intrusion when we went to Boston than was possible for anyone there to emulate. I left all who were dear to me in the West, and I did not want to make new friends. I went there for a purpose and as a stranger I could throw my whole energy into its accomplishment.

31

Spokane Splash

We are in Hawaii, not exactly the West of my lumbering stagecoaches, though they have them here with fine horses and seats of worked leather. But even in this tropical land I discovered sturdy cowboys moving large herds of cattle against the backdrop of volcanoes and of course the quiet sandy beaches. It feels like a honeymoon, so much better than the trip from Illinois to Omaha all those years before. Maybe we'll truly have a new start when we head to Spokane. Or will Pard surprise me and keep me in the tropics?

New Year's Day, my birthday, 1900

It was December again before Robert said, "Hawaii. For this Christmas." He'd returned from his foray to various spots west and east. It was a drizzling day in Marengo, spitting snow. A warm, sandy beach sounded wonderful. I'd settled my parents' estates and we three sisters had small amounts to invest on our own. Robert and I used our passes to book a Pullman across the continent to arrive on a steamer that sailed across the Pacific.

When it was decided we should leave Argos with my niece's family in San Francisco to save him the strain of travel in his later years, I thought my heart would break. I made it my decision, though it had been Pard's suggestion. The choice came after watching that dear dog play with my niece and her children and seeing his eyes clouded and knowing his time to leave this earth could not be far behind. I could not stand it if it happened while we were on the road or in Hawaii, or Alaska, or wherever our future paths might take us hither and yon. And a hotel is not the greatest playground for a large, old dog. I hugged his neck. "Goodbye, old friend. You have a good life with my niece." He twisted and licked my neck and then we left.

I still grieved both my parents—and leaving Argos behind added to that sadness—but we were now wealthier than we'd ever been, and that was supposed to keep me always in my happy lane. It didn't. I said as much to Robert.

"It's natural for you to feel saddened. Your mother was dear to you." He had gathered a cup of tea from the steward, made his way weaving with the ship's sway as we headed to the islands. So far, seasickness had stayed away. "And Argos your good friend."

"It's been a year. I should be over it, don't you think?"

He handed me the cup and saucer. Sat across

from me on the divan. "Hawaii will do you good. Put sad memories of death and loss behind you. Come spring, we'll make a splash in Spokane."

I rather liked that image of "splashing" but wasn't sure how that would happen. We arrived on Christmas Eve. Then on the eve of my birthday, at a hotel in Waikiki, I managed to get my dear Pard to dance with me to a ukulele playing "Auld Lang Syne." He kissed me, held me closer without his usual brief squeeze before releasing me.

"It's a new century and a new beginning, Dell."

"To get you up and dancing? I guess it is."

"No, Spokane. That's where we'll put down roots. I promise."

I didn't want to hope too much, but planting roots anywhere is an act of hope.

※※※

On our last days, after the luau and a ride to the top of a volcano and watching young dancers move their hips to festive music, we decided to go out on the ocean with one of Pard's old comrades in the military, another railroad colonel named Stearns and his daughter. Mrs. Stearns declined to don her bathing costume and join us on a log canoe with each of us using our paddles. An outrigger would keep us from being swamped, we were told.

But that day, our boat was slammed by a twenty-foot swell, and we were dumped into the sea, hitting a coral reef before we could resurface, gasping for air. Pard hung on to me, pulling me to the upside-down boat, grabbing me when another wave tore at us. One of our native paddlers grabbed the Stearns girl and swam with her to shore while the other tried to manage the broken outrigger as the colonel, Pard, and I hung on.

I could not swim.

Pard pushed me astride the boat bottom, where I tossed up gallons of sea water. Then realizing his mistake—that neither he nor Colonel Stearns could easily cling to an overturned boat—he tried to convince me to come back into the sea.

Go back into the water? Risk that we could turn the canoe over before we sank ourselves? But Pard's shouts of assurance, his eyes holding mine and with a belief that he would not ask me to do something menacing without the conviction of the rightness of it, gave me courage. And I left behind the security and slipped back into the sea. He held me up while the two men turned the boat over, water sloshing over the sides we clung to.

In those moments, I didn't know if I would survive and I longed for the peace I'd found on that terrible stage ride in Colorado years before. The colonel hung on. Pard kept his arm around me and lifted me when I appeared to lose strength. Eventually, the waves took us shoreward where our young companion and her rescuer cheered us on.

Then as we seemed near to rescue, the colonel

gasped. "Oh, Mrs. Strahorn! Oh, Mrs. Strahorn!" He hung in front of me. I feared he was slipping away into a warm watery grave.

"We're almost there," I shouted. "Hang on." His wife paced on the shore.

"Oh, Mrs. Strahorn, I fear—" he gulped a bit of water, spit it out—"I fear . . . I am losing my suit."

Ah, the demands of the culturally refined. "Worry not about your trousers, Colonel. I've seen men's underdrawers."

"But I don't wear them, dear lady. All I have on is my bathing suit."

The constant waves grabbed against his swimsuit that he didn't dare reach to pull up for fear the waves would steal his grip on the boat.

Pard shouted, "If that's all we lose on this voyage, we are indeed lucky, Colonel."

I began a hysterical laughter that Pard joined in and so did the colonel. What else was there to do?

❧❧❧

It was as close to dying as I'd come in recent years. And it did seal to my mind the shortness of life, of our responsibility to live fully, generously, and with joy. I vowed to do that and also thanked my dear husband over and over that he had kept his partner afloat. I guess he always had.

We arrived by train into Spokane, a city that

had grown dramatically since we'd been there years before. A great fire had swept through the business district in 1889, but instead of it leaving ashes and shambles behind, the city grew from it, using the ash as humus. Washington was a state now. Women had the right to vote in the territory in 1883, then the Supreme Court knocked it down in 1887. But here was a city—ready to leave behind whatever it must to go forward into this new century.

In addition to the Northern Pacific and Great Northern railroads that already served the city, Pard imagined what a grand terminal Spokane would be if three other railroads were to be induced to bring their steam engines: The Milwaukee Road, the Canadian Pacific, and his dear Union Pacific. And he hoped to build that North Coast Line to link Portland to Spokane. Even while we lolled beneath the palm canopies, considered the mainland only when the mail boat arrived—or so I thought—Pard was dreaming again. He hadn't chosen Spokane for the landscape and climate and people as I had. He had chosen it for the railroading potential.

We stayed at the Spokane House like many others new to the area, identifying a neighborhood to live in. At least I thought that was the reason we were still at the hotel after three months into the new year. He'd been busy with his schmoozing of yet more investors.

"Why don't we find a modest home," I said. "Get out of this hotel."

"No, no, we'll have a mansion when the time comes. But right now, there's too much to do. Get involved, Dell. Suffrage is alive here. Sing your heart out."

"I'd like to sing in my own home. Sit before a fireplace, keep my feet warm."

Ever since Yellowstone, my toes easily numbed, as did my fingers when hit by a drop in the thermometer.

"Don't be impatient." He shushed me with his hand as though I was a child.

"Impatient? We finally have the resources—you say—but they can't be spent on a home for us?"

"We don't want to look too—immoderate. It's all about pacing, Dell." He pulled his shoes off, stayed sitting on the bed. "We appear wealthy because of our careful management. That draws investors. After we've moved things along, friends see others comfortable with me and my business acumen, we make our splash with a lavish mansion where you serve people, make them comfortable for when I close the big deals. But for now . . ." He patted my hand as though I were a pup. "Pacing."

Something inside derailed me from my happy track. "Pacing? Have I not paced my entire life at your beck and call?" I'd never asserted myself, allowing Robert to make all the decisions while I niggled along beside him or worse, behind him. It was a lightning bolt: I suddenly knew. We weren't "Pardners." My heart pounded. Maybe if I had been involved with the canal company at Caldwell we could have stayed. Maybe if I'd stood firm, we'd be raising twins now. Robert put Robert first. He was a friendly snake oil salesman who dealt in land and railroads instead of elixirs and oils. Why hadn't I seen that before?

"You . . . you're selfish, Robert. If you treated your railroad partners as you do me, keeping them in the dark about things, always putting yourself first, why would they stay with you?"

He blinked. "Well, I . . . keep them apprised. I accede to their wishes now and then as a partner must. I didn't think I deprived you of that courtesy, Dell. We've been through everything together."

"It's difficult to negotiate as 'pardners' if someone is walking in front of you on the path. That's hardly together. It's rather an independent trek even if the one in front occasionally looks behind to see if the follower has fallen." I pulled a shawl around my shoulders.

"Where are you going? It's nearly midnight."

"Going for a walk. Alone. If I fall, I know how to pick myself up."

He didn't follow me and the walk near the falls with its pounding splash gave me time to calm and reminded me of our overturned boat in the crushing waves. I had believed myself safe atop the water-slogged canoe but had to trust Robert's view that I was not. I had accomplished that leap of faith believing in my Pard, though not yet mastered it. Pastor Boone would say that is the journey we're on in life: knowing when to trust another on the path with us as we "find our way clear" to God's direction, living fully in life. So what was my life's work? I hadn't yet found it. And that wasn't Robert's fault.

From *Fifteen Thousand Miles by Stage*, vol. 2, by Carrie Adell Strahorn (page 268)

An old Squaw called "Old Mary" was said to carry one hundred twenty years . . . was too old to fish. But she used often to climb the mountains for berries and was an active element of life wherever she went.

32

Rent by the West

I am ever so grateful that my own family ties with my sisters stay strong. And yes, with Pard too, though I came to understand that while he adores me, buys me jewels and gems, takes my literary advice, marvels when I "hold a room" while he stands quietly by the fireplace, watching, is proud of me and loves me, his adoration does not extend to meeting my greatest desires: a home of my own, having a family. I live with those uncertainties and losses and do my best to not subtly hold him accountable for the lack in my life. We are responsible for who we are and what we become. We must know what matters and have the courage to act on that. Oh, I understand circumstances intervene, but it is how we respond to those circumstances that marks our character, that decides if we will pursue a desire or let it drift out to sea.

May 30, 1900

If you should happen upon a census record of 1900, you might imagine a conundrum. The census taker came in June to the hotel in Spokane and recorded Robert and me as living there. Robert was home at the time and he answered the questions. But I appear on another census document as "Carrie Strahorn, head of household."

I had my trunks sent up by the hotel manager the morning after our conversation about our need to pace ourselves and thus wait yet longer for a home. Robert noticed the trunks being packed.

"Please. Reconsider, Dell." His pleading had no effect on the deliberateness of my sorting. Of course, he had no idea. I'd never told him how I felt, not really, and I couldn't find the words this time either, beyond what I had already said. I knew I needed to use that railroad pass and leave. I wasn't certain where I'd end up. I wasn't going to walk across the continent like that Norwegian mother and daughter, that was certain.

But I needed time. Those ties that had bound us had frayed through the years of Omaha, Denver, Hailey, Caldwell, Fairhaven, Boston, years when we lived together, shared meals, loved each other, though at a distance as the years ensued. I nursed him, we spoke of inane things like his clients and my voice instructor's idiosyncrasies. We had grand memories, but we'd passed each other in the night. Maybe it was our near death in Hawaii that put me on a trajectory away from the wealth we'd accumulated and more toward what any of it meant.

I didn't blame him for the emptiness I felt. That emptiness was of my doing. He was a child in a toy shop with his railroads while I . . . I stood outside with my face pressed against the proverbial window, wishing I had something I loved as much. Not anymore.

His eyes were shiny as tumbled black onyx. His total inability to grasp how much I wanted at last to have a home of my own as the only motherly thing left to me became too much.

"Where will you go? Back to Hattie's, I suppose." He crossed his arms over his chest, assumed my sisters would draw me in. "Illinois will be splendid this time of year. Hot. Humid. Bugs."

"Don't you malign my Illinois bugs," I said. "They have fireflies in Marengo, something this West doesn't have." *I'm defending bugs?*

He took my hands, held them. "Just tell me you'll come back."

"Let me go, Robert."

"But you'll return?"

His angst was palpable, it felt like a too-tight corset over my chest. I could so easily nurture him as I always did, but this time, I couldn't. But I could lessen his pain's intensity.

"I'm going to Caldwell."

"Caldwell? Oh. Certainly. Caldwell." He stepped away from me, ran his hands through his still-thick hair. His hat line marked his forehead. "Visit some friends there. Stay at the hotel."

"I intend to purchase a house. A modest one, of course."

He blinked but recovered quickly. "Of course, yes, a good investment. I'll have money ordered to the bank. Just telegraph me. Or call."

"My parents remembered me in their will. I need to do this on my own."

"Oh, Carrie, what are you doing to me?" He actually pulled at his hair.

"I'm doing nothing *to* you, Robert. I'm doing something *for* myself."

I left the trunk I'd been packing and sat on the divan in our hotel rooms. "Come here." I patted the seat next to me and he flopped onto it. "I don't know how to explain it, but I have to go where I once felt both excited about something larger than myself that I had a part in, and where I overcame a great loss. To remind myself that I can."

He frowned. "A great loss? Oh, having to sell the canal company. That was tragic."

Tears burned behind my eyes.

I patted his hand and stood. "Time to finish up." I used my most cheery voice. I looked at my breast-pin watch. The violet traveling suit would do, though the cuffs were frayed. "Don't you have an appointment with someone about an electric and water system of some kind?"

He stood, scratched frantically at his vest, found his watch fob and opened the case. I'd given it to him for our fifteenth wedding anniversary. *Will he forgo the meeting?* "Yes, you're right as usual. Look, I'll have the carriage brought around to take you to the depot."

"You're so generous, Robert."

He frowned but remained silent, missing my sarcasm, which was good because I didn't really want to continue in that vein. My intention was to go forward, not only leave him behind.

"Let me know as soon as you're there, what you need. I can visit—"

"No. Please. I want time alone. Not with you, nor my sisters."

"I'll miss you, Dell. You know that."

"You'll do fine as you have a dozen times when we've been separated."

"But those were me leaving you so that I could write or make a deal. Did I tell you that I've got interest in a gold mine in Sumpter, Oregon? Investors. I'm investing there."

I didn't say anything.

"Fairhaven. That's it, isn't it? You're still mad about what happened. Maybe I did exaggerate with those drawings showing lumber mills and railway approaches and smokestacks where there were only docks and forest."

I patted his arm. "It's been our way, priming the pump for dreamers to quench their thirsts. But bitter water sometimes shows up where fresh is intended." I could grow all nostalgic in a minute, but so could my Pard, especially if the subject of development came up. He had his way of avoiding pain too.

"I'm off." I left him and our rooms, told the hotel porter to please bring down my trunks. I took the carriage to the depot and boarded the train. I was strong and certain. Every journey must begin there.

❄❄❄

Once I stepped off the train in Caldwell, the emptiness came back; not a panic exactly, but a *what have I done?* ache formed in my stomach. I'd never lived on my own, not ever. I swallowed away the discomfort. I was here. I could do what I wanted, which was to check into the hotel and then walk out to our cottage in Sunnyside, see how many of the trees had made it; visit the Presbyterian church and check on the progress of the College of Idaho, of which Reverend Boone now served as president. I'd visit the cemetery to see if I recognized any new names.

"Dell Strahorn, I'm so glad I got here before you went off to the hotel." It was Carrie Blatchley, breathless. "Here, let James secure your trunks." She signaled a man in a uniform, who tapped his fingers to his cap. She leaned into me. "I know, we're getting fancy in Caldwell having chauffeurs in uniform, and electric street cars and all. It's kind of fun." She hugged me. "It's been too long. How are you?"

"I . . . how did you know?"

"Robert telephoned. He said you were coming for a visit. We are delighted. You should have let us know. Annie will be pleased to see you too. The Boones live right next door, you know. You'll stay with us, of course."

"No. I . . . the hotel has a suite for me, until I decide what I want to do."

She pooched her lower lip out. "Please. We've plenty of room and I've missed you. Besides, the sight and sound of giggling girls will be a fine elixir for tired eyes behind those spectacles. Still forgetting to clean them, I see."

My hands went automatically to my glasses as I said, "Giggling girls? When did you and Henry . . . that is, I didn't know. How wonderful for you both. I would have sent baby gifts."

She laughed her wonderful flute-like laugh. "Not babies, Dell. They're students. We've given up half our house as a dormitory for the college, built an addition. You'll love them and they'll love meeting you."

I was easily malleable. I went home with Carrie.

Annie Boone with her three children came over as soon as our carriage arrived before a grand house on Belmont. It wasn't nearly as imposing a structure as some I'd visited but felt welcoming, with its white picket fence and geraniums blooming red.

"This is Mrs. Strahorn, Marie," Annie said to her daughter. Annie's blonde hair was wrapped up around the top of her head much like I wore mine. Simple ivory combs held the soft curls in place while a hat squashed my chestnut locks. "She helped your aunt Carrie and a few other of Mama's friends start the church your papa preaches at sometimes."

"And the college," Carrie said.

"Oh, I can't lay claim to any of that," I said.

"You got my husband to stay or it wouldn't exist."

I thanked her for that thought.

"How do you do, Mrs. Strahorn," Marie said with a curtsy. "I'm already eleven." Marie was the oldest of three Boone children. She was slightly younger than the twins, Kate and Kambree Bunting, would be. *My twins.*

"Eleven is a very important age. Are you a reader? There are many good books to read when one is eleven."

"I do like books. And I like to write, don't I, Mama?"

"Yes, you do. She's quite good, for her age," Annie said to me as she accepted a teacup and saucer. "This is Sarah." A toddler sat on her lap and Annie carefully put the cup down on the table. Another child, probably three or four, stood beside his mother. "This is shy James."

Carrie poured my tea. "You have to sing in the choir Sunday. Surprise Hester. She doesn't know you're here yet. It'll be like old times." We heard laughter and the clatter of footsteps. "The students. They'll come in through the back. We built the addition two stories so we could house more. Our little college is growing and doing well, but finding places for students to live has been a challenge."

"One day the college will build a dormitory," Annie said.

"Can I live in it?" Marie asked.

"You won't need to. You can live at home with us and go to school."

Lucky you, I thought and meant it.

It was an afternoon where I felt warm and welcomed, even if annoyed yet again at Robert. He had meant to be kind asking Carrie to meet me, but he was without awareness of how he diminished my abilities with his cloying.

≫※≪

Carrie's husband arrived home and we'd finished a lovely meal of lamb with rosemary potatoes and fresh mustard greens.

"Thank you for the invitation to stay here, but I need a little thinking time. We've had such an up-and-down life these past years I wanted to return to my Caldwell roots, alkali though they may be. The hotel will be a good place for contemplation."

"Your Robert's now investing in Spokane, is he?" Henry Blatchley tapped tobacco into his pipe.

"He wants to build a coastal short line to connect Spokane to Portland. He estimates $30 million. I . . . those numbers boggle my mind. I'm looking for a little house here in Caldwell for maybe $100 at most."

"I'll see what I can find for you."

"No. Please, Henry." I touched his suited sleeve. "I appreciate your help, I do. I want to do this on my own . . . or not. I may just visit, then go on to Hailey or who knows where."

He looked at Carrie. She nodded. "I see. Well, call on me if you need to."

"I will."

I did take a walk that next beautiful May morning. The air was as I remembered it, but there were many more trees, the canals flourished and bridges crisscrossed where there hadn't been a need before. At our cottage, I remembered how Argos had romped and played and how I had one evening fallen into a small irrigation ditch while out calling for him to prevent his playing with coyotes. Argos had passed on at my niece's in California. I wished I'd had his bones buried in our old backyard.

Those had been good years for us, Robert and me. Maybe I missed our joint enterprises as we'd had in our beginnings. Maybe twenty-three years of marriage of uncertainty left me in a fuddle. What had been different about Caldwell?

My work. Helping build up that church and being able to let go of it when it was finished. It was something good for someone else, not just for Robert's clients or to promote the railroad's interests. It made a difference. And I'd enjoyed the activity of serving, being hospitable to people, having them visit my home. The Wood River Presbytery had accepted our congregation and gone further with forming the college. Carrie had said she and Henry intended to bequeath property and an endowment to the college if they still had money when they died. "It gives me comfort knowing I can contribute now with our little dormitory," she had said. Maybe I could do something like that as well.

The following day, I visited a real estate agent and asked to see a small house I'd walked by on the way to our old cottage. It had a fenced-in yard and a small garden area. After seeing the interior, I knew it would be a perfect getaway place for me for when I needed time to remember the things that mattered. I wired the bank in Marengo that sent cash for the purchase and was in it and thriving when George Little came to my door to ask the census questions. I felt quite pleased to see him write "Head of Household" on the form. That Sunday I sang in the choir.

It was a healing summer.

※※

Carrie Blatchley and I took bamboo fly poles and fished the Boise River, where she showed me how to match the hatch, as she called it. "You look carefully at the bugs that flutter over the water and that the fish are paying attention to and then you offer them a fly that resembles that. It works every time."

"It sounds like promotional material for the railroad."

She laughed. But the stripping of the line, the quiet comradery, the scent of pine and shades of willow soothed my soul, and I wondered why I didn't do more of this. Robert and I used to fish, though often it was a promotional activity with senators and corporate presidents with us too. I didn't have time to listen to my own thoughts. There was something comforting about this fishing with flies that Carrie said she tied herself. "And you could learn how too." That summer, I did.

Hester's husband still owned the expanded livery and he loaned me a horse so I could ride in the early mornings, sometimes at sunset, beside the Wood River. Developing a relationship with such a big animal gave me confidence I'd lost in Fairhaven and Boston and even in Spokane.

I also made an appointment to speak with Reverend Boone.

Not being a reflective person, meeting with the Reverend took quite an effort. But I tried on my own to reconcile my marriage vows, my love for Robert—and I did love him—with a deep sense of emptiness that I had put upon his shoulders rather than find another way to be the person I was created to be. A helpmate, yes. But surely, more.

"Your voice is a gift to all who hear you sing," President Boone told me. We sat in his office at the college, the sounds of student chatter in the background. "And your passion for the church has met many needs, including students'."

"All indirectly, though."

"Nothing wrong with that. Think of the quiet women of the Bible from dressmaker to cook to foot washer to water carrier. Each did what she could do, never forgot what she could do, and did it. I'm here because of your words and your work, because you did what you could do."

"That's something, I guess."

"Quite a bit of something." He got up from behind the desk and pulled a chair to sit beside me. "You're a hospitable woman, Dell, and that kind of gift can't be minimized. You see people, put them at ease."

"Too bad I can't do that for myself." I smiled. "Something gets in my way."

"Why don't you write about your life? An auto-biography has a way of pulling threads together that you otherwise might miss. I'd like to read such a book."

"Would you?" He nodded.

"Writing about why you're even here now in Caldwell might bring you insights our Lord would be pleased to reveal."

❧❦

Hester concurred when I told her that I was thinking of writing a memoir.

"Have you journaled?" Her hair had turned gray in the passage of years, the silver only adding to her beauty. We sat on my little back porch dotted with wicker rockers and colorful pads. My ore served as a centerpiece that held down the center napkin against the occasional gust.

"Little paragraphs here and there," I answered. "Enough to remind me of what was happening though."

"An autobiography is a legacy, really."

"But for who? I have no children who might care."

"There are others, Carrie. Friends, your nieces. Historians, perhaps. Write it for yourself, your own love story."

I laughed. "I'd best be careful what I say if friends find themselves in it."

Hester picked up the ore, moved it from hand

to hand. "Find the diamonds inside and let them shine. Let the irritating souls you've come across be nameless. And be kind to yourself. A memoir is no place to whine but rather give us wisdom we can all share without having to go through the pain ourselves."

I did then begin to write in earnest but not all of happy-lane experiences deciding I could always edit painful details out later. And when at night I listened to the coyotes call or watched the summer moon rise to fill the sky, it occurred to me that Robert might never be able to do for me what I needed when I needed it. And in fact, neither he nor any husband should be required to. Or any other person for that matter: a mother for her children; a sister for her sibling. What happiness I'd find inside my marriage—or even with myself—required giving myself credit when I felt credit was due and not relying on Robert or my sisters or the sweet friends I'd made to fill me up. Nor on the gifts of having a child of my own, whether born to me or adopted or fostered. Those poor little things could waste away trying to meet my needs—if that was why I longed for them. A husband weaker than Robert might have wasted away too. After all, if we were created as fearfully and wonderfully made, then surely that included all the gifts and talents and tools necessary to live creatively and fully. To be enough. To be loved enough, competent enough; to soak in enough—and then to pour love out.

I had much here in Caldwell. I bought an English bulldog puppy, white with a brown splotch around one eye and ear. I named her Daisy. Taught her to "b-flat" instead of "down," just as I had Argos. She took walks with me, made me laugh at her antics. I felt myself invigorated by the pace of the days, the control I had over time, and the writing of my memoir. *I could do what I'm doing here with Robert daily in my life as well as when he isn't.* I simply had to make the commitment to care for myself and not wait for anyone else to do it for me.

I enjoyed my morning tea I made myself, loved my back porch that looked out on a patch of green into the wide vistas. I adored inviting young Marie Boone to bring her books and read with me. Delia Gwinn still made those marvelous croissants. Mrs. Meacham had passed on, but there were new people to listen to who sang in the choir. And Hester read early drafts of my autobiography that gave me confidence to carry on. I'd found my way clear to writing my own love story.

※※

Robert and I wrote letters back and forth. He'd asked when I was coming home, a question I didn't have an answer to. But when the time was right, I felt assured that I'd hear that inner voice making it clear what I should do.

And then one day while I was out weeding in the garden, a carriage pulled up. It was Robert. He had a woman with him.

From *Fifteen Thousand Miles by Stage*, vol. 2, by Carrie Adell Strahorn (page 301)

What hardships have been endured and heart-strings crushed and broken; what family ties have been rent by the great movement to the West!

33

The Promise of a Rainbow

Stories, I believe, are the most powerful way we have of organizing human experience. As I began to do what President Boone suggested I do, write my memoir, I found myself wrapped up in stories. Of terrible winters and being stuck in Hailey with my helper, making our way out through drifts so deep, men walked before us to make trails for our horses. Robert had gone on ahead and it was several weeks before we met up again. What I'd leave in and what I'd leave out of my memoir became a happy occasion of self-consulting. I'd discover who I really was inside those stories.

September 1, 1900

I have always liked rainbows, both their color and their promise of God's eternal love for mankind. When I saw Robert step out of the carriage, my heart skipped a beat as it had when I'd first met him. He'd come those years before to bring me to his then fiancée Carrie Lucy, my University of Michigan classmate who was dying. I was struck by the way grief carved his face that day and was encouraged when my eye caught a rainbow behind the carriage following an Illinois summer shower. Then I thought it meant my friend would live; but it had meant a different kind of promise.

No rainbow arched behind my husband nor the woman whose arm threaded through his, her hat feather waving in the Caldwell breeze. She wore a beige linen traveling suit with a pink shirt and cameo brooch at her throat. I swallowed. Of all the perils we'd experienced in our twenty-three years of marriage, I had never had cause to imagine his affections might stray. But I'd never left him before either.

She looked a little older than either Robert or me. I didn't recognize her face nor gait.

At Robert's smile, my face grew hot.

"It's good to see you, Dell." I could barely hear him over the sound of my pounding heart. Daisy barked and danced at his feet. He hesitated, then dropped the woman's arm from his, bent to lend the back of his hand to the dog to sniff. Daisy calmed and Robert stepped to hold me, kiss my wet cheeks. "You look as beautiful as ever, even with garden gloves, hat, and apron. And who is this?"

"Daisy. B-flat," I told her. "And you might have let me know so I could have cleaned up." I wore a long braid instead of my usual coiffured hair.

"And risk having you tell me not to come?" He stepped out of the way. "This is Mrs. Browne."

A widow. She reached out both hands to hold my garden-gloved ones. "A pleasure to meet you, Mrs. Strahorn. I've heard so much about you." Daisy snorted her way between us, her whole body wiggling.

"And Mr. Browne?" *Not very hospitable of me.*

"He's had a touch of the stomach upset, but he'll be fine by dinner, he promised. He's back at the hotel."

Confusion must have reigned on my face, but I managed to invite them inside. Daisy romped ahead of us. Mrs. Browne—Ann—smiled at her surroundings and said, "What a lovely home. The leaded glass windows are perfection with that stagecoach and horses."

"It's comfortable."

"Your husband tells me that you and he started this town."

"With a few other investors and hardy pioneering souls," I said. "Please, sit. Let me get us some coffee or tea?" I removed my gloves, washed my hands, and put on the kettle.

"Tea," Ann said. "Some say my husband and I built Spokane Falls but there were already fifty-four people there. Seven families. When we pulled up to the one questionable street—I'd come from Portland—my heart went down. I thought I was coming into a desolate place. We

378

had baby Guy. It was 1878 and we lived for a year with the Post family."

"Caldwell was alkali desert then. We stayed in a tent."

What are the Brownes doing with my husband in Caldwell? Why is Mrs. Browne sitting in my parlor?

"They went on to build the magnificent city Spokane is," Robert said. He cleared his throat. "Mr. and Mrs. Browne have a lovely home they're selling to the right people. It's on First Street, and Dell, I think it would be the perfect home for us. We'll call it Strahorn Pines—but only if you'd like."

"It must be in the trees then."

"Robert assures me that you'd turn it into something spectacular. We raised our children there so it's special to us, but we fully expect others to make their own mark on it."

"It needs your touch, Dell. It does."

"We came to meet you, Mrs. Strahorn, because your Robert didn't want to commit to the purchase unless you approved. I hope you will. Is that an elm tree you've planted?"

"Yes. We planted all these trees."

She stood and looked out the window. "And started the Presbyterian church, your Robert says. He's quite a supporter of yours. Spokane's Women's Club needs strong women like you, Mrs. Strahorn."

"Will you join us for dinner at the hotel, Dell?" Robert's invitation carried a sweet note of uncertainty.

Was I strong enough to go back and not lose what I'd gained this summer? *Myself.* I spoke a silent prayer.

"Yes," I said. "I'm sure we'll have more to talk about."

※

We did. There was an ease to the conversation with the Brownes. Mr. Browne spoke Robert's language of finance and banking and development and railroads. We had both attended the University of Michigan, he in law and me in music; Mrs. Browne came from a wealthy Portland family, lumber in her background. She chimed in, spoke of children, grandchildren, suffrage, and added, "Putting us on the gold standard will be very good."

Mr. Browne heard his wife's mention and chose to respond with an honest statement. "I lost money in the Panic of '93. The bank closed."

"But he personally guaranteed the deposits and no one else lost money," Mrs. Browne said.

"I had other businesses. And those people would have been destitute if I hadn't kept my commitments."

I liked his integrity. I could imagine them as friends and realized how much proximity meant to the establishment and sustenance of relationships with friends. I'd walked right back into laughter with Delia and Carrie and Hester and even with Annie Boone, who I hadn't known all that well. But we'd had sustained times, worked through issues with our committee, planned events together. Entertained each other. I'd mostly only chummed with my sisters before Caldwell. Well, Pard and I played too, but in recent years, those excursions had been more obligations than adventures. And in Boston, staying in one hotel all those years, we'd lost the surprise in each other and in our lives. Perhaps Robert's wanting to pick out our home was his way of bringing surprise back into our marriage. And he had waited before acting. I gave him credit for that.

After dinner, we said good evening to the Brownes. "I hope you'll see your way into becoming the mistress of our . . . your home," Mrs. Browne said. "And bring your many talents back to Spokane."

"I'll think about it, certainly," I said. "I understand how a home can mean so much to a family."

Robert stood as they left, then said he'd call a carriage to take me back to my house. "Unless you want to spend the night in my hotel room."

"Are you propositioning me, Mr. Strahorn?"

"I am, Mrs. Strahorn."

"Then let me counter. Why don't you spend the

evening with me at my home? We can talk about acquiring an architect for this house you plan to buy. Is there room for a dog?"

His eyes lit up. "Yes. Oh, yes. Any number of dogs. We can discuss architects . . . among other things." He put his elbow out and I took his arm as he opened the carriage door. He pulled the step down, then took my hand and helped me in. I let him.

≫≪

"I'll join you in a week," I told Robert the next morning. "I want to close up this house or maybe make it available to one of the college teachers. If students have difficulty finding housing, I suspect the teachers may as well."

"Very civic minded." He brushed the crumbs from his mustache. He looked out of place in my little house, his tallness filling it. "The Browne house," he said, changing the subject. "It has three stories. I'd like to see steam heat in it and billiards, a bowling alley and buffet palace in the basement."

"Is it that large? And how much will the renovations cost?"

"I want it to be one of the finest houses between Minneapolis and Portland. But you have to choose it, to make it yours. Ours. Whatever you want, that's what we'll do."

"As I have with my little Caldwell house."

"As you have here." He paused, then looked at me, those black eyes shining. "I was afraid you wouldn't come back. I . . . I brought along the Brownes because I couldn't bear it if I'd had to return to Spokane alone without you or the promise you would return to me."

"And my heart sank when I saw you with an attractive woman on your arm."

"You didn't think that I—"

"I didn't know. Perhaps I'd given you cause, leaving you. But I'm grateful she wasn't a replacement for me."

"There will never be a replacement for you. You're my partner and always will be." He kissed my fingers. "Don't ever doubt it."

"And the cost?"

"Don't worry about it. The budget for remodeling is $100,000."

I gasped. "Robert—"

"We can afford it. I promise. The money is in the bank."

"I'll like to see the accounts."

"Absolutely. Anything you want."

❧❧❧

Robert had arranged for the driver to pick him up so he could catch the train and ride back with the Brownes. I came along and told them all goodbye.

"You will come to tea soon."

383

"Within the month," I told Mrs. Browne. They boarded and Robert and I stood on the platform. He held my hands.

"Why don't I wait and travel with you?" Robert said.

"Go on. Get the papers signed for the house."

"You don't want to look at it first?"

"It was less about having a home of our own than about who I am with you, home or not. I have a better understanding of all that now. I think I've matched the hatch that will make the flow go so much easier."

And so, it did.

❧❦

The Browne house on West First Avenue was astonishing. The structure sat in the trees and we called it The Pines, though others called it Strahorn Pines or simply Strahorns. Mrs. Browne had recommended Kirtland Cutter as an architect. I met him at the house and liked him. He was a few years younger than me, and he took me around by carriage to several homes he and his partner had designed so I could see the possibilities. He'd made a name for himself rebuilding after the big Spokane fire of 1889.

"Sometimes out of flames the new has a chance to flourish," he told me.

"It's good to be able to push away the bad with

something good," I agreed. "We've never lived through a fire."

"Spokane lost the entire downtown. I'd suggest a fourth floor, Mrs. Strahorn." We stood in front of our new home. Pard had left us to it. He was off making plans for his North Coast Railway and another idea, one in Central Oregon near Bend; another not far from Crater Lake.

"A fourth floor?"

"You could then put that bowling alley in the basement. That would be quite a dramatic draw." He often spoke in alliterative phrases. He parted his hair in the middle and didn't always wear a hat, which gave him a boyish appearance. A storm thundered in the east and shafts of color in a linear rainbow broke the horizon. "And steam heat, the first in Spokane."

"I hadn't thought of a dramatic draw being in the basement."

"I see handsome hand-carved beams and wood-work, damask-covered walls with rare oriental rugs, mosaic floor tiles."

"Oh, I know of an old palace in Italy. We might be able to get tiles from there."

"We'll work well together, Mrs. Strahorn. Your husband has said I have a blank check."

"We still need to be . . . wise," I said.

He nodded. "It's likely to take a couple of years to do all we want. I can get sixty carpenters working at once if need be."

"Just so at the end there are enough bedrooms. We'll have many guests, I'm sure." Daisy trotted around, following us.

"Nine or ten bedrooms with the master suite, of course. Will that be enough?"

"I should think so." We walked in the upstairs hall, looked at the maid's room, then made our way to the kitchen. He made notes about the pantry and a small mudroom near the back door. "Daisy will have a place here but of course in our bedroom as well." He smiled. "And I hope to see if Whitworth University students could use rooms. What's the use of a large house without young laughter and the happy barks of a dog within its walls?"

"That's a splendid idea, Mrs. S. What a prize for those students to have time with you."

I hadn't told Robert yet about the student invitations. I would find a new way to mother in this West. A crystal chandelier cast a rainbow across the empty foyer as the architect, Daisy, and I made our way down the grand staircase. I took the rainbow as a sign.

From *Fifteen Thousand Miles by Stage*, vol. 1, by Carrie Adell Strahorn (page xv)

The main purpose has been to record some of the humorous and thrilling events during many years of pioneer travel, leaving out most of the heartaches and disappointments, the excessive fatigue and hardships, and giving more of the rainbow glow to an adventurous life on the frontier.

34

Surprises

I had to live the best chapters for my auto-biography and that was making The Pines our home and sharing it with others.

May 12, 1901

The house became my artistic palette, but I made certain to make and maintain real friendships. I took trips back to Caldwell for weekends, staying with the Blatchleys, fly fishing as an escape. Once or twice I dragged Robert with me, packed a picnic lunch, and we ate on the banks of the Boise. The carpenters worked through the winter months and I was there to cheer them on—and give advice. I bought a horse, a thoroughbred named Morning Song. I called him Song for short.

In Spokane, I joined the Daughters of the American Revolution, as my own history included a great-great-grandfather who had fought for our country. At a suffrage meeting, I met the famous, now elusive and often talked about Helga Estby who, with her daughter, had walked to New York City. We society women admired her greatly, but she was shunned by her Norwegian neighborhood for having left her family to make that historic walk. And I understood she no longer spoke with the daughter who had accompanied her. It all seemed very sad to me. How easily our fortunes could change.

❧❦

I expressed concern about shifting fortunes to Robert one morning when Kirtland (the architect and I were on a first-name basis by then) told me what it would cost to have bathrooms attached to the many bedrooms.

"That's fine," Robert told me. "It's only money." We walked beneath a scaffolding where men had worked earlier in the day on plastering the walls. The house was silent now, with a May sunset turning the world pink inside and out. We'd been at the remodeling for more than a year.

"Yes, but there could be a limit to ours. We've been there before when we slipped out of the hotel in Fairhaven and I don't want to go there again." I'd looked at the books and monitored the expenses, but to my questions about where the money came from Robert had been as elusive as mist. "As much as I don't understand finance, I wonder if you ought to take time and really teach me. I do trust God to take care of us, but still, if we foolishly spend lavishly—"

"Dell." He interrupted me, then stared as though thinking. "Look. We have a blank check

389

from Harriman. For all of this." He spread his hand. "He . . . he bailed us out in Boston."

"The Union Pacific did? You said you'd made some money buying warrants."

"I did. I did. Harriman advanced the money. I've paid him back. And now he's financing my North Coast Railroad and The Pines is collateral—"

"Harriman owns this house?"

"It's in our name. We have the deed. I covered it with his ample assistance paying me for the work I'm doing. But I've also mortgaged it."

I frowned. "Mortgaged it?

"It's a common practice, Dell. Nothing to worry about. But you can't say anything. If we're to get all three railroads here, we can say nothing about Harriman's involvement, because he and James J. Hill of the Great Northern hate each other. It's going to take all my finesse to make this happen. Meanwhile, we do have money of our own but most of this—" he waved his arm again to take in *our* house—"most of this remodeling is Harriman's doing. He agrees we need a lavish place for us to entertain, to bring in the right people, to make Spokane the grand city it'll be. And he wants that major depot here as much as I do. We're partners, but he's the silent one. It's ironic that people call me the Sphinx."

I dropped down onto a pile of fresh-cut lumber. "I've heard that. I thought people were being coy about what they really wanted to say out loud: 'Where is Strahorn getting all his money?' I've had women ask as much in their side-way language. I always tell them you made your money in bonds and warrants in Boston."

"I did. But it was Harriman behind it. I made a killing. We are millionaires, Dell. But these big investments—oh, not the $100,000 in the remodel, that's nothing—I mean the railroad depot, the North Coast Line, my Oregon line I'd like to see, all of that—Harriman's behind it. Remember when we went to Klamath Falls?"

That had been in the '80s.

"It was to touch base with Harriman. His lodge on Pelican Lake. Now, he deposits money in an account. I take it out and put it in our personal account. And I pay our bills with it and bills for the railroad ventures. And I buy up what Harriman wants me to. That's all the finance you really need to know."

"The house? This house?"

"It's ours. But Harriman's money helped and we'll repay him with your grand parties and your being the greatest hostess of the West as we wine and dine investors, sell ideas and dreams. We cannot talk about him. With anyone. Later, when all three lines are here, then it can come out. But not before. But I know I can trust you. You're my partner." He grinned.

I had stopped calling him Pard in Boston. It

seemed out of place when we were in the East, but now I realized I had already known that *we* were no longer the partners we'd once been. Coming to Spokane hadn't changed that. At that moment, I missed my father terribly. I would have liked to have talked with him, sorted out all of this. For five years Robert had been partnering with Edward Harriman of the Union Pacific and I'd known nothing about it.

Perhaps I deluded myself, but what did it really matter where the money came from? Some people made money raising wheat and corn; others by selling fabric at the mercantile. Still others built hotels and made their money through people who stayed in them as we did while we worked on the house. Still others were teachers or librarians or police officers whose salaries came from taxes paid by those who made money enough to pay them. And in return, they paid taxes. It was all as interconnected as a railroad hub with tracks coming from faraway places bringing passengers and goods in and taking others out. And yet . . .

"I'll keep your secret, certainly, Robert. You know that. I feel a little chagrined that it's taken you this long to share it."

"I didn't want to burden you, Dell."

"Information is never a burden, Robert."

He dropped his eyes.

"Well, I will do my best to be that hostess you

envision. If I can sleep in a room with twenty-six men and live to tell about it, I guess I can plan a party for a couple of hundred people and live to tell about that too."

"That's my girl." He hugged me to him.

"But I do have one suggestion. And I do hope it doesn't have to pass through the hands of Mr. Harriman."

"Name it. A lavish mural painted on the living room walls by a renowned artist? Gold-plated furniture in the drawing room? What about leaded-glass windows? Greek statues?"

"I hadn't thought of any of that except the windows, but it's intriguing. No, I want to see if Whitworth University needs student housing. I'd like to keep three of those nine bedrooms to house young ladies' laughter."

"Great idea! You can hire them as maids for the parties."

"No. I won't want to interfere with their studies. We'll hire real maids and chauffeurs and chefs and housekeepers and pay them good wages and keep Mr. Harriman's money in circulation."

※※※

While I knew that all we'd acquired had come because of business, after a time I did see it as a kindness extended by those Robert had worked with and befriended enough to keep us not just afloat but lavishly swimming.

One evening in 1902 at the Davenport Hotel, I arrived for a small party Robert had arranged. "It's a business dinner," he said. "Wear that Giuseffi gown with the blue overlay. It shows off all your curves." He winked.

But when I headed toward the door of the private dining room where I expected to meet our guests, the maître d' directed me to the ballroom.

"Hattie? What are you doing here? And Mary?" *My sisters are here?* I looked around. There stood, applauding, dozens of friends from Caldwell and Hailey and beyond. Robert had sent a private car for the Caldwell crowd and a stage for the Hailey crew to get to Caldwell for the occasion, which he reminded me was our twenty-fifth wedding anniversary. Then in front of everyone, he handed me the key to The Pines.

"It's finished. And it's my anniversary present to the most remarkable woman who ever graced the West. Or East for that matter."

"Where are all the other keys?" I said. "It has two dozen doors."

Everyone laughed as I hoped they would. And, well, I knew it wasn't quite finished and I was a bit irked that Robert had stolen my thunder. But I'd plan the first party *in* The Pines, at least.

We hadn't moved in yet, but I had met the three young women who would be using our "dormitory bedrooms," as classes would be starting soon. They'd brought their trunks and chosen their bedroom views. I looked forward to their presence. But I had yet to hire the maid or chauffeur. The housekeeper and chef were in place.

Kirtland Cutter was at the party, as were the Brownes, whom I'd grown quite fond of, them and their houseful of children. Many of Robert's railroad friends attended (though not the elusive Mr. Harriman, who I wasn't sure had even been to Spokane). But so were the Blatchleys and the Littles and the Gwinns. And Peter and Hester came too. All would be staying at the hotel. I wished I'd known, as I'd have rushed up efforts to have our guests stay in our new home. But I think Robert liked the idea of the surprise and his big moment. It was sweet of him, even if overly dramatic to hand the key to me and make his announcement that "Strahorn Pines" was *his* twenty-fifth wedding anniversary present to me.

"And I have a surprise for you too," I told him. "I didn't expect to be telling you in front of everyone, in case you don't like it."

"I'd like anything you gave me," he said. The crowd applauded.

"I didn't bring it with me, obviously not knowing all of you would be here." I spread my hands to take in the shining faces of our friends. "But it does involve transportation, the heart of Robert's life." He grinned, anticipating. "It's two tickets aboard the ocean liner *Americana*. We are headed to Europe, Mr. Strahorn. That's *my* anniversary present to you."

"I . . . I don't have a passport, Dell."

Everyone laughed and it was funny. This empire builder, developer, massager of the West had never left the country. He needed to.

"One's been ordered for you. We pick it up at the Waldorf Astoria in New York next month. You're not the only one who can plan an event. We'll be gone for six months. And when we come back, we'll be moving into The Pines and all of you are invited back."

Loud applause and cheering erupted. Robert shook his head, kissed me, and whispered, "I can't possibly leave for six months, Dell."

"Yes, you can, Robert," I whispered back. "I've already spoken to the electric plant company director. All will be well. And as for your railroad business, there's the transatlantic telegraph, though I hope to keep you occupied in Florence and Venice and Rome and Pompeii and Paris so that you forget about railroads if only for a few moments a day."

"I don't know—"

"Shh, we have guests." I put my finger to his lips. "We can discuss it later."

He put on his winning smile, waved at everyone, signaled the waiters to bring in dessert, and we mingled at the tables.

The evening was magical. For the memories written across all those faces of my sisters, nieces and their husbands, and precious friends. The senator and Pace Caldwell had come from Leavenworth, Kansas. It had been years since I'd seen them. What machinations Robert had gone through to bring the former Yellowstone ranger (who had offered us the haymow for that cold night) and his wife here I couldn't imagine. But the couple had named their first child after me—a daughter—for "the first woman to have graced our humble home, after my wife, of course," the ranger said. "We felt honored to be invited."

Even a few forgiving souls from Fairhaven arrived.

"We came for you," Frances Larrabee said. "Charles still smarts a little at the Great Northern passing Fairhaven by, and he holds your Robert as a part of that sting. But you, we love." She kissed me on both cheeks. "And it's wonderful to see you again."

"You're still doing well?"

"Marvelously. There's a vote planned next year to make our three towns into one called Bellingham. I hope it passes. You'll have to come celebrate with us if it does."

She didn't dwell long on what was surely a betrayal and Robert's part in it. And when I asked if she was doing well, she spoke immediately of the town, the region, the projects of her husband. It must be in a woman's nature to keep seeking that happy lane and not swerve into the bar ditch of emotion.

It was a night of reminiscence, and in the morning, we gave tours of The Pines. I hadn't thought that I would ever live in a home as grand as a museum where people came to ooh and ahh, but it was fun to listen to Kirtland expound upon his design, why he did what he did, where he acquired the Italian tiles and the gold-leaf light fixtures, that floor-to-ceiling mirror as big as a stage-stop barn door. "That's the Strahorn coat of arms on the fixtures," he noted. All eyes looked upward.

"Isn't Strahorn Scot?" the senator asked. Robert nodded. "They must be turnin' o'er in their graves with their lavish American laddie."

Everyone laughed, including Robert. We'd commissioned an artist to make up the coat of arms. Robert was about to respond when three young women started down the staircase, stopping in a bunch when they saw all the people staring up at them. "Our girls," I said and introduced them. "They are students at Whitworth University and will hold down the fort while we're traveling. Well, they and Mrs. Buchel, our housekeeper. We won't show you the staff's quarters. But Mr. Cutter has given them all a lovely place to live and Mrs. Buchel will not abide wild parties. You girls know that, right?"

"Yes, Mother Strahorn," they said in union and then giggled. I loved the sound.

Later, we said a dozen goodbyes and sent our guests on their way. I'd be meeting up with Hattie and Mary and my nieces for an early dinner at the Davenport Hotel. I had gone upstairs to what would be our bedroom. The bed was there and furniture, but I was still choosing linens to go with the damask walls. Robert had followed me up.

"That was quite a gathering, wasn't it, Dell?"

"Hmm." I held two swatches of woven material against the window wall, checking the color. I planned to pick up what I wanted in Toscana, Italy, at the Busatti Family weaving factory. They'd made uniforms for Napoleon—under duress—and had been weaving linens ever since.

"There isn't any way I can be gone for six months, Dell. You know that."

"No, I don't know that. You've never taken a real vacation. You're not getting any younger and neither am I. You can make it into a working trip if you want. Evaluate the train systems in Europe. See if there are investment possibilities in a Swiss hotel for when you're finished with your adventures here." I tugged at his tie. "Just enjoy being with me, tasting the wines of Tuscany, eating good food. Maybe we can help press grapes. I can imagine you with your pants rolled up and purple feet. Or olives. We can bring back exotic plants for the gardens. I haven't even started with the gardens yet."

"Dell . . ."

"I haven't asked you for much, Robert. This house doesn't even count because it's what you and Harriman want, though I have had a grand time of it. And will. Those girls will see to that. But I want us to have a few months where I'm not in competition with avarice." He winced. "Perhaps that's harsh. I know it's taken that kind of energy, commitment if you will, to bring about all the development you've been a part of. We've been a part of. But for a time, six months at most, let's just be you and me, Dell and Robert, two people who care deeply for each other and find pleasure in being together. Can you give me that?"

What would I do if he said no? Would I go on my own? Would it mean the end to a relationship of love and devotion and the beginning of years when we "worked" together and that was all?

I didn't fill the silence.

"You haven't asked much of me and you have gone the extra mile every time," he finally said. I petted Daisy. "I'll go. I will." Then, turning on a penny to a new subject, "That one," he said, pointing to the beige-and-gray-striped material I held in my hand. "Let's use that linen. I like its boldness."

From *Fifteen Thousand Miles by Stage*, vol. 1, by Carrie Adell Strahorn (page xv)

We shall ever have a kindly feeling in our hearts for the many friends on the frontier who smoothed our thorny way by generous and thoughtful hospitality.

35

Dedicated to Change

We traveled in Europe, spent Christmas in Rome, my birthday in Venice, purchased pottery in Cortona. As old as Europe is, it's been held up by the history of people more conquered than conquerors. But still it endures. I hoped Robert could see that perseverance as we traveled by train hither and yon in those walled cities. Whether the three railroads he so wanted to come to Spokane came or not, life would go on. We would go on. Europe and my faith gave me that.

December 1, 1902

It was indeed a grand trip and Robert did pay good attention to us as a married couple. He allowed me to plan, but during the first months he was like a buffalo in a wagon: confined, uncertain. It reminded me that he had left school young and was basically self-taught in the literary vein. His business instincts had put him into the realm of the very wealthy, but here, with no goal in sight but to vacation, he didn't know what to do.

"Let me plan our schedule," I told him. "You tell me what you'd like to see and I'll make the arrangements."

"I don't really know."

"Then practice spontaneity."

"Last time I was spontaneous, you put me on a cowcatcher across the Dale Creek Canyon and I almost lost my lunch."

"But you talk about it all the time. You loved it."

"I loved having done it, not doing it."

We laughed together at that. He was sweet and attentive and never strayed an eye at the young things in Spain whose dark eyes snapped at him when they danced, nor did he sleep on the ferry we took to Greece like I saw most men doing on the deck. He read and we talked and he asked how my memoir writing fared.

"Good. I write perhaps one thousand words a day, on the days that I write."

"Will I get to read it before you send it to the publisher?"

"Would you want to?"

"I can correct your statistics and edit your long sentences." He grinned.

"You, kind sir, are not one to talk about long sentences or, even worse, long titles. Remember that collection of articles for *The New York World* that New West Publishing wanted?"

He combed his mustache with his fingers,

smiling. "Yes. My old Omaha publisher. The title is *Gunnison and San Juan: A late and reliable description of the wonderful gold and silver belts and iron and coal fields of that newest and best land for prospector and capitalist, Southwestern Colorado: With facts on climate, soil, forests, scenery, game, fish, cities, towns, populations, development, routes, rates of fare, employment, wages, living expenses, etc.: as presented in a series of letters written to the 'New York World.'*"

"I can't believe you can remember that whole thing."

"They're like children. Of course, I remember the title of each book."

"They loved you or they'd have changed that title quick as a flick of a lamb's tail. I've chosen a much simpler title for mine. *Fifteen Thousand Miles by Stage.* Sounds adventurous and romantic, don't you think?"

"Unless you've ridden on a stage." He put his book down onto his lap. "How will you deal with, well, some of the incidents? Like the Boise-Caldwell battle or the Fairhaven disaster?"

"I won't malign you, Robert, or your work, if that's what you're worried about. Nor our friends. If I must say something uncomplimentary, I'll couch it in humor or not name anyone at all. I wrote 'a minister did not support our efforts in Caldwell and both his daughter and son were

404

helping with the Presbyterian Society.' No need to call out his un-Christianlike attitude nor discuss a family wound."

"What about our wounds, yours and mine?"

These words surprised. "They've healed up. No scars."

"Would you tell me if they hadn't?"

I considered those deep black eyes and felt my own begin to water. "I've had a struggle with the Bunting babies, and your subsequent comment that you didn't want a child not of your own making." I inhaled the sea air. "It's one of those irreconcilable issues."

"Important ones."

"Yes. But I have learned, I hope, that the resolution isn't in your doing what I want. Or my pressing you until you do it, resentfully most likely. But in taking responsibility for finding a way to meet that mothering need some other way. The Presbyterian church served that, I think. And now, the girls from the college. I'll . . . like having them around. I have my bulldog." He grinned. "I've grown new flesh around the deepest wounds. As I said, no scars."

He patted my hand. "I do have a place I'd like to go, now that I think of it. To the archaeological site of Ephesus, in Turkey. It hasn't been worked very long, but I've heard that tourists are already visiting there, imagining where Paul was imprisoned when he wrote those letters to the

Ephesians. They hope to uncover the library this year."

"How do you know that?"

He shrugged. "I read the scientific journals. Ephesus is an intriguing mix of science and religion."

"You are a remarkable man," I said. "I'll see what I can arrange."

"If we build Union Station in Spokane, then you can call me remarkable. That's what I'll be focused on for the next few years. That and a short line for Central Oregon. I left them out when we pushed for the southern and the Columbia Gorge routes. Much to do." He picked his book back up, read for a time, then said, "They can call me the Sphinx all they want, but if Harriman is outed as the backer, it'll fall apart because Hill doesn't know the UP is involved. And I don't mind having people think I'm that flush. It's our secret, Dell." I nodded. "You and me. Can I get you a hot chocolate?"

I told him that would be nice and he left to find a steward. I was wrapped up in a blanket, a book on my lap. He trusted me. And I trusted him, though it didn't mean he might not still take us back to that path of poverty with his investments. *A railroad in Central Oregon, through those lava beds?* I wouldn't jump that rope before I saw it come to pass.

I did wonder, though, how I'd handle all the

railroad business in the book. Or how much I'd really say about the ups and downs of our financial life. I decided to be elusive. I'll round the facts rather than set them straight.

When we returned to Spokane, leaving from Liverpool on April 20, 1903, I did set myself down to work on the memoir more diligently. After my mother's death while I was staying to tend to her estate, I found all the letters I'd written to her. I had details I'd forgotten, about traveling to New Mexico and Alaska or the time Pard and I called a steamer purser to put the Caldwells, with whom we were traveling at the time, in the bridal suite but to not say anything to them about it, as they were "sensitive because of their age." The purser told everyone else though, and people were so sweet to them, treating them as newlyweds. Pard never confessed to them, even though they commented on all the little extras that had shown up in their cabin each day, and how people smiled at them. "They must think we're doddering old fools," the senator opined, and even then, Pard never told him.

There were interruptions in my writing, of course, those next years. Robert's North Coast Line was finished. He bought up rights-of-way to railroad depot access in Seattle and other cities, so when the main lines came in, he would benefit.

These purchases he said were from our own pots of money. He started that Central Oregon line while he ran the electric and water companies he owned in Spokane. I couldn't keep track. So I didn't.

I had management concerns of my own. Keeping a good staff proved to be a full-time occupation. Our coachman left us in 1909 shortly after we hired him and trained him in the way we wanted, and we had to find another. Our gardener was still with us, the one we hired in 1909. I planned and executed lavish parties for up to four hundred people who walked the gardens, mingled in the ten rooms open to living (and not sleeping), played billiards in the basement and croquet on the lawns. My chef and I worked together on elaborate settings with agate-handled cutlery at one event, silver at another. I always placed individual crystal vases at each setting, made certain the centerpieces never rose above eye height. The chef's sauces rivaled Paris.

I thought we had a schedule and could resume my writing.

Then my sister Hattie's husband died and we insisted she come live with us. She would have the bedroom overlooking the gardens.

"Beautiful," Hattie said. After we settled her in her room, we moved out onto the little patio each room had. Wrought-iron chairs and tables were designed to match each bedroom theme.

Hattie sighed as she gazed at the azaleas in bloom, the topiary, then sank into a chair. "He was there one minute and gone the next. What did I miss?" She closed her eyes, leaned her head back.

"I'm sure you missed nothing. You're a doctor, not God. You looked after him better than anyone could have."

"He wasn't even fifty." A couple of college girls lounged on the cast-iron benches below us, chattering. Our original three boarders had graduated and we'd had a party for them at The Pines. Each year we'd gained a few more whom I encouraged and helped support.

I held my sister's hand, deciding that when people are grieving it's best to say nothing but sit and listen. Let their sorrow find the words it needs to without any help from well-meaning chattering family or friends.

Hattie was good about turning the tables. "And how are you and Robert?"

"Good. We're good. We have our parallel lives that intersect over dinner or when we have an evening at home. I've given up understanding all the financial matters, and it's a kind of faith I have not in him but in the Divine. If I'm faithful with our tithes and I sing in the choir and look after the needy, well, then it's my prayer that we'll be alright. We were alright in Boston, eventually. And even if we lose it all, we'll be alright."

"God took care of you."

"Yes, though Robert still seems to think it was Harriman." We laughed.

Early in the morning, I began writing again while Robert slept or walked the gardens and we'd have breakfast together. I loved that alone time in the dark hours, that chunk of ore on my desk a reminder. I watched the sun come up and took my reverie back into the past as a kind of vacation. My mother's letters that I'd kept and those I'd written to her and my articles all brought back memories.

And when Harriman died unexpectedly at age sixty-two . . . well, that set us on a course of stabilizing what Robert had worked so hard to put together. But his efforts paid off and Pard's plan to bring those three railroads continued as though the giant of the railroad and financial world was still with us. I was pleased with myself that I hadn't wasted worry on something God had already managed.

⫸⫷

I finished my memoir in 1910, the year we hired additional staff, including a new chauffeur. Frank Weiss came with two children and without a wife. Five-year-old Oscar and one-year-old Willis arrived at the interview with him. All three had red hair, blue eyes, and a dimple on the left cheek only, just like their father. Those boys were Frank's sons.

"I'm so sorry, Mrs. Strahorn. I had arrangements for the lads. A Norwegian girl will watch them, but she got sick today of all days. I couldn't afford to miss this interview. Oscar, you come sit now. See, Willis is behaving." The baby clung to his neck, sneaked looks at me, yawned.

"You're . . . widowed?"

"No, ma'am, sorry to say. My wife up and left. Doctors said she never recovered from Willis's arrival. We've done alright these past months. I have help. Sorry about today."

I had checked his references, which were excellent. And I liked the look of him, the way he gentled Oscar to come sit beside him, patted little Willis while he talked to me. Before the interview was over, I knew I'd hire him and would be getting more than I'd pay for.

Oscar and Willis wheedled their way into our lives and shifted our world. If you must ask how they did so, then you've never been around children much . . . or dogs. My beloved bulldog Daisy had full rein through The Pines, her black-and-white body (a writer's colors) chasing Oscar's scampering feet and holding court when Willis took his first steps across the Italian tiles. We hired a nanny for them. It was a home. My home. Our home, peopled with family. The shortest path to home, I've learned, is with family and friends walking beside us. It was one of the happiest periods of my life.

From *Fifteen Thousand Miles by Stage*,
vol. 1, by Carrie Adell Strahorn
(dedication page)

This book is lovingly dedicated to my
dear husband Robert E. Strahorn whose
constant chum and companion it has been
my greatest joy to be for more than thirty
years in the conquering of the wilderness.

36

What She Didn't Say

Much of the wide-open space we'd traveled through by stage is gone. The cowboys are few. The sheep even fewer. I only saw one herd of buffalo and it held up the train, but they went the way of the wilderness too. Indians are gone or rounded up and put on reservations. Seems a shame. I don't like to think of our part in all that. Manifest Destiny was the war cry that removed them and brought settlers as though it was a right. My mind has found a place to lament those passings as well as celebrate the future of the West. I hope my memoir delights others as it has me. Only Daisy's passing marred my joy. I miss her.

July 1, 1910, at The Pines

I began work with the publisher, hoping *Fifteen Thousand Miles by Stage* would come out the following year, 1911. I decided to only write about our lives between 1877 and 1880 for volume 1 and cover 1880 to 1898 for volume 2, though we'd release them both at the same time. I didn't want a six-hundred-page book. Who would read that, let alone hold it? If they held such a book at night in bed, it could break their noses when dropped on a face that sleep overtakes. Or tries to. I wouldn't write about The Pines or of our lavish life in 1910 or 1911 either. And I wouldn't tell stories of Oscar and Willis sleeping in their quarters above the carriage house or how I taught them to ride our horses. Nor how they loved our second Daisy and how she loved them back. No sense in dwelling on an opulent life in a memoir about discovering the West in a stagecoach. Stories of well-fed children putting sticky fingers onto the French artist's murals in the large living room and ordering Daisy to "b-flat" had no place in my memoir. Neither did the Halloween party where we dressed the Greek statues in witches' hats and cowboy chaps. Better to let the reader linger over the strength and resilience of those pioneer women looking after their babes, doing whatever it took for them to keep alive, a task made more difficult when their men read one of Robert's books and left the green of Kentucky to head to the harsh lands of Montana or Idaho or Oregon. Besides, it wasn't meant to be a book about me but about the West.

The publication process wasn't a great surprise, since I'd helped with Robert's books, checking facts, writing up tables of contents, and whatnot. For *Fifteen Thousand Miles*, I collected dozens of photographs to include. Then Robert got the great idea to put sketches in the book for events we didn't have photographs to illustrate.

"Like the time my horse went head over heels into that ravine, remember that?"

"No. Because it happened while you were in the Sioux war and I wasn't there," I reminded him.

"You included the story in the book though." He had yet to read the manuscript, but I'd shared snippets with him.

"Because it was a fascinating example of the West and what can happen. Who could I get to illustrate it?"

"That cowboy artist from Montana. His works are selling well. C. M. Russell. His young wife manages his business now."

"Behind every successful man . . ."

"Is a railroad magnate willing to loan money."

"Loan?"

"A figure of speech." He patted my hand. "Why don't you contact Russell? I think they're in Great Falls."

I did that. Then I sent the artist the manuscript and identified a few places where I thought a sketch would enhance the work. He had suggestions of his own, including one I didn't really like, the one of me being scraped off my horse, wounding my pride. But he captured so much. The sadness of a broken pioneer wagon. The rugged cowboy branding. And in the sketch he created of that business near Spokane with the sick Indian woman whom I gave stomach powders to (and her husband said he'd trade some horses for me on the morrow), he made me look as lithe as my niece instead of the "fluffy woman" I always was. I did like Russell's rendition of me as thin.

Charles ended up doing fifty sketches for the first volume alone. And our artist friend received nice recognition when the *New York Times* review came out. That same review said very kind things about my work and called me "The Mother of the West." Robert added that I was "The Queen of the Pioneers."

I wasn't really. Women like Mrs. Bunting were.

❧❦

Robert took the publication and the acclaim that followed in stride. And for our thirty-fourth anniversary, he planned a publication party at the Davenport Hotel. I didn't have to do a thing, though I would have liked to. After all, hospitality was my gift and sharing The Pines was my serving platter.

But that night he marveled us all when he presented me with a sterling-silver-and-gold-covered copy of my book. He'd had a stagecoach embossed on the front, matching the Russell drawing on my cover. And 174 guests had already signed the six sterling silver pages. He'd had to get those signatures in advance of the event so the engraving plates could be made. Robert had again sent that special car to bring our friends from the Wood River Valley to celebrate. There were plenty of oohs and ahhs over his gift and how clever and sweet he was to have planned for it. He also said some of the kindest words of me he'd ever spoken, that he 'couldn't have done what he'd done without me.'"

Later, my oldest sister Mary said to me, "Robert always has a way of putting himself as the lead horse, doesn't he?" She and Hattie and I sat in the living room at The Pines, lounging on the leather. Robert had gone up to bed and I held the heavy silver book on my lap, my fingers tracing the names.

"What do you mean? He was sweet to have planned the party and arranged for this. He's proud of me and I of him."

"Oh, I know. But this should have been your night, your big event. You wrote the book," Mary said. "Two, for goodness' sake, and they've gotten marvelous reviews." She picked at a silk thread of her burgundy dress. "Tonight, everyone raved about how thoughtful *he* was. Your memoir and you writing it is what should have held the floor. Not Robert's adoring gift."

"He loves doing splashy things," I defended.

"I don't doubt it. But why not hold the party here, let you enjoy doing what you do best, making everyone feel welcome so they ooh and ahh at what you've done—the marvelous books and holding court in your finally permanent lovely home."

"I don't mind playing second fiddle to Robert. He's my Pard," I said. I realized I was telling the truth. I admired my husband.

"You don't have to play cheery with me, Carrie." I must have looked chagrined, because she changed her tone and said, "Oh, never mind. Now is not the time for me to express my big-sister views. It was a lovely party and the book is an extravagant acknowledgment of both your publication and your adventurous lives together. It's a very good remembrance of your experiences. I look forward to sharing it with our friends who only half believed the stories I told them of my visits to you."

"My friends thought I was exaggerating like Mark Twain too," Hattie said. "They still think the West is a foreign country."

"I suppose it is—or was," I said. "But we're civilized now." Our second Daisy did her little snorting sniffs as she waddled over to lie at my feet. "We have the same ups and downs as any couple anywhere who writes a symphony of their lives, with crescendos and adagios repeating the themes."

"How are Robert's businesses doing these days?" Mary asked.

"Fine. We're fine." I wasn't going to tell either of my sisters of that little nudge I felt with his work to build the Oregon line out of Klamath Falls. I loved Crater Lake, the jewel in Oregon's crown, but I wished he would have kept his interests in Spokane instead of spreading himself so thin. But that was Robert and always would be. A wife comes to accept that or spend her life suffering.

Those next years were full of parties, managing a staff, working to remember history through the Daughters of the American Revolution, singing in the First Presbyterian choir. I'd helped the Women's Club raise funds for a new clubhouse but stepped away as things got rolling. It was their project and I didn't want my presence to dominate. Mary would likely add to that sentence, "Unlike Robert who loved being the center of attention" and who perhaps did see everything as a promotional opportunity.

The decade that followed was a challenge to him. The Great Northern put many impediments in Robert's way as he tried to build his Oregon, California, and Eastern line, which kept putting him further and further into debt. But of course he never ought to have started it without millions of dollars to invest. We simply didn't have that depth of personal wealth. But I'd given up trying to hold my "lead horse" back. He was the one who set the pace and I trotted along. But I was trotting in quite a lovely setting those years. I didn't travel with him anymore, as I had two young boys to spoil and a mansion to run.

Robert had another huge success when Union Station was finished and three major lines claimed their railroad dynasty with Spokane as their center. Robert got to pound in the golden spike during a big celebration where he gave a speech and train whistles pierced the air. It was 1914 and I was quite proud of him. The second printing of my memoir came out that year too. Robert's coast-line was complete—well, his and Harriman's—and he truly was the railroad builder he'd always wanted to be.

Of course, it was not enough for Robert, and that next year, he extended his investments in Central Oregon near Bend, a line he hoped would meet up with California tracks and link western Idaho and ultimately the East. He hadn't asked my advice about that. We were no longer "partners" in that sense. I had my world in The Pines, which I thoroughly loved, and he had his schmoozing the halls of investors.

Hattie had moved to Los Angeles to stay with her daughter there, but the year Robert planned a big "Railroad Days" event in Klamath Falls, she came up. We'd seen each other in Illinois the month before for Mary's funeral. The map of our older sister was gone. I was the elder sister now.

I took the train south to turn over the shovel of dirt that marked the beginning of the next phase of the line. Thirty miles of the 360 miles Robert had to lay between Klamath Falls and Ontario, Oregon—another town we'd started—was complete. He'd bought a locomotive, a passenger car, boxcars, and flat cars for freight that could be used between California and Klamath Falls. He called it the beginning of the Strahorn Central Oregon System. Robert always loved a party, with him giving speeches and the city fathers clapping his back. I suppose he thought looking prosperous would invite investors, maybe even James J. Hill himself. But Hill was as wily as Harriman of the UP. Buying his own rights-of-way before Robert could.

Hattie and I and Robert took a side trip to Crater Lake. Seeing it again reminded me of what a glorious life I'd led. One should never die before seeing such a sight as that blue water. We stayed at the Lodge that had opened the year before, but I had seen that wonder of the world before a building broke the cauldron's timbered edge.

I returned to Spokane without Robert, who had "things to do" in Klamath Falls. But I didn't mind. The staff at The Pines became my family. The Weiss boys were so much a part of our lives that when the 1920 census taker came around in

January of the new decade, the two boys were listed as "sons of Robert and Carrie." I didn't correct it. Frank, their father, was identified too as a resident, which he was. He was a good dad. He never missed a beat putting those boys first. He was the best chauffeur. Perhaps the genuine affection I felt for Oscar (already fifteen) and Willis (eleven by then) showed itself while the census taker wrote down our housekeeper's name, the first and second maids' names, and the cook's, as well as Robert's and my legal name, Carrie A. I suspect Robert liked his occupation listed as "railroad builder." I liked seeing Oscar and Willis listed as "sons of Robert and Carrie." They weren't those precious twins Kate and Kambree, but they were here for me to love.

It was leaving the boys that pained me more than anything when Robert came to tell me the news I never hoped to hear. "Hill is a wily businessman, Dell." Robert paced our bedroom while he talked, running his hands through his hair. It was 1920. "He owes nothing, never took bank loans to build his railroads, never got involved in accepting government land. He did it on his own. He can hold out and keep me from getting that track laid out of Bend." I petted Daisy as she lay on the settee beside me. She didn't usually jump up there. She was already ten years old and I didn't encourage furniture assumption by canines. She must have sensed something I hadn't and I let her stay, her pudgy body radiating heat through my silk Chinese dressing gown.

We'd had a lovely dinner with friends where Robert railed about the Great Northern owners. He was particularly agitated that night. I did what I usually did: listened, never said "I told you so."

The small royalty payment from my book each month had been a boon to my sense of security and independence, and I still had funds in the Marengo Bank.

I should let old silver tarnish in private. Still, I've grown fond of telling the whole story. For it isn't the trouble or the riches we have in life but how we respond to them that gives life meaning. At least I think that's so. It took me a time to get there, but I have.

Finally, Robert pulled a chair up to sit in front of me, leaned forward, his forearms on his knees. "Dell. Carrie." He cleared his throat. His eyes looked tired, puffy around the edges. We were both getting on in years, already in our sixties. My hair was piano-key white. "I've got to raise more capital to pay construction costs for the line." He continued, "Hill's waiting for me to admit that I'm undercapitalized, have no more investors, have maxed out my own credit line at the banks. He wants to buy it cheap and finish the line himself. I can't let that happen."

I waited for him to say he was going to sell the line. The dog looked up at me with her watery eyes and lapped my cheek. "Oh, you." I patted her white head.

"Dell. The construction loans on the short line are due and what Hill offered isn't enough to cover them. I've—we've—got to sell The Pines."

I blinked. "Sell The Pines? But . . ."

"I know, I know. It's terrible. I'm terrible. I thought I had it covered. I mortgaged it. That lava rock outside of Bend, it's a killer for laying tracks. Once the line's operational, I'll make a fortune. I'll buy back The Pines, but the note is due now. And, well, Hill. That Hill." He shook his head.

"Sell our home? Where—where will we go?" I could feel my heart stop beating, I really could. But, of course, it kept right on.

"San Francisco. I wouldn't ask you to stay here and be forced every day to explain our, well, our circumstances. And I fully intend to buy it back. I've got a couple of ideas already, but the bank, well, you know banks. I just need another investor or I could sell to Hill, but he'd only pay me a pittance of my investment. We'll plan a little extended vacation in San Francisco. I've got rooms for us there. And a little cash. We'll be comfortable."

"Another Single Room Occupancy arrangement."

"It's temporary. And Hattie can come up from Los Angeles and stay with you when I'm back here working things out."

"Yes, my family can help heal the wounds, as you'll be occupied."

"I'm so sorry, Dell. I am." He reached for my hands, but I subtly moved them to bring Daisy onto my lap. "I did everything I could to prevent this."

No, you didn't. But blame and accusation do no good. Those twin emotions only keep one from a commitment.

He sat beside me then, pushing Daisy out of the way. I'd have preferred the dog's comfort at that moment. But I did what I always did: gave comfort as I could. Robert leaned his head on my shoulder. I patted his back.

"I really do have good ideas. I will buy this back from the bank, before they can ever try to sell it. I will, Dell. I will. This is so difficult for me."

"I know you'll do your best," I said.

"Can you ever forgive me?"

"It's what I signed on for, Robert. For richer, for poorer."

"That's my girl. I knew you'd understand." He sat up to kiss my cheek; never commented on my tears. My eye caught that chunk of ore I'd gotten so many years before. I was capable of so much. I needed to remember that.

Epilogue

I write this not in the room where I wrote most of *Fifteen Thousand Miles by Stage* in my beautiful Pines but in a Single Room Occupancy hotel in San Francisco. Hattie is with me and her daughter. I haven't been feeling so well, lots of swelling of my ankles and my kidneys tiring. Very annoying. Robert is in Spokane or maybe Klamath Falls or back east. He'll join us for Christmas, I'm sure. He writes that he has a plan to buy The Pines back. We'll see. I have my scrapbook with photos of that home, my horses, our trip to Europe. I love showing it to any who will listen. It brings me joy to look at these memories. I have had my time there, a glorious time, but home is where family gathers and where love blossoms even in a desert.

Willis and Oscar have visited their "mother," which pleases me to no end and if I'm well enough next spring, Hattie and I will travel to Clatsop Beach in Oregon and the boys will join us. Our rooms here are of a much better quality than the one we shared in Boston all those years ago, and Daisy loves the settee. And certainly, my sleeping room excels over the stage stops of my earlier days. After all, it's a hotel suitable for a lady and her housedog, without the presence of twenty-six western men. My chunk of ore reminding me of what I'm capable of sits beside my bed. In our many moves, I lost the crocheted bird, our marriage favor. Like a good Presbyterian, I have seen my way clear to supporting Robert in whatever his endeavors have been. But I'll support my own desires as well. I write a little, even sold an article to the San Francisco *Chronicle*, a travel piece for young ladies about how to keep their decorum in the western climes but to still allow themselves to have a grand life and as much exhilaration as comes from riding out front in a steam engine's cowcatcher. I've added a few suggestions about the importance of staying in the happy lane.

We have a splendid view—when the fog lifts—as I'm sure it will. It always does.

Carrie Adell Green Strahorn, 1922

Author's Notes
and Acknowledgments

Years ago, my sister (deceased these twenty-one years) shared an audiotape of a trip she'd taken with her family, commenting at various sites they visited in the West. At one point, my sister stopped the tape and turned to me and said, "I can't believe I sound all sweet and light with what I'm saying when what I was actually feeling at that moment was that I wanted to disappear." I was struck by how one could make a tape—or write a memoir—of sweetness and light while beneath the words were feelings much different. I never forgot those moments with her as she spoke of what was really happening for her on that journey.

Then several years after that, a faithful reader, Carol Oxley, told me about *Fifteen Thousand Miles by Stage 1877–1880* and *1880–1898*, written by Carrie Adell Strahorn, illustrated with Charles Russell sketches, and published in 1911. The two-volume memoir received critical acclaim, sold through its first printing with a second edition issued in 1914, and earned Carrie a place in western history. Her adventurous life on the road with her writer/railroad advance man/investor Robert Strahorn won national appeal and she was called "Mother of the West" and "Queen of the Pioneers." Her story of being a Victorian lady traveling by stage, rail, horseback, steamship, and walking, too, piqued my interest. Carol loaned me her copies that I read and remembered to return. I then ordered my own reproduction copies and put them in my possible story pile.

Fast-forward twelve years. I read the books again and had this unanswered question: What was really going on behind the scenes of that memoir? Was Carrie sharing how she really felt or was she like my sister, only sharing the sweet and light? I decided to read between the lines to find out.

My thanks go to Carol Oxley, who occasionally asked how that book was coming. My thanks also go to CarolAnne Tsai, a researcher who came into my life at the right time and who found an array of resources, from a student's thesis on Carrie to portions of Robert's own memoir written when he was ninety years old to census records and dozens of newspaper accounts of this fascinating couple. CarolAnne's assistance continues to be invaluable and I thank her for her encouragement and her friendship.

CarolAnne also put me in touch with John Caskey, author of several books, including *The Amazing Strahorns: Literary Pioneers of the American West*. I thank him for his insights and willingness to arrange events to celebrate Carrie in Spokane. Railroad financing was complex, especially in those days of the titans who competed for access to the West. Mr. Caskey is a historian of note about Spokane and its railroad history and the Strahorns. I'm grateful to him.

I'm also grateful to Jan Boles, archivist at the College of Idaho, begun as the Caldwell College, a Presbyterian university. She shared photographs from Carrie's scrapbook and identified other resources about the Strahorns and long-time college president William Judson Boone. A lecture given by Louie Attebery, professor emeritus of English, at a reunion of Finney Hall at the College of Idaho in 2010, provided a colorful history of the institution, Reverend Boone's theology (he was a botanist comfortable with both "Darwin and Deuteronomy"), and a physical description that brought Carrie's mentor to life (https://www.collegeofidaho.edu/about). John Lundin and Stephen Lundin's paper "Strahorn, Robert E. (1852–1944)—Railroad Promoter in Washington and the Northwest" (available at historylink.org/file/10159) gave me the best understanding of the railroad machinations and Robert's part in them. Thank you to musician Mary Ostrander as well, for her loan of the "b-flat" command. These historians, writers, archivists, and musicians made this novel richer, but any errors or omissions are all mine.

In addition to thanking my editor, Andrea Doering, who always asks the best questions and gives the best direction, I also want to thank the Revell team in totality and especially Barb Barnes, Michele Misiak, Karen Steele, Cheryl Van Andel, Hannah Brinks, and so many others who help bring these stories to life and to readers. You are all amazing. My prayer team, Judy Schumacher, Carol Tedder, Judy Card, Loris Webb, Gabby Sprenger, and Susan Parrish, are stalwart companions on this writing journey and I am grateful. My friend Hilary Rothert provided books and discussions about the lavish entertaining Robert and Carrie would have hosted, and while the novel does not go into much detail, the requirements of serving four hundred people is alarming for those of us not born with hostessing genes.

Leah Apineru of Impact Author continues to make my social media presence available, along with my website manager Paul Schumacher. Thank you both tons! Janet Meranda has been my special copy reader and I am grateful for the catches she makes in what I always hope is a flawless manuscript I turn in! And to my readers, my gratitude. Where would an author be without dear readers? And to my most faithful reader, researcher, map maker, and true partner, my husband Jerry, thank you.

My readers always like comments to distinguish

fact from fiction, so I share these few while encouraging reading of John Caskey's book and Carrie's memoir. Carrie was an early graduate of the University of Michigan in Ann Arbor; she did marry the former fiancé of her college friend whom she hoped to nurse to health but did not; Carrie's father was a doctor in Marengo, Illinois, near Chicago, one of the first to use anesthetic as a military surgeon west of the Mississippi. Her younger sister Hattie became a doctor and her older sister Mary was a mother and journalist. Carrie did publish letters and articles in various newspapers across the country both as Dell Strahorn and as A. Stray and Emerald Green. Carrie did remain a lady, and her good sense of humor and wit saw her through some trying occasions.

I relied on Therese O'Neill's *Unmentionable: The Victorian Lady's Guide to Sex, Marriage and Manners* to give me insight about how difficult it would have been to be a woman of child-bearing age wandering the true wilderness of the West in the 1870s and 1880s. Such intimacies weren't spoken of in Oregon Trail diaries nor in Carrie's book. I kept Carrie's musing about such issues in this novel PG rated.

Carrie's stories in her memoir inspired my own speculation about them, seeking her motivation, intent, feelings about the events. For twenty-five years she traveled across the West, always trying to remain a lady with her long skirts, bustle, and hat. The incident with the runaway stage and the man who felt compelled to ride seventy miles in the opposite direction of where he'd planned to travel is in her memoir. The Yellowstone experience, the twenty-six men, being the only woman traveling during the snowstorm of 1877–78 are all included in her memoir. Her experience with electricity in Laramie she notes as occurring in 1878, but electricity came first to Wyoming in Cheyenne in 1883. I left her memory intact, even though it must have been a later trip she recalled. Carrie's father did send her the dog who loved tramps and Carrie was a good shot with a pistol. Her sisters often spent time with her in the West. Her singing abilities and trips to Europe are all as reported.

The offering of the twins to the Strahorns was also a fact, though I gave the twins their names, loaned from two contemporary girls. Both girls' families won the right to name a character in one of my books as an auction item for a fundraiser. Kaitlyn Miles's family supported "Raise the Roof" for a Coos Bay, Oregon, school district facility. Kambree Palmer's father's boss, Chip Wahlberg, purchased the auction item to support the Asotin, Washington, library and gave the naming right to the Palmers. Interviews with each girl gave me a picture to help create those tiny twins and project their love of reading and music onto their characters.

Robert did call her "Dell"; she called him Pard, but she also called him Robert and in letters to her mother referred to him as Robin. I decided using Robin as well as other names would be too confusing. As John Caskey noted, "Dell" and "Pard" are not particularly affectionate terms. I chose to have Carrie write her comments as Carrie, as that's how she signed her memoir. While I read only excerpts from Robert's unpublished memoir, *Ninety Years of Boyhood*, it is noted that he devoted but three sentences to his beloved "Dell":

> Here intervened the first real crushing, heartrending sorrow of my life, the sudden death of my deeply loved, superb wife, who had been my inseparable companion, my greatest inspiration and staunchest support for nearly fifty years. The earth, which at times seemed only dangerously slipping before was now indeed gone from under. How attempt to picture the glory surrounding, permeating and emitting from such angelic womankind?

Robert remarried a year after Carrie's death in 1925 and in that same memoir wrote twenty-six pages about his second wife and their two years of travel in Europe. He was his own kind of entrepreneur.

The sickness that pervaded Robert's life did affect their travel and Carrie's looking after her husband, deciding where to travel to get him well. Robert had the mumps (reported in the Omaha paper) and tuberculosis; he was a journalist during the Sioux campaigns and did seem to have an affinity for going into business with military men. The couple had no children, but in reading between the lines, that was not as Carrie wished it. Her comments in her memoir regarding children are poignant and defensive if she saw inappropriate treatment by others of children.

Upon Carrie's death, Robert donated $35,000 to the City of Marengo for a Strahorn library in honor of Carrie and another $65,000 to fund the library building at the College of Idaho in memory of Dell Strahorn. Since 1967, the building has been called Strahorn Hall. In 1970, the Daughters of the American Revolution in Spokane researched Carrie's ancestry, hoping to name a chapter after her. However, it was named instead for Carrie's great-grandfather, Jason Babcock, who served during the Revolutionary War. In 2013, the DAR chapter encouraged and published the Caskey-Victor book *The Amazing Strahorns*, which gave me great details and wisdom into this couple and is another memorial to Carrie.

The Strahorns did indeed "birth" towns in the

West, including Caldwell, Idaho; North Weizer, Idaho; Ontario, Oregon; and Shoshone Falls, Idaho. The latter had been a stage stop, but the Strahorns developed it into a railroad and tourist terminus at the "Niagara of the West." The Idaho and Oregon Land Development Company, Robert's first investment company, bought the town of Hailey, Idaho, and owned the power and water plant. They expanded Hailey by building the hotel near the hot springs that became a tourist attraction. The failures at Fairhaven are as described, as is the humiliating departure and the Strahorn years in Boston. Robert was a successful writer, promoter, and some said a bit of a flimflam man, in addition to being charming and a visionary. The lost manuscript in Fairhaven is also true.

I believe that Carrie's greatest joy was in organizing the Presbyterian women's group of Caldwell that went on to raise money for a church and to call a pastor. It was identified as the only Presbyterian church to be started by women without the assistance of male elders and without the benefit of first having a missionary. When the church was accepted into the Wood River Presbytery, men were of course the elders and trustees. The women presented were the original committee, except for the addition of Hester Adeline Brown. Hester was named for the grandmother of Hestor (spelling changed for her descendant) Lindberg, who won the auction at First Presbyterian Church, Bend, Oregon, to help renovate the church's commons area. Hester became a friend to Carrie along with actual historical persons. The Blatchleys did turn their home into a dormitory and later donated money to the College of Idaho for new facilities.

Carrie's other great joy was The Pines. She rarely traveled with Robert after they moved into the mansion, finding a full life entertaining and riding her horses and enjoying her bulldog. She kept a scrapbook of her travels and of The Pines. How she chose to leave it is as portrayed.

Robert did throw anniversary parties for Carrie and he was so pleased with the success of her memoir that he had the silver edition made of the cover and back with the 174 guest signatures engraved. The artifact is in the collection at the Museum of Arts and Culture in Spokane. Charles Russell drew the illustrations.

The census information of 1900 is as described in both Spokane and Caldwell. Census takers often wrote down everyone at home, which might include visitors from afar. But in Caldwell, it is notable that Carrie was listed as "Head of Household," usually indicating there were no other occupants. The Weiss boys being "children of the Strahorns" is from the actual census record of 1920. Clearly, they were the sons of the chauffeur who for some reason were identified as the Strahorn children. Carrie didn't correct the assumption.

The Strahorns bought the Browne house and remodeled it under the direction of Kirtland Cutter, a prominent architect in the West. Known as The Pines, it had twenty-two rooms, electricity, steam heat, a bowling alley and buffet area in the basement, Italian tiles, a French artist mural, and so much more. It was a lavish and lush mansion tended by a housekeeper, first and second maids, a chef and chauffeur. After the Strahorn deaths, The Pines was converted into apartments and purchased by the Eastern Washington Historical Society in 1970. It was placed on the historic register in 1974 and then torn down the same year to provide room for expanded facilities and parking. For a more detailed history and a photograph, visit http://properties .historicspokane.org/property/?PropertyID=2017.

Robert made money and Robert lost money. He successfully built the North Coast short line as he had hoped, but he then invested in the Oregon California and Eastern Railway and the land-scape demands and the impediments put up by James J. Hill drained Robert of money and the ability to move forward. Large railroad magnates like Harriman and Hill would often wait for the failure of these short line investors, then swoop in and buy them for pennies on the dollar. This is what happened to Robert in 1920.

It's said that Robert did buy back The Pines, but Carrie never lived there after her and Robert's move to San Francisco sometime around 1920. Carrie died in San Francisco in 1925 of kidney failure. She was seventy-one. Robert had her ashes brought back to Spokane and a widely attended service was held for her at the First Presbyterian Church. The newspaper account of the funeral noted that Carrie's friend Reverend Boone gave the eulogy in which he commented on her ability to have "good cheer in unfavorable circumstances" and of "her power to recover from defeat." Her ashes were placed in a mausoleum at Riverside Memorial Park. It is the same mausoleum where Robert placed his second wife's ashes and left word for his own to be placed there too. He was frugal in death if not in life. Robert died in 1944.

Carrie did become famous in her time and I felt the Nye poem in the front matter speaks to that fame. Once Carrie remembered what she could do, and did it, she captured a history and a people that would otherwise have been lost to us. I, for one, am grateful. I hope you will be too as you read my version of her life and perhaps seek out her memoir, *Fifteen Thousand Miles by Stage*.

READER'S GUIDE

1. What was Carrie's desire in wanting to live a full life? Did she achieve her hopes and dreams? What propelled her forward and what got in her way?

2. Carrie quotes Von Goethe: "Knowing is not enough, we must apply. Willing is not enough, we must do." Do you agree? Why or why not?

3. How would you describe the relationship between Carrie and Robert? Was it a "good marriage"? What was good about it? What was troubling, if anything?

4. Did Carrie do the right thing in how she responded to the Bunting twins?

5. Could Carrie have put down deeper roots in places besides Omaha, Caldwell, and Spokane while living in the Single Room Occupancy hotels? How might she have done that?

6. How did Carrie's spiritual journey inform her physical journey and vice versa?

7. What steps did Carrie take to fulfill her hopes to be a parent, to have a home of her own, to be her own person? What else might she have done?

8. Have you had to move often and try to

make new friends? What helps? What hasn't worked?

9. Why didn't Carrie want to write letters and pass them around to a group of women to share experiences about books? Have you ever done something like that to maintain friendships across the miles?

10. What of Carrie's life speaks to you today?

Author Interview

What was the hardest thing about writing a memoir within a memoir?

JK: "A memoir," wrote Brenda Peterson and Sarah Jane Freymann in *Your Life Is a Book: How to Craft and Sell Your Memoir*, "is a love story. It's the story we tell ourselves about ourselves." When I finally realized Carrie's love story was about the West rather than about her life with Robert, it made writing about their lives easier. I could explore their relationship as the memoir she might have written if she'd been free to do so.

How did you decide to organize the material the way you did?

JK: Originally, the format began with the quote from the actual memoir, *Fifteen Thousand Miles by Stage*. But in revisions, at the wise suggestion of my extraordinary editor, Andrea Doering, I put those quotes at the end. I hoped that the reader would see what Carrie hadn't been able to say in the memoir by reading what *I'd* written. This change meant I had to write journal entries to begin each chapter to allow readers to know where in time and space that chapter began in Carrie's mind but without giving too much away. Carrie's musings *about* her life—the main text of *Everything She Didn't Say*—sometimes resulted in my choosing different quoted passages at the end. It was complicated, but Carrie kept teaching me more things even in the revision stage. Covering forty years of her life with only twenty years covered in her memoir was also a challenge that I hope I met.

Did writing your own memoir help or hinder you in writing this novel?

JK: My memoir, *Homestead*, was my first published book in 1991. It was about following your heart even when the world around you thinks you've gone off the deep end. We left suburbia and professional jobs and moved to 160 acres known as Starvation Point in the wilds of Oregon in the 1980s, one hundred years after Carrie's memoir was written. I had decided in the beginning that I would not complain or whine in my memoir despite the trials and tribulations of building a life at the end of eleven miles of dirt road, seven miles from our mailbox. So I appreciated at some level Carrie's always "staying in the happy lane." But I would have preferred more insights from her trials, more epiphanies that others might learn from. I also understood her reluctance to share the pain. It made me sensitive to what poet Emily Dickinson meant when she wrote, "Tell all the truth but tell it slant." There was also my sister's startling stories about how her audiotape offered landscape details in a happy tone while burying the difficulties she faced in relationships on her journey. I wanted always to be authentic but also didn't want to harm others in my writing of them. I share that desire with Carrie.

You've written many novels based on the lives of real historical women. What appeals to you about them and how did Carrie fit into that?

JK: I've long been drawn to biographies and the rich experiences of women who went before us, both the ordinary and the better known. But finding detailed material about historical women is very difficult. I can locate information about their husbands, fathers, brothers, and sons, but little of them. This paucity of detail about women led Virginia Woolf to write that "women's history must be invented . . . both uncovered and made up." That's what I do, uncover and make up. But there is always an unanswered question that puts me onto a particular woman. Sixty-six-year-old Tabitha Moffat Brown (*This Road We Traveled*) being named the Mother of Oregon *after* she headed west on the Oregon Trail intrigued me. How did that happen? For Carrie, I wanted to know what it would have been like to travel all those miles by stage, but more, what did she have to give up? And why didn't she talk about it? What might she have said if it had been her memoir and not a story about the West?

You offered the ability to name a character as a fund-raising item. How do you incorporate such names?

JK: It actually adds to the challenge of creating characters that for some are as real as the historical ones. Of course, they are all fiction. In this novel, I was able to incorporate three, and the historical documents gave rise to where I might place them in the plot. There were really those two twins, unnamed in Carrie's memoir but very important, as this was one of the few times when Carrie's deep longing comes through. Adding a friend named Hester to the Presbyterian women seemed a natural fit too. It's my belief that the Caldwell community gave Carrie her greatest joys and perhaps greatest sorrows. Besides, it's a way for my stories to bring a little generosity to nonprofit organizations I see as doing good things.

What can we expect in a Jane Kirkpatrick novel?

JK: Let's see. No profanity. I like to challenge myself to see if I can create the emotions that might bring a character to swear without doing so. No sex, though passion. I have an agreement with my characters: I won't reveal any of their sexual idiosyncrasies and then they agree not to reveal any of mine! I spend a lot of time choosing the epigrams in the front because I think that's the first chance I have to tell a reader what I think the story is about. But it's also the last chance, because once a reader reads the book, they'll decide what it's about. And finally, I weave four threads of a story: landscapes, relationships, spirituality, and work. All these threads are critical to the text for me. I also want to leave readers feeling hopeful.

Do you have any particular strategies that help you write a book a year?

JK: I follow a practice taken from a book called *Structuring Your Novel* by Robert Meredith and John Fitzgerald that asks me to answer three questions before I start: (1) What is my intention? (What's this story about?) (2) What is my attitude? (What do I feel deeply about?) And (3) What is my purpose in writing this story? (How do I hope a reader might be changed?) I may take many pages to write the answers but try to get it down to three sentences each. I post them at the top of my computer so when I get lost or start to listen to Harpies telling me that writing this book was a terrible idea, I can look up and see what I thought at the time this story was about, what I cared about, and what's my purpose. That way I can keep going.

Where do you live? And have you traveled to the places Carrie traveled to?

JK: I live in Central Oregon now, near Bend, the site of the fateful short line that ultimately was Robert's greatest challenge. I have traveled to a great many of the places Carrie shared in her memoir. I think Yellowstone as Carrie saw it would have been grand indeed.

How many books have you written and what is your favorite?

JK: Carrie's story is my thirty-first, and my favorite is the one I'm working on now.

Jane Kirkpatrick is the *New York Times* and CBA bestselling author of more than 30 books, including *All She Left Behind*, *The Memory Weaver*, *This Road We Traveled*, and *A Sweetness to the Soul*, which won the prestigious Wrangler Award from the Western Heritage Center. Her works have been finalists for the Christy Award, Spur Award, Oregon Book Award, and Reader's Choice awards, and have won the WILLA Literary Award, the Carol Award for Historical Fiction, and the 2016 Will Rogers Medallion Award. Jane lives in Central Oregon with her husband, Jerry. Learn more at www.jkbooks.com.

Center Point Large Print
600 Brooks Road / PO Box 1
Thorndike, ME 04986-0001 USA

(207) 568-3717

US & Canada:
1 800 929-9108
www.centerpointlargeprint.com